MADAME RÉCAMIER

AND HER FRIENDS

Art Repro. Co.

Madame Récamier, (ætat 23)
From the painting by Gérard.

MADAME RÉCAMIER

AND HER FRIENDS

BY

H. NOEL WILLIAMS

AUTHOR OF "MADAME DE POMPADOUR," "MADAME DE MONTESPAN," "MADAME DU BARRY," "QUEEN MARGOT," "QUEENS OF THE FRENCH STAGE," "LATER QUEENS OF THE FRENCH STAGE," "FIVE FAIR SISTERS," ETC.

"Il y a dans la temme une gaieté légère qui dissipe la tristesse de l'homme."—BERNARDIN DE SAINT-PIERRE

WITH PORTRAIT

NEW YORK
CHARLES SCRIBNER'S SONS
1907

NEW AND REVISED EDITION

PREFACE

THERE are few more interesting figures in the social life of the nineteenth century than that of Madame Récamier. Distinguished alike for her beauty, her virtue, her charm of manner, and her goodness of heart, she reigned for upwards of fifty years the almost undisputed queen of Parisian society. "One cannot expect to find in future times," says her friend, the Duchesse d'Abrantès "a woman like her—a woman whose friendship has been courted by the most remarkable persons of the age; a woman whose beauty has brought to her feet all the men who have once set eyes upon her; whose love has been the object of universal desire, yet whose virtue has remained pure; a woman whose unsullied reputation never suffered from the attacks of jealousy or envy; a woman who lost none of the affections which had been pledged to her, because in her days of gaiety and splendour she had the merit of being always ready to sacrifice her own enjoyments to afford consolation—which no one could do more sweetly and effectually—to any friend in distress. To the world Madame Récamier is a celebrated woman; to those who had the happiness to know and to appreciate her she was a peculiar and gifted being, formed by Nature as a perfect model in one of her most beneficent moods."

One would naturally have supposed that so striking and attractive a personality would have claimed no inconsiderable amount of attention from English and American writers; but such is far from being the case. Although frequent mention is made of her by George Ticknor, Mary Berry, Maria Edgeworth, and other contemporary writers, and although she has always been a favourite with contributors to periodical literature, yet with the exception of a short study by Madame Mohl, an intimate friend of her later years (London: 1862), and an abridged translation by Miss Luyster of Madame Lenormant's *Souvenirs et Correspondance tirés des papiers de Madame Récamier* (Boston: 1867), there is no work in our language of which she is the subject.

Nor can either of these works be considered altogether satisfactory. Madame Mohl's little book does not pretend to be anything more than an essay—in fact it originally appeared in the *National Review*; while Miss Luyster's translation, excellent as it is, unavoidably reproduces many of the defects of the original.

Madame Lenormant's book, indeed, although it contains a mass of interesting information, and must always remain the chief authority for any "Life" of her celebrated aunt, is not only involved and diffuse in style and faulty in construction, but is open to the charge so frequently brought against biographies written by near relatives—that of excessive partiality; and, in the present instance, this partiality extends not only to Madame Récamier herself, but to more than one of her intimate friends.

Again, at the time Madame Lenormant wrote it was found impossible to include the letters written by Benjamin Constant, the famous publicist and statesman, to Madame Récamier—by no means the least interesting portion of the latter's correspondence—owing to the opposition of the Constant and Récamier families, who had gone so far as to obtain an injunction restraining their publication.

These remarkable letters, of which, through the courtesy of Baron d'Estournelles, I am enabled to give a selection in the present volume, have since appeared, though not without a further contest in the Law Courts, together with Benjamin Constant's *Journal Intime*; the *Souvenirs* of the Duc de Broglie; the *Mémoires* of Alexis de Tocqueville; Madame Lenormant's *Madame Récamier, les Amis de sa Jeunesse*, and *Coppet et Weimar*; the *Mémoires* of Madame de Rémusat, and many other works which contain much additional information about Madame Récamier and her friends. And I am, therefore, inclined to think that the time has now come when it is possible to offer to English readers something approaching an adequate account of one of the most remarkable among the many remarkable women of whom France is justly proud.

It may possibly occasion some surprise that this volume differs from most works of its kind, inasmuch as, although it comprises a number of letters addressed to Madame

Récamier by her various distinguished friends, there are very few written by herself. The explanation of this is that, with the exception of those to her niece, Madame Lenormant, and other members of her family, few of which are of much general interest, scarcely any of Madame Récamier's letters have been preserved. What became of the very large number which must have been written at different periods to Mathieu de Montmorency, Prince Augustus of Prussia, Ballanche, Benjamin Constant, and Chateaubriand is uncertain. But it is believed that they were in each case returned after the death of the recipient, and formed part of two bulky manuscript volumes, containing Madame Récamier's own reminiscences, which she had, until her sight began to fail, intended to publish, but which were destroyed by her directions shortly before her death in 1849.

The absence of these letters is the more to be regretted, as from the few which are in existence, and the manner in which literary friends, like Madame de Staël, Ballanche, and Chateaubriand, speak of those which they were accustomed to receive from her, it would appear that she must have been a singularly charming correspondent, even in an age when letter-writing was still accounted one of the fine arts.

"To compile a real account of Madame Récamier," says the writer of the brief article devoted to her in the *Encyclopædia Britannica*, "would necessitate the ransack of all the memoirs, correspondence, and anecdotage concerning French political and literary life for the first half of the nineteenth century." This, it will readily be admitted, is a formidable task and one requiring an amount of leisure which seldom falls to an author's lot. Nevertheless, this volume is the result of a more careful sifting of available materials than will perhaps appear upon the surface.

H. NOEL WILLIAMS.

LONDON, *April* 1901.

CONTENTS

CHAPTER I

Birth and parentage—The convent of La Déserte—Juliette joins her parents in Paris—A youthful escapade—Her beauty as a child—A visit to Versailles—Her taste for music—A marriage of convenience—Jacques Récamier and the guillotine—A singular story

"HER angelic face can bear no other name; one look suffices to bind your heart to her for ever."

Such was the dictum pronounced by no less a person than Lamartine on Madame Récamier, without a doubt the most remarkable figure in French society during the first half of the nineteenth century, the idol of Prince Augustus of Prussia, of Mathieu de Montmorency, of Simon Ballanche, and of René de Chateaubriand; the confidante of Moreau, Bernadotte, and Murat; the bosom friend of Madame de Staël; about whose charms Lucien Bonaparte and Benjamin Constant raved, and to whom Wellington made love in his bad French. Before the throne of this uncrowned queen, kings and princes, statesmen and orators, authors and artists, warriors and diplomatists bowed the knee, while she received their homage with an easy grace and gentle dignity which commanded at once their admiration and their respect.

Madame Récamier's long career falls naturally into three periods, coinciding with three well-defined epochs in French history. During the first and second of these—

that is to say, from her appearance in society after the Reign of Terror to the restoration of the Bourbons in 1814, and again from the latter date to the revolution of 1830—her life is so closely connected with the politics of her country that it is hardly possible to speak of her without dwelling to some extent on the great events which were passing around her. Like a fine silver thread, as one of her contemporaries aptly observes, her career runs through the web of history, and cannot be drawn out without dragging some shreds of the coarser tissue along with it. During the third period, which may be said to cover the last eighteen years of her life, and in which her most intimate friends had retired from the political arena, we see her the centre of a literary coterie, which recalls the salons of the reign of Louis XIV., the friend and confidante of poets and philosophers, as she had formerly been of diplomatists and politicians, and extending her hospitality to distinguished foreigners from all parts of Europe.

Although during these later years, her beauty had waned, while her means were comparatively slender, the extraordinary fascination she exercised over all with whom she was brought into contact remained as potent as ever, and an invitation to her receptions was as much prized as when half the celebrated men in France were at her feet, and every luxury which money could purchase was at her command.

Jeanne Françoise Julie Adélaïde Bernard—to give her her full name, though she was known throughout life by her first *nom de caresse* of Juliette—was born at Lyons on December 4, 1777. Her father, Jean Bernard, was a notary of that city, but, beyond the fact that he was extremely good-looking, he does not appear to have been in any way distinguished. Her mother (whose maiden name was Manton), from whom Juliette inherited that bewitching loveliness and charm of manner which was to secure for her a European reputation, was a singularly beautiful and attractive woman, with an aptitude for business most unusual in one of the gentler sex, which enabled her to amass by successful speculation a snug little fortune, and, what according to the younger Disraeli is far harder of accomplishment, to keep it.

In 1784 Jean Bernard was, through the influence of Calonne, a great admirer of the notary's handsome wife, appointed a collector of customs in Paris, where he and his wife henceforth resided, while their little daughter was placed in the convent of La Déserte at Lyons, in which community one of Madame Bernard's sisters was a nun. Juliette always retained the most affectionate and grateful remembrance of the days spent at the convent, as one of the few fragments of her journal which have been preserved testifies :

"The night before my aunt was to fetch me," she writes, "I was taken to the Lady Abbess's chamber to receive her blessing. The next day, bathed in tears, I passed over the threshold of that door which I could scarcely remember opening to admit me. I found myself in a carriage by the side of my aunt, and we started for Paris. I left with regret that tranquil and innocent period of my life to enter upon one of turmoil. The memory of it comes back to me like a vague, sweet dream with its clouds of incense, its innumerable ceremonies, its processions in the gardens, its chants, and its flowers.

"If I have spoken of these early years, notwithstanding my intention to be brief in all matters relating to myself, it is on account of the immense influence which they have exercised on my whole life. It is without doubt to those vivid impressions of faith received in childhood that I am indebted for the fact that I have retained my religious convictions in the midst of all the conflicting opinions which I have met with. I have listened to them, understood them, admitted them, as far as they were admissible, but I have never allowed doubt to enter my heart." [1]

Juliette was about ten years of age when she joined her parents in Paris, where they were living in good style, having a box at the Théâtre Français, and giving supper parties twice a week. The Voltairean philosopher, Simonard, a great friend of the family, and his son, a little boy about Juliette's own age, shared their house ; and one day soon after her arrival, the latter, who seems to have been somewhat of a scapegrace, persuaded her to join him in a raid on a neighbour's grapes. This was by no means the first time that Master Simonard had levied toll on this particular garden, and on the present occasion, as ill-luck would have it, the irate owner was on the watch, with the result that the marauders were caught red-handed. Young Simonard managed to effect his escape, but his companion was less fortunate, and was taken prisoner. Her captor, however, who was a very gallant old gentleman, was not proof against the tears of so lovely a child ; and, instead of punishing her, as she undoubtedly deserved, begged her to cry no more, promised to say nothing about her escapade to her parents, and sent her home with her pinafore full of fruit.

Indeed, even at this early age, Juliette seems to have been remarkable for her beauty and grace, and became the pet of La Harpe and other literary men who frequented the Bernards' house ; and to this fact may be attributed

[1] *Souvenirs*, i. 2.

her taste for literary society, to which she is in no small degree indebted for her lasting celebrity. Her mother, who appears to have attached an extraordinary importance to the power of personal attraction, compelled the poor child to spend many weary hours at her toilet table, and allowed no opportunity to slip of exhibiting her little daughter's budding charms to the admiring eyes of the Parisians.

At that time the unfortunate Louis XVI. was already the slave of his people, and was ready to make almost any sacrifice to please his capricious subjects and bolster up his tottering throne. The public were even admitted to the dining-room at Versailles, to stare at the royal family taking their meals with all the ceremonial of the ancient monarchy. On one occasion Madame Bernard and Juliette entered among the crowd, and Marie Antoinette was so struck with the child's beauty, that after dinner she sent one of her ladies to the proud mother with a request that she would allow her daughter to go to the queen's apartments, where Juliette and the little Madame Royale, who happened to be both about the same age, were measured to see which was the tallest. The dignity of the little princess is said to have been somewhat ruffled at being compared with a child who had, as she expressed it, "been taken from the rabble."

Although Madame Bernard paid so much attention to her child's personal appearance, she was far from neglecting her education, and indeed supervised her studies with the greatest care. Juliette had a very decided taste for music, and received instruction from the first masters of the day. She performed on both the harp and the piano, and took singing lessons from Boïeldieu. Her voice, we learn, though lacking in power, was good in tone and expression.

She soon gave up singing and the harp, but remained all her life devoted to the piano. Her memory was excellent, and she was fond of playing without notes at twilight. Thus when her sight began to fail, as it did about ten years before her death, she was still able to enjoy music, and by its aid console herself for the loss of other pleasures.

She was also a most accomplished and graceful dancer, and it must have been worth going a long way to see her perform her shawl dance, which served her friend Madame de Staël as a model for the dance in *Corinne*.

"One day during the sad winter of 1812-13, which she passed as an exile at Lyons," says Madame Lenormant, her niece and adopted daughter, "she gave me an idea of this dance in order to drive away her *ennui*, and also, no doubt, to recall the memory of other days. With a long scarf in her hand, she went through all the different attitudes wherein the light fabric becomes in turn a girdle, a veil, and a drapery. Nothing could be more graceful, more becoming, or more picturesque than this succession of harmonious poses, worthy to be perpetuated by the pencil of an artist."[1]

At the age of fifteen, Juliette received an offer of marriage. Her suitor was a wealthy Paris banker named Jacques Récamier, who, like the Bernards themselves, came originally from Lyons, where his father had formerly carried on a highly lucrative business in the hat trade. Jacques Récamier was a handsome, pleasure-loving man of forty-three, generous to a fault, and, at the same time, oddly enough, quite incapable of any deep feeling. One day, we are told, he would lend a friend money to almost any amount; the next, if the same friend happened to die, he would coolly murmur, "Another drawer shut!" and straightway forget all about him.

[1] *Souvenirs*, i. 18.

Juliette seems to have received her middle-aged suitor's addresses without reluctance. She had known him for several years; he had always been exceedingly kind to her when a child, and she was indebted to him for many of her most costly toys and most gorgeously attired dolls. She felt quite sure in her own mind that he would prove equally indulgent as a husband; and so, after a little hesitation, she consented to become his wife.

The banker, on his part, seems to have regarded the lovely young girl mainly in the light of a daughter, whose beauty refreshed his eyes, while the admiration it excited among his friends and neighbours flattered his vanity. ("*Il voulut par son mariage éblouir et éclipser le monde dans lequel il vivait,*" says Rondelet.[1]) Moreover the tie which bound them to each other was never anything but a nominal one.

The wedding took place in the month of April 1793; scarcely a time, one would have supposed, for marrying or giving in marriage. The Reign of Terror was at its height; all society was broken up and scattered to the four winds of heaven, and all family ties annihilated. People saw their relatives and friends being dragged to the block, themselves living in hourly dread of a similar fate, and were yet too paralysed by fear to resist the tyranny of the executioners.

Jacques Récamier used to go almost every day to the Place-de la-Concorde to watch the guillotine being fed with human prey beneath a colossal statue of Liberty, according to his own account, in order to accustom himself to the fate which he had every reason to expect would soon be his own, but more probably because such gruesome scenes had a peculiar fascination for him, as they had had

[1] Rondelet's *Madame Récamier*, p. 10.

for George Selwyn. He was present at the execution of the King; he saw the fair head of Marie Antoinette fall into the fatal basket, and nearly all the men with whom he had been intimate in business or society guillotined one after the other; but he himself, his wife, and her family were spared, chiefly, it is believed, through the influence of Barère, one of the leaders of the Terrorists, who was a great friend of the Bernards. Jean Bernard, it may be remarked, was probably the only *receveur des finances* of Louis XVI. who escaped the guillotine.

The fact of Juliette's marriage taking place at such a time, and the peculiar relations which were known to exist between her and her husband, gave rise to a very singular story, which, extravagant as it may seem, found credence among a great number of Madame Récamier's contemporaries.

It was asserted that Juliette was in reality Jacques Récamier's own child, and that his object in marrying her was to ensure her possession of his fortune in the not unlikely event of the guillotine claiming him as one of its victims.

Into the merits of this story we do not propose to enter, and it will, therefore, be sufficient to observe that the reputation which the fascinating Madame Bernard bore—both Calonne and Barère are said to have been her lovers—was not of a kind to entirely preclude such a possibility; and that the fact that no mention is made of the civil marriage, performed in 1793, being supplemented by a religious ceremony when the churches were re-opened—a practice which was general among all respectable people—is in itself somewhat significant, the more so as Madame Récamier was throughout her life a strict observer of the ritual of her Church.

CHAPTER II

Paris after the Reign of Terror—Madame Récamier's extraordinary beauty—Sensation it arouses—The *quête* at St. Roch—Fête at the Luxembourg in honour of Bonaparte—Dinner given by Barras—Madame Récamier meets Madame de Staël—Purchase of Necker's house in the Rue du Mont Blanc—Mary Berry's description of it—Lucien Bonaparte's fête—"The First Consul thinks you charming"—Lucien Bonaparte—His great abilities—His passion for Madame Récamier—Letters of Romeo to Juliette—Juliette rejects Romeo

Owing to the disturbed condition of Paris, the first four years of Juliette's married life were necessarily passed in comparative seclusion, for during that terrible time retirement and insignificance afforded the only sure means of safety, and most people preferred to forego social functions and remain at home rather than run the risk of attracting the notice of the bloodthirsty *Comité de Salut Public.*

But at length the Terror came to an end, and the work of order and reconstruction began. The exiles, or at least such of them as had not committed themselves beyond hope of reprieve, and were prepared to conform, outwardly at all events, to the new order of things, returned; the commercial magnates emerged from their retirement; the prison doors were opened; and the Parisians, incorrigible in their frivolity, threw themselves with a zest sharpened by the privations of terror, war, and famine, into a perfect vortex of pleasure, crowded once more to the theatre, the promenade, and the ball-room, and danced, and gambled, and flirted as if none of them had lost a friend or a relative for years.

It was now that Juliette Récamier began to cause that sensation which was to give her, in after years, such an extraordinary influence over French society. During this period of retirement her beauty had ripened, and she had passed from childhood into all the splendour of womanhood. The following description, from the pen of Madame Lenormant, of her appearance about this time does not seem, even after making all due allowance for the fact that the writer was both her niece and most enthusiastic admirer, to be in any way an exaggerated one :

" A figure supple and graceful ; throat and shoulders of exquisite form and proportions ; beautiful arms though somewhat slender ; a little rosy mouth ; pearly teeth ; black hair that curled naturally ; a delicate and regular nose, but *bien-français ;* an incomparable brilliancy of complexion ; a frank, arch face, rendered irresistibly lovely from its expression of goodness ; a well poised head ; a carriage slightly indicative of both indolence and pride, so that to her might be applied St. Simon's compliment to the Duchess of Burgundy :

"Her step was like that of a goddess on clouds."

Such was Madame Récamier at eighteen."

The success of a woman did not then depend on the verdict of an exclusive society. The Revolution had changed all that. Salon life no longer existed. The finest houses in the Faubourg St. Germain might have been hired for almost nothing ; the whole Hôtel de Luynes was rented at only six hundred francs a year, for people's purses were as empty as the national exchequer. A few bankers and contractors, whom the war had enriched, were, indeed, the only persons who had houses fit for the reception of company; and the only places where the beauty and fashion of the new society could show itself were in the Tuileries grounds during the day, and, at night, at the theatres and the subscription balls, held at illuminated gardens like Tivoli and Beaujon, where any one might go for three francs, and take a lady for one franc more. At such gatherings as these Madame Récamier's presence was looked upon as an event of no small importance, and, wherever she went, her beauty called forth murmurs of curiosity and admiration.

On one occasion, after public worship had been re-established, she was asked to hold the plate at St. Roch for some charitable *quête*. She consented, and knelt, as was usual, in the middle of the church. When the time came for the collection to be made, the church was filled to overflowing; the people stood on the chairs, the benches, and even the altars of the side-chapels, and hustled one another unmercifully to catch a glimpse of the lovely *quêteuse:* indeed, the two gentlemen, who had, according to custom, been deputed to protect her, had all their work cut out to prevent her being crushed to death by her too enthusiastic admirers. The sum collected amounted to something like twenty thousand francs, an immense sum having regard to the state of people's fortunes at this period.

On December 10, 1797, the Directory gave a fête in honour of Bonaparte, who had just returned from his victorious Italian campaign. It was held in the great court of the Luxembourg, where a statue of Liberty had been erected, at the foot of which sat the five Directors, habited in Roman costume, with short togas and bare legs, a garb which they must have found somewhat trying on a cold winter's day. The ministers, ambassadors, and public functionaries occupied benches placed in the form of an amphitheatre, and behind them were the reserved seats for the invited guests, amongst whom were Madame Récamier and her mother. All the front windows of the building, the court, the garden, and the adjacent streets were thronged with people.

Talleyrand, who was Minister for Foreign Affairs, read to the future Emperor an address of congratulation, and Bonaparte replied in a characteristic speech, brief and forcible, which was, of course, loudly acclaimed. Madame Récamier, who could not from where she sat distinguish the features of the hero of the occasion, took advantage of the moment when Barras was replying to the general to rise from her seat in order to obtain a better view of him. The crowd, who had hitherto had no eyes for any one but Bonaparte, immediately turned to admire the beauty of the day, and a low murmur of admiration ran round the court. This sound did not escape Bonaparte, who glanced about him to see who it was who could possibly be diverting attention from himself; and when he perceived a young woman, dressed in white, standing on a bench, he bent upon her one of his terrible frowns, and the careless young beauty sat down crimson with confusion. Thus, at the very outset of her career, Madame Récamier had the satisfaction of rivalling the conqueror of Europe himself in popular admiration.

In the summer of 1796, Jacques Récamier rented a furnished château at Clichy, where he established his young wife and her mother. He himself remained in Paris, but drove out every day to Clichy to dinner. The château was large and beautifully situated in a wooded park which sloped down to the banks of the Seine, and here the Récamiers kept open house, and every Sunday gave a large dinner party to their more intimate friends.

Madame Récamier mingled but little in the very mixed society of the Directory. She was, however, present, in the spring of 1799, at a reception at the Luxembourg given by Barras, who since the affair of the 18th Fructidor had been practically dictator of France, at which her host paid her marked attention, and the poet Despaze, who was among the guests, improvised a quatrain in her honour.

Madame Récamier took advantage of the favourable impression she had created to intercede with the Director on behalf of a poor priest, whose release she desired to obtain; and Barras, who never could refuse anything to a pretty woman despite the poor opinion which he professed to entertain for the sex, granted her request. Poverty and misfortune always had for Madame Récamier the same attractions which wealth and prosperity have for the ordinary run of mortals, and this was only one of many instances in which she used the influence which her beauty and popularity gave her to promote the happiness of her less favoured fellow-creatures.

As Jacques Récamier's fortune and the fame of his wife's beauty increased, he found his town house in the Rue du Mail too small for his requirements, and hearing that Necker, with whom he had long had business relations, was desirous of selling his hôtel in the Rue du Mont Blanc (now the Chaussée d'Antin), he entered into negotiations for its purchase. It was this transaction which was the means of bringing Madame Récamier and Necker's famous daughter, Madame de Staël, together, and was the beginning of a friendship which lasted until the death of the brilliant authoress of *Corinne* and *De L'Allemagne*, who seems to have been completely fascinated by the fresh young beauty whose attractions were so different to her own. Madame Récamier has left us an interesting account of this first meeting, which took place at the Récamiers' château at Clichy.

"One day, and that marks an epoch in my life," she says, "M. Récamier arrived at Clichy with a lady whom he did not introduce by name, and whom he left alone with me in the salon, while he went to join some people who were in the park. This lady came about the sale of a house. Her costume was peculiar; she wore a morning gown and a little dress hat trimmed with flowers. I took her for a foreigner. I was struck with the beauty of her eyes and her expression. I was unable to analyse my feelings, but I am sure that I was thinking more of finding out, or rather guessing, who she was than of addressing to her the usual commonplaces, when she said to me, with an air at once charming and impressive, that 'she was truly delighted to make my acquaintance; that her father M. Necker'—at these words I recognised Madame de Staël. I did not hear the rest of her sentence. I blushed and was extremely embarrassed. I had just been reading her *Lettres sur Rousseau*, in the perusal of which I was intensely interested. My looks were more expressive than my words; she both awed and attracted me. I was conscious at once of her genuineness and her superiority. She, on her side, fixed her splendid eyes upon me, but with a friendly scrutiny, and paid me some compliments on my appearance that would have been too exaggerated and direct had they not seemed to escape her unconsciously, thus giving to her praises an irresistible fascination. My embarrassment did me no harm ; she understood it, and expressed the hope of seeing a great deal of me on her return to Paris, for she was on the point of starting for Coppet. This interview was only a passing one, but it left a deep impression upon me. I thought only of Madame de Staël, so much did I feel the influence of that strong and earnest personality."[1]

The arrangements for the purchase of the hôtel in the Rue du Mont Blanc having been completed, Jacques Récamier put it into the hands of Berthaut, the architect, with directions to have it enlarged and furnished in the Greek style, then so fashionable. Berthaut, who was allowed *carte blanche* in the matter of expense, acquitted himself with admirable taste, and, as since the Revolution luxury had almost disappeared, the house became one of the sights of Paris. From all accounts, however, it would seem to have been simplicity itself compared with the prodigal magnificence of later years. Of this house Mary Berry, who was in Paris during the Peace of Amiens, gives the following description :

" Went to the house of Madame Récamier. We were resolved not to leave Paris without seeing what is called the most elegant house in it, fitted up in the new style. There are no large rooms nor a great many of them ; but it is certainly fitted up with all the *recherché* and expense possible in what is called *le goût antique.* But the candelabra, pendules, &c., though exquisitely finished, are in that sort of minute frittered style which I think so much less noble than that of fifteen or twenty years ago. All the chairs are mahogany, enriched with ormolu, and covered either with cloth or silk ; those in the salon trimmed with flat gold lace in good taste. Her bed is

[1] *Souvenirs*, i. 24.

reckoned the most beautiful in Paris: it, too, is of mahogany, enriched with ormolu and bronze, and raised upon two steps of the same wood. Over the whole bed was thrown a coverlid or veil of fine plain muslin, with rows of narrow gold lace at each end, and the muslin embroidered as a border. The curtains were muslin, trimmed like the coverlid, suspended from a sort of carved *couronne des roses*, and tucked up in drapery upon the wall against which the bed stood. At the foot of the bed stood a fine Grecian lamp of ormolu, with a little figure of the same metal bending over it, and at the head of the bed another stand upon which was placed a large ornamental flower-pot, containing a large artificial rose-tree, the branches of which must nod very near her nose, in bed. Out of this bedroom is a beautiful little *salle-de-bain*. The walls are inlaid with satin-wood, and mahogany, and slight arabesque patterns in black upon satin-wood. The bath presents itself as a sofa in a recess, covered with a cushion of scarlet cloth, embroidered and laced with black. Beyond this again is a very little boudoir, lined with quilted pea-green lustring, drawn together in a bunch in the middle of the ceiling."[1]

The winter which followed the *coup d'état* of the 18th Brumaire, in which the last remnants of the Republican institutions were swept away, and the thin end of the wedge of despotism firmly inserted in the Constitution, was a very brilliant one in Paris. Balls, fêtes, receptions, amusements of all kinds increased in number in proportion to the growing indifference of the people to liberty and all the great objects for which so much of the best blood in France had been shed. The Bonapartists, knowing full well that when the public mind is wholly given up to

[1] Miss Berry's "Journal and Correspondence," i. 191.

pleasure it is but little disposed to concern itself with the working of political institutions, did all in their power to encourage the prevailing love of gaiety, and themselves entertained in a style to which the Parisians had long been strangers. It was in pursuance of this policy that Lucien Bonaparte, who had lately been appointed Minister of the Interior, gave a grand fête in honour of the First Consul, to which Jacques Récamier and his young wife were invited. It was here that Madame Récamier met, for the first and only time in her life, the man who was to exercise so sinister an influence on her own fortunes and those of her friends.

On this occasion Madame Récamier wore a white satin gown, with a necklace and bracelets of pearls. She always had, it appears, a very decided preference for white, and wore it at all seasons, varying only its material, shape, and trimmings. In like manner, she preferred pearls, of which she possessed some splendid specimens, to all other jewels, and even in the time of her husband's greatest prosperity never wore diamonds. Perhaps, as Madame Lenormant observes, she experienced a certain feminine satisfaction in surrounding herself with objects whose dazzling whiteness was eclipsed by the brilliancy of her own complexion.

Soon after her arrival, and while she was talking with her hostess, Madame Bacciochi, who, owing to the indisposition of Lucien's wife, was doing the honours, she noticed a gentleman standing by the fireplace in the salon. In the dim light she took him for Joseph Bonaparte, whom she had frequently met at the house of their common friend, Madame de Staël, and bowed pleasantly to him. Her greeting was returned, but with a faint expression of surprise, and, the next moment, she was conscious of her mistake, and that she had been bowing to the First Consul. Her impression of him was very different from the one which she had received at the Luxembourg two years before; and she was struck with the simplicity of his manners and his pleasant expression. Presently Napoleon beckoned Fouché to his side, and said a few words to him, looking at Madame Récamier meanwhile, and making it evident that he was talking about her. Shortly afterwards Fouché came behind her chair, and whispered, "The First Consul thinks you charming."

Madame Récamier would have been more than human if she had not felt a thrill of gratification at receiving this tribute to her charms from the man whose name was on every one's lips, and a little incident which occurred later in the evening still further disposed her to judge him favourably.

While he was talking to the flatterers who surrounded him, he held the hand of Lucien's little daughter, a child of four years old. He had unintentionally ignored her presence until the child, tired of her captivity, began to cry, whereupon Bonaparte exclaimed, in a tone of tender regret, "Ah, *pauvre petite*, I had forgotten thee!" More than once in after years, Madame Récamier recalled this excess of apparent kindheartedness, and contrasted it with the harshness of his treatment of herself and others.

When dinner was announced, Napoleon rose, and led the way into the dining-room without offering his arm to any lady. The guests followed, and seated themselves almost without regard to order. Bonaparte himself sat at the middle of the table, with his mother, Madame Letitia ("Madame Mère," as she was afterwards called), on his right. On his left a place remained vacant, which no one presumed to occupy. Madame Récamier, to whom her hostess, as they were passing into the dining-room, had said a few words the meaning of which she had failed to grasp, took a seat on the same side of the table as the First Consul, but at some distance from him. Napoleon then turned angrily towards the persons still standing, and said brusquely to Garat, the famous singer, pointing to the vacant place at his side, "Come, Garat, sit down there!" At the same moment, Cambacérès, the Second Consul, seated himself next to Madame Récamier, whereupon Napoleon remarked, loud enough to be heard by every one in the room, "Ha! ha! Citizen Consul, next to the prettiest."

Dinner was soon over. Bonaparte ate very little and very fast; and at the end of half an hour rose from the table and left the room. Most of the guests rose too, and, in the commotion which ensued, he came up to Madame Récamier, and asked: "Why did you not sit next to me at dinner?"

"I should not have presumed to do so," she replied.

"It was your place," rejoined Bonaparte.

"That was what I said to you before dinner," added Madame Bacciochi, who was standing by.

A move was presently made for the music-room, where the ladies formed a circle facing the performers, while the men stood behind them. Bonaparte sat near the piano in solitary state. Garat sang, with admirable expression, a passage from Gluck, which was loudly applauded. After this several artistes played. Bonaparte, however, did not care for instrumental music, and after a piece played by Jadin, his patience was exhausted, and he began to thump the piano, calling out "Garat! Garat!" This summons could not but be obeyed, and Garat sang a song from Orpheus, and surpassed himself.

Madame Récamier, who was devoted to music, was so fascinated by Garat's wonderful singing that she paid but little attention to the crowd which thronged the rooms.

Whenever she raised her eyes, however, she found those of Bonaparte fixed upon her with a persistency which ended by making her decidedly uncomfortable. When the concert was over he approached her, and remarked, "You are very fond of music, madame." He seemed disposed to continue the conversation, but Lucien coming up, Napoleon moved away, and Madame Récamier returned home. This meeting was not without important consequences to our heroine, as will presently be related.

Lucien Bonaparte, who thus interrupted what might have proved a very interesting conversation, was at this time four-and-twenty, taller and altogether of finer physique than his brother, whom he resembled in appearance, though his features were not so strongly marked as those of Napoleon. Lucien was, of course, quite overshadowed by the fame of the First Consul, but he was, nevertheless, for his years, an exceptionally able man: indeed, the Revolution, the mother of so many precocious statesmen, produced none more brilliant than the second brother of Napoleon. An eloquent and powerful speaker, with an indomitable resolution which refused to yield a single inch to popular clamour, he rapidly made his mark in the Council of Five Hundred, to which he had been elected in 1798, and in the following year, a few weeks before the *coup d'état* of the 18th Brumaire, he became its President. On that eventful day, when the timidity of Sieyès and the ill-timed interference of Napoleon threatened to ruin all the plans of the conspirators, it was Lucien who stepped into the breach, and, by his coolness, promptitude, and courage, saved the Bonapartists from inevitable destruction.

A cynic has observed that however wisely and prudently

a man may behave in the ordinary affairs of life, in diplomacy, in finance, or in politics, in affairs of the heart he is just as prone to make himself supremely ridiculous as the most brainless of his sex; and Lucien Bonaparte's relations with Madame Récamier afford a remarkable illustration of the truth of this axiom. He had met her for the first time, some months before, at a dinner party given by M. Sapey at Bagatelle, and had at once fallen desperately in love with her. Unfortunately for the object of his passion, he made not the least attempt to disguise the state of his feelings, which in consequence speedily became the talk of Paris.

Lucien opened the siege of Madame Récamier's heart with a bombardment of *billets-doux*, couched in the most grandiloquent language, in which the writer assumed the name of Romeo, presumably because hers was Juliette. Of these romantic epistles, the following will serve as a specimen:

"LETTERS OF ROMEO TO JULIETTE

"By the Author of the Indian Tribe

"'Without love life is one long slumber'

"What, more love letters!!! Since those of St. Preux and Héloïse, how many have appeared! . . . how many painters have striven to copy that inimitable masterpiece. It is the Venus de Medicis, which a thousand artists have essayed in vain to equal.

"These letters are not the fruit of long labour, and I do not dedicate them to immortality. They are not the offspring of eloquence or of genius, but of the most sincere passion. They are not written for the public, but for a beloved woman. They reveal my heart: it is a faithful glass, wherein to behold myself is a never-ending delight. My letters express my feelings, and in giving expression to those feelings I am happy. May these letters interest her for whom I write. May she hearken to my entreaties. May she, with pleasure, recognise herself in the portrait of Juliette, and think of Romeo with that delicious agitation which proclaims the dawn of love."

First Letter of Romeo to Juliette.

"Romeo writes to you, Juliette. If you refuse to read it you will be more cruel than our parents, whose long quarrels have just been settled. Doubtless these dreadful quarrels will not be renewed.

"A few days ago I knew you only by reputation. I had seen you sometimes at churches and fêtes. I knew that you were the most beautiful of women. A thousand tongues repeated your praises, but these praises and your charms had struck without dazzling me. Why has peace delivered me into your power? Peace . . . it now exists between our families, but trouble reigns in my heart.

. . . . .

"I have seen you again! Love seemed to smile upon me. Seated on a round bench I spoke with you alone. I thought I heard a sigh escape from your bosom. Vain illusion! Convinced of my mistake, I beheld indifference with a tranquil brow seated between us. The passion which masters me is expressed in my speech, but yours bears the kind and cruel impress of raillery.

"O Juliette! Life without love is only one long slumber. The most beautiful of women ought to be compassionate: happy the man who will become the friend of your heart!"

Poor Romeo must have felt extremely foolish when his

Juliette handed him back his first love-letter, in the presence of a number of common friends, praising the talents of the writer, but advising him not to waste in works of imagination the time which he might more profitably devote to politics.[1] However, he was not the man to be discouraged by the want of success which had attended his romantic epistles; and so, abandoning his *nom-de-guerre*, he wrote Madame Récamier letters the purport of which she could not pretend to misunderstand. These she showed to her husband, and proposed to forbid Lucien the house. But Récamier represented to her that to quarrel openly with the brother of the First Consul would undoubtedly compromise him, and, perhaps, jeopardise his business, and advised her not to repulse Romeo too harshly. So, for her husband's sake, she bore, with more or less patience, the importunities of the infatuated young man, meeting his most impassioned declarations with peals of merry laughter, but was, nevertheless, greatly relieved when, tired of so unsuccessful a pursuit, his ardour cooled, and at length, becoming conscious of the ridiculous part he was playing, he left her in peace. Some months later, he sent his friend M. Sapey to ask Madame Récamier to return his letters; but the lady very wisely refused to give them up in spite of entreaties and even threats; and Madame Lenormant tells us that she, in her turn, preserved them "as indisputable proofs of her (Madame Récamier's) virtue."[2]

1 Some little time after this, at the beginning of the Peace of Amiens, Lucien retaliated rather neatly on Madame Récamier for thus turning him into ridicule. At a supper given by Ouvrard, the financier, he raised his glass to toast the most beautiful of women. When all eyes were turned towards Madame Récamier, undeterred by her embarrassment, he exclaimed: "Eh, bien, messieurs, c'est la Paix."

2 *Souvenirs*, i. 34.

CHAPTER III

Popularity of Madame Récamier's receptions—Her friends—Adrien de Montmorency—Mathieu de Montmorency—His early career—His conversion—His unselfish affection for Madame Récamier — His letters — La Harpe — Madame Recamier's kindnèss to him—His unfortunate marriage—Practical joke played upon him at Clichy—Madame Récamier sits to David for her portrait—And to Gérard—Amusing incident during the sittings—Madame Récamier's father becomes Postmaster-General—He intrigues with the Royalists, and is arrested—An interrupted dinner-party—Bernadotte intercedes with the First Consul—Madame Récamier's adventure in the Temple—A friend in need—Her father is released

JACQUES RÉCAMIER'S position as a wealthy banker gave him in those days a position which he, of course, could not have occupied under the old *régime*, and his wife's renown as a beauty, and the fact that her salon was regarded as a sort of neutral ground, where all parties might meet, added to the popularity of her receptions, and their hôtel in the Rue du Mont Blanc became the rendezvous for all that was most distinguished in social, political, and literary circles. There the Duc de Guignes, Adrien and Mathieu de Montmorency, Christian de Lemoignon, Louis de Narbonne, La Harpe, Madame de Staël, and others of the returned exiles rubbed shoulders with Barère and Fouché, the Terrorists; Murat, Masséna, and Moreau, and the generals of the late war; Lucien and Joseph Bonaparte and their sisters; and Eugene and Hortense Beauharnais; while many distinguished foreigners came to pay homage to the most charming hostess in Paris.

With the two Montmorencies Madame Récamier was on especially friendly terms. They were cousins and great friends. Both had recently been struck off the list of *emigrés*. The youngest, Adrien, afterwards Duc de Laval, was then about thirty years of age. He was widely read, and might have passed for a wit, but for an impediment in his speech. With his old-world manner and lofty ideas of honour he was an admirable representative of the old noblesse, and his veneration for the family of which he was the head amounted almost to idolatry. When his son died, he is said to have suffered as keenly from his pride of race as from his affection as a father. After the Restoration, he entered the diplomatic service, and represented his country with credit, if not with distinction, at Madrid, Rome, Vienna, and London.

His cousin, Mathieu, afterwards Duc de Montmorency, was a much abler man, and altogether a more interesting character. He was born in 1760, and, when little more than a boy, accompanied Lafayette to America, serving with the Auvergne regiment, of which his father was at that time colonel. He was an intimate friend of Madame de Staël, and belonged to that small class among the French aristocracy which had embraced liberal ideas. It was, indeed, on a motion brought forward by Mathieu de Montmorency, then deputy to the States-General, that the National Assembly abolished, on the night of the Fourth of August, the privileges of the nobility—privileges which he, as a Montmorency, was, of course, vitally interested in maintaining.

In 1792, he emigrated to Switzerland, as by that time France had got too hot to hold even so ardent a disciple of progress as himself, and while there learned that his brother, the Abbé de Laval, to whom he was most devotedly attached, had been guillotined. Mathieu was inconsolable at his brother's death, of which, mindful of the part he had taken in promoting the Revolution, he accused himself of being the cause. From that moment he was a changed man, and, whereas he had hitherto led a gay and dissipated life, he now became, under the influence of Madame de Staël, an austere and fervent Christian.

Between Mathieu and Madame Récamier the most perfect sympathy always existed ; indeed, his pure and unselfish affection for her is, perhaps, the most interesting phase of the early part of her life. He was quick to perceive the temptations to which a young and lovely woman, whom destiny had precluded from the natural affections of a wife and a mother, must necessarily be exposed, and, accordingly, did his utmost to impress her with his own religious convictions, the while he watched over her with a more than paternal solicitude. Mathieu de Montmorency's letters are a rare example of a love whose purity is equal to its sincerity.

MATHIEU DE MONTMORENCY *to* MADAME RÉCAMIER.

"How charmingly you know how to express your sentiments, and how charming those sentiments are! What balm you know how to apply to the wounds that, in another way, you inflict upon a sincere friend! Ah, madame, you regard and estimate me with the prejudices of the most kind and indulgent of natures, which, in fact, leads you to set too high a value upon my merits instead of judging me impartially. But, in your eyes, I am willing to appear a thousand times better than I really am. I would like to unite all the privileges of a father, of a brother, of a friend, to obtain your friendship, your entire confidence, for one object alone—in order to influence you for your own happiness, and to see you entering on the only road which is able to guide you thither—the only road worthy of your heart, of your mind, of the sublime mission to which you are called ; in one single word, to induce you to take a firm resolution. For everything depends upon that. Must I confess it to you? I seek eagerly, yet in vain, for some indication of it in your actions, in all those little involuntary details of conduct, not one of which escapes me. Nothing reassures me, nothing satisfies me. Ah! I know not how to conceal it from you: I come away feeling terribly depressed. I shudder at perceiving you threatened with the loss of true happiness, and myself with the loss of a friend. God and yourself forbid me to altogether despair: I will obey; I will pray without ceasing. He alone is able to open your eyes, and to convince you that a heart that truly loves Him is not so empty as you imagine. He alone is able to inspire you with a genuine inclination—not a transient, but a continuous and permanent one—for those duties and occupations which will be entirely in keeping with the goodness of your heart, and which will occupy in a pleasant and profitable manner much of your time.

"I was not jesting in the least when I asked you to assist me in my work on behalf of the Sisters of Charity. Nothing could be more delightful or of greater service to me. It would throw a peculiar fascination over my work, which would overcome my idleness, and give me a new interest therein.

"Do nothing but what is good and kind; nothing that will cause any heart-breaks, or leave any regrets behind. But, in the name of God, in the name of our friendship, renounce what is unworthy of you, and what under no circumstances can bring you happiness."

MATHIEU DE MONTMORENCY *to* MADAME RÉCAMIER.

"Be assured that it is impossible to set any limits to the infinite mercies of Him to whom you desire to address yourself in all sincerity, nor the marvellous and totally unexpected changes that He works in hearts regenerated by a true piety. I count the days that separate you from this regeneration so ardently looked forward to by your true friends. I also count the days that pass by without seeing you, and I accept the appointment for Tuesday.

"Allow me to remind you of the books that I have had the pleasure of lending you. Do not omit to read a few pages of them every morning. I fancy that I have also spoken to you of *Les Réflexions sur la miséricorde de Dieu*, by Mademoiselle de La Vallière, in which you will be doubly interested on account of its sentiments and its author. You have told me that your softened heart often turns to God. Continue and foster this excellent habit. I trust that our thoughts have already met, and will often meet on this road. My dearest wish, which you will pardon me for expressing, is that you may always find your evening gaieties and many of the people who are called pleasant a little tiresome. Is not that a very unkind wish? However, pray believe that my intentions are good.

"I am not without fear of the daily effects of these

frivolous surroundings of yours, which can do you no good, and which are unworthy of you. When you have read nothing serious during the day; when you have scarcely been able to spare a few moments for meditation, and have passed three or four hours of an evening in an atmosphere contagious from its very nature, you persuade yourself that your convictions are still unsettled, that it is necessary to begin over again an examination, which, once made, ought to be relied upon as a sure foundation, incapable of being shaken. Thus you lose heart and get discouraged. Ah! I entreat you, in the name of that deep interest which you do not doubt, in the name of my many sad personal experiences, not to give way to these fatal tendencies. Take care that you do not draw back, and thus render your future inconsolable. Nor is this all; do not advance very rapidly, if you feel you have not sufficient strength to do so, but at least move a few steps forward. Put your faith in the most earnest of prayers, and, at the same time, in the wisest of counsels. I hope you have not forgotten your promise to devote half an hour every day to consecutive and serious reading—these two conditions are indispensable—and also a few moments to prayer and meditation. Is this too much to ask for the greatest—one might say the only—interest in life?"

Another of Madame Récamier's most intimate friends was the famous critic La Harpe, whose *Lycée ou Cours du Littérature*, in spite of the bitterness with which the author assailed contemporary writers, long remained a standard of literary criticism. Madame Récamier always had a great attraction for literary men. Her taste in art and literature was far from contemptible; and the naïve, spontaneous admiration she was accustomed to express was a kind of incense very acceptable to men of letters. She had, moreover, for the sufferings of wounded vanity a pity and sympathy seldom accorded them. "No one," says Madame Lenormant, "knew so well how to pour balm on the wounds that are never acknowledged, how to calm and soothe the bitterness of rivalry or literary animosities. For moral chagrins and imaginary sorrows, so intense in some natures, she was *par excellence* the sister of charity."[1]

Her attachment to La Harpe, whom she had known from her childhood, was very sincere. She admired his talents and appreciated his wit—which was more than could be said for the majority of his contemporaries, as it was of a peculiarly mordant description—and was always kind and attentive to him. He was a frequent visitor at Clichy, and when he resumed his famous lectures at the Athenæum, which his proscription after the *coup d'état* of the 18th Fructidor had interrupted, Madame Récamier always made a point of attending them. Her presence, of course, proved a great attraction, and the lectures were delivered to a numerous and fashionable, if not very intellectual, audience.

Madame Récamier, probably, felt that La Harpe had a greater claim upon her consideration than any of her other friends, as it was through her own husband's propensity for matchmaking that the poor old man had been drawn into a most unfortunate marriage.

It happened that Jacques Récamier had an old friend, a certain Madame de Longuerue, whose husband had died, leaving her in very poor circumstances. This lady had a very beautiful daughter, for whom, however, it was difficult to find a husband owing to her lack of fortune; and

[1] *Souvenirs*, i. 53.

the good-natured banker conceived the idea of marrying her to La Harpe. The girl, who, not unnaturally, felt that a celebrated name was hardly likely to compensate her for accepting a husband thrice her age, protested; but Madame de Longuerue, having artfully concealed the state of her daughter's feelings from La Harpe, at length succeeded in gaining her consent to the match. At the end of three weeks, however, the bride sued for a divorce on the ground that she hated her husband, a plea which was held quite sufficient to justify the dissolution of the connubial knot during the Revolutionary era, when divorces were so easily obtained and so common that we read of women who had been married four or five times. Poor old La Harpe, who appears to have been really attached to his young wife, was terribly upset; but he threw no obstacle in the way of the divorce, and forgave the girl the scandal of the rupture.[1]

Like Mathieu de Montmorency, La Harpe had been wild at one time, and had changed his mode of life almost as suddenly. The world, however, seems at first to have

[1] Unless the following picture of the critic's mode of life is an exaggerated one, we can understand why young Madame de La Harpe was so anxious to obtain a divorce:

"We went with Madame Récamier and the Russian Princess Dalgourski to La Harpe's house to hear him repeat some of his verses. He lives in a wretched house, and we went up dirty stairs, through dirty passages, where I wondered how fine ladies' trains and noses could go, and were received in a dark, small den by the philosopher, or rather *dévot*, for he scorns the name of philosopher. He was in a dirty-reddish nightgown, and very dirty nightcap, bound round the forehead with a superlatively dirty chocolate-coloured ribbon. Madame Récamier, the beautiful, the elegant, robed in white satin trimmed with white fur, seated herself on the elbow of his armchair, and besought him to repeat his verses. Charlotte has drawn a picture of this scene."—MARIA EDGEWORTH *to* MRS. SNEYD, January 10, 1802.

been but little disposed to credit the sincerity of his conversion. The following anecdote is related by Sainte-Beuve, who had it from Madame Récamier :

"It was at the château of Clichy, where Madame Récamier was spending the summer. La Harpe had come there to stay a few days. The question came up (the same one that everybody was then asking) whether his conversion was as sincere as he professed, and it was resolved to put it to the proof. It was the age when practical jokes were the fashion, and one was planned which seemed perfectly fair to these lively and thoughtless young men. It was well known that La Harpe had always been very fond of women, and that that had been one of his great failings. A nephew of M. Récamier, one of the youngest and, apparently, the best looking, dressed himself in woman's clothes, so as to represent a fine lady, and, thus disguised, installed himself in M. de La Harpe's room—that is to say, in his bedroom. Quite a long story had been made up to account for so strange an intrusion. She had just arrived from Paris ; she had a most urgent favour to ask ; she could not make up her mind to wait till the next day. To be brief, M. de La Harpe when the evening came left the salon, and went upstairs to his room. The expectant and silent auditors were already on the watch behind a folding-screen to enjoy the fun. But what was the astonishment, the disappointment, and, to some extent, the remorse of these foolish youths, including the *soi-disant* lady seated in a corner of the fire-place, on perceiving M. de La Harpe on entering the room take no notice of anything, but simply kneel down and say a long prayer. When he rose from his knees and approached the bed, he caught sight of the lady, and drew back in astonishment. But in vain did the latter endeavour to stammer out some words of her part. M. de La Harpe cut it short, explaining that this was neither the time nor the place to listen to her. He put her off till the morrow, and courteously bowed her out. Next day he did not mention the visit he had received to any one at the château, nor was anything said to him on the subject."[1]

In 1800 Madame Récamier sat for her portrait to the famous painter David. The sketch he made, which depicts the young beauty reclining on a couch, with her head turned towards the onlooker, is a very pleasing one, but it was thought by many scarcely to do her justice, and David himself, it appears, was not wholly satisfied with it. It is, however, full of interest as an example of the leader of the French school of this period. It was retained by the painter, and offered for sale with the rest of his pictures by his executors in 1829, when it was purchased by M. Charles Lenormant, the husband of Madame Récamier's niece, for six thousand francs, and a few months later sold for the same sum to the Museum of the Louvre.

A far better known and altogether more satisfactory portrait is the celebrated full-length one by Gérard, which is generally acknowledged to be one of the most beautiful creations of that talented artist. Gérard, who, like most famous painters, was of a nervous, irritable temperament, was greatly annoyed by the number of fashionable people who came to his studio, begging permission to see the picture, and even to be present during the sittings. For some time he bore these interruptions in silence, but at length his patience was exhausted.

One day, just before the portrait was finished, there was a knock at the door, and a voice—that of Christian

[1] *Causeries du Lundi*, v. 108, 109.

de Lemoignon, one of Madame Récamier's most devoted admirers—was heard craving admission. Poor Gérard, who had made up his mind to an uninterrupted morning's work, was furious. Going to the door, his pallet in one hand and his *garde-main* in the other, he flung it open, and in a voice hoarse with passion exclaimed, "Come in, monsieur, come in, but afterwards I shall destroy my picture!" He almost pushed the intruder into the room, repeating his threat, and it is more than probable that he would have kept his word, as he was almost beside himself with anger, had not Lemoignon had the tact to apologise for his intrusion and withdraw, with the remark that he should be in despair if he were unfortunate enough to deprive posterity of one of M. Gérard's masterpieces.

It was during this same year, 1800, that Madame Récamier's father, M. Bernard, was appointed Postmaster-General, of which office, however, he was deprived in 1802, on a charge of countenancing a secret Royalist correspondence which had been circulating in the South of France. He was arrested, and thrown into prison, and matters would, undoubtedly, have gone hardly with him but for his beautiful daughter's exertions on his behalf. Madame Récamier left among her papers an interesting account of this event:

"In August 1802," she says, "my father was at the head of the Post Office. Just at this time the Government was alarmed by a very active correspondence carried on by the Royalists: a number of pamphlets or brochures, written in the same cause, were circulated in the south, without the authorities being able to discover by what means they were transmitted. It had long been suspected that it was through the intervention of a public functionary the head in fact of the department, for it was under cover of my father that all these clandestine writings were passing.[1] He had never taken any of his family into his confidence, and both my mother and myself were entirely ignorant of what was going on.

"One day Madame Bacciochi, the sister of the First Consul, who was anxious to make the acquaintance of La Harpe, asked me to invite her to dinner to meet him. I consented, though we were not on terms of sufficient ntimacy to warrant her making such a request; but the ladies of the First Consul's family had already begun to assume the airs of princesses, and seemed to imagine that they conferred honour upon those who entertained them. The only ladies present were Madame Bacciochi, Madame de Staël, and my mother, while the gentlemen were M. de La Harpe, M. de Narbonne, and Mathieu de Montmorency.

"The dinner passed off pleasantly, as one would presume it would do from the presence of M. de La Harpe and Madame de Staël, and in view of the taste which Madame Bacciochi at that time affected for literature.[2]

1 "The publications were edited in Paris by an abbé named Guyot, who took advantage of the friendship subsisting between M. Bernard and himself to transmit them to all those places with which M. Bernard kept up an official intercourse, whence they were thrown into general circulation."—*Mémoires de Duc de Rovige*, iii. 7.

2 "Madame Bacciochi was dressed on this occasion [Madame Junot's wedding dinner] with a degree of eccentricity which even now is fresh in my mind. She had presided in the morning at a female literary society; and, proposing to establish a peculiar costume for the associates, she considered the readiest way to effect her purpose was to have a pattern made, and appear in it herself: and in this new dress she afterwards came to my mother's: such a medley of the Jewish, Roman, Middle Age, and modern Greek costumes—of everything, in short, except French good taste—was, I think, never seen."—*Mémoires de Duchesse d'Abrantès*, i. 412.

"Just as we had risen from the table to go into the salon, a note was handed to my mother. Being somewhat uneasy about what it might contain, she glanced through it, and, giving a cry of pain, fainted away.

"I ran to her, and when the remedies which we freely applied had restored her to consciousness, anxiously questioned her. She handed me the note which she had just received. It contained the news of the arrest of my father, who had just been confined in the Temple prison. This was a great shock to all present. Though overwhelmed by so terrible an event, the consequences of which I did not dare to contemplate, I felt the necessity of overcoming my grief, and, summoning up all my strength, I approached Madame Bacciochi, who seemed more embarrassed than concerned. 'Madame,' I said to her in a voice broken by emotion, 'Madame, Heaven, which has made you the witness of our misfortunes, intends, beyond doubt, to make you our deliverer. I must see the First Consul this very day; it is absolutely imperative, and I rely on you, madame, to procure me this interview.'

"'But,' said Madame Bacciochi, with embarrassment, 'it seems to me that the best thing for you to do is to see Fouché, and find out exactly how matters stand; then, if it is necessary for you to see my brother, you may come and tell me, and we will consider what had better be done.'

"'Where shall I be able to find you, madame?' I replied, not allowing myself to be discouraged by the coldness with which she spoke.

"'At the Théâtre-Français, where I am going to join my sister, who is waiting for me.'"

Poor Madame Récamier, accordingly, ordered her carriage and drove to Fouché's house. From that astute personage, however, she received but little consolation. He informed her that her father's position was a very serious one, but that he himself could do nothing to help her. He advised her to see the First Consul without a moment's delay, and obtain his promise that the *mise en arraignment* should not take place. If she waited till the next day, he would not answer for the consequences.

In an agony of apprehension, Madame Récamier re-entered her carriage, and drove to the theatre to find Madame Bacciochi, her last hope. The journal continues:

"When I reached the Théâtre-Français I could scarcely stand. The noise, the crowd, the lights produced a strange and painful sensation. Wrapping myself in my shawl, I was conducted to Madame Bacciochi's box, where I was admitted during an *entr'acte*. She was there with Madame Leclerc,[1] and, on recognising me, could not conceal an expression of keen annoyance; but I was sustained by too strong a feeling to pay any attention to that.

"'I have come, madame,' I said, 'to claim the fulfilment of your promise. I must see the First Consul this very evening, or my father is lost.'

"'Well,' replied Madame Bacciochi carelessly, 'let us see the end of this tragedy; when it is over I am at your service.'

"There was nothing to be done but to wait. I sat down, or rather I sank down, in the remotest corner of the box. Fortunately for me, it was a stage box, very deep, and dark enough for me to be able to give myself up without

[1] Pauline Bonaparte, Napoleon's youngest and favourite sister. She married General Leclerc in 1801, and after his death, which occurred in the following year, became the wife of the Prince Borghese, a wealthy Italian nobleman. She was extremely beautiful, and was the original of the Venus Victrix of Canova.

restraint to my distressing thoughts. I then observed, for the first time, in the corner opposite to mine, a man whose large black eyes were fixed on me with so deep and kindly an interest that I was touched. After having endured so much coldness, it was some consolation to me to meet with a little kindness and compassion.

"At this moment Madame Leclerc turned abruptly towards me, and asked if I had seen Lafont before in the rôle of Achilles. Then, without waiting for a reply, she added, 'He is very handsome, but to-day he is wearing a helmet which does not become him in the least.'[1]

"At this idle question, and these frivolous and cruel words, which showed the most complete indifference to the situation in which I was placed, the unknown gentleman could not control a gesture of impatience; and, having doubtless resolved to cut short my agony, bent towards Madame Bacciochi, and remarked to her, in an undertone, 'Madame Récamier appears to be in distress. If she will permit me, I will escort her home, and will myself undertake to speak to the First Consul.'

"'Yes, of course,' answered Madame Bacciochi eagerly, delighted to be relieved of this disagreeable duty. 'Nothing could be more fortunate for you,' she added, turning to me. 'Confide in General Bernadotte; there is no one better able to help you.'"

Bernadotte, for her unknown friend was none other

[1] The celebrated actor Pierre Lafont was born at La Linde, in Périgord, in 1775. After performing for three or four years in the provinces, he came to Paris towards the end of the year 1799; and, in the following May, appeared at the Comédie Française as Achilles in *Iphigenia in Aulis*, and scored an unqualified success. He excelled both in tragedy and comedy. He was generally believed to be the lover—or rather one of the lovers, for "la jolie Paulette" was very free with her favours—of Madame Leclerc.

than the future King of Sweden, drove with Madame Récamier, who had, of course, gratefully accepted his offer of mediation, to her house, and then left to proceed to the Tuileries, promising to return as soon as he had seen the First Consul.

Madame Récamier found her own salon full of people, who had come to inquire the particulars of M. Bernard's arrest, which was already common property. She had not the courage to face them, however, but retired to her room to wait for Bernadotte, and, as she tells us, to count the minutes until his return. He came at last in triumph, and informed her that he had, although not without considerable difficulty, obtained a promise from the First Consul that her father should not be arraigned; and he hoped to procure his release in the course of a few days.

Next morning Madame Récamier, anxious to impart the good news to her imprisoned father, hastened to the Temple, where he was confined, and persuaded one of the turnkeys, named Coulommier, to allow her to see him for a few moments. Scarcely, however, had she been admitted to his cell when Coulommier rushed in, pale and frightened, and, opening a door in the wall, thrust her into what appeared to be a small dungeon, where he left her in total darkness. Presently she heard voices in her father's cell; then the opening and closing of a door, after which all was still.

Poor Madame Récamier remained shut up in her dungeon for two hours—it seemed to her more like two years—for she was half stupefied with thinking of all the horrors that had been committed in the Temple, and imagining that Coulommier had been detected in some breach of duty, and had been himself imprisoned, in which case no one might discover where she was until it was too late. At the end of that time she heard the sound of keys, and, to her joy, Coulommier came and released her, explaining that, just after she had entered her father's cell, the Prefect of Police had sent some gendarmes to conduct M. Bernard to the Préfecture, and that he had had no alternative but to conceal her, or run the risk of dismissal from his post, or, possibly, of a worse fate.

Bernadotte, in the meanwhile, had not relaxed his exertions, and, a few days later, he came to Madame Récamier's, holding in his hand the order for her father's release; and asked, as his only reward, permission to escort her to the Temple to free the prisoner. Madame Récamier, it is needless to say, overwhelmed the kind-hearted general with thanks, and he became from that moment one of her most intimate friends.

Although he obtained his freedom, Jean Bernard was, of course, dismissed from his office, nor does there seem to have been the slightest doubt but that he was deeply implicated in the Royalist conspiracy.

CHAPTER IV

Madame Récamier queen of Paris society—Her beauty and virtue—Charles James Fox's high opinion of her—Fox in Paris—His interviews with Bonaparte—Amusing incident at the Opera—An Irishman's impressions of Madame Récamier—Mary Berry's description of her—Paris during the Peace of Amiens—A drawing-room at the Tuileries—Demidoff's ball—The masked balls at the Opera—Madame Récamier's adventure with the Prince of Würtemberg—Madame Récamier visits England—Enthusiasm she arouses—Embarrassing situation at Covent Garden—Amusing letter in the *Gentleman's Magazine*—Rupture of the Peace of Amiens—Growing power of Bonaparte—Intrigues of Bernadotte against him—Animosity between Bonaparte and Madame de Staël—Reasons for this—Banishment of Madame de Staël—Bernadotte renews his intrigues—Madame Moreau's ball—Bernadotte's efforts to win over Moreau — Trial of Moreau, Pichegru, and Cadoudal—Madame Récamier's account of it—Banishment of Moreau—The First Consul sends for Bernadotte—Bernadotte's account of their interview

THE first seven years of the nineteenth century may be regarded as the period of Madame Récamier's reign as queen of Parisian society. Her husband's banking house had now become one of the wealthiest in France, and she only had to express a wish to see it immediately gratified; so that at their country-seat at Clichy, and at their hôtel in the Rue du Mont Blanc she was able to entertain in regal style all the most distinguished people in Paris.

Juliette was now in the zenith of her beauty and popularity. She was by this time entirely free from a slight bashfulness from which she had suffered when she first appeared in society, and her manners were charming, while she seems to have been as good as she was beautiful. It is true that, according to our English ideas, she must have been a desperate flirt, though this does not appear to have arisen from any craving for admiration, but rather from a desire to be loved by her friends—a desire not unnatural in a woman married to a husband more than twice her age, and entirely engrossed in the management of his business. She, certainly, does not seem to have been so indifferent to the many celebrated men who laid their hearts at her feet as she had shown herself to the advances of Lucien Bonaparte. But, on the other hand, it has not been suggested—by any one, that is to say, whose opinion carries any weight—that she ever exceeded the bounds of harmless flirtation: indeed, we have a striking testimony to her virtue from a contemporary—who was certainly by no means prone to credit any lady with that quality unless she had given very substantial proof of possessing it—Charles James Fox, who pronounced her to be "the only woman who united the attractions of pleasure to those of modesty."

Fox visited Paris during the Peace of Amiens, that brief lull in the terrible storm which deluged Europe in blood for so many years. He was accompanied by his wife (formerly Mrs. Armistead), his marriage to whom, although it had taken place, privately, seven years before, had only just been publicly announced, and John Bernard Trotter, a young Irishman who, subsequently, became his private secretary, and to whose "Memoirs of Fox" we are indebted for many interesting details of the great

Whig statesman's last years. The principal object of his visit seems to have been to make researches in the Archives for his projected history of the Stuarts, but he found time to mix freely in Parisian society, where, as his predilection for France was, of course, well known, he was greeted with enthusiasm. He had several interviews with Bonaparte, who, always anxious to conciliate the English Whigs, and create if possible a Bonapartist faction in that country, received him with marked cordiality. Fox's conversations with Napoleon, however, do not seem to have raised his opinion of the First Consul, whom he describes as "a young man intoxicated with success."

Fox soon became on very friendly terms with Madame Récamier and her immediate circle, and was a frequent visitor at Clichy. One afternoon Madame Récamier called for him in her carriage, and insisted on taking him for a drive along the Boulevards. "Before you came, Mr. Fox," said she, "I was the fashion ; it is a point of honour, therefore, that I should not appear jealous of you."

Some days after this drive, while Fox was sitting with Madame Récamier in her box at the Opera, a Frenchman entered, and handed each of them a copy of an ode, in which the English statesman was eulogised under the title of Jupiter, and his fair companion under that of Venus. On reading this extraordinary effusion, Fox felt naturally somewhat embarrassed ; but Madame Récamier only laughed, and assured him that she cared not a jot for the opinion of the good people of Paris. She was, undoubtedly, far too careless of her reputation, and it is hardly surprising that some of her most innocent friendships should have been construed into intrigues.

If Fox was favourably impressed by Madame Récamier,

his friend and travelling companion, Mr. Trotter, seems to have been completely overpowered by her charms, for in the "Memoirs," already referred to, we find her thus described:

"The lovely phantom, breathing a thousand delicious charms, yet flits before me—and so ingenuous and unaffected! shunning the ardent gaze, and, if conscious of her dazzling beauty, unassuming and devoid of pride; rich at the first of female virtues—a kind and noble heart."[1]

It is interesting to compare the susceptible Irishman's description of Madame Récamier with that of Mary Berry, who also met her, for the first time, during the Peace of Amiens:

". . . Madame Récamier, a rich banker's wife, who has the finest house in Paris in the *new* style, and is herself the decided beauty of the *new* world, for if she can be called handsome, it is entirely a *figure de fantasie.* She has a clear complexion, is young, tall, dressed with much affectation of singularity in the extravagance of the mode; her manners are *douceureuses*, thinking much of herself, with perfect carelessness about others; for, besides being a beauty, she has pretensions, I understand, to *bel-esprit.* They may be as well founded, and yet not sufficient to burn her for a witch."[2]

This sounds rather ill-natured; but Madame Récamier had a way of monopolising the adoration of the opposite sex at any ball or dinner-party at which she happened to be present, which ladies who met her for the first time must have found somewhat galling, and which even "an angel inside and out," as Horace Walpole declared Mary Berry to be, could not easily forgive.

[1] Trotter's "Memoirs of Charles James Fox," p. 341.

[2] Miss Berry's "Journal and Correspondence," ii. 177.

Paris was very gay that spring. No sooner was peace concluded than numbers of English people flocked across the Channel, eager to behold the city which had been the theatre of such stirring events, and the dictator whose name was on everybody's lips. To such lengths was the anxiety to see Napoleon carried that people actually came to France for a few hours, went to a review of the troops, saw the First Consul, and returned to England. Not only England, however, but every country in Europe contributed its quota of visitors; and the various ambassadors were simply overwhelmed with applications from people who wished to be presented at the Tuileries. Miss Berry has left us an interesting account of a kind of drawing-room held nominally, of course, by Josephine, but really by Napoleon.

On this occasion the ladies to be presented were ranged in a circle at one end of the salon, round which Bonaparte passed, accompanied by the two *Préfets du Palais*, and *followed*, at a respectful distance, by Josephine. One of the Préfets announced the name and nationality of each lady in turn, after which the First Consul talked to her for two or three minutes about the Opera, the respective merits of French and Italian actors, the benefits to be derived from horse-exercise, and such like topics; and then passed on to the next. Madame Bonaparte, who, we are told, "wore, by way of being in a smart *demi-parure*, a pink slight silk gown, with a pink velvet round spot upon it, a small white silk or satin hat, with three small white feathers, tied under the chin, and carried a handkerchief and no fan in her hand," also spoke to each lady in turn. As, however, she had no attendant to announce to her any of their names, the ceremony would appear to have been rather an informal one in her case.

But whatever innovations may be introduced at Court, they are almost certain to find imitators in society. There happened to be in Paris at this time a wealthy young Russian named Demidoff, who entertained on a most sumptuous and regal scale. This Demidoff gave a magnificent ball at the Hôtel de Montholon, to which all Paris was invited. A feature of this entertainment was that a *bouquetière* was stationed in the ante-chamber, who presented each lady with a splendid bouquet of hothouse flowers, with an intimation that she was at liberty to exchange it for a fresh one as often as she pleased during the evening. What was the astonishment of the guests, however, especially the English portion of them, to find on their arrival that it was their *host* and not their hostess who received and did all the honours, and that poor Madame Demidoff occupied quite a secondary position.

At this period the masked balls at the Opera were all the fashion, and were attended by the best people in Paris. Ladies went to them in masks and dominoes, but gentlemen in ordinary evening dress. The term *bal* was somewhat of a misnomer, for there was little or no dancing ; and the amusement of the evening depended on the mystery which surrounded the fair portion of the audience, who were permitted to freely accost and even attach themselves to any gentleman present. It was here that a lady could gratify a long cherished grudge, and, secure in the protection of her disguise, indulge in some very unpleasant home thrusts, or even reveal a secret passion, while the ugly little mask concealed her modest blushes. The fortunate or unfortunate individual thus addressed, of course, did all in his power to discover who the lady could be in whose bosom he had aroused these amorous or vindictive feelings, and many were the strange adventures which were met with at the Opera balls.

Madame Récamier attended several of these balls, under the escort of her brother-in-law Laurent Récamier, and met with a number of piquant adventures, and made several acquaintances which afterwards ripened into friendships. Among them was the young Prince—afterwards King of Würtemberg—who had been presented to her at one of her grand balls at the Rue du Mont Blanc, but with whom she had not on that occasion had the opportunity of exchanging more than a few words. Under cover of her disguise, she accosted him one evening, and, after they had conversed for a while on ordinary topics, asked him what he thought of Madame Récamier.

The Prince replied that he thought her very lovely, but that she was too inanimate to please him. Thereupon Madame Récamier, emboldened by her mask, commenced a very lively and fascinating conversation, with the result that the Prince was completely captivated, and entreated her to unmask. This she declined to do, but gave him a ring, saying that she would claim it at another ball (not a masked one) to be given a few days later. The Prince's astonishment and confusion may be imagined, when he discovered, on the evening in question, that the insipid beauty of the Rue du Mont Blanc and the vivacious owner of the ring were one and the same person.

In the spring of 1802 Madame Récamier with her mother paid a visit to England. Furnished with excellent introductions by the old Duc de Guignes, who had been ambassador at St. James's thirty years before, and a great favourite in society, and still more recommended by her reputation as a beauty, she was warmly welcomed in London. Georgiana, Duchess of Devonshire, still one of the most beautiful women of the day, "*quoique privée d'un œil qu'elle couvrait d'une boucle de ses cheveux*," was especially friendly, and Madame Récamier's first appearance in public was in the duchess's box at Covent Garden. The Prince of Wales, the exiled Duc d'Orléans, and his two young brothers, the Duc de Montpensier and the Comte de Beaujolais, were also of the party, and the "first gentleman in Europe" paid the lovely stranger the most marked attention.

As soon as Madame Récamier entered the box every glass was turned in her direction, while a low buzz of curiosity and admiration ran round the house, whereupon the Prince suggested that it would be advisable for the party to leave before the conclusion of the play, in order to escape the too obtrusive admiration of the crowd. The duchess concurred, but when they rose to leave, the audience rose too, and, regardless of the fact that the performance was not yet over, left their seats and flocked into the vestibule, determined to have as close a view as possible of the beautiful Frenchwoman. So great was the crowd that poor Madame Récamier was nearly swept off her feet; but, fortunately, managed at length to reach her carriage in safety.

Madame Récamier's reception at Covent Garden was only a foretaste of what was in store for her. Whenever she appeared in public she was followed by large and admiring crowds; her engagements, her remarks, her every movement were as faithfully chronicled by the newspapers as if she had been a royal personage; while her portrait, engraved by Bartolozzi, was to be seen in every shop window, and made its way from England to the Ionian Islands ("Beauty returning to the land which gave it birth," one of her admirers gallantly remarked),

India, and even China. The following amusing letter, which appeared in the *Gentleman's Magazine* for November of that year, and was, apparently, intended as a protest against the classic garb in which Madame Récamier sat for her portrait, will give some idea of the interest which her visit aroused in England :

"*October* 9.

"MR. URBAN,—Every husband, father, and brother in his Majesty's dominions owes thanks to the author of 'Remarks on Female Manners' reviewed on p. 846 : and you, Sir, must also claim a due share of praise for your endeavours to stir up the public indignation against such levities as seem to be now *systematically* introducing amongst us. We were informed by the Newspapers, the beginning of last spring, that a lady of exquisite beauty and elegance would walk in Kensington-gardens on the following Sunday. The next week we were told by the same papers that the public curiosity was so excited that the lady suffered the greatest inconvenience from the throng which surrounded her, whose rudeness was so great as even to lift up her veil that they might gaze upon her face.[1] Now, Mr. Urban, was not all this consequence *intended* by the *previous* notice, and has not the same lady left behind her an infamous proof of her own desire to draw aside the veil? Witness the exposure of her indecent portrait, now exhibiting in all the print-shops of the metropolis : but which I trust will not find its way into the houses of any of our English families who have the least regard to chastity, and the preservation of that

[1] A newspaper of the day in extenuation of this outrage says that "great part of the crowd consisted of Italian corset-makers, men-milliners, and shoemakers, who were endeavouring each to catch the fashion of her shoe and the quality of her veil."

characteristic modesty which heretofore distinguished the British female.

"As to the lady in question, I hope it will be some mortification to her vanity to be told that the *figure* of herself which she has left behind has drawn forth no better praise than what is contained in the following miserable epigram, written under the portrait (or, if Mr. Urban has no objection to mention names, under the portrait of Madame Récamier):

> "Can *modest* females *en chemise*
> Court public notice? Surely not.
> Such only can expect to please
> Those like themselves *les sans culottes*.

"Yours, etc.
"B. S."

A few months after Madame Récamier returned home, England and France were once more locked in a death grapple, and all communication between the fashionable worlds of London and Paris was cut off for eleven long years.

The year which followed the renewal of hostilities was an eventful one for Madame Récamier and her friends. It was becoming daily more apparent that nothing short of the vacant throne would be likely to satisfy the ambition of Bonaparte, and the prospect was one which filled the old Republicans with alarm and apprehension. They recognised, however, that to oppose Bonaparte at this stage of his career courage of no ordinary kind would be required; for not only had he shown himself perfectly unscrupulous in his dealings with his political opponents, but every advantage was now on his side. The army was devoted to their victorious leader; the Press had been effectually muzzled; and the vast majority of the nation, heartily sick of revolutionary changes, would be far more disposed to resent than to support any attempt to interfere with the man whom they regarded as the champion of order against anarchy.

The centre of the Republican opposition to Bonaparte at this time was Madame Récamier's new friend Bernadotte, who had been one of the first to divine the real intentions of the First Consul. Bernadotte's plan was to proceed by constitutional means. He proposed that a memorial, signed by a number of the leading men in France, should be presented to Bonaparte, representing that the friends of liberty had paid too high a price for it to allow such sacrifices to be turned to the glorification of one man, however well he may have deserved of the State. Should Bonaparte return a favourable answer to this memorial, and express his willingness to abide by the terms of the Constitution, their purpose would have been achieved: if not, a resolution calling upon him to resign, or imposing fresh limitations on his power, could be brought forward in the Senate.

This proposal sounded to Madame Récamier, whom the general made his confidante, both "just and generous," but unfortunately Bernadotte could not find a single Republican senator with the courage of his convictions. They agreed that the power of Bonaparte "had increased, was increasing, and ought to be diminished"; but to subscribe to a resolution to that effect, which would definitely commit them to a struggle with so formidable an antagonist, was quite another matter; and they one and all refused their signatures to the document.

It must not be supposed that the First Consul long remained in ignorance of what was going on. Few things escaped the vigilant eyes of his secret police. He had no wish to strike at Bernadotte, who was but a poor schemer, though a brave soldier, and, moreover, connected with his own family, having married Madame Joseph Bonaparte's sister, Desirée Clary, an old playfellow of the First Consul. As for the other conspirators, he despised them as timid doctrinaires, who had brought their country to the verge of ruin in the past, but were impotent when confronted with a man of courage and resolution. There was one person in the Opposition ranks, however, whom he both feared and hated, and of whom he now determined to make an example. This was Madame de Staël, in whose salon Bernadotte and his friends had been in the habit of meeting.

The exact date of the beginning of what has been styled Madame de Staël's duel with Napoleon is not very easy to determine, but the probability is that it dates from the early days of the Consulate. "When Bonaparte became First Consul," says Madame de Rémusat, "Madame de Staël was already celebrated for her opinions, her mode of life, and her writings. Such a man as Bonaparte would naturally excite first the curiosity and then the enthusiasm of a woman so alive to anything out of the common as Madame de Staël. She was enraptured, and eagerly sought his acquaintance. She thought that one who united so many remarkable gifts with so many favourable opportunities would be a powerful promoter of liberty, which was her idol; but she alarmed Bonaparte, who did not choose to be either closely watched or clearly interpreted." [1]

[1] Bourrienne puts the beginning of the quarrel much earlier, and Madame de Staël's conduct in a far from favourable light. "Madame de Staël," he says, "had not been introduced to him (Bonaparte), and

Bonaparte, in fact, disliked clever women, and received Madame de Staël's friendly advances with studied coldness, and disconcerted her with the brevity and downrightness of his speech. The lady, however, was not one to accept defeat lightly, and she tells us how, hearing that the First Consul had expressed himself unfavourably about her, she had, before going to a dinner-party at Berthier's at which he was to be present, "written down a number of tart and piquant replies which she might make to the questions which she supposed he would address to her." On this occasion, however, Bonaparte avoided her, and gave her no opportunity for retaliation, and, in a passage of arms which took place soon afterwards, and in which Madame de Staël was herself the aggressor, gained a very decisive victory.

The authoress had asked him with that direct mode of attack which Byron found so trying, "Whom do you think the greatest woman alive or dead?" and was met with the sarcastic retort, "Her, madame, who has given

knew nothing more of him than what had been published respecting the young conqueror of Italy when she addressed to him letters full of enthusiasm. Bonaparte read some passages of them to me, and, laughing, said: 'What do you think, Bourrienne, of these extravagances? This woman is mad.' I recollect that in one of her letters Madame de Staël, among other things, told him that they certainly were created for each other; that it was in consequence of error in human institutions that the quiet and gentle Josephine was united to his fate; that nature seemed to have destined for a hero such as he a soul of fire like her own. These extravagances disgusted Bonaparte to a degree which I cannot describe. When he had finished reading these fine epistles, he used to throw them into the fire, or tear them to pieces, with marked ill-humour, and would say, 'Well, here is a woman who pretends to genius—a maker of sentiments, and she presumes to compare herself to Josephine. Bourrienne, I shall not reply to these letters.'"—"Memoirs of Napoleon" (Colonel Phipps's translation), ii. 365.

most sons to the State!" "They say you are not very friendly to the sex," she resumed. "I am very fond of my wife," he replied, and abruptly turned away.

There was nothing in these replies to call forth any particular resentment, for Napoleon's lack of good breeding was always especially manifest in his conversation with women, whom he delighted to embarrass by peremptory remarks which admitted of no reply, and even by rudeness of language, which could not fail to both perplex and mortify them. Bourrienne tells us that he often addressed to them such remarks as "How red your elbows are!" "What a strange head-dress you wear!" "Pray, tell me, do you ever change your gown?"—familiarities which few of them dared to resent.[1] Madame de Staël, however, was not as other women, and it is said that she never forgave Napoleon these sarcastic answers, and vowed vengeance. Her reprisals took the form of biting *bon-mots* directed against the First Consul and his family, which, of course, never failed to reach Bonaparte's ears. Wit and sarcasm are deadly weapons enough, if effectually manipulated, and in the hands of Madame de Staël they cut

[1] "The celebrated Sophie Gay, a friend and defender of Madame de Staël, was less timid before him, and repelled his cynicism by her ready repartee. She was on intimate terms with his sister Pauline, and met him at her house at Aix-la-Chapelle. In passing near the young authoress, he said to her very brusquely and with the eagle glance before which most women cowered, 'Madame, my sister has told you that I do not like intellectual women.' 'Yes, sire,' she responded, not at all disconcerted; 'yes, sire; but I do not believe her.' The Emperor was surprised, and made another attempt. 'You write, do you not? What have you produced since you have been in this country?' 'Three children, sire,' she proudly replied. He passed on, pretending to smile. The lady's wit was too much for his own. One of these children was Delphine, well-known in our day as the accomplished authoress, Madame Girardin."—*Biographie Universelle*, xvi.

deeper than iron or steel, and wounded Bonaparte in the one spot in which he was vulnerable—his vanity. He had no means of counteracting these attacks except by resorting to extreme measures, and these he finally took. It is only fair to Bonaparte to observe, however, that it is very doubtful whether Madame de Staël would have had any reason to complain of his treatment of her had she not deliberately gone out of her way to provoke her enemy. Bonaparte, indeed, was desirous of disarming her hostility and winning her over to his side. "What *does* she want? Why does she not join us?" he asked his brother Joseph, who was on intimate terms with Madame de Staël, and commissioned him to sound the lady on the subject. When Joseph reported what Napoleon had said to his friend, she replied, "The difficulty, monsieur, is not what I want, but what I *think*."

At length Benjamin Constant's (the famous publicist) speech in the Senate, in which he denounced the First Consul, although without specifying him by name, as aiming at arbitrary power, and which was generally believed to have been prompted by Madame de Staël; the appearance of her father's (Necker) *Dernières Vues de Politique et de Finance*, which gave great umbrage to the First Consul; and, finally, her friendship with disaffected men like Bernadotte and Moreau, exhausted Bonaparte's patience, and in the autumn of 1803 Madame de Staël was banished forty leagues from Paris.

This harsh and arbitrary act, revealing as it did despotism in its most odious form, made the friends of liberty more than ever apprehensive of the results of Bonaparte's assumption of absolute power. Bernadotte, Madame Récamier tells us, showed her a list of Republican generals upon whom he thought he could rely, but Victor

Moreau, the hero of Hohenlinden, the one man above all others whose co-operation was essential to the success of his plans, was not among them. He had refused to join. Bernadotte had several interviews with Moreau, both at the latter's country house at Grosbois, and at Madame Récamier's, and used every argument he could think of to induce him to take the lead against Bonaparte, but all to no purpose. The Republican general, though admitting the gravity of the situation, was fearful of provoking civil war, and disinclined to take part in any movement which might redound to the advantage of the hated Bourbons.

In the early part of the winter Madame Moreau gave a ball. All the foreigners in Paris were there, but Madame Récamier was struck by the absence of everybody connected with the Government. Both Moreau and Bernadotte, too, seemed preoccupied; and during a quadrille the latter offered her his arm to go and get a little air, "although," remarks the fair conspirator, "it was our thoughts that needed breathing-space."

"We retired into a small salon," she continues, "where only the sound of the music came to remind us of where we were. I confided to him my fears. He had not yet given up hope of Moreau, whose position both for determining the course of any movement, and for moderating its possible excesses, he considered so excellent; but he was irritated at the thought that so many advantages might be lost.

"'Were I in his place,' he said, 'I would go this evening to the Tuileries, and dictate to Bonaparte the conditions on which he might govern.'"

Moreau happened to pass by at that moment, whereupon Bernadotte called to him, and repeated all the reasons and arguments he had made use of to influence him.

"'With your popular name,' said he, 'you are the only one amongst us who can face Bonaparte supported by the whole people. Think what you can do—what we can do with you as our leader, and then decide!'"

Moreau reiterated what he had often said: that he felt the danger with which liberty was menaced; that it was necessary to keep a watchful eye upon Bonaparte's movements, but that he feared civil war. He held himself in readiness; his friends might act, and, when the time for action arrived, he would be at their disposal. They might count on him as soon as the first movement was made, but, for the present, he did not feel called upon to take the initiative. He even disclaimed the importance which they thought fit to attribute to him.

The conversation lasted a long time and grew warm. Bernadotte lost his temper, and said to Moreau:

"'Ah, you are afraid to espouse the cause of liberty. And Bonaparte, say you, will not dare to attack it. Ah, well, Bonaparte will make game both of liberty and you! She will perish in spite of our efforts, and you will be involved in her ruin without having fought for her.'"

Madame Récamier tells us that she retained a vivid recollection of this conversation, and when, in the following spring, Moreau was implicated in the trial of Georges Cadoudal and Pichegru, she remained convinced that he was as innocent of all connection with that conspiracy as he had been of the intrigues of Bernadotte.

Madame Récamier had not intended to be present at the trial, but Madame Moreau, happening to mention that her husband had often looked for her among his friends in court, she determined to go. We will let her relate her impressions of this *cause célèbre*.

"I was accompanied," she says, "by a near relation of M. Récamier, a magistrate named Brillat-Savarin.[1] The crowd was so great that not only the hall and the galleries, but all the approaches to the court-house were thronged with people. M. Savarin took me in by the door that opened on the amphitheatre, facing the prisoners, from whom I was separated by the whole length of the hall. I glanced hurriedly and fearfully over the benches of this amphitheatre to find Moreau. The moment I raised my veil he recognised me, and, rising from his seat, bowed. I returned his greeting with respect and emotion, and hastened down the steps to take the seat reserved for me.

"The prisoners were forty-seven in number, and, for the most part, strangers to each other. They occupied the raised seats facing those on which the judges sat. Each prisoner was seated between two gendarmes: there was much deference in the manner of the two who guarded Moreau. I was deeply touched to see this great captain, whose reputation was, at that time, so great and so untarnished, treated as a criminal. It was no longer a question of Republic and Republicans; it was—with the exception of Moreau, whom I am convinced was an entire stranger to this conspiracy—Royalist fidelity which struggled against the new power. Nevertheless, the cause of the ancient monarchy had for its leader a man of the people—Georges Cadoudal.

[1] Anthelme Brillat-Savarin, a member of the Court of Cassation from 1802 till his death in 1826. He was a famous gastronomist. His well-known work, *Physiologie du Goût*, an elegant and witty compendium of the art of dining, has been translated into several languages.

"That intrepid Georges! In looking at him I thought that that head, so freely, so energetically devoted, was destined to fall on the scaffold, and, perhaps, be the only one not saved, since he made no effort on his own behalf. Scorning to defend himself, he only defended his friends. I heard his answers, all bearing the impress of that ancient faith for which he had fought so bravely, and had been ready long ago to lay down his life. Accordingly, when they endeavoured to persuade him to follow the example of the other prisoners, and to ask for pardon, 'Will you promise me,' he replied, 'a better cause to die for?'

"In the ranks of suspected persons were M. de Polignac and M. de Rivière, objects of interest on account of their youth and disinterestedness. Pichegru, whose name will be associated in history with that of Moreau, was, however, missing from the side of the latter, although one might fancy that one saw his spirit there, for it was known that he had died in prison.[1] Another death, that of the Duc d'Enghien, added to the terror and grief existing in many minds even among the most devoted partisans of the First Consul.

"Moreau did not speak, and after the session was over, the magistrate who had escorted me came to take me away. I passed the bar on the opposite side to that by which I had entered the court, thus passing along the whole length of the raised benches on which the prisoners sat. At that moment Moreau was coming down, followed by his two gendarmes and some other prisoners; he was only separated from me by a railing. He spoke a few

[1] Pichegru was found strangled in his cell on the morning of April 6. There does not appear to be any justification for the Royalist report that he was made away with by Bonaparte's orders. It is far more probable that he took his dishonoured life with his own hands.

words of thanks in passing, that in my agitation I scarcely heard. I understood, however, that he was grateful for my having come, and begged me to come again. This conversation was destined to be our last."[1]

Madame Récamier did not attend the trial again, for, early the next morning, she received a message from Cambacérès, begging her, for Moreau's sake, not to return to the court. The First Consul, it appeared, had, in reading the report of the session, seen her name in the list of those present, and had asked sharply, "What business had Madame Récamier there?" and it was thought by Madame Moreau that every mark of interest shown in her husband would only increase his danger.

At the close of the trial all business was suspended; the whole population was in the streets, and the one topic of conversation the fate of Moreau. It was the general opinion that Bonaparte only desired Moreau to be condemned to death in order to pardon him; but, on this being repeated to Clavier, one of the judges, he replied, "And who then would pardon us?"

The night preceding the sentence, during the whole of which the court continued sitting, all the approaches to the Palace of Justice were blocked by surging crowds, animated by the most intense excitement. When the decision of the judges was made known, it was found that twenty of the prisoners had been condemned to death, of whom ten perished with Georges Cadoudal on the scaffold. The others, most of whom were connected with great families, whom Bonaparte was anxious to conciliate, were imprisoned in fortresses, the ladies of the First Consul's family having gone through the farce of obtaining this commutation.

[1] *Souvenirs*, i. 104.

Moreau's sentence was banishment for life to America. No one seriously believed that he was implicated in the conspiracy, although he had undoubtedly been approached by Pichegru and Cadoudal with the view of securing his co-operation ; but his military reputation, second only to that of Bonaparte himself, was naturally obnoxious to the First Consul, who saw in him a stumbling-block in the path of his ambition which must be removed at all costs.

One day soon after Moreau had been arrested, Bernadotte came to Madame Récamier in great alarm to inform her that he had just received a message from the First Consul, requiring his presence at the Tuileries. He had apparently forgotten all about his grand scheme for safeguarding the Constitution, and was fearful lest his frequent interviews with Moreau at the latter's country house should have compromised him with the Government. Madame Récamier made him promise to return and let her know the result of his interview with Bonaparte, and anxiously awaited him.

When he arrived he seemed preoccupied, but more easy in his mind. In answer to her inquiries, he told her that Bonaparte had received him cordially, and proposed that he should throw in his lot with him, pointing out that the country had now declared in his favour, and that opposition to his plans could only end in disaster. He had concluded by asking Bernadotte whether he would march with him and with France, or hold aloof.

Madame Récamier, who seems to have summed up her friend's character with tolerable accuracy, and suspected that personal ambition was at the root of all his intrigues, was not in the least surprised when Bernadotte added, a little shamefacedly, for she had been a witness of all his vapouring about liberty and republican principles, that he had felt that he had no alternative but to promise Bonaparte a loyal co-operation.

After Napoleon became Emperor honours were showered upon Bernadotte. He was made a Marshal of the Empire, and in 1806 created Prince de Ponte-Corvo; nevertheless ill-feeling always existed between him and Napoleon, and the latter found means to give proof of this, even in the favours he bestowed upon him.

CHAPTER V

Napoleon becomes Emperor—He desires that his Court shall rival that of the ancient monarchy—Madame de Rémusat's and Madame de Staël's accounts of it—Creation of a nobility—Napoleon wishes to attach Madame Récamier to the Court—Sinister motives attributed to him—Fouché's visits to Clichy—His conversation with Madame Récamier—Advises her to apply for the post of *dame du palais* to the Empress—His insinuations—Annoyance and alarm of Madame Récamier—Visits Caroline Murat at Neuilly—Fouché also of the party—Caroline seconds Fouché's efforts—She lends Madame Récamier her box at the Théâtre Français—The Emperor's undisguised admiration for Madame Récamier—He commissions Fouché to offer her the post of *dame du palais*—She declines it—Fouché's anger and threats—Jacques Récamier's bank in difficulties—His application for assistance refused by the Bank of France—Récamier's bank stops payment—Courage of Madame Récamier under her reverses—Universal sympathy which she arouses—Her letter to Camille Jordan—Napoleon's characteristic remark—Letters from Madame de Staël and Bernadotte

On May 18 of that year the curtain was rung down on the farce of republican government, and the Empire of Charlemagne was revived in the person of the Corsican adventurer who had so long been monarch in everything but name.

It was scarcely to be expected that Madame Récamier would witness the despot who had so recently deprived her of two of her most cherished friends ascend the vacant throne with any great degree of satisfaction, but true to the principle which she had always observed of ignoring, as far as possible, all political distinctions, she continued to extend her hospitality to both the members of the new aristocracy and the representatives of the old *régime.* Unfortunately, as it proved for her, the latter predominated among her friends, and thus gave to her receptions a complexion which the fair hostess herself would have been the first to disclaim.

Napoleon was fully resolved to leave no stone unturned to add to the splendour of his Court, which he intended should emulate that of the ancient monarchy. The ponderous regulations of Louis XVI. were taken down from their shelves in the library of St. Cloud, and carefully consulted in order that a code of etiquette might be drawn up for the use of the new Court. The Empress sent for Madame Campan, who had been First Lady of the Bedchamber to Marie Antoinette, and questioned her minutely concerning the manners and customs of the late Queen of France; and Madame de Rémusat tells us in her memoirs that she was instructed to take copious notes of Madame Campan's answers, and then pass them on to the Emperor, who was collecting similar memoranda from all sides.

When once launched on a course of ceremonial, the work went merrily on. "Whoever," says Madame de Staël, "could suggest an additional piece of etiquette, propose an additional reverence, a new mode of knocking at the door of an antechamber, a more ceremonious method of presenting a petition or folding a letter, was received as if he had been a benefactor of the human race. The code of Imperial etiquette is the most remarkably authentic record of human baseness that has been treasured up by history."

It was one of Napoleon's favourite maxims that an aristocracy is the chief prop of a throne; and no sooner had he assumed the Imperial crown than he proceeded to create a new nobility to replace that of the old *régime*. Talleyrand became Prince de Benevento; Berthier Prince de Neufchatel; Murat, whose father was a little innkeeper in Perigord, and whose mother went out charing at a franc a day, was made Grand Duke of Berg; Savary, who had superintended the murder of the young Duc d'Enghien, received as his reward the duchy of Rovigo; while counts were created by the dozen[1] and barons by the score, and endowed with the revenues of the conquered territories and the confiscated property of the *emigrés* to enable them to support their new dignities.

If rigid ceremonial and high-sounding titles had been all that was required to give distinction to the Court of the First Empire, there would have been enough and to spare. There is, however, another element which has to be taken into consideration in the formation of a Court. That element is woman. In that direction Napoleon soon found that his power, great as it was, had its limitations. He could create dukes, and barons, and counts; he could enrich the humble and ennoble the obscure; but he could not make plain women beautiful or dull women witty. His ill-advised harshness had deprived his Court of the first wit in France, and he was, therefore, doubly anxious that the first beauty, courted as she was both by the old nobility and the new society, should adorn his palace. Moreover, he was fully alive to the fact that the salons of Paris were distinctly hostile to his Government, and that at

[1] All the members of the Senate indiscriminately were ennobled, and given what Cambacérès, in announcing the imperial edict, called "the majestic title of Count."

receptions like those of Madame Récamier his ambitious schemes were wont to be discussed, and treated with scant respect. He, therefore, sent for Fouché, who had lately been reinstated in his old office of Minister of Police, and instructed him to make overtures to Madame Récamier with the object of inducing her to join the Imperial Household.

A far less creditable motive than that of merely undermining Madame Récamier's social influence, and, at the same time, of adding lustre to his Court has frequently been ascribed to Napoleon, and it is significant that this view of the matter is taken not only by the lady's intimate friends, who were for the most part hostile to the Emperor, but also by impartial chroniclers of those times, like Bourrienne and Madame Junot. Whether Napoleon really hoped to succeed where his brother Lucien had so conspicuously failed it is very difficult to say; but it is certain that Fouché, who had as little scruple about pandering to his master's vices as Cardinal Dubois had to those of the Regent Orléans, believed such to be the case, and acted accordingly.

When, in the summer of 1805, the Récamiers moved as usual to Clichy, Fouché became a frequent visitor. Madame Récamier had no particular liking for the Police Minister, who had been one of the worst of the Terrorists, and whose name was held in abhorrence by all the Lyonnais on account of the cruelties perpetrated by him in their city in 1794; and she was, moreover, not a little surprised that so busy a man should be able to find leisure for country visiting. Still she was not unwilling to avail herself of his influence to aid some of the unfortunate people who had embroiled themselves with the Government, and were constantly applying to her to make intercession for them with her powerful friends.

One afternoon Fouché begged for a private interview, and Madame Récamier gave him an appointment for the following day. He arrived punctually, and was shown into the salon where his hostess was awaiting him.

The Police Minister opened the conversation by deploring the opposition to the new Government displayed by so many of the habitués of Madame Récamier's salon—a feeling which, he observed, had been gradually increasing ever since the dismissal of her father, M. Bernard, from the Post Office. This antagonism—for which there was no adequate reason, since Napoleon had treated M. Bernard with great indulgence—had, he declared, seriously annoyed the Emperor. He strongly advised her to avoid every shadow of offence, as Napoleon was easily irritated, and concluded by reminding her that her friend the young and lovely Duchesse de Chevreuse had, like herself, shown more than coldness to the new dynasty, but had been promptly reduced to submission by a threat that her property should be confiscated. "Now," added the crafty Minister, "the house of De Luynes and their kinsmen, the Montmorencies, are only too glad to accept for the Duchesse de Chevreuse a place as *dame du palais* to the Empress Josephine. The Emperor since the day when he first met you has never forgotten you. Be prudent, and do not wound his feelings."

Madame Récamier, not a little astonished at this advice, thanked the Minister for the interest he took in her welfare, and disclaimed all concern in politics; but asserted that it was impossible for her to abandon her friends. The conversation did not go any further that day, and presently Fouché took his leave.

Some time afterwards, when Fouché was walking with his fair hostess in the park at Clichy, he said to her, with a smile:

"Can you guess whom I was talking with about you for nearly an hour last evening? With the Emperor."

"But he scarcely knows me!"

"Since the day when he first met you, he has never forgotten you, and although he complains that you have ranged yourself on the side of his enemies, he does not lay the blame on your own feelings, but on your friends."

Fouché then insisted that Madame Récamier should tell him her real feelings with regard to the Emperor.

She replied, with perfect frankness, that at first she had been attracted towards him by the glamour of his victories and the great services he had rendered to France, and that, on the one occasion on which they had met, she had been favourably impressed with his simple and natural manners; but that his persecution of her friends, the exile of Madame de Staël, the banishment of Moreau, and the execution of the poor young Duc d'Enghien had checked her enthusiasm for him, and alienated her sympathies.

Without appearing to pay much attention to what Madame Récamier had said, Fouché then boldly broached the subject which had brought him thither. He advised her to apply for a place at Court, and took it upon himself to assure her that her request would be immediately granted.

This unexpected overture struck Madame Récamier with astonishment and dismay, for she felt an invincible repugnance to the position it was suggested she should fill. Apprehensive of giving offence, however, she couched her refusal in the most courteous language at her command, observing that she was highly flattered at the Minister's proposal, but that the simplicity of her tastes, her natural timidity which contact with the world had not succeeded in overcoming, her love of independence, and, above all, her husband's position in commercial circles, which involved constant entertaining, all precluded the possibility of her accepting so important a post.

Fouché, however, made light of all these objections, protesting that the office would leave her entirely free; and then, seizing with adroitness on the only inducement which would be likely to weigh with so generous a woman, he pointed out the important services which she would be in a position to render to the oppressed of all classes, the many grievances she would be able to bring before the Emperor which might otherwise escape his notice. He laid great stress upon the ascendency which a woman of so noble and disinterested a character, and endowed with such ravishing charms ought to be able to exercise over the mind of the Emperor. "He has not yet," he added, "met a woman worthy of him, and no one knows what the love of Napoleon might be if he attached himself to a virtuous woman. Assuredly he would permit her to exercise over his mind a mighty influence, which would be wholly for good."

Fouché grew quite eloquent in expatiating on the great benefits to humanity which would be sure to follow the conquest of the Emperor's heart, and did not notice the growing disgust with which his companion was listening to his odious insinuations. However, fearful of offending him, she succeeded in mastering her righteous indignation, and, with an affectation of good humour, told Fouché that he was altogether too romantic and overrated the influence of pretty women; and the Police Minister left her, by no means dissatisfied with the result of his mission.

Poor Madame Récamier was terribly upset by what had passed, but buoyed herself up with the hope that Fouché's offer had been made on his own responsibility, and not on that of his master. She, however, sent for Mathieu de Montmorency, the one friend in whose discretion she could place implicit confidence, and told him all that had occurred. Montmorency recognised at once the danger of her position, but could only advise her to await further developments, and, in the meantime, to exercise great prudence and reserve.

Shortly after Fouché's visit, Madame Récamier, in response to a message from the Princess Caroline (Madame Murat), went to call upon her at Neuilly, the country seat which her brother had lately given her. The princess received her very cordially, and invited her to breakfast with her a few days later. When she arrived on the morning in question, she found, to her intense annoyance, that Fouché was also to be of the party; and she suspected that a trap had been laid for her—a suspicion which was confirmed when, on rising from the breakfast-table, her hostess proposed a walk, and suggested that the Police Minister should escort them.

After a little desultory conversation on ordinary topics, Fouché, as she had anticipated, returned to the attack. He told the princess of the proposal he had made to Madame Récamier, and of the latter's objections, and begged her to use her influence with her friend to induce her to accept a post in every way so desirable.

The princess expressed herself much pleased at Fouché's project, and—what must have appeared to her guest not a little singular, since she pretended that this was the first she had heard about it—brought forward "a hundred arguments" to persuade her to consider it in a favourable light. She concluded by saying, "in a tone of most sincere friendship," that, if Madame Récamier would apply for the post of *dame du palais*, she would endeavour to get her into her own service, as Napoleon had placed the establishments of his sisters on the same footing as that of the Empress. In this way, she added, she would be able to screen her from the jealousy of Josephine, whose suspicions might be aroused if so beautiful a lady of honour was placed about her own person.

Madame Récamier, although now more than ever determined that nothing should induce her to consent to such an arrangement, thought it best to temporise, and, therefore, promised to give the matter further consideration, with which the princess and Fouché were fain to be content. As she was leaving, the former, remembering that her friend had always expressed great admiration for Talma's acting, offered her the use of her own box at the Théâtre Français, which was on the grand tier, exactly opposite to that of the Emperor, whenever she cared to avail herself of it; and, next day, the following note was forwarded to the management of the theatre:

"NEUILLY, *October* 14.

"Her Royal Highness, the Princess Caroline, informs the management of the Théâtre Français that, from this date until a new order be issued, her box is to be open to Madame Récamier, to those who accompany her, or to those to whom she may give permission. Persons belonging to the household of the Princess, unless admitted or expressly named by Madame Récamier, cease from this moment to have the right of presenting themselves.

"CH. DE LONGCHAMPS,

"*The Secretary of Orders to the Princess Caroline.*"

Madame Récamier only made use of the box twice.

On both occasions it happened, either by accident or intention, that the Emperor was also present, and levelled his lorgnettes so persistently at the lady opposite, that it was rumoured among the courtiers, always on the watch to note their master's slightest movement, that the banker's beautiful wife was on the road to high favour.

Meanwhile Fouché continued his negotiations, and one day came to Clichy in high spirits, and, taking Madame Récamier on one side, said, with a triumphant chuckle:

"You can no longer refuse; it is not I now, but the Emperor himself who offers you the post of *dame du palais*, and I am commissioned to offer it in his name."

So little did Fouché imagine the possibility of a refusal, that he walked away to join the rest of the company without even waiting for a reply.

It was now no longer possible for Madame Récamier to avoid giving a definite answer; and so, when her husband came to Clichy to dine that evening, she informed him of the offer that had been made her, and of her great reluctance to accept it.

The banker fully sympathised with her feelings in the matter, and left her free to act as she thought best; and, accordingly, the next time Fouché presented himself at Clichy, she told him, courteously yet firmly, that she had finally decided to decline the honour the Emperor wished to confer upon her.

The Police Minister was furious, and, carried away by his indignation, broke out into a storm of reproaches against Madame Récamier's friends, especially Mathieu de Montmorency, whom he accused of having "prepared this insult for the Emperor." He indulged in a violent tirade against the old nobility, to whom he said the

Emperor showed a fatal indulgence, and left Clichy vowing vengeance.

Madame Récamier was soon to discover what this refusal was to cost her. One Saturday, in the autumn of the following year, Jacques Récamier came to his wife, looking very much disturbed. He told her that his bank had lately become involved in a series of misfortunes owing to the financial panic in Spain; and now things had come to such a pass that, unless, by the following Monday, he could obtain from the Bank of France the accommodation for which he had that day applied, he would be compelled to suspend payment. The sum he required to tide over his difficulties was a comparatively small one—a million francs (£40,000)—and, as he had ample security to offer, and the Bank of France had lately shown itself desirous of doing everything in its power to re-establish public credit, he had little fear of his application being refused. Still he could not help feeling extremely anxious; and begged Madame Récamier to do all the honours of their usual Sunday dinner-party, which it was impossible to countermand at so short a notice without exciting suspicion, as he himself felt that he would be unable to summon up sufficient courage to be present. He would go into the country until he got his answer on the Monday.

Such a revelation was, naturally, a great shock to the young wife, accustomed from childhood to a life of ease and luxury, whose every whim it had been the delight of her husband to gratify as soon as expressed, and who had never been permitted to trouble her pretty head about money matters. But she did her utmost to cheer her disconsolate spouse; and, on the following evening, when her guests arrived, they found her as lovely and smiling as ever, and no one would have suspected the terrible effort that it cost their hostess to preserve her composure, or the ruin which menaced the house where they were being so hospitably entertained.

A few hours later her worst fears were realised. The all-important loan was harshly refused, and, on the same day, Récamier's bank stopped payment.

The sensation caused by this catastrophe was immense, for the bank was one of the wealthiest in France, and many smaller houses, both in Paris and in the provinces, were involved in its fall. In financial circles general astonishment was expressed at the refusal of the Government to assist Récamier, and thus prevent what they well knew must cause widespread disaster. There can be little doubt, however, that Napoleon, who manipulated banks and bourses as readily as he did armies and navies, was responsible for this otherwise unaccountable action on the part of the authorities of the Bank of France.

Madame Récamier, aware that she herself was indirectly the cause of her husband's failure, bore this terrible reverse of fortune without a murmur, and while Jacques Récamier voluntarily surrendered everything to his creditors, who, as a proof of their esteem and confidence, nominated him head of the liquidators of the bank, she parted with her jewellery to the last trinket. The splendid house in the Rue du Mont Blanc was at once advertised for sale, but as a purchaser for so valuable a property was not immediately forthcoming, Madame Récamier gave up her own apartments, which were let furnished to Prince Pignatelli, reserving for herself only a small drawing-room on the ground floor, the windows of which opened on to the garden. The house was finally sold, two years later, to M. Mosselman, the banker, in whose counting-house the famous strategist Jomini was at one time a clerk.

The following letter, addressed to her old friend Camille Jordan, will show with what fortitude Madame Récamier endured a misfortune which would have utterly crushed most women :

"Dear Camille,—Your letter has come as a very charming consolation to me in the midst of my troubles. I have read it to M. Récamier, who has been much touched by the kindly interest you take in us. The affection of my friends sustains my courage. Although my misfortune was a totally unexpected one, I am quite resigned to my fate ; and I have had the happiness of being able by my care and attention to soften the grief of my husband and family. And, besides, dear Camille, ought not I to thank God that in keeping in store for me such bitter calamities, He has given me friends to enable me to support them ? . . . "J. R."

The attentions which Madame Récamier received at this time of unmerited misfortune were highly creditable to French society. She was the object of universal sympathy and respect ; her door was simply besieged with callers, and she became, if it were possible, an even greater object of admiration than she had been before. "They would not have shown so much respect to the widow of a marshal of France killed on the field of battle ! " Napoleon sarcastically observed, when Junot, Duc d'Abrantès, joined him in Germany, full of the catastrophe which was the talk of Paris, and the widespread interest the innocent victim of it was arousing.

Madame de Staël wrote to her friend a letter full of womanly sympathy :

"Geneva, *November* 17, 1806.

"Ah, my dear Juliette, what grief have I experienced at the dreadful news which I have received! How I curse my exile which prevents me from being near you and pressing you to my heart!

"You have lost all that pertains to the ease and luxury of life; but, were such a thing possible, you are more beloved and more interesting than you were before this misfortune overtook you. I am going to write to M. Récamier, who has my sympathy and respect. But tell me, will my hope of seeing you here this winter be only a dream? If you would care to pass three months in a circle where you would be fondly cared for. . . . But in Paris also you inspire this same feeling. Still, at least, I will go to Lyons, or as near as my forty leagues will allow me, to behold you, to embrace you, and to tell you that I love you more tenderly than any woman I have ever known. I have nothing to say to you by way of consolation, unless it is to assure you that you will be more beloved and honoured than ever; and that those admirable characteristics of yours—generosity and kind-heartedness—will, in spite of yourself, become known through these misfortunes as they never would have been without them.

"Certainly, in comparing your present position with what it was, you are a loser; but, if it were possible for me to envy any one whom I love, I would gladly give all I have to be you. Beauty without an equal in Europe, reputation without a stain, a proud and generous heart—what a wealth of happiness still left in this sad world through which one passes bereft of so much one values! Dear Juliette, let our friendship become a closer one. Let it be no longer simple, generous services that have all come from you, but a regular correspondence, a reciprocal need of confidence, a life together. Dear Juliette, it is you who will be the means of my returning to Paris—for you will always be an all-powerful person, and, as you are younger than I am, you will close my eyes, and my children will be your friends. My daughter has mingled her tears with yours and mine this morning. Dear Juliette, we have enjoyed the luxury which surrounded you; your fortune has been ours, and I feel myself ruined since you are no longer rich. Believe me, there is still happiness left when one knows oneself to be beloved. Benjamin[1] wishes to write to you; he is deeply moved. Mathieu[2] has written me a very touching letter about you. Dear friend, let your heart be at ease in the midst of these misfortunes. Alas! neither death nor the indifference of friends threaten you, and those are incurable wounds. Adieu, dear angel, adieu! With reverence do I kiss your lovely face.

"NECKER DE STAËL-HOLSTEIN."

Bernadotte, who was with the army in North Germany, also wrote to offer his condolence.

"A sprain of my right hand at first prevented me from replying to your letter. Scarcely had I recovered the use of it when operations recommenced, and I was struck on the head by a bullet. This wound has kept me in bed for a month.

"I am far from deserving your reproaches, as General Junot will, perhaps, bear witness. I heard through him of the beginning of your troubles, the evening before Austerlitz.[3] I left him, at eleven o'clock at night, with

[1] Benjamin Constant. [2] Mathieu de Montmorency.

[3] This must have been a slip of the pen. It was Auerstadt that the marshal meant. Austerlitz was fought in the previous year.

the assurance that I was going to write to you on my return to my tent; and he charged me with a thousand messages. My head and heart were full of your affairs, and I described to you all the pain which your reverse of fortune occasioned me. While I was writing and thinking of you, the thought occurred to me that, at dawn of day, I was to aid in deciding the fate of the world. When friendship, tenderness, and sympathy excite a loving heart, it feels deeply all that it expresses. Since then I have not ceased to give you my prayers and best wishes; but, although fated to love you for ever, I dared not run the risk of wearying you with my letters. Adieu! If you still think of me, believe that you are my chief thought, and that nothing equals the sweet and tender friendship I entertain for you."

The kindness and sympathy she met with on every side were, of course, very gratifying to Madame Récamier, but unfortunately money made all the difference, and without money she was well aware that, although she might retain her friends, she could no longer continue to lead society.

CHAPTER VI

Coppet—Sainte-Beuve's description of it—Madame Récamier visits Madame de Staël—Prince Augustus of Prussia—He falls in love with Madame Récamier—He tries to induce her to obtain a divorce—Her letter to her husband—His reply—Madame Récamier returns to Paris—Prince Augustus's letters—She refuses to marry him—Her rendezvous with him at Schaffhausen—Meets him again in 1814—She gives him her portrait by Gérard—His letter to her before his death—Madame Récamier's conduct considered—She visits Madame de Staël at Chaumont and Fossé—*La petite poste*—Madame de Staël's visit to the theatre at Blois—"Surrounded by a Court"—Publication and suppression of *De L'Allemagne*—Madame de Staël is banished from France—Her despair

THE traveller in Switzerland, passing along Lake Leman—that lovely lake immortalised by Byron—from Lausanne to Geneva, sees, on its north-western shore, a little village, all the habitations of which seem to nestle to a central stately structure. The village is Coppet, and the central edifice the Château de Necker, once the home of Madame de Staël.

"What Ferney was to Voltaire," says Sainte-Beuve, "Coppet was to Madame de Staël, but with a much more poetic halo around it, and with a nobler life. Both reigned in their exile, but Coppet has counteracted and almost dethroned Ferney. We of the present generation rank Ferney below Coppet. The beauty of the site, the woods which shade it, the sex of the poet, the enthusiasm that we breathe there, the elegance of the company, the glory of their names, the rambles by the lake, the mornings in the park, the passions and the mysteries that we may suppose inevitable there, all combine to enchant our conception of this abode. Coppet is the Elysium with which all the soul-children of Jean-Jacques would fain endow the lady of their dreams."[1]

It was, at once, a refuge for the persecuted and an intellectual centre, where proscribed politicians and distinguished men of letters from all parts of Europe came to pay homage to the foremost woman of her time. There were often as many as thirty people in the house, including strangers and friends. The most frequent visitors were Benjamin Constant, August Wilhelm von Schlegel, Comte Sabran, Simonde de Sismondi, the historian, Bonstetten of Geneva, Prosper de Barante, and Mathieu de Montmorency. Discussions on a variety of subjects, literary, philosophical, and political, began at eleven o'clock in the morning, the hour when the company assembled for breakfast, were resumed at dinner, or in the interval between dinner and supper, and continued until midnight. Famous authors read chapters from their manuscript works, poets recited their masterpieces, and tragedies and comedies, often written for the occasion by Madame de Staël or one of her friends, were performed by the house-party.

It was to this charming mansion that, in the summer of 1807, Madame Récamier, who had recently suffered a severe blow though the death of her mother Madame Bernard, from whom she had never been separated since childhood, came in response to a warm invitation from its

[1] *Critiques et Portraits littéraires*, iii. 342.

illustrious *châtelaine*, in search of the rest and change she so much needed; and it was here that she was destined to meet with a most romantic adventure.

It happened that, at the time of her visit, the mistress of Coppet had extended her hospitality to another victim of misfortune—Prince Augustus of Prussia, the nephew of Frederick the Great, a handsome and chivalrous young man of four-and-twenty, who had been taken prisoner at the battle of Saalfeld, where his brother Louis had been killed, and was now held as a kind of hostage by Napoleon.

The prince's heroism on that fatal field, his intense grief for the death of his brother, to whom he had been devotedly attached, and the misfortunes of his country all combined to surround him in Madame Récamier's eyes with a halo of romance. The prince, on his part, fell desperately in love with the beautiful Parisian, and, in spite of the difficulties which his high rank naturally suggested, conceived the project of inducing her to divorce her husband and to marry him. He took his hostess into his confidence, and that lady, whose poetical imagination prompted her to favour a scheme that was calculated to diffuse a sort of romantic interest over Coppet, readily promised him her support.

To our modern ideas such a proposal seems both repulsive and preposterous, more especially as Madame Récamier had no cause for complaint against her husband, but at the time of which we are writing it would be regarded very differently. In Prussia divorce was authorised both by the ecclesiastical and the canon law, and, at the beginning of the nineteenth century, custom had made it so common in Germany, upon grounds of complaint quite independent of moral conduct, that no obloquy whatever attached to it. There was nothing, therefore, very extraordinary in Prince Augustus venturing to hope that Madame Récamier would be willing to comply with his wishes, as Madame de Staël had probably told him the strange story that was current. Moreover, as we have said, the tie which bound Madame Récamier to her husband was a purely nominal one, and one which the Catholic Church itself pronounces void; and so, either because she returned, in some measure at least, the prince's ardent affection, or, more probably, because she was tempted by the brilliant prospect held out to her, she yielded to his entreaties so far as to consent to write to her husband, asking him to release her.

Jacques Récamier replied that he would set her free if such was really her wish; but, at the same time, he begged leave to remind her of the care and affection he had always lavished upon her, and pointed out the bitter grief such an estrangement would be to him.

This tender and dignified letter made a great impression on Madame Récamier, and filled her with remorse and compassion. She pictured to herself the indulgent companion of her girlhood—who, with all his faults, had been the kindest and most generous of husbands—stripped of the great fortune with which it had been his delight to gratify her every whim, old and lonely. To abandon him under such circumstances seemed impossible, and, accordingly, though not without some regrets for the great position she was relinquishing, she decided to decline the prince's offer. She went back to Paris at the end of the autumn with her mind made up, but without informing her royal adorer, who had shortly before the receipt of her husband's letter returned to Berlin, of the futility of his hopes, relying upon time and absence to soften his disappointment.

Meanwhile, the lovelorn prince, in blissful ignorance of her decision, was endeavouring to obtain his family's consent to the marriage, and frequent letters reminded his beloved Juliette of her promise, and painted in glowing terms the golden future which he was so eagerly anticipating.

"I hope," he writes, "that you have already received my letter, No. 31, wherein I could but feebly express the happiness which yours has given me: but, still, it will convey to you some idea of the emotion which I felt at receiving it and your portrait. I gazed for hours on this enchanting portrait, and dreamed of a happiness that must surpass all the delights that the imagination can offer. What fate can be comparable to that of the man you love!"

It was a task of no little difficulty for a Prussian prince to carry on a correspondence with a lady who was the object of Napoleon's resentment, and therefore certain to be to some extent under police surveillance, without exciting the suspicions of Fouché's myrmidons, and consequently incurring the displeasure of the Emperor. We, therefore, find him taking every precaution when writing to conceal his identity. Thus he alludes to the King of Prussia as "my relative" or "my cousin"; to the Queen as "my cousin's wife," and to the Prussian Government as "our firm." In a letter announcing the appointment of Hardenberg as Prime Minister, he says, "Some advantageous changes have been made in our firm lately; we have secured an excellent head clerk, but the good results we expect from this are still distant."

The prince was, of course, impatient to once more behold his enchantress; but the King of Prussia, fearing that, if his young cousin set foot on French territory, he would be arrested, absolutely forbade him to cross the frontier, and an attack of small-pox, which nearly proved fatal, put an end to the prosecution of his suit for a time at least.

Madame Récamier, on her side, now that she was no longer under the influence of Coppet and its romantic surroundings, became convinced of the wisdom of her decision. The religious scruples, which the prince's arguments had never quite silenced, even when supported by his handsome presence, were strengthened by reflection; she shrank, too, from the scandal of a divorce, while the thought of quitting her beloved Paris was repugnant to her. She therefore wrote the prince a letter intended to show him that his hopes were vain.

"*J'ai été frappé de la foudre en recevant votre lettre,*" the poor young man replies; but he did not accept his dismissal—at least he insisted on seeing her once more. Madame Récamier, however, refused to grant even this request until the autumn of 1811, when she consented to meet her adorer at Schaffhausen.

The infatuated prince at once set out for Switzerland, without even waiting to obtain leave of absence from his military duties, but the lady chose to exercise the feminine prerogative of changing her mind, and did not keep the appointment. The prince was deeply mortified at her treatment of him. "At last I hope I am cured of a foolish passion that I have cherished for four years," he writes to his friend and confidante Madame de Staël. To Madame Récamier he writes more in sorrow than in anger.

PRINCE AUGUSTUS OF PRUSSIA *to* MADAME RÉCAMIER.

"SCHAFFHAUSEN, *October* 1811.

"You have cruelly disappointed me. What I cannot understand is that not being able or not wishing to see me, you did not condescend to tell me so, and spare me a useless journey of three hundred leagues. I leave to-morrow for the high mountains of the Oberland and the Petits Cantons. The wild nature of these districts will be in harmony with the sadness of my thoughts, of which you are the object. If, at last, you deign to reply to my letter, please write to the city where I usually live, and to which I intend to return before long."

In spite of this rebuff, Prince Augustus continued to correspond with Madame Récamier until they met again, in 1814, when he entered Paris with the allied armies. He was then in command of the Prussian artillery, and before reaching the city besieged successively Maubeuge, Landrecies, Phillipeville, Givet, and Longevy. From each of these places he wrote to Madame Récamier, showing how eagerly he was looking forward to their reunion.

"To-morrow," he writes, "I open the trenches round Maubeuge, and in eighteen days I shall reduce it, even supposing the defence obstinate. The desire of beholding you once more will be a very powerful incentive to me to push on the siege."

The friendship between the prince and Madame Récamier was renewed, but, though his admiration for her was as great as ever, nothing more was said about a divorce; indeed, the former appears to have already sought consolation for his disappointment in a kind of left-handed marriage, the result of which—two daughters—were in after years well known in Berlin and Paris society, and on intimate terms with their royal father's first love. In 1818, however, the prince commissioned Gérard to paint the picture of "Corinne," which he presented to Madame Récamier, "as an immortal souvenir of the passion with which she had inspired him, and of the glorious friendship which united Corinne and Juliette." In exchange for this picture, Madame Récamier sent him the famous portrait of herself by the same painter. The prince had it hung in the gallery of his house in Berlin, but after his death, which occurred in 1845, it was by the terms of his will returned to the donor.

Some months before that event, when, although at the time in perfect health, he seems to have had some presentiment of his approaching end, he wrote to Madame Récamier a touching letter, in which he declares that "the ring which she had given him he would wear to his grave"; and there can be little doubt that, notwithstanding her refusal to bear his name, she always remained mistress of his heart.

It cannot be denied that in this affair with Prince Augustus Madame Récamier comes before us in a very unfavourable light; and it is significant that her niece, Madame Lenormant, usually so ready to explain away any circumstance which casts the least reflection upon her aunt, has practically nothing to say in exoneration of her conduct, but takes refuge in a judicious silence. Much, however, may be forgiven a woman so peculiarly situated as was Madame Récamier; and it is quite conceivable that at the time she wrote the letter to her husband asking him to release her from her marriage vows, she really believed that he would welcome the severance of a tie which must have been a very considerable strain on his then limited resources.

On the other hand, nothing can possibly condone the fact that for many months after she had apparently made up her mind to reject the prince's offer, she continued to keep him in suspense, unless, as one of her contemporaries suggests, she had reason to imagine that he was not quite so faithful to her as the ardent tone of his letters would lead one to suppose.

Madame Récamier passed the years 1808 and 1809 partly in Paris, and partly at Coppet and Angervilliers, where her friend Madame de Catellan lived. Madame de Staël was at this time engaged upon her great work, *De L'Allemagne*, and did not leave Coppet during that time. She was very fond of music and the drama, and often organised amateur theatricals among her guests, as a relaxation from her literary labours. Pictet de Sergy speaks highly of her acting, and declares that she was admirable both in comedy and tragedy.

"The great hall of the *rez-de-chaussée* of the château was," he writes, "converted into a complete and permanent theatre; and there she and her friends acted not merely comedy, but frequently tragedy. The Marquis de Sabran, being of diminutive stature, appeared nearly crushed under the helmet of Pyrrhus; Madame Récamier represented Andromache, while Madame de Staël personated with marvellous effect Hermione. From time to time Madame de Staël left her feudal home, and transported all her noble *cortège* to Geneva, where they gave representations in the great building called the *Douane*, on the Place du Molard. All the best society in the city came down from the Rue des Granges or the Taconnerie into this large hall of the common people—a place which they seldom condescended to visit, especially at night—

borne thither by an irresistible curiosity. There I still see Madame de Staël imposing and terrible in the rôle of Phaedra, and Benjamin Constant, but not, as they have lately reported him, personating Hippolytus in blue spectacles which he absolutely refused to lay aside. The Genevese were enthusiastically grateful to Madame de Staël for her kindness in bringing among them her actors and theatrical properties. I agree with her cousin that in tragedy she produced truly great effects."

While Madame Récamier was at Coppet, in the autumn of 1809, Racine's *Phèdre* was performed. Madame de Staël played the title-rôle, while Madame Récamier took the part of Aricie. The classical costume was, of course, admirably adapted to her style of beauty, and she was pronounced a great success, in spite of her almost painful nervousness.

The following summer Madame de Staël came as near Paris as her forty leagues would allow her in order to superintend the printing of *De L'Allemagne*, which was to appear in three volumes. She took up her residence at the old château of Chaumont-sur-Loire, near Blois, where Cardinal d'Amboise, Diana of Poictiers, and Catharine de Medicis had formerly lived. The present owner of that historic mansion, a M. Le Ray, a personal friend of Madame de Staël, was at this time with his family in America.

Madame Récamier, in response to a letter from her friend, inviting her to the château of Catharine de Medicis, "who did more harm in the world than you have done," joined her there on her way back from the baths at Aix towards the end of the summer, and found herself one of a large house-party, including Adrien and Mathieu de Montmorency, Prosper de Barante, August Wilhelm von

Schlegel, Comte de Sabran, and Benjamin Constant. Soon after her arrival, however, the owner of the château and his family returned unexpectedly from America, whereupon Madame de Staël and her guests removed to a farmhouse called Fossé, which had been placed at their disposal by a M. de Salaberry, an old officer of the Vendean wars.

M. de Salaberry had hitherto led a very lonely life, and was regarded by his neighbours as a hermit. Madame de Staël and her party, however, were nearly all musical; one had brought a guitar and another a harp; and on the evening of their arrival organised a kind of impromptu concert. So astonished were the neighbouring peasants at hearing such unusual sounds that they came flocking to the house to find out what it could all mean; and, while Madame Récamier was singing, she suddenly made the discovery that a large and appreciative audience had gathered on the lawn outside the house.

It was during her visit to Fossé that she and Madame de Staël invented a new form of amusement, which subsequently became quite fashionable, called *la petite poste*. After dinner the company used to gather round a table covered with a green cloth, and write little notes to one another. One day a gentleman of the neighbourhood, who had never given a thought in his life to anything beyond hunting and shooting, called to take Madame de Staël's sons into the woods with him, and was shown into the room where the whole house-party was seated round the table intent on their new diversion. For some minutes he regarded them with amazement, trying vainly to comprehend what this busy but silent company could be doing. Then Madame Récamier, in order to put the visitor at his ease, wrote him with her pretty hand a charming little note. But the sportsman, fearing she wished to make fun of him, excused himself from receiving it, on the plea that he could not read writing except by candle-light. "We laughed a little," says Madame de Staël, "at the rebuff which the benevolent coquetry of our beautiful friend had received, and thought that a note from her hand would not always have met with the same fate." [1]

But even this harmless party was soon to be broken up by the malice of Napoleon. Madame de Staël had a most fatal celebrity. At that time the opera of *Cinderella* was creating a perfect furore in Paris. A provincial company gave a representation of it at the little theatre at Blois, and Madame de Staël went to see it. On leaving the theatre at the conclusion of the performance, she was followed by a crowd of curious people, anxious to get a view of the celebrated exile. The stupid police immediately informed the authorities in Paris that she went about "surrounded by a Court."

Shortly after this incident, she finished correcting the last proofs of *De L'Allemagne*, the composition of which had occupied her nearly six years, and was in high spirits at the thought of its appearance. The book had passed with a few alterations through the hands of the public censor; she had made all arrangements with a publisher in Paris; its popularity was expected to be so great that ten thousand copies had been printed for a first edition; everything seemed to be going on smoothly, when her implacable enemy again pounced down upon her; the whole of the edition was confiscated and destroyed by the police; the Prefect of Loire-et-Cher came to Fossé to require her to deliver up the manuscript, though, fortu-

[1] Madame de Staël's *Dix Années d'Exil*, p. 224.

nately, he was satisfied with a rough copy; and, to put the *comble* upon all, the authoress was ordered to leave France in three days for ever.

Utterly prostrated by this double blow, the unfortunate woman returned to Coppet—Coppet the home of romance, the haunt of genius, where every luxury which money could procure was at her command, but which this true daughter of Paris would willingly have exchanged for a garret in the Rue du Bac. Before leaving Fossé, however, she wrote to Madame Récamier, whose turn it now was to play the part of comforter.

MADAME DE STAËL *to* MADAME RÉCAMIER.

"DEAR FRIEND,—I have fallen into a state of frightful melancholy. I am in utter despair at the thought of my approaching departure, and, for the first time, I realise all the misery of a condition which I fondly imagined would be easy to bear. I counted also on the success of my book to sustain me, and, now, here are six years of labour, study, and travel almost entirely wasted. Do you fully comprehend the singularity of this affair? It is the first two volumes, already approved by the censor, that have been seized, and M. Portalis[1] knows no more than I do what all this means. So I am exiled because I have written a book which has been approved by the Emperor's censors. Nor is this all. I could have printed my book in Germany. I came of my own free will to submit it to the censorship, under the impression that, if it came to the worst, they would only prohibit the work. But can people be punished who come voluntarily to submit to their judges? Dear friend, there is Mathieu,[2] the friend

[1] The Censor. [2] Mathieu de Montmorency.

of twenty years, and I must leave him. And you, dear angel, who have loved me on account of my misfortunes, who have only known me during the period of my adversity, who render life so sweet—I must leave you also. Ah, mon Dieu! I am the Orestes of exile, and fate pursues me! But God's will must be done, and I trust that He will sustain me. For the last time I am listening to that music of Pertozza that recalls your sweet face, that charm which you possess apart from your beauty, and so many of the pure and tranquil pleasures of this summer. For the last time I press you once again to my heart, and then the unknown future begins. I will summon all my courage; but thus to die to all one's memories, to all one's affections, this is a terrible effort.

"I am encompassed by such a cloud of sorrow that I know not what I write. . . . I dare not finish. I should be tempted to say, like M. Dubreuil to Pechméja, 'My friend, thou above all shouldst be here.'"

CHAPTER VII

Bernadotte becomes Crown-Prince of Sweden—His letter to Madame Récamier—Royal admirers—Ludwig, Crown Prince of Bavaria—George, Grand-Duke of Mecklenburg-Strelitz—His adventure with Madame Récamier's *concierge*—His letter to her in 1845—Animosity of Napoleon against Madame Récamier—The Government persecute Madame de Staël—She resolves to fly to Sweden—Madame Récamier determines to go to Coppet—Her friends endeavour to dissuade her—Mathieu de Montmorency is exiled—Madame Récamier arrives at Coppet—Madame Récamier is exiled from Paris—She goes to Châlons—Monotony of her life there—Letter from Madame de Staël—Madame Récamier removes to Lyons—The Duchesse de Chevreuse—Her harsh treatment by Napoleon—The Duchesse de Luynes—Her skill as a compositor—Simon Ballanche—His ugliness—His devotion to Madame Récamier—Annoyances to which Madame Récamier is subjected as an exile—A pressing invitation—Extraordinary conduct of her host—His subsequent explanations—Visit from the Duchesse d'Abrantès—Anecdote of Talma and the Bishop of Troyes—Mathieu de Montmorency comes to Lyons—Madame Récamier starts for Italy

WHILE Madame Récamier was with Madame de Staël at Fossé, her friend Marshal Bernadotte, since 1806 Prince de Ponte-Corvo, was unanimously elected heir to the childless Charles XIII. by the Swedish Diet, who hoped by so doing to propitiate Napoleon and preserve the independence of their country. At the beginning of

October he set out for Stockholm, whence he wrote to Madame Récamier to bid her farewell.

THE CROWN-PRINCE OF SWEDEN *to* MADAME RÉCAMIER.

"STOCKHOLM, *December* 22, 1810.

"MADAME,—On leaving France for ever, I am filled with regret that your absence from Paris has deprived me of the pleasure of receiving your commands and bidding you farewell. You were engaged in consoling a friend for an approaching and, doubtless, life-long separation ; and I felt constrained to postpone writing to you until some future date. M. de Czernicheff has kindly undertaken to convey to you my respects. We have long talks about you, your estimable qualities, and the tender interest you inspire in all who approach you. Adieu, madame, pray receive the assurance of the affection which I have always professed for you, and which neither time nor the ice of the north can extinguish.

"CHARLES JEAN."

Some time before this Madame Récamier had made the acquaintance of two other royal personages, Ludwig, Prince-Royal—afterwards King of Bavaria—and George, Grand-Duke of Mecklenburg-Strelitz. The former, who is now, probably, best remembered through his infatuation for the notorious adventuress Lola Montez—an infatuation which ultimately cost him his throne—came to Paris in the winter of 1808, and was extremely anxious to be presented to the celebrated beauty of whom he had heard so much. Madame Récamier, however, knowing that the Emperor still regarded her salon and its habitués with anything but a friendly eye, and unwilling to get the young prince into trouble, declined to receive him ; and the latter, therefore, had recourse to the intervention of a friend, who, aware of the royal visitor's artistic tastes, wrote to Madame Récamier the following diplomatic epistle:

MADAME DE BONDY *to* MADAME RÉCAMIER.

"The Prince of Bavaria is extremely anxious, madame, to carry away with him a correct impression of the lady whom he has so long desired to know, and M. de Bondy has been charged by His Royal Highness to ask your permission to call at your house *to see your portrait.* M. de Bondy would have asked your consent himself, but he has been obliged to accompany the Prince to St. Cloud. He has therefore commissioned me to make the request. This time it is an *official demand* and no longer a favour. M. de Bondy trusts that you will not refuse to the Prince the privilege of admiring the *chef d'œuvre* of Gérard, which you have accorded to many persons; and, if you will permit him, he will accompany His Highness to your house either on Saturday or Monday morning, whichever you prefer; or on any other day convenient to you. Should you be so *ill-natured* as to go out precisely at the hour appointed, the Prince may conclude that, if report has not deceived him in regard to the charm of your appearance, it has exaggerated the affability of your manners; and I do not think that the sight of your picture will diminish his regret at not making the acquaintance of the original. But this is not my business: I am only commissioned to plead for the amateur in art. I await your reply with impatience, and will hand it to M. de Bondy on his return from St. Cloud.

"Believe me, madame, very sincerely yours,

"H. DE BONDY."

After this letter, of course, Madame Récamier had no alternative but to receive the prince, of whom she formed a favourable impression, as did Madame de Staël, who describes him in one of her letters as "un bon homme qui a de l'esprit et de l'âme"; but she does not appear to have admitted him to the same degree of intimacy which she accorded to the Grand-Duke of Mecklenburg-Strelitz, who visited Paris about the same time.

Madame Récamier made the duke's acquaintance at a *bal-masqué* at the Opera, and, after talking to her for the greater part of the evening, he begged permission to call upon her. She refused to allow him to do so, however, for the same reason which had prompted her to decline the proffered friendship of the Prince of Bavaria—the fear of compromising him with the Emperor, whom he had come to Paris on purpose to propitiate. Undeterred by her refusal, the young man wrote begging her to reconsider her decision, and, at length, flattered by his persistence, she consented, and named an evening when she received only her most intimate friends, and there would be little chance of any one reporting his visit to Napoleon.

The grand-duke arrived at the appointed hour, and, to avoid recognition, left his carriage at some distance from the house, and proceeded thither on foot. Finding the door open, he attempted to glide past the porter's lodge without being seen; but the *concierge* was on the alert, and the grand-duke had not gone far before he heard a gruff voice calling out to him to stop. Unwilling to be known even to the porter, he paid no attention, but quickened his pace. The porter, his suspicions aroused, followed. The grand-duke began to run. The *concierge*, now fully convinced that the intruder was a thief, ran after him. The grand-duke reached the main staircase, and rushed up; but his pursuer was too quick for him. Before he reached the salon door, the enraged *concierge* seized him by the collar; and the unfortunate young man was being very roughly handled when Madame Récamier, hearing the noise of the scuffle, came out to see what was the matter, and released her royal visitor.

The grand-duke visited Madame Récamier again on several occasions, and wrote to her frequently gracefully worded little notes:

"May I dare? Will you be so kind and generous? May I venture to come again to-morrow at the same time? I make this request with diffidence; but if you knew how strong is my feeling, and how much it has cost me to keep away, perhaps, you will not only pardon me, but say that my request is justified. I came to this city with a heavy heart. My experiences here have been painful. Do you wish me to carry away a grief heavier to bear than all of them, from having seen an angel without daring to approach her? Pray, do not consider me deserving of so cruel a fate, and pardon, if you can, my apparent presumption. There is no one more capable of appreciating you than myself, or of cherishing for you all those feelings which you deserve, and which, alas! you will always inspire in every noble and sensitive heart. I repeat that I write with diffidence, but not without a ray of hope."

The admiration with which Madame Récamier inspired the grand-duke was very far from being a mere passing fancy—the light offspring of propinquity and youth. Thirty-seven years later we find him writing to her from Strelitz to beg her to send him the famous portrait of herself by Gérard, which, after the death of Prince Augustus of Prussia, had been returned to the donor.

THE GRAND-DUKE OF MECKLENBURG-STRELITZ *to* MADAME RÉCAMIER.

"STRELITZ, *December* 1, 1845.

"MADAME,—If I have ever experienced a feeling of diffidence it is to-day, when I have resolved not only to write but to ask a favour of you; yes, a great and very important favour. When I think of the number of years that have elapsed since I have had the happiness of seeing you or of hearing from you directly, the step which I am about to take seems very much like a rash one. I even feel, alas! that if you were to ask after reading my signature, 'Who is this Grand-Duke of Mecklenburg-Strelitz?' I should have no right to complain. This is what reason says to me, but what says the heart? Shall I confess it to you, madame? It says the contrary. It tells me very plainly that the ravishing beauty with which nature has endowed you is but the reflection of an adorable soul; and that such a soul cannot forget the person whom it at one time deemed worthy of its esteem and affection.

"Among the precious recollections which I owe to you, there is one above all others that the memory never ceases to recall with all the charm that attaches to it. It is the eminently noble, generous, and amiable manner with which you treated me after Napoleon had said publicly in the salon of the Empress Josephine, that 'he should regard as his personal enemy any foreigner who frequented the salon of Madame Récamier.' I can say without exaggeration that I still think of this with emotion, and that, on my knees, I desire to assure you anew of my humble gratitude which will endure for ever.

"'But what is this favour which you wish to ask

me?' I fancy I hear you inquire. It is your portrait, madame, that same admirable portrait with which you honoured the late Prince Augustus of Prussia, and which I understand is to be returned to you. I repeat madame, that I make this request with great diffidence; that I should have, perhaps, never have had the courage to ask it did I not have it so inexpressibly at heart. But if the worship of your memory can give any one the right of possessing this treasure, pray believe, at least, that no one has a better claim to it than myself. Nor is it I alone who would have the right. My wife, my children, all my family appreciate you as you deserve. They have listened with delight to my reminiscences of you. We all look upon you as the embodiment of perfect beauty and perfect goodness.

"I have not the courage to add another word to my letter; but your heart is formed to understand it.

"George, Grand-Duke of
"Mecklenburg-Strelitz."

Madame Récamier declined to permit so valuable a souvenir of herself to pass a second time out of the possession of her family, but the grand-duke's letter is interesting as evidence that, at the time to which he refers, Napoleon, so far from being satisfied with having ruined Madame Récamier and her husband, was still further incensed against her by the heroic fortitude with which she had borne her reverses, and the universal sympathy which they had evoked. Moreover, he was compelled to admit that, in spite of her changed circumstances, Madame Récamier's social influence was practically unimpaired; and, as he could not endure the idea of a society which did not derive all its *éclat* from himself, he seems in time to have actually come to regard the poor lady with the hatred of a rival. Of this malignity she was soon to have a further proof.

After the sentence which banished her from French soil had been passed upon her, Madame de Staël, as we have mentioned, had returned to Coppet. From the moment she arrived there, "dragging her wing like the pigeon in La Fontaine," she was subjected to a series of petty persecutions calculated to break the spirit of the proudest woman. One prefect of Geneva, M. de Barante, treated her with great civility: he was dismissed, and his successor immediately went to the other extreme. She accompanied her youngest son to Aix in Savoy, where the physicians had prescribed for him a course of the baths: before she had been there ten days, she received a peremptory order to return to Coppet. She consoled herself with the society of Augustus Wilhelm von Schlegel, who for the past eight years had been educating her son: he was promptly accused of having insulted the French nation, inasmuch as, in an essay which he had written, he had given preference to the *Phaedra* of Euripides over the *Phèdre* of Racine, and was ordered to leave Geneva. At length the poor woman's life became perfectly unendurable, and she determined to leave Coppet, and take refuge with her husband's relatives in Sweden.

On being informed of Madame de Staël's resolution, Madame Récamier at once decided to set out for Coppet to bid her talented and unfortunate friend farewell. But, in order not to excite the attention of the police, who at that time exercised the strictest surveillance over all persons suspected of the least hostility to the Government, she gave out that her destination was Aix in Savoy, from the waters of which she had derived considerable benefit the previous summer; and asked for a passport to that town.

The passport was granted, but the object of her journey could be easily divined, and she received no lack of warnings from her friends. Esménard, one of the chiefs of the Police, and an ardent admirer of Madame Récamier, made strenuous efforts to dissuade her from visiting Coppet, pointing out that her presence there could be of no possible assistance to her friend, while it might entail serious consequences to herself, as the Emperor would be sure to visit with his displeasure any one who held communication with a proscribed person, especially one so obnoxious to him in every way as was Madame de Staël.

Madame Récamier, however, ridiculed the suggestion that the visit of an innocent woman to an unhappy friend on the eve of departure for a distant country could possibly be construed into an act of hostility to the Government; and declared that, whatever might be the consequences, she could not bring herself to refuse Madame de Staël this last proof of affection. Accordingly, on August 23 she started for Coppet.

A few days before Madame Récamier left Paris, Mathieu de Montmorency arrived at Coppet, also on a farewell visit to its *châtelaine*. The prefect of Geneva at once notified the Government of his arrival there, and by return of courier Montmorency received an order of exile from the Minister of Police.

Poor Madame de Staël tells us that she "shrieked with agony" on learning of the misfortune which she had brought upon the kind-hearted Mathieu, and bitterly reproached herself with having been the means of separating him from his family and friends. While she was in this state, she received a letter from Madame Récamier, announcing that she was on her way to Aix, and intended breaking the journey at Coppet, where she would arrive in two days' time.

Madame de Staël, fearful lest Montmorency's fate should befall her beloved Juliette, at once despatched a messenger to intercept her, and implore her not to come to Coppet. To drive past Madame de Staël's windows and yet not to see her appeared to Madame Récamier altogether out of the question, and it was with tears in her eyes that the mistress of Coppet beheld her friend enter the house where hitherto her arrival had been so welcome.

Madame Récamier only remained one night at the château, and then, instead of continuing her journey to Aix, set out on her return to Paris. But, brief as had been her stay, it had been duly notified to the Government, and, on reaching Dijon, she was met by her husband, who informed her that she had been exiled forty leagues from Paris.

To any one who realises what Paris means to a Frenchwoman—that to her it is the world without which the rest of France is but one huge void—will readily understand that to a woman like Madame Récamier, who might almost be said to live for society, such a sentence was in reality worse than complete exile. Like the Peri at the gate of Paradise, she might gaze, so to speak, on the joys of the blessed, but might not enter to share therein. Nor was this all. Under the odious system inaugurated by Napoleon, the friend of the exile became as criminal as the exile himself, and, thus, Madame Récamier found herself cut off not only from Paris, but also from the society of all her friends, with the exception of those who happened to be in the same unfortunate position as herself.

Madame Récamier, however, continued her journey to Paris, in spite of the prohibition which she had received, and took an affectionate farewell of her friends. She preserved the strictest incognito, and saw no one but the members of her own family, but the police were far too wideawake for her presence to remain long unnoticed, and, ere forty-eight hours had passed, her husband received the following official communication:

"PARIS, *September* 17, 1811.

"I request you, sir, to inform me, immediately on receipt of this, where Madame Récamier is to be found at the present moment, that I may execute the order of which I gave you notice on the 2nd of this month.

"Your obedient servant,

"PASQUIER,

"*Councillor of State, Prefect of Police,*

"*Baron of the Empire.*"

After this it was clearly out of the question for Madame Récamier to remain any longer in Paris, and, accordingly, the following day, she set out for Châlons-sur-Marne, accompanied by her little niece, Amélie de Cyvoct, whom she had recently adopted. It is to the works of this lady, who married, in 1825, M. Charles Lenormant, a distinguished antiquary, that we are indebted for much that we know about her celebrated aunt.[1]

Châlons, where Madame Récamier took a suite of rooms at the Pomme d'Or, was a dull little country town, but it was not without its advantages. In the first place,

[1] *Souvenirs et Correspondance tirés des papiers de Madame Récamier*, *Madame Récamier les Amis de sa Jeunesse*, and *Coppet et Weimar*. Madame Lenormant also edited *Les Lettres de Benjamin Constant à Madame Récamier*.

it was just outside the forty leagues' radius, and not very far from the Château de Montmirail, the seat of the Duc de Doudeauville, who was a great friend of Madame Récamier, and whose son, Sosthènes de La Rochefoucauld, had married Mathieu de Montmorency's daughter, and shared that family's devotion to their "*amiable amie*." In the second place, the town was governed by a good-natured prefect, who might be inclined to regard the visits of Madame Récamier's friends with an indulgent eye, in the absence of any special instructions to the contrary.

Madame Récamier, however, did not see much of the La Rochefoucaulds, as she was fearful lest they should suffer for their kindness to an exile; but her husband, her father, old Simonard, Junot, Duc d'Abrantès, Madame de Catellan, and several other relatives and friends braved the displeasure of the Government and came from Paris to see her; while her cousin, Madame de Dalmassy, left Switzerland to spend a week at Châlons, and Auguste de Staël brought her news of his mother, whom he represented as inconsolable at the thought of the persecution she had drawn upon her and Mathieu de Montmorency.

In spite of the kindness of her friends, time hung very heavily upon Madame Récamier's hands, for there was no society or public entertainments of any kind at Châlons, and the only relief to the monotony of her life was on the occasions when she went to the church, where she had made friends with the organist, to play the organ at high mass. Her love of music, as we have said, was always a great consolation to her.

After she had been about nine months at Châlons, she received a letter from Madame de Staël urging her to remove to Lyons. "At present," her friend wrote, "I am extremely anxious that you should come to Lyons. If I take my passage in the frigate,[1] I shall be able to have another heart-break in embracing you there. You will be on the road to Italy, and you will have friends who are not to be despised, for they are very good for the nerves. Alas! generous victim, I have experienced what you suffer; and you can, therefore, trust me in regard to the compensations of such a situation. The prefect of Lyons is a very kind-hearted man, and quite a gentleman. I advise you strongly, therefore, to go to Lyons."

Madame Récamier decided to follow her friend's advice, and, a few days after the receipt of her letter, left for Lyons, where she was warmly welcomed by her husband's relatives, who were much respected in that city. She found there, also, several old friends, among them the Duchesse de Chevreuse, an exile like herself, her mother-in-law, the old Duchesse de Luynes, and Camille Jordan, whom the *coup d'état* of the 18th Brumaire had driven out of public life.

The poor young Duchesse de Chevreuse had, much against her will, been persuaded by her relatives to accept the post of *dame du palais* to the Empress Josephine. The duchess, however, who was as proud as she was beautiful, brought with her to the new Court all the disdain and hauteur of the old *régime;* and when the Emperor showed himself not insensible to her charms, received his advances with marked coldness.[2]

[1] Madame de Staël appears to have had some idea, at this time, of making her way to the coast, and escaping to England in one of the English cruisers.

[2] "Madame de Chevreuse was pretty, although red haired, and very clever, but, having been excessively spoilt by her family, was wilful and fanciful. Her health, even then, was delicate. The Emperor tried by coaxing to console her for having been forced into the Court, and at times he would appear to have succeeded, but at others she would take

After the family of the deposed King of Spain was brought to Fontainebleau, Napoleon intimated his desire that the duchess should be transferred to the service of the Spanish queen ; whereupon she haughtily replied that, although she had no objection to being a prisoner, she must absolutely decline to become a gaoler. This answer sent her into exile. When Madame Récamier met her at Lyons, her banishment had already lasted four years, and her health, never very strong, had quite given way, owing, in a great measure, to her constantly fretting over her troubles. She, in fact, died some months later.

Madame de Chevreuse's mother-in-law, the old Duchesse de Luynes, and Madame Récamier soon became great friends. The duchess was a clever and eccentric old lady, who preferred male to female attire, and had a printing-press of her own at her château at Dampierre, where she not only set up type herself, but had the reputation of being a skilful compositor. One day, while at Lyons, she paid a visit to the works of a printer named Ballanche, and, while passing through the compositors' room, suddenly tucked up her dress—she was attired that day, by way of a change, in woman's clothes—placed herself before a case, and, to the intense admiration of all the workmen, set up the type for a whole page, imitating even the movement of the body peculiar to the compositors of that

no pains to conceal her dislike to her position. She had an attraction for the Emperor, which others would have vainly endeavoured to exert, the charm of combat and of victory, for she would sometimes seem to be amused with the fêtes and splendour of the Court, and when she appeared there in full dress and apparently in good spirits, then the Emperor, who enjoyed even the smallest success, would laugh and say, 'I have overcome the aversion of Madame de Chevreuse.' But, in reality, I do not think he ever did."—*Memoirs of Madame de Rémusat*, ii. 85.

day, and accomplishing her task with the most astonishing rapidity.

Simon Ballanche, the son of the above-named printer, was destined to achieve fame both as a philosopher and a poet, and—what he probably valued a great deal more—to become one of Madame Récamier's most intimate friends. Ballanche was an extraordinarily ugly man, owing to a deformity of one side of his face, the result of an accident; but his fine eyes and pleasant expression compensated, in some degree, for this defect. He was presented to Madame Récamier by Camille Jordan, who was enthusiastic in praise of his recently published *Fragments*, and was at once completely fascinated by the lovely Parisian.

The unaffected simplicity and grace of her manner, the charm of her conversation, the kindly interest which this woman, so different from any whom he had hitherto met that she seemed almost like a being from another world, took in his somewhat obscure aspirations, won his heart and made him her slave for ever. Michelet—another printer's son, by the way—tells us that he once put the question off-hand to Ballanche, "*Qu'est que c'est la femme?*" The philosopher blushed like a child, hesitated a moment, and then replied, "*C'est l'initiation.*" And such assuredly was Madame Récamier to him. She led this shy, retiring, austere thinker into a new world; she taught him that there were more things in heaven and earth than were dreamed of in his philosophy; she inspired his best efforts, and encouraged him to accomplish work which, otherwise, he would have been too modest even to attempt.

"Give me leave to cherish for you the feelings of a brother for a sister," he says in one of his letters. "I look forward to the moment when I shall be able to lay at your feet, along with this brotherly affection, the little all that is in my power to accomplish. My devotion to you is sincere and whole-hearted." And such it undoubtedly was for the rest of his life. He spent as much of his spare time in her company as she would allow him, and looked forward to the hour or two when he was admitted to the presence of his enchantress to console him for the literary solitude in which the remainder of his day was passed. When she travelled, he was always ready to accompany her did she need an escort, and when he could not be with her, it was seldom that a courier arrived without bringing her a letter from this, perhaps, the most devoted and unselfish of all her friends. To be with her was to be in heaven; without her life would have been a burden too grievous to be borne. "You know well," he says in another of his letters, written at a time when her health was causing her friends much uneasiness, "that if you were to die, it would be necessary to lose no time in digging a grave for me, as I should soon follow you." This was not mere Gallic exuberance of expression; it was the sober truth. There was no false sentiment about Simon Ballanche.

And Madame Récamier, it is pleasant to relate, with that delicacy and tact so peculiarly her own, having once ascertained his real worth, and the depth and purity of his affection for herself, admitted him to her friendship on a footing of perfect equality with the most distinguished of her associates, such as the Montmorencies and the La Rochefoucaulds.

The printer-poet, although he had no flow of small talk, was far from being an uninteresting companion, but his manners were somewhat homely, and he was profoundly ignorant of the usages of polite society. The day after he had been presented to Madame Récamier he called upon her, and found himself alone with his charming hostess. Unfortunately, Ballanche's boots had that morning been cleaned with a preparation which imparted to them as disagreeable an odour as those of Sir Roger Williams, to whom Queen Elizabeth, on the occasion of his presenting an unfavoured petition, is said to have observed, with more candour than courtesy, "Faugh! Williams, I prithee begone, thy boots stink," and to have been met with the witty retort, "Tut! Tut! madame, 'tis my suit that stinketh." Madame Récamier had the advantage of better breeding than good Queen Bess, but the noxious odour was too much even for her sense of politeness, and, at length, she timidly confessed to her visitor that the smell of his shoes made her ill.

Ballanche was not in the least offended at her admission, but at once rose, apologised profusely, and left the room. In a minute or two he returned without his shoes, and, quite unconscious that he was committing any solecism, resumed his seat, and continued the conversation. Just at that moment several other visitors were announced, and Ballanche was, of course, under the necessity of explaining to them his unusual and somewhat suspicious appearance.

The hope of seeing Madame de Staël had been the principal reason which had induced Madame Récamier to come to Lyons. She appears to have had some idea of sharing her friend's flight to Sweden, and wrote offering to join her at Coppet. Madame de Staël, however, had reasons of her own for not desiring the company of even Madame Récamier at this juncture. She had lately contracted a rather undignified second marriage with a young Swiss officer named Rocca, invalided home from the

Spanish war, whose helpless condition had aroused first her sympathy, and afterwards that feeling which is supposed to be akin to it. The only reply Madame Récamier received was a brief note, announcing that Madame de Staël had made her escape from French territory.

"I bid you adieu, my guardian angel," she writes, "with all the warmth of my heart. I commit Auguste to your care. I trust that he will see you, and that I shall see him again. It is on you that I rely to console him, and to bring about our reunion when such an event becomes possible. You are an angelic creature. If I could live near you, I should be only too happy. Fate drags me away. Adieu!"

Although Madame Récamier saw a good deal of society, such as it was, at Lyons, and visited and received without any interference from the authorities, the lot of an exile under Napoleon's tyrannical rule was bound to be a humiliating one, and, when in the company of her friends, she was never quite free from the fear that those who were showing her kindness might at any moment be made to suffer for their generosity. The more timid and selfish of her neighbours, too, studiously avoided her; and this could not fail to be extremely galling to a woman hitherto so admired and sought after. One such case she was fond of relating as an illustration of the petty despotism of those days.

Shortly after she came to Lyons a certain gentleman, with social aspirations, who had been an occasional visitor at her house in Paris, hearing of her arrival, and ignorant of the reason which had brought her thither, hastened to the Hôtel de l'Europe, where she was staying, eager to pay his respects to so celebrated a leader of society. He found her in the company of her sister-in-law Madame

Delphin, and Eugène d'Harcourt (afterwards the Duc d'Harcourt), who had come to Lyons on purpose to see her ; and, after paying her many extravagant compliments, informed her that he was about to give a *fête-champêtre* at his country house, a few miles from Lyons, and entreated her to grace it with her presence.

Madame Récamier, who since her husband's failure had avoided large assemblies, declined, pleading a prior engagement with Madame Delphin and Eugène d'Harcourt. Her visitor, however, would take no refusal, and she did not get rid of him until he had extracted a promise from the whole party to attend his fête.

On the appointed day Madame Récamier and her friends hired a carriage, and drove out to the fête. When they entered the grounds, they found their host seated on the balustrade of a ring-game of which he was counting the strokes. Instead of rising to receive his guests, he merely nodded to them in a patronising kind of way, and again turned his attention to the game. Astonished beyond measure at such an extraordinary reception from a person who, a few days before, had been so extremely anxious for their company, they forthwith ordered their carriage and returned to Lyons.

Not long afterwards Madame Récamier again met her late host at a dinner-party, at which he happened to be placed next to her. He hastened to apologise for his behaviour at the fête, remarking quite frankly, "What could I do ? I had learned that you were an exile. I do trust you are not offended."

Madame Récamier was so amused at this unconscious meanness that she answered, laughing :

"Monsieur, it is impossible to be offended with such a person as you are."

This the good man took as a compliment, and declared that she was the most amiable woman he had ever met.

The frequent stopping of travellers at Lyons furnished some distraction for Madame Récamier. It was to this that she owed a visit from Madame Junot, now Duchesse d'Abrantès, who was on her way from Aix to Paris. The duchess and Madame Récamier had not met since Jacques Récamier's failure, and the former was much touched at finding her friend, whom she had last seen in her magnificent hôtel in the Rue du Mont Blanc, surrounded by every conceivable luxury, occupying a single apartment at an inn, but still as beautiful, as graceful, and as charming as ever.

"Madame Récamier," she says, "had in her apartment a pianoforte, drawing materials, work-frames, books, &c. These alternately occupied her time, but could not entirely exclude melancholy recollections. Madame Doumerc ran her fingers over the keys of the pianoforte, and produced those sweet sounds which she knew so well how to draw from the instrument.

"'Ah!' exclaimed Madame Récamier, 'revive some of the recollections I share in common with you both. Sing me a song, but let it be French not Italian.'

"Madame Doumerc requested me to accompany her in one of Boïeldieu's romances, the words of which were written by M. de Longchamp when he was banished to America by the Directory. They are expressive of the deepest melancholy, and I could perceive they drew tears from the eyes of the fair exile." [1]

That winter the celebrated actor Talma came to Lyons to fulfil an engagement at the Grand Théâtre. He had been on friendly terms with Madame Récamier in Paris

[1] *Memoirs of the Duchesse d'Abrantès*, iv. 243.

and she invited him to dine with her. The Abbé de Boulogne, Bishop of Troyes, one of the most famous preachers of the day, was also of the party. The bishop had never been to a play in his life, but he was well acquainted with dramatic literature, and was delighted at meeting the celebrated tragedian.

After dinner he asked Talma to recite something, which the actor did, choosing, out of respect to the good bishop, one of his rôles in which religious sentiment was expressed. The abbé was delighted, and when Talma, in return, begged for an extract from one of his sermons, willingly consented. Talma listened with great interest to the preacher, praised his delivery, made some remarks upon his gestures, and added, "It is very good down to here, monseigneur (pointing to the bishop's chest), but the lower part of the body goes for nothing. One can easily see that you have never given a thought to your legs."

Towards the end of January 1813 Mathieu de Montmorency came to Lyons, and, noticing that his friend seemed far from well, advised her to spend the remainder of the winter in Italy. Madame Récamier had long wished to visit the enchanted land of Dante and Petrarch, of Raphael and Michael Angelo ; and, now that Madame de Staël was beyond her reach, there was nothing to keep her at Lyons. She therefore started for Italy early in February, with her little niece and maid. Montmorency accompanied her as far as Chambéry ; and, after he had left her, she divided her time between the scenery and a little travelling library, the books composing which had been selected for her by Simon Ballanche. One of these books, it is interesting to note, was *Le Génie du Christianisme*, the brilliant author of which was to become in later years the most cherished of all her friends.

CHAPTER VIII

Madame Récamier's impressions of Turin—She arrives in Rome—State of the city during the French occupation—The Torlonias—Canova, the sculptor, and his brother—Madame Récamier's friendship with them—Visit of Ballanche to Rome—Madame Récamier goes to Albano—The condemned fisherman—Madame Récamier's efforts to save him—Madame Récamier sets out for Naples—The post-horses at Velletri—Meeting with Fouché—Arrival in Naples—Cordial reception by the King and Queen—Character of Caroline and of Joachim Murat—Murat joins the coalition against Napoleon—A painful scene at the palace—"Then I am a traitor!"—Madame Récamier intercedes for a criminal—She returns to Rome—The Beatrice of Canova—The Allies enter France—Madame Récamier again visits Naples—M. Mazois and the brigands—Entry of Pius VII. into Rome—Extraordinary enthusiasm of the people—Madame Récamier returns to Paris

MADAME RÉCAMIER's first stop was made at Turin, where Prince Borghèse, Pauline Bonaparte's second husband, who had in 1808 been appointed by Napoleon Governor-General of Piedmont, Genoa, and Parma, had fixed his Court. From Turin she writes to Camille Jordan.

MADAME RÉCAMIER *to* CAMILLE JORDAN.

"TURIN, *March* 26, 1813.

"It is impossible, dear Camille, to write a more charming letter than the one I have received from you. You cannot imagine the feeling of sadness which came over me on reaching the summit of Mont Cenis, and beginning the descent of the opposite slope. It seemed to place an eternal barrier between myself and those I love; and I was so miserable when I reached Turin that I thought I was going to be ill. I began to recover my spirits two days ago, to make plans for the future, and to escape for a little while from that gloomy train of thought, which I have determined to avoid as much as possible.

"I am also beginning to take some interest in my surroundings, and to receive a few visitors. Italian influences commence to make themselves felt here, not on the climate, but on people's morals. The married ladies have *cicisbeos* to keep them company, and abbés for their major-domos. Prince Borghèse, whom every one speaks of as "the" Prince, has, they say, the most pompous little Court in Europe. The scandals, the toilets, the intrigues of this little Court appear to engross all people's thoughts, and to be the sole topic of their conversation. Our friend, the Comte Alfieri, is a wonderful success as Master of the Ceremonies. The old Piedmontese nobility and the French officials are always meeting at Court, and there is no longer much love lost between them. The conceit of these nobles and officials reminds one of the great world of Paris, but they are much more ridiculous, inasmuch as they move in a much smaller sphere, and are not allied to any political party. I do not believe there is any country in the world where people attach more importance to outward display. Their houses are palaces, and they cling to the old custom of keeping an immense number of servants. But when you pay them an informal visit, you are considerably astonished, after traversing antechambers, reception-rooms, and galleries, to find the mistress of the house in a little back room lighted by a single candle.

"'The' Prince leads a most secluded life, except when he has to attend official gatherings. He spends all his time shut up in a suite of rooms on the ground floor of his palace. He has lived this retired life for two years. They say that all that time the Venetian blinds of the lower room of his suite have always remained closed. A single man-servant enters this lower room each morning, and it is provided with fresh flowers every day, and . . ."

[*The rest of this letter is missing.*]

On leaving Turin, Madame Récamier visited Parma, Modena, Bologna, and Florence, and arrived in Rome at the beginning of Holy Week. She engaged rooms, at first, on the Piazza d'Espagna, but, a little later on, removed to a suite on the first floor of the Fiano Palace, on the Corso, where her salon soon became a centre of attraction to the few foreigners then in Rome.

Rome was at this time bereft of its Pontiff, who was a prisoner at Fontainebleau, in the palace of Francis I.; and the capital of the Christian world was only the chief town of the Department of the Tiber. Sympathy for the unfortunate Pius VII. was universal among the Romans, and all classes were united in hatred of the French rule. Many of the aristocracy and clergy had left Rome; the disturbed state of Europe kept foreigners away, and a mournful spirit seemed to hover over the whole city.

Madame Récamier had letters of credit and introduction to the principal banker Torlonia, "a banker in the morning and Duke de Bracciano at night," an extraordinary character, who in business was as avaricious as a Jew usurer, and in private life as sumptuous as the most magnificent grand-seigneur. He lived in a splendid palace on the Corso, filled with almost priceless works of art, where he dispensed lavish hospitality, and boasted, at the same time, of his mean acts, the contemplation of which seemed to afford him as much pleasure as that of his pictures and curios. Here Madame Récamier visited him, and was most cordially received by the banker and his wife, who, in her way, was almost as singular a personage as her husband.

"The duchess," says Madame Lenormant, "had been very lovely, and, though no longer young in 1813, was still handsome. She was good-natured, and, like the Italian women of that day, a strange compound of infidelity and devotion. In a confidential moment, she related what care she had taken to prevent her husband's peace of mind being disturbed by her conduct, and added, 'Oh! he will be very much astonished at the Day of Judgment.'"[1]

The Torlonias were extremely kind to Madame Récamier, and through them she became acquainted with several of the leading families among the Roman aristocracy.

One of the first visits which Madame Récamier paid in Rome was to the studio of the famous sculptor Canova. She had no special introduction to him; but all strangers were admitted to his *atelier*. The sculptor himself worked in an inner room, secure from all interruption. Madame Récamier, however, was so charmed with the specimens of Canova's skill which she saw around her that she wished to see the workman also, and, accordingly, sent in her name. Canova immediately came out, holding his paper

[1] *Souvenirs*, i. 220.

cap in his hand, and, bowing gracefully, invited her into his own studio, where she found his half-brother the Abbé Canova, who acted as secretary and reader to the sculptor, and was so devoted to him that he followed him about like his shadow.

Canova, who was a passionate admirer of beauty, returned Madame Récamier's visit the same evening; and the acquaintance thus formed soon ripened into a warm friendship, and it was seldom that the sculptor failed to pass part of his evening with the beautiful Frenchwoman.

He lived on a second floor on the Corso, in large rooms, comfortably rather than luxuriously furnished, and full of fine engravings. He was extremely simple in his tastes, and went but little into society. Generous to the verge of prodigality, he spent the greater portion of his princely income in assisting struggling fellow artists and men of letters, and was, in consequence, universally beloved. His half-brother, the abbé, who had considerable literary attainments, shared his admiration for Madame Récamier, and, every day during her stay in Rome, composed a sonnet, which he dedicated to "*la bellissima Zulietta.*"

In the early part of July, Madame Récamier received a flying visit from Ballanche. His father was unable to spare him for more than a few days, so, in order to lose as little as possible of his brief holiday, he travelled from Lyons without stopping day or night. On the day of his arrival, the evening being beautifully fine, Madame Récamier suggested a drive to show him St. Peter's and the Coliseum by moonlight. Canova, who took the most minute care of his health, was one of the party, and appeared enveloped in a thick cloak to protect himself from the balmy evening breeze. But Ballanche came without his hat, and, on being asked where it was, replied unconcernedly that he fancied it was at Alexandria. He had, in fact, left it there, and had never even thought of replacing it, so little attention did he pay to the ordinary details of life.

When August came, and Rome was becoming deserted owing to the heat and the malaria, Canova placed part of his *locanda* at Albano at Madame Récamier's disposal, an offer which she gladly accepted. Her rooms overlooked the Campagna, and commanded a magnificent view of the vast undulating plain and the distant sea. In this lovely spot the ex-leader of fashion was quite happy with no other company than that of her little niece, though Canova and his brother came out from time to time for a breath of country air, generally remaining three or four days.

It was while she was at Albano that an incident occurred which affords a striking illustration of that goodness of heart which endeared Madame Récamier to all with whom she came in contact.

One Sunday evening she was returning from church when she saw an excited crowd of peasants grouped round the low doorway of a cottage; and, in reply to her questions, she was told that a fisherman of the coast, accused of giving information to the English, had just been confined in the cottage, which served the purpose of a prison, and was to be shot at daybreak. At that moment the prisoner's confessor, the priest of Albano, came out of the cottage, and catching sight of Madame Récamier, whose alms had several times passed through his hands, hastened towards her, hoping that she might possibly have some influence with the French authorities.

Madame Récamier accompanied the priest into the prison, where she found the condemned fisherman, a young and handsome man, heavily manacled and almost beside himself with fear. His eyes seemed to be starting out of his head, his teeth chattered, the sweat rolled in great beads off his forehead, and his whole appearance indicated the most intense agony.

On seeing the terrible distress of the unhappy man, Madame Récamier was deeply touched, and promised the priest to do everything in her power to obtain a commutation of his sentence. The priest then explained to the prisoner that the lady was French, that she was kind and generous, that she was full of compassion for him, and would intercede for his pardon.

At the word "pardon," the condemned man became a little calmer: "*Pietà! Pietà!*" he cried. His confessor made him promise to compose himself, to pray to God, and take a little food, while his protectress went to Rome to make intercession for him.

As the execution was fixed for the following morning, there was plainly not a moment to be lost. Madame Récamier forthwith hurried home, ordered post-horses, and set out for Rome. At that time the Campagna between Albano and Rome was infested by brigands, and travelling by night far from safe; but she was not molested, and reached the city in safety. She drove at once to General de Miollis, the commander-in-chief of the French troops, but, though he received her very courteously, he professed himself unable to help her. The power of pardon, he said, rested entirely with M. de Norvins, the prefect. To his house, accordingly, she went, but he was not at home, and all attempts to find him were unsuccessful. She, therefore, left a message begging him to come to her rooms at the Fiano Palace as soon as he returned, and drove thither to await him.

It was very late before the prefect arrived, and she saw at once by his manner that her errand would be a fruitless one. His only reply to her passionate entreaties was to advise her not to forget her own position, and to remind her that it ill became an exile to endeavour to save the Emperor's enemies from punishment. She returned to Albano the following morning, feeling terribly depressed by the failure of her mission of mercy, and haunted by the face of the unfortunate fisherman, whom she had seen a prey to all the terrors of death.

When she arrived the tragedy was over. The priest of Albano called upon her in the course of the day to bring her the victim's blessing. Up to the very last moment, it appeared, he had refused to abandon hope, turning his bandaged eyes towards Rome, as if expecting to hear the sweet voice of the *Signora Francese* returning with his pardon.

In October Madame Récamier returned to Rome, where the check which Napoleon's ambitious schemes had received and the continuous reverses of the French armies formed the one topic of conversation, and kept every one in a state of constant excitement. A victim of Napoleon's tyranny, Madame Récamier had every reason to desire his overthrow, which would leave her and her friends free to return to their beloved Paris. But personal considerations did not cause her to forget that she was a Frenchwoman ; and she would never permit a single word derogatory to the national honour to be uttered in her presence.

The autumn brought a few visitors to Rome, including M. de Chateauvieux, whom she had met at Coppet; the Prince de Rohan-Chabot, the Emperor's chamberlain, one of the few great noblemen who, from prudential reasons, had joined the Imperial household ; and Sir John Coghill, the antiquary, who was travelling in Italy in quest of Etruscan vases and ancient inscriptions. The two latter were on their way to Naples, and urged Madame Récamier to complete her Italian tour by a visit to that city. She demurred at first, being a little doubtful as to the reception which she, as an exile, might expect from the king and queen, her old friends Joachim and Caroline Murat; but, on being reassured on this point by M. de Rohan, she left for Naples in December, in company with Coghill and his family.

At Velletri, their first halting-place, they found to their surprise the horses for both their carriages already harnessed and awaiting them. Coghill, who occupied the foremost carriage, with true British imperiousness, forthwith secured them, without troubling himself to inquire for whom they were intended. The same thing occurred at every successive stage, and at length they discovered, from some remarks that the postilions let fall, that a courier had preceded them, and ordered the horses to be in readiness for some great unknown personage who was expected.

In this manner they reached Terracina, where they intended to pass the night, but had not been there long when two carriages drove up, and a loud and angry voice exclaimed, "Where are those insolent people who have robbed me of my post-horses along the whole route?"

On hearing this voice, which sounded strangely familiar, Madame Récamier put her head out of the window, and beheld her old enemy Fouché stamping up and down the courtyard in a white heat of indignation.

"Here they are," she answered, laughing heartily. "It is I, Monsieur le Duc."

On recognising Madame Récamier the old Minister of

Police drew back, a little ashamed of his anger, but the lady, without appearing to notice his embarrassment, invited him into her room. Fouché was hurrying to Naples on a mission to Murat, the object of which was to maintain that vacillating sovereign in his allegiance to Napoleon; for the earth was beginning to tremble under the feet of the conqueror, and the kings whom he himself had created were beginning to show unmistakable signs of restiveness. Murat himself was being warmly pressed by both England and Austria to join the coalition against Napoleon ; and it was only some honourable scruples that had hitherto kept him from doing so. It was of the utmost importance to the Emperor not to lose such an ally, and his envoy had good reason for his haste.

Fouché asked Madame Récamier rather sharply what she wanted in Naples, and proceeded to warn her against meddling in politics.

"Yes, madame," said he, "remember that when we are weak, we ought to be amiable."

"And when we are strong, we ought to be just," she retorted.

Fouché continued his journey, and Madame Récamier arrived safely in Naples the following day.

Scarcely was she installed in the rooms on the Chiaja, which had been taken for her by Rohan, when a page came from the queen, bearing a basket of magnificent fruit and flowers, and a message from both sovereigns inquiring after her health, and expressing their desire to see her as soon as she was sufficiently rested. The following morning, accordingly, she presented herself at the palace, and was most cordially welcomed by the king and queen. Both Caroline and her husband vied with one another in showing her kindness. There was always a welcome for her at Court, where the queen insisted on giving her precedence over all the other ladies, much to the disgust of the latter; a box at the Opera was placed at her disposal, and a special party to Pompeii was organised for the purpose of displaying its antiquities to the fair visitor.

Caroline Murat, though not so handsome as her sister Pauline, perhaps next to Madame Récamier the greatest beauty in France, was a very lovely woman with dazzlingly white skin and beautiful fair hair, and united to her personal attractions administrative capabilities of no mean order. Her government of Naples, when entrusted with the regency during her husband's absence at the seat of war, was distinguished by a prudence and energy which caused Talleyrand to remark that "she had the head of a Cromwell on the shoulders of a pretty woman."[1] Her husband, on the other hand, although as brave a soldier as ever drew a sword, was absolutely destitute both of political ability and of moral courage. "You are a good soldier on the field of battle, but, beyond that, you have no energy," wrote Napoleon to him on one occasion. He seems, indeed, to have been entirely under the domination of his clever and ambitious consort, and, when deprived of her counsels, to have been like a ship without a rudder.

At the time of Madame Récamier's arrival in Naples, Murat had finally decided to throw in his lot with England and Austria against his old master and brother-in-law.

[1] "The Queen of Naples was a woman of considerable shrewdness, energy of character, and talent. I use this expression in reference to political life only. That excepted, she was as ignorant as a woman can well be, or, I ought rather to say, as women were a hundred years ago. Though wanting in the most ordinary education, yet, if a grave political question came under discussion, she would speak like a well-informed statesman."—*Memoirs of the Duchess of Abrantès*, iv. 354.

The interests of his dynasty, indeed, imperatively demanded such a step, for it was the only course by which he could avoid being involved in the downfall of Napoleon, now plainly inevitable. The Neapolitans themselves desired peace at any price, and loudly demanded separation from France. Murat was extremely popular with his subjects, especially with the fishermen and the *lazzaroni* of the Carmine, but their affection was alienated by the fear of war and the English invasion. Large crowds began to assemble in front of the palace, clamouring for peace, and accompanying their demands with threatening gestures. The queen, too, who was not inclined to allow any sentiment of gratitude or honour to stand between her and her ambition, ably seconded the people's wishes, and used all her influence to induce her husband to betray their common benefactor, with the result that, on January 11, poor Murat, consoling himself with the reflection that his first duty was to his own subjects, signed the treaty which bound him to the coalition.

On the day on which the treaty was to be made public, Madame Récamier was alone with the queen in her apartments when the king entered in a great state of agitation. He was deadly pale, his hair was in disorder, his eyes rolled wildly, and, to all appearance, he was under the influence of some overpowering excitement. Rushing up to Madame Récamier, he seized her by both her hands, and, hoping against hope that she would approve the decision he had already made, he began, as coherently as he could, to explain the situation in which he was placed, and concluded by asking her what course she would advise to adopt.

"Sire," she answered, "you are a Frenchman. To France you must be true."

"Then I am a traitor!" cried the unhappy man, and

opening a window of the palace which overlooked the sea, he pointed to the English fleet sailing majestically into the Bay of Naples, and then, covering his face with his hands, burst into tears.

Murat seemed perfectly bewildered with despair and grief. The queen, much firmer, though not less moved, ran towards him, exclaiming:

"In the name of Heaven, Joachim, be silent, or, at least, speak lower! In the next room there are a hundred ears ready to catch every word you utter. Be silent! Have you lost all self-control?" Then, finding that her words produced no effect upon her husband, she went to a table, filled a glass from a carafe of orange-flower water, poured some drops of ether into it, and brought it to the distracted monarch.

"Drink this and compose yourself," said she. "The crisis has now arrived. Murat, remember what you are. You are King of Naples. Do not lose sight of the duty you owe to your subjects and your family."

After a time Murat, who perhaps had some premonition of the terrible fate which awaited him, grew calmer, and left the room to make some alteration in his dress. No sooner had the door closed behind him, than the queen threw herself into Madame Récamier's arms, and, with tears in her eyes, exclaimed:

"You see, I am obliged to have courage for him as well as for myself. At a time, too, when my courage is scarcely sustained by my affection for my children—when I am hourly distracted by thinking of my brother, who believes me to be guilty of treason towards him. Oh, pity me! I have need of pity, and I deserve it. If you could search my heart, you would understand what torture I am doomed to bear."

Madame Récamier returned to her hotel much moved by the painful scene which she had just witnessed. Suddenly her attention was attracted by a great commotion in the street. She ran to the window, and saw Murat on horseback in the midst of an immense crowd. The intelligence of the treaty of alliance, confirmed by the presence of the English ships in the harbour, had spread, and the populace, whose attitude had recently been so threatening, were now cheering the king. Later in the day the king and queen ordered their carriage, and drove round the town, where they were everywhere received with enthusiasm; and at night appeared at the theatre in company with the Austrian Envoy Extraordinary, the negotiator of the treaty, and the English admiral. Two days later Murat quitted Naples to take command of the Neapolitan army, leaving his wife to act as regent.

One morning, soon after the king's departure, Madame Récamier, coming to the palace in response to an invitation from the queen, was ushered into the royal bedchamber, where Queen Caroline, who was rather unwell, was still in bed. The queen's bedchamber, which commanded a view of the bay, was, like all her other apartments, fitted up most luxuriously. It was hung with white satin, which harmonised with the dazzling complexion of its mistress, while the bed curtains were of richly worked tulle, lined with pink satin. Queen Caroline frequently received visitors while in bed, as she had been in the habit of doing in Paris, and at the moment when Madame Récamier entered, the Minister of Justice was standing by her side, handing her some papers relating to his department which required her signature. As she was about to sign one of these documents, she paused and said, "You would be very unhappy, dear Madame Récamier, were you in my place, for I am about to sign a death warrant."

"Oh, madame!" cried her visitor, rising, "you will not sign it. Since Heaven has brought me into your presence at this time, it wishes to save this unfortunate man."

The queen smiled, and, turning to the Minister, said: "Madame Récamier does not wish this wretched man to die. Can we pardon him?" After some discussion, the party of clemency carried the day, and the pardon was granted.

Madame Récamier was fond of recalling this incident as one of the happiest moments of her life, and regarded it as some compensation for her unsuccessful efforts on behalf of the poor fisherman of Albano.

Madame Récamier returned to Rome in time for the ceremonies of Holy Week. The Canovas were, of course, overjoyed at seeing her again, and made her promise to come to the studio to see the works executed during her absence. She went, but was somewhat surprised to find little or nothing new until she came into the private studio, when the sculptor, about whom there was an air of mystery, drew aside a curtain, and displayed two clay busts of Madame Récamier, one with no ornament but the hair, the other with the addition of a veil.

"See if I have not thought of you!" exclaimed Canova, with the air of an artist who believes in his success.

The busts had, of course, been executed from memory, and, as one of the lady's friends observes, "the sculptor had not attempted to copy Madame Récamier's features so much as to embody the lineaments of her soul." [1]

[1] *Fraser's Magazine*, July 1849.

Unfortunately, Madame Récamier did not consider the busts faithful likenesses, and said as much. The sculptor was deeply wounded. He dropped the curtain, and never referred to them again. It is not known what became of the plain bust, but Canova added a crown of olives to the one with the veil, and when, some time afterwards, Madame Récamier asked him what he had done with it, he replied, "It did not please you, so I have made a Beatrice of it." Such was the origin of the *Beatrice of Dante*, one of the most exquisite works of this famous sculptor. After Canova's death his brother, the Abbé Canova, sent a copy of it to Madame Récamier, with the following lines:

> "Sovra candido vel, cinta d'oliva,
> Donna m'apparve. . . .[1]
>
> DANTE.

"*Ritratto di Giulietta Récamier, modellato di memoria, da Canova, nel* 1813, *e poi consecrato in marmo col nome di Beatrice.*"

Meanwhile France was invaded, and Napoleon's position was daily becoming more critical. Caroline Murat, half regretting her own and her husband's treachery, and apprehensive that perhaps after all it might fail to save their throne, wrote to Madame Récamier, begging her to come and comfort her. She went, and, while at Naples, learned that Napoleon had abdicated, and had been sent to play at being king on the little island of Elba.

There was now, of course, no obstacle in the way of Madame Récamier's return to Paris, although her sentence of exile had not yet been formally revoked; and,

[1] "Under a white veil, crowned with an olive wreath, a woman appeared to me."

accordingly, she took an affectionate farewell of her royal friend, and left Naples for Rome *en route* for France. Just as she was on the point of starting, however, intelligence was brought that a band of brigands was committing depredations in the neighbourhood; whereupon Queen Caroline insisted that M. Mazois, one of the officers of her household, should escort her guest. The journey to Rome was accomplished without hindrance, but on his way back to Naples, M. Mazois and his servants were less fortunate. They were attacked and overpowered by the banditti, who were in much greater force than had been supposed, and robbed of everything, even their clothes.

Before Madame Récamier finally quitted the Eternal City, she had the privilege of beholding such a spectacle as is seen only once in a lifetime—the return of Pius VII. to his capital. She witnessed the pageant from the top of some raised seats that had been erected beneath the porticos of the two churches which form the entrance to the Corso, opposite the Porto del Popolo. The enthusiasm of the whole city was indescribable. All the great Roman nobles and young men of rank went out to meet the Pope at Storta, the last stage from Rome, where the horses were taken out of the Pontiff's carriage, which was then drawn to the city and through the streets to St. Peter's, amid the acclamations of the people. The august old man who was the object of all this passionate loyalty was on his knees, his whole bearing suggestive of the deepest humility: and when at length St. Peter's was reached, and the liberated Pontiff knelt before the altar, while the *Te Deum* resounded through the vaulted arches, there was hardly a dry eye in the whole vast assembly.

On her way to Paris Madame Récamier stopped for a few days at Lyons, where Ballanche and Camille Jordan had been impatiently awaiting her arrival; and attended a grand fête, which was given in honour of the restoration of the Bourbons. At Lyons she received a note from Madame de Staël, who had hastened back to Paris as soon as she was assured of the fall of her old enemy. "I am ashamed," she wrote, "to be in Paris without you, dear angel of my life. After so many trials, the sweetest prospect that lies before me is that of seeing you, for my heart is always devoted to you."

Madame Récamier arrived in Paris on June 1, after an absence of nearly three years.

CHAPTER IX

Society at the Restoration—Old familiar faces—Madame de Staël—Mathieu de Montmorency—Madame Moreau—Fate of Victor Moreau—Honours bestowed upon his widow—The Duke of Wellington the hero of the day—Madame Récamier's account of her acquaintance with him—His admiration for her—His "unmeaning notes"—"*Je l'ai bien battu*"—Benjamin Constant—Influence of women over him—Madame Récamier invokes his assistance on behalf of the Murats—He falls madly in love with her—His extraordinary letters—Madame Récamier's treatment of him considered—Napoleon returns to France—Madame Récamier refuses to leave Paris—Letter from the Queen of Naples—The fate of Murat—Benjamin Constant's violent article in the *Journal des Débats*—He flies to Nantes—But returns, and is reconciled to Napoleon—He becomes a Councillor of State—"*Le Benjaminisme*"—Probable reason for Constant's tergiversations

MADAME RÉCAMIER returned not only to Paris, but to something of her former wealth, for in the interval her husband had in a measure recovered his losses, while she had inherited her mother's fortune of some 400,000 francs, which had maintained her in exile. In person she was as lovely as ever; and the prestige of her self-sacrificing friendship for Madame de Staël, and the sympathy which Napoleon's cruel persecution of her had aroused, enhanced the fame of her beauty, and her salon was as brilliant and as crowded as ever.

Solitude and reflection had opened to Madame Récamier

fresh and more permanent sources of pleasure. During the dreary months she had spent at Châlons and Lyons she had been afforded opportunities for study which had been denied her while living in the whirl of Parisian gaiety; and her taste for intellectual society had been greatly stimulated by intercourse with such men as Ballanche and the Canovas. She determined, henceforth, to confine herself as much as possible to the society of refined and cultivated people, and to withdraw from the fashionable and somewhat dissipated circles she had formerly frequented. To do so was now far easier than before the Restoration, for society was beginning to return into its old channel. During the Empire the salons had never attained to anything approaching the brilliance which had distinguished them under the old *régime*, partly owing to the suspicion with which Napoleon regarded them, and partly owing to the vulgarity of the ladies of the Imperial Court. Now, however, allowing for the difference of manners, they soon became of as much importance as before the Revolution.

To Madame Récamier's social successes were added the pleasures of renewed friendships. Madame de Staël was one of the first to welcome her, and was, of course, overjoyed at once more beholding her "dear angel." Mathieu de Montmorency had also returned, and had just been appointed *Chevalier d'Honneur* to the Duchesse d'Angoulême, and was looked upon as one of the leaders of the ultra-Royalists; while among many other old friends, to whom the gates of Paris had been opened by the fall of Napoleon, was Madame Moreau, now, alas! a widow.

After his expulsion from France in 1804, Moreau and his wife had retired to America, where for nine years they lived happily enough. Unfortunately, Madame Moreau, who was an extremely ambitious woman, would not allow her husband to rest, but persuaded him to open negotiations with his old comrade Bernadotte, who had joined the coalition against Napoleon.

At Bernadotte's suggestion, Moreau entered the service of the Czar, and agreed to direct the operations of the campaign of 1813. Fortunately for his fame as a patriot, he did not live to invade his country, as he was mortally wounded, while making a reconnaissance in company with the Czar, before Dresden, on August 27, and died a few days later. His last words, "*Soyez tranquille, messieurs; c'est mon sort,*" would seem to imply that he did not altogether regret being removed from his equivocal position as a general in arms against the troops which he had so often led to victory. His body was embalmed at Prague and conveyed to St. Petersburg, where the Czar caused it to be buried in the Roman Catholic church in that city. Alexander also bestowed upon the widow a pension of 100,000 francs.

After the Restoration, Louis XVIII., wishing to testify his respect for the memory of the Republican general, offered Madame Moreau the title of "Duchess." This she refused, but accepted that which would have belonged to the soldier had he survived, and was, accordingly, created *Maréchale de France*, the only time this dignity has been conferred upon a woman.

Society was very gay that year in Paris. The national pride was undoubtedly wounded by the presence of foreign soldiers in the capital of France, especially when people happened to be as unfortunate as the poor Duchesse d'Abrantès, who had an officer of Cossacks billeted upon her, who drank a bottle of brandy at every meal, and went to bed in his boots and spurs; but the Parisians consoled themselves with the reflection that their own troops had bivouacked in every capital in continental Europe. Moreover, disgust with Napoleon's insatiable ambition and the conscriptions, which had sent so many thousands of gallant young men to their death, was such that the whole country breathed more freely now that the despotic Government was no more.

With the returned exiles the English were the fashion, and Wellington the hero of the day. The duke was a frequent visitor at Madame de Staël's, and it was here that Madame Récamier first met the conqueror of the Peninsula, who, like every one else, seems to have at once succumbed to the charms of the world-renowned beauty. One of the fragments of Madame Récamier's journal which has been preserved contains some interesting memoranda relating to her acquaintance with the duke.

"*The Duke of Wellington.*

"Madame de Staël's enthusiasm for the Duke of Wellington. I see him at her house for the first time. Conversation during dinner. He pays me a visit the following day. Madame de Staël meets him here. Lord Wellington's visits become frequent. His opinion of popularity. I present him to Queen Hortense.[1] *Soirée* at the house of the Duchesse de Luynes. Conversation with the Duke of Wellington before a glass door. M. de Talleyrand and the Duchesse de Courland. *Empressement* of M. de Talleyrand towards me. The feeling

[1] Queen Hortense did not leave Paris on the downfall of Napoleon, and, mainly through the pressure brought to bear upon him by the Emperor Alexander, Louis XVIII. consented to create her Duchesse de St. Leu, giving her at the same time her estates as an independent duchy.

of aversion I have always entertained for him. Madame de Boigne stops me as I am leaving, followed by the Duke of Wellington. Continuation of his visits. Madame de Staël wishes me to obtain influence over him. He writes me unmeaning notes, which all resemble one another.[1] I lend him Mademoiselle de L'Espinasse's letters, which have just appeared. His opinion of these letters.[2] He leaves Paris. I see him again after the battle of Waterloo. He calls upon me the day after his return. I did not expect him. Annoyance this visit occasions me. He returns in the evening, and is denied admission. I again refuse to see him the next day. He writes to Madame de Staël to complain of my treatment of him. I do not see him again. It is reported that he is very much impressed with a young English lady, the wife of one of his aides-de-camp. Return of Madame de Staël to Paris. Dinner at the Queen of Sweden's with

[1] Of these "unmeaning" notes the following one will serve as an example:

"PARIS, *June* 13.

"I confess, Madame, that I am not very sorry that business matters will prevent my calling upon you after dinner; since each time I see you, I leave you more deeply impressed with your charms, and less inclined to give my attention to politics!!! I shall call upon you to-morrow, provided you are at home, upon my return from the Abbé Sicard's, and in spite of the dangerous effect such visits have upon me.

"Your very faithful servant,

"WELLINGTON."

[2] "J'étais tout hier à la chasse, Madame; et je n'ai reçu votre billet et les livres qu'à la nuit, quand c'était trop tard pour vous répondre. J'espérais que mon jugement serait guidé par le vôtre dans ma lecture des lettres de Mlle. Espinasse, et je désespère de pouvoir le former moi-même. Je vous suis bien obligé pour la pamphlete de Mme. de Staël.

"Votre très-obéissant et fidel serviteur,

"WELLINGTON."

her and the Duke of Wellington, whom I then see again. The coolness of his manner towards me. His attention to the young English lady. I am placed at dinner between him and the Duc de Broglie. He is sullen at the beginning of dinner, but grows animated, and, finally, becomes very agreeable. I observe the annoyance of the young English lady, who is seated opposite to us. I cease talking to him, and devote myself entirely to the Duc de Broglie. I see the duke very seldom. He comes to call on me at the Abbaye-aux-Bois on his last visit to Paris."

Madame Récamier was undoubtedly flattered by the attention paid her by the duke, but Madame Lenormant tells us that, in spite of his fame, she did not find him "either animated or interesting," and, consequently, did not follow Madame de Staël's advice "to obtain influence over him," "which," adds her enthusiastic niece, "without a doubt she could have easily gained." On his return to Paris after Waterloo, Wellington hastened to call upon her, but Madame Récamier's patriotism was wounded by his visit, and when, thinking that she would be delighted at the defeat of her old persecutor, Napoleon, the duke exclaimed, "*Je l'ai bien battu*," her aunt, if we are to believe Madame Lenormant, closed her doors against him in disgust.

That same year, 1814, brought Madame Récamier another admirer in the person of Benjamin Constant, the famous orator and publicist, whose services she had engaged at the request of the Murats to plead the cause of their dynasty, the fate of which the Congress of Vienna was about to decide. Constant was a man of brilliant parts, but of a fickle and emotional temperament. Throughout his life, we are told, he was "subject to feminine influences, as varied as they were powerful." When little more than a boy, he lost his heart to Madame Charrière, to whom, according to M. Melegari, his latest biographer, he was in the habit of inditing "*lettres sèches et spirituelles.*" At twenty-three, he married a young German girl, whom he divorced three years later. He then became acquainted with Madame de Staël, and aspired to become her second husband, threatening to kill himself if she rejected his suit. The authoress of *Corinne* remained obdurate, however, in spite of his threats, and, instead of taking his life, Constant consoled himself by marrying a sister of Count Hardenberg, a lady who had already made two experiments in matrimony. Now, at forty-seven, he fell madly in love with Madame Récamier, and for many months bombarded her with love-letters, which, in point of absurdity, quite throw into the shade those which Lucien Bonaparte had penned fifteen years before. These letters have had a singular fate: they have been the subject of three law-suits.

Soon after Madame Récamier's death, her niece, Madame Lenormant, to whom she had bequeathed all her letters and papers, with directions to utilise them "according as her judgment dictated," attempted to publish them. Both the Constant and the Récamier families objected, however, and sought and obtained an injunction restraining their publication. It was not until thirty years had passed that another attempt was made to give them to the world, this time with success, in spite of the renewed opposition of the two families. Then M. d'Estournelles, Benjamin Constant's great-nephew, feeling that their publication was scarcely calculated to increase his celebrated kinsman's reputation, claimed to be allowed to insert a preface, entreating the reader not to judge the publicist or the statesman by these epistles. But this application was also set aside by the courts; and now all who care to do so may peruse *Les Lettres de Benjamin Constant à Madame Récamier*, a selection from which, as no English version of them has appeared, may not be without interest to the reader.

BENJAMIN CONSTANT *to* MADAME RÉCAMIER.

"*September* 1814.

"To-morrow evening! To-morrow evening! How much, how much that evening means to me! For me it will commence at five o'clock in the morning. To-morrow? —nay, it is to-day! Thank God, yesterday is over. Nine o'clock will find me at your door. Perhaps I shall be told you are not in. In that case, I shall return between ten and eleven.[1] Shall I again be told that you are not at home? I think of no one save you. For the last two days I seem to have seen no object but your face. All the past, all your fascination that I have always dreaded, has taken possession of my heart. I am speaking the truth, when I tell you, that I can scarcely breathe while I am writing to you.

"I have but one thought; you have willed that it should be so; that thought is of you. Politics, society, everything is forgotten. Perhaps you think me mad; but I recall your glance, I repeat to myself your words, I see again that girlish air so full of grace and refinement. I have reason for my madness—I should be mad not to be so. *Mon Dieu!* if you were not the most indifferent of women, what a life of suffering I might be spared! To love is to suffer; but it is also to live, and for a long time I have not lived. Once more, till this evening!"

[1] At this time Madame Récamier used to receive after the Opera.

BENJAMIN CONSTANT *to* MADAME RÉCAMIER.

"SAINT CLAIR, *October* 2, 1814.

"Forgive me for being so near you.[1] I will not come any nearer; no one shall see me. I will shut myself up in my room at the inn, and there await your answer. I will wait six hours for one line in your writing, and then return to Paris. I cannot live without you. I wander about, wounded unto death, utterly incapable of recovering my strength. But I much prefer to tire myself out on horseback than to pine away in solitude, or in the midst of a world that no longer understands me, in which I have no longer any interest—a world that does nothing but wonder at my wretchedness, and attribute it to the most ridiculous causes. I shall never get better, of that I am certain; but I await the answer that is to relieve you of my presence here. Tell me to go, and you shall be no longer plagued by a man whose life and whose reason you have ruined in one short month.

"Have you received the letter I wrote you yesterday? If you have not got it yet, you can easily guess its contents. Had I your love, I should be able to endure everything, even absence. But I have no support, no consoling thought, and am dying of grief. Do you wish me to call to-morrow with Auguste[2] and Victor de Broglie?[3] My doing so will excite no comment, and my refusal to come might attract more attention than my arrival would do. But, in that case, be kind enough to take a short walk with me, or let me have an hour's talk with you.

[1] Madame Récamier was staying with her friend Madame de Catellan at Angervilliers. St. Clair is a village a few miles from that town.

[2] Auguste de Staël, Madame de Staël's eldest son.

[3] The Duc de Broglie, who married Albertine de Staël, Madame de Staël's only daughter.

"I am wearying you; I am vexing you by my importunity. If the dreadful obstacle with which you have threatened me is not to be overcome, I will go away. You shall see me no more. I must at any price spare you pain. Send me one word in answer to this, one line in your handwriting. Tell me if I may come. But do not let me come unless you have a word of comfort for me. Pardon again, and pity me. Never man loved as I love, or suffered as I suffer. Adieu; I shall go back again as soon as my messenger returns.

"If the others do not come, alas! I shall not come any more."

"*October* 1814.

"I venture to remind you that you have promised to receive me alone to-day at four o'clock. It is absolutely necessary for me to speak to you about several matters; and I have not had a moment in which to do so. I am going to ask your advice, and truly it is time I did so, for my life is ruined, and I have but one thought—to speak to you, and you continually avoid me. However, ordinary friendship gives me the right to a few words of conversation with you, and you will do me a service, a true service, in granting me those few words. You have given me two hours to discuss the business of the King of Naples.[1] I ask you for one for myself. Condescend to give a thought to the state in which I am, and to the sufferings which I have been enduring for the last six weeks, and listen to me this once."

[1] The brochure written by Benjamin Constant in defence of the Murats appeared anonymously. It was cited in the English House of Commons during the debate on the affairs of Naples. Queen Caroline sent the author an honorarium of 20,000 francs and a decoration. He refused to accept either.

BENJAMIN CONSTANT *to* MADAME RÉCAMIER.

"*October* 1814.

"Was I sufficiently resigned to my fate yesterday? Did I leave early enough, and have you deigned to give a thought to what I was bound to suffer? However, if you will condescend to keep your promise, I will keep mine. I do not wish your kindness to me to cost you a single regret, and I feel bound to add to your happiness, even at the expense of my own. . . . One day, perhaps, you will be just; to-day be happy, and be kind.

"I am dining then with you. You have promised to allow me to come before dinner-time, for a moment's conversation, I hope. I want also to make my peace with M. Ballanche, whom I left rather abruptly while he was talking to me about his verses on Pythagoras. Have you read the letter I sent you yesterday? In each of my letters I ask you a thousand questions, but you never send a line in reply, neither do you refer to them when we meet. Thank Heaven, it is three o'clock, and M. de F—— is no longer at your house!"[1]

BENJAMIN CONSTANT *to* MADAME RÉCAMIER.

"*November* 1814.

"Acknowledge that you were fully aware of your power, and of the magical state of subjection to which you have reduced me, when I asked if you would be at home to any one this evening, and you replied, 'Not to you at any rate'! *Mon Dieu!* what have I done to be treated like this, and yet not to have the courage to complain?

[1] Comte Auguste de Forbin, a painter of some distinction, and Constant's rival in Madame Récamier's affections.

" . . . I am going to spend at least three days without seeing you. I know not how I shall be able to endure them. Be kind to me to-day at least. From what people have said to me this evening, I am sure that those cruel precautions which you insist on are quite unnecessary. No one has any suspicion of my real feelings towards you. They attribute my unhappiness to a totally different cause. I tell you again that my going to Angervilliers will not create the least scandal. Will you not allow me to escort you this morning a little way on your road? Then I shall have a few minutes more in your society. At any rate, be kind to me. My terrible unhappiness has astonished everybody, and will end by ruining me. You have made me a trifle calmer. Do not spoil your own handiwork. Never was heart so devoted as mine. Try and do me some good. You can make of me what you will."

BENJAMIN CONSTANT *to* MADAME RÉCAMIER.

" *November* 1814.

"Is there, then, no answer to my letter?

"I cannot part from you under a misunderstanding like this. My miserable heart is breaking. One moment's conversation to cement a friendship which will last for ever."

" *November* 1814.

"In Heaven's name, an answer! Oh, that I might see you! I will not speak to you about anything you object to. I have hardly sufficient strength to prevent myself from fainting. As soon as I see you, I shall be better. Suffer me to see you, then, and be myself once more. Do not utterly crush a man, who has never done you any harm, and who was, a little time ago, a man of some distinction. One word, a quarter of an hour's talk, in God's name."

BENJAMIN CONSTANT *to* MADAME RÉCAMIER.

"*November* 1814.

"I am as grateful to you as if you had saved my life. As a matter of fact, for the last two hours I had ceased to live. I have been pacing up and down my room, catching hold of the furniture to prevent myself from rushing to your house, and a visitor who called was so terrified at the state of agitation in which he found me, that he advised me to consult a doctor for the affection of the nerves from which he imagined me to be suffering. Oh! it is impossible to live devoured by such a passion.

"You order me not to call to-day. I submit. Be grateful to me; for, after this morning, I should have had indeed need to speak out, to cast myself at your feet, to implore you not to become what I am always fearing you will become when I am some time without seeing you. I can scarcely breathe; but you have written to me at last, you have given a thought to me. I obey then. . . .

"I should be able to see you between dinner-time and the ball; but no; I wish to prove to you that I can obey at whatever cost to myself. I am in Heaven in comparison with the condition in which I was an hour ago. For pity's sake do not kill me. I live on so little! Never man loved or suffered as I do. To-morrow, then, at two o'clock. Accept my thanks for having rescued me from the frenzy which was consuming me. To-morrow, to-morrow! I shall keep on repeating those words all day.

"If you have any message for me, I shall be at home until just on six o'clock. You understand that I have not abandoned all hope of seeing you to-day. But no; I will abandon it. My wish is to obey you. Till to-morrow! Nevertheless, I shall stay at home until six o'clock."

BENJAMIN CONSTANT *to* MADAME RÉCAMIER.

"*November* 14, 1814.

"I believe that you do not read my letters: I implore you to read this one. It concerns my reason and my life—matters of little importance to you—but it also concerns a life which is more precious to you than mine.

"It is five o'clock in the morning; I have passed a night of hellish torment. You do not believe in my wretchedness; it is far worse than anything that I can describe to you; and if God were to permit me to die this instant, I should bless Him for His goodness. I pray fervently to Him to let me do so; I ask only this favour of Him, for I hold life in abhorrence. But all this is of no consequence to you. Go on reading, however, I beg you.

"You have sent me away at half-past eleven o'clock, when I might have remained with you without your suffering any inconvenience, without any person remarking it. When I am at your house in the company of other people, you send me away for fear that any one should be surprised at my remaining behind the others. You have sent me away when I have come to you, dolt that I was, my heart full of a foolish joy at having some pleasant little piece of news to relate to you. You don't wish to be alone with me, but I have found you alone with that man, whose name I have no wish to mention. You do not love me; I know it. You interrupt me when I begin to speak; your only desire is not to witness my grief. Were I to die while at a distance from you, it would trouble you very little.

"I am willing to relieve you of my presence; I promise you I will do so. I have made all arrangements; my mind was made up long ago. But until then, in the name of that devotion which you despise, in the name of that heart which you are rending, out of pity for yourself, be kind to me, and do not show me, every time I see you, that I am as dirt in your eyes in comparison with the man against whom I can hardly contain myself.[1]

"I have no desire to kill him ; but my blood boils in my veins when I see him laughing at my folly, him, the scourge of my life, who has not dared to revenge himself upon me, and who has not had the courage to shed a single drop of his blood for your sake. I tell you, I have no desire to kill him. I wish to go away without taking vengeance for the frightful injury he has done me. But you do not understand me. In your presence I am timid ; I pretend to be cheerful in order not to displease you ; but despair is in my heart, and all my reason has forsaken me. I love no one save you. I live only for your sake ; the rest is agony and convulsion. Suffer me during the few—the very few—days I shall be here to see you and speak to you freely. Then I shall look forward to the day of my departure ; I shall welcome it with joy as a last resource, and, if it fails me, at any rate, I shall die far away from you, which is all you care about.

"But I can control myself no longer. You do not wish me to take vengeance. Condescend, then, to give me some reason for renouncing it. You have promised me an hour this morning and one this evening, the same as you have given that man. In God's name do not disappoint me. I love you madly : forgive me for doing so. You are everything to me on this earth. Consider that, if you repulse me, I have nothing in the world to lose.

[1] M. de Forbin. Constant challenged him to a duel, but Madame Récamier interfered, and the meeting did not take place.

If your door is closed to me, I know where that man's is, and one of us shall not cross the threshold alive. Pardon me for writing such a letter; it is the expression of the most awful suffering; it is dictated by the desire to spare you pain. Do not be afraid of my complaints. When I am with you a single word is sufficient to reduce me to submission. I will speak of nothing that you do not wish me to speak of. But bear with me, tolerate me, until my departure, which I shall take care to hasten.

"Believe me, I am making a sacrifice for your sake. After the happiness of possessing you, the desire that is nearest my heart is to kill the man who has ruined my life, and afterwards to die. Forgive me, once again. I know not what I am writing. I will relieve you of the burden of my presence, do not doubt it. This devotion which annoys you, this love which wearies you, I, in short, whom you loathe, all shall vanish away."

Benjamin Constant *to* Madame Récamier.

"*December* 14, 1814.

"Here is a letter from Madame de Catellan, which I enclose to show you that other people find some pleasure in my society. I stand in precisely the same position in regard to you as a certain lady once stood to me. She used, also, to send me the pathetic letters which people wrote to her; but you are not in the position in which I was placed. She demanded that I should break my bonds, and forsake the person to whom I was legally bound. I do not demand of you anything of the kind. To-night, during which I have again examined the evidence of my frenzy, has proved to me that all I require is to see you, and talk to you freely for a few minutes every day or every other day. In the name of morality, religion, and conscience, you cannot refuse me: that is the only way to calm me, and to calm me completely for the time being. I only saw you for a moment this morning, and I have gathered sufficient strength to last me till this evening. If I can talk to you for a quarter of an hour this evening about the plan I propose trying, I shall have sufficient to last me until to-morrow. But I swear to you that, strive as I may, it will be dangerous for you to refuse this request. I shall, on my part, do my utmost to cure myself, but I have not sufficient strength. You alone can give it me. I will be so cheerful, so self-contained, and so pleasant, that I shall be able to prevent your self-sacrifice being too trying a one. But consider, I implore you, that it is not by spurning the passion that overwhelms my heart that you will cure me; but by doing exactly the contrary."

BENJAMIN CONSTANT *to* MADAME RÉCAMIER.

"BRUSSELS, *November* 8, 1815.

" . . . My despair at your silence has caused me to make a mistake so ridiculous that, in spite of all my sadness, I am unable to keep from laughing. I had begun a letter to you with these words: 'I warn you that your neglect is driving me to despair, and that I shall not live unless you come to my help. Have a care for yourself also. Neither you nor I know what death means, and when you have driven me to it, &c.' I had, at the same time, written to M. Meuss, a correspondent of M. Récamier, asking him to take care of some property of mine during my journey to Hanover. In the agitated state in which I was I mistook the letters, and I sent to M. Meuss the one intended for you. Fortunately he had gone out, and I have been able to get back my letter. But when I picture to myself the worthy banker receiving my letter, and reading that his forgetfulness was driving me out of my senses, and that I should kill myself if he neglected me, I cannot think of his astonishment without laughing."

As none of Madame Récamier's letters to Constant have been preserved, we have no means of ascertaining on what sort of fuel this devouring flame was nourished. Madame Lenormant, as might be expected, denies that her aunt gave her importunate adorer "the slightest encouragement," and, immediately afterwards, naïvely admits that "at their first interview Madame Récamier exerted herself to please, and succeeded but too well." An extract from Constant's diary, which St.-Beuve quotes in his *Derniers Portraits*, confirms this :

"Madame Récamier takes it into her head to make me fall in love with her. I am forty-seven years of age. Rendezvous which she gives me under the pretext of some business relating to Murat. Her manner to me that evening. 'Dare to make love to me!' says she. I leave her house madly in love. My whole life is *bouleversée*. Invitation to Angervilliers. Coquetry and cruelty of Madame Récamier. I am the most wretched of men. My frightful mental sufferings prevent me from writing a line of common sense. I am beginning to lose money at play, because I can think of nothing but Madame Récamier."[1]

The Duc de Broglie, too, declares that Madame Récamier carried on a "*coquetterie flagrante*" with Benjamin Constant and Auguste de Forbin at the same time; and that at a *bal masqué*, at which, contrary to the usual custom, the men as well as the ladies wore masks, she,

[1] Constant was a terrible gambler. In his *Journal Intime* he speaks of winning and losing as much as 30,000 francs at a sitting.

much to his surprise, singled him out for special preference, so that, as he was in disguise, Constant thought he was Forbin, and Forbin thought he was Constant, and were both consumed with jealousy on account of the favour which each thought was being shown to his rival.[1]

Truth, therefore, compels us reluctantly to admit that Madame Récamier did flirt outrageously with Constant, though, probably, not more so than with a score of other men. And we should also remember before condemning her that Madame Récamier was not an ordinary flirt. Like Madame de Sevigné, she possessed the rare talent of being able to persuade a lover to be content with friendship; and Constant's case is, perhaps, the only one in which any of her innumerable adorers suffered for their infatuation. If any persons had a right to complain of her conduct, they were the wives of some of her married admirers; but, then, *les convenances* entered so largely into French matrimonial unions in those days, and *madame* was generally so very complacent a lady, that we question whether, even in this quarter, very much harm was done.

With regard to Constant, it would appear probable that Madame Récamier for once overrated her power of changing the lover into the friend, and that, when she became conscious of the desperate passion with which she had inspired him, she was afraid to repulse him too abruptly lest he should really destroy himself, as he was perpetually threatening to do. Madame Récamier, however, in later life, admitted that she had treated Constant badly, and she wished his letters to her to be published after her death in order to justify him. But, when we take into consideration the fact that Constant had on at least one occasion attempted to commit suicide, when a

[1] Duc de Broglie's *Souvenirs*, i. 288.

lady had rejected his addresses; and that he was the creator of Adolphe, who expounds the publicist's own views with regard to the relation of the sexes, and is surely one of the most worthless scamps to be met with in fiction, we cannot believe that he is entitled to any large amount of sympathy.

When, in March 1815, all Europe was astounded at the news of Napoleon's return from Elba, and the *emigrés*, lately so exultant, fled like naughty schoolboys when their master's step is heard returning to the schoolroom, Madame Récamier courageously refused to voluntarily exile herself, and remained in Paris, though Madame de Staël besought her to fly with her to Coppet, and the Queen of Naples wrote offering her an asylum in that city.

"We are very tranquil here," wrote the queen. "Our people love us, and we love them. A change of government, moreover, would involve acts of vengeance and other calamities. They dread more than ever anything that may tend to bring back Ferdinand."

Poor Queen Caroline little knew that, at the very moment she was penning this letter, her husband was meditating that act of criminal folly which was to cost him both his throne and life.

When the Congress of Vienna met, the previous year, Murat soon found that his removal from the throne of Naples was one of the principal objects of France; and neither the solemn treaty with Austria, into which he had entered, with so many misgivings, while Madame Récamier was at Naples, nor the old affection of Metternich for Caroline, nor the brilliant causistry of Benjamin Constant were likely to prove serious obstacles to its realisation.

Furious at finding that his treachery to his old master and benefactor was likely to prove unavailing, Murat no sooner heard of Napoleon's landing than he turned round once more, and, with incredible rashness, led his army against the Austrians. He advanced as far as the Po, but was utterly routed by the Imperialists under Neipperg, afterwards the second husband of Marie Louise, at Tolentino, and compelled to fly to France. Napoleon, however, had not forgiven him for his desertion in 1814, and not only refused to see him, but gave orders that he was to leave French territory at once.

Murat then went to Corsica, where he remained in hiding for some weeks, refusing Metternich's offer of an asylum provided he would pledge his word not to leave the Austrian dominions. In the autumn he landed in Calabria, with the intention of making an effort to recover his kingdom, but was taken prisoner, and, after a mockery of a trial by a court-martial, shot on October 13. "He died as he had lived," says Bourrienne, "a brave but theatrical man, with his last breath giving the order to the firing party to spare his face." [1]

Madame Récamier was probably strengthened in her resolution to remain in Paris by a letter she received at this time from her friend Queen Hortense, promising to intercede for her with the Emperor should the occasion arise. She had no reason to regret her decision, for Napoleon, even if he was aware of her presence, thought it best to ignore it, and left her in peace.

Few people had more cause to dread Napoleon's return than had Madame Récamier's infatuated slave Benjamin Constant. He had been banished for his opposition to him during the Consulate; he had fought against him,

[1] Bourrienne's *Memoirs of Napoleon*, iv. 289.

and had treated him more roughly in his brochure *De l'Esprit de Conquête* than even Chateaubriand had done in *De Bonaparte et des Bourbons.* To crown all, on March 19, the same day that Louis XVIII. fled from Paris, there appeared over Constant's well-known signature in the *Journal des Débats* a violent article, in which Napoleon was compared to Attila and Genghis Khan, and which concluded with the words that have become historical:

"I have seen that liberty is possible under a monarchy. I have seen the people rallying round the king. I will not, like a miserable turncoat, crawl from one power to another, cover my infamy with sophistry, and stammer out profane words to ransom a shameful life."

It has been repeatedly asserted that Constant wrote this article solely to please Madame Récamier, and a letter he sends her the next day, in which, after telling her that a few days will see him either a proscribed fugitive or the occupant of a dungeon, and begging her to give him a little of her time in the meanwhile, he concludes by asking her if she is satisfied with what he has written in the *Débats*, seems to confirm this; while the Duc de Broglie declares that he saw Constant strutting up and down Madame Récamier's salon, brandishing the newspaper containing his famous article in the face of his rival Forbin, as if challenging him to emulation of his reckless daring.

Before Napoleon reached Paris, however, Constant, yielding to the entreaties of his friends, fled to Nantes, with the intention of taking ship for England. But, when he arrived there, the dictates of his heart appear to have got the better of the counsels of prudence. "To live perhaps for years," says his biographer, M. Melegari, "without again beholding her who had caused him so much misery proved too much for his courage. He preferred to brave every danger, and to return to Paris."[1]

On his return a temptation, for which he was in no way prepared, was awaiting him. Napoleon, instead of demanding his head, began to make overtures to him on the basis of constitutional liberty. He was sent for to the Tuileries, greeted as cordially by the Emperor as if he had been one of his most devoted adherents, and invited to draw up a plan of constitutional government. A few days later, the *Moniteur* announced that Benjamin Constant had become one of the Emperor's Councillors of State.

The result of this reconciliation between the publicist and his old enemy was the *Acte Additionnel*, which pleased no one save a few *doctrinaires*, and was called by the Parisians in derision "*Le Benjaminisme*."

Poor Benjamin Constant has been held up to odium both by his contemporaries and by historians on account of these remarkable tergiversations ; but we are inclined to think that he has been too hardly used. If it is admitted that his article in the *Débats* was inspired entirely by the desire to propitiate Madame Récamier—which is probably the case—then there was nothing very remarkable in his attaching himself to Napoleon, for, as a staunch supporter of liberty, he might very well have imagined that there was a better chance of constitutional government under a restored Napoleon, who might be inclined to profit by bitter experience, than under a restored Louis, surrounded by fanatical priests and revengeful *emigrés*. Constant, moreover, was a curious compound of generosity, ambition, and vanity, and he was as wax in the hands of so keen a judge of human nature

[1] Introduction to Benjamin Constant's *Journal Intime*, p. 52.

as Napoleon, who seems to have succeeded with very little difficulty in convincing him of his good faith, and of his need of his assistance in carrying out the proposed reforms.[1]

Very different was the reception which the Emperor's overtures met with from another of Madame Récamier's friends—Madame de Staël—to whom he wrote begging her to return to Paris "as her presence was required for constitutional ideas." "You have done without a Constitution or me for twelve years," she replied, "and even now you are not fonder of one than the other."

But, however strong may have been Constant's love of liberty, however great his ambition and vanity, they were as dust in the balance in comparison with his hopeless passion for Madame Récamier. A few days after he had decided to throw in his lot with the Emperor, and had accepted office at his hands, we find him writing to Madame Récamier offering to resign his post the next day if such was her will.

Could anything be more abject?

[1] "Benjamin writes to Madame de Staël that he firmly believes that he will establish a liberal Constitution, and that a change has come over Bonaparte."—CHARLES CONSTANT *to* his sister ROSALIE, April 17, 1815.

CHAPTER X

Madame de Krüdener—Her early life—*Valérie*—Her conversion—Her extraordinary ascendency over the Emperor Alexander—His visits to her at the Hôtel Montchenu—Unsuccessful efforts of Talleyrand and Metternich to counteract her influence—Her evening *séances* become the fashion—Chateaubriand's opinion of her—Her sympathy for Benjamin Constant—Her friendship with Madame Récamier—Proposes to establish a "*lien d'âme*" between Constant and Madame Récamier—But fails—Constant becomes a mystic—And a devil-worshipper—The Duc de Broglie's account of his conduct—Madame de Krüdener goes to Switzerland—Her letter to Madame Récamier—Her last years and death—Madame de Staël returns to Paris—Popularity of her receptions—Her illness and death

WHEN the allied sovereigns returned to Paris after Waterloo, there came with them Madame de Krüdener, "the keeper of the Emperor Alexander's conscience," and one of the most remarkable women of the period. This lady, who was the widow of Baron de Krüdener, a distinguished Russian diplomatist, had been an extremely beautiful and fascinating woman, and, although now past middle life, still retained something of her former charms. She had at one time resided in Paris, where she had mixed in the gayest society, and had achieved a considerable literary reputation by the publication of a remarkable novel called *Valérie*, "a work," says Sainte-Beuve, "of prodigious success in the highest circles in France and Germany, and which can be read three times in a lifetime—in youth, middle age, and old age."[1] This book is generally believed to have been a record of her own early married life, which had been by no means a blameless one, although her husband—who, it may be mentioned, as an illustration of the lax morality of the time, had been twice married and twice divorced before he met her—had treated her with a forbearance hardly conceivable in our own age, and had refused to avail himself of his legal remedy. Madame de Krüdener, however, in spite of her frailty, seems to have been the possessor of a naturally sensitive conscience, which never allowed her to rest content with her frivolous

[1] The phenomenal success which *Valérie* met with in Paris was due in no small measure to the singular manœuvres in which its authoress indulged in order to advertise it. "For several days she made the rounds of the fashionable shops, asking sometimes for shawls, sometimes for hats, feathers, wreaths, or ribbons, all *à la Valérie*. When they saw this beautiful and elegant stranger alight from her carriage, and inquire for fancy articles which she invented on the spur of the moment, the shopkeepers were seized with a polite desire to oblige her by every means in their power. Moreover, the lady would soon pretend to recognise the articles she had asked for; and if the unfortunate shop-girls, confused by such unusual demands, seemed puzzled and denied all knowledge of the article, Mme. de Krüdener would smile graciously, and commiserate them for their ignorance of the new book, thus converting them all into eager readers of *Valérie*. Then, laden with her purchases, she would drive off to another establishment, pretending to search for things which only existed in her imagination. Thanks to these manœuvres she succeeded in arousing such ardent competition in honour of her heroine that, for at least a week, the shops sold everything *à la Valérie*. Her own friends, the innocent accomplices of her stratagem, also paid visits to shops on her recommendation, thus carrying the fame of her book through the Faubourg St. Germain and the Chaussée d'Antin."—Eynard's *Vie de Madame de Krüdener*, i. 136.

surroundings ; and, on her return to her estates in Livonia, in 1805, her sense of the vanity of earthly things gradually deepened, and she became a member of the Moravian community. In 1808 she fell under the influence of Jung Stilling and Oberlin, and ultimately resolved to adopt the vocation of an itinerant preacher.

Her obvious sincerity, her intellectual attainments, and her social position enabled her to command attention wherever she went, especially in Switzerland, where she made many converts. At Heilbronn, in the spring of 1815, she obtained an audience of the Emperor Alexander, and rapidly acquired a most extraordinary ascendency over the mind of that somewhat impressionable monarch, who, although he had not escaped unscathed the contamination of the immoral Russian Court, had never abandoned his early religious convictions, and had for years been seeking some more satisfying spiritual consolation than the lifeless, though gorgeous, services of his own Church afforded.

On his return to Paris, the change which had come over the hitherto gay and pleasure-loving sovereign was at once apparent, and caused the most unbounded astonishment. Whereas, during his previous visit, Alexander had mixed freely in society, where he had been the gayest of the gay, he now eschewed every form of private entertainment, and abstained, as far as possible, even from official festivities. While the Empress was absent in England he shut himself up in his apartments at the Elysée Bourbon, where he devoted himself to State business and devotional exercises, and received only those whom it was impossible to exclude. His reason in thus temporarily retiring from the world seems to have been a sense of his inability to resist the temptations with which he was surrounded. "Pray for me," he said one evening to Madame de Krüdener; "pray to the Almighty to strengthen me against the evil influences of this city. Up to the present I have resisted its seductions, but man is so weak, that unless he is sustained by grace, he succumbs to the temptations which beset him on every side. I feel the necessity of avoiding society; that is the reason I asked for a retired residence. In the apartment which I occupy I find a great deal of peace; I work, I study the Scriptures, I commune with God in prayer, and I put my trust in His merciful and tender protection in all that He helps me to avoid."

Every alternate evening, as soon as his official duties would permit, Alexander, accompanied only by a single servant, used to walk across from the Elysée Bourbon to the Hôtel Montchenu, in the Faubourg St. Honoré, where Madame de Krüdener was staying; and was received by his spiritual directress in a little sitting-room, adjoining the salon, in which she was accustomed to receive those who desired to confer with her privately on religious matters. Here the Czar frequently remained until a very late hour, the time being spent in prayer and in the study of the Bible. By his express wish, Madame de Krüdener always spoke to the Autocrat of All the Russias as freely as she would have done to the humblest of her disciples. "Do not be afraid, madame," he would exclaim when sometimes the lady hesitated, fearing that her enthusiasm was carrying her too far. "Scold me well, and by God's grace I will carry out all your instructions."

On Sundays Madame de Krüdener had a place reserved for her in a room overlooking the Emperor's private chapel, in the Elysée Bourbon, where, with her features concealed by a white veil, she remained throughout the service in order that her soul might be united in prayer with that of her royal disciple.

The intimate relations which existed between the Emperor and Madame de Krüdener, as may well be supposed, speedily became the talk of Paris, and gave rise to many conflicting rumours. The diplomatists at that time assembled in the French capital were naturally much exercised in their minds as to the real significance of this unexpected development, and had recourse to all the private sources of information at their disposal in order to unravel the mystery. That the connection was anything but an ordinary intrigue they at first refused to believe; and when, at length, they were assured that it was one of a purely religious character, their scorn and astonishment knew no bounds. However, they were fully alive to the important political consequences which might follow these evening *séances;* and both Talleyrand and his rival Metternich, fraternising for the nonce in the face of a common danger, laid their heads together to discover some means to wean the Czar from his allegiance to his middle-aged enchantress. To this end the most renowned beauties of Paris and Vienna were pressed into the service of the astute diplomatists, and paraded for the delectation of the Russian monarch. But in vain was the net spread: Alexander rose superior to all such intrigues.

Although at this period unbelief was rampant in Paris, its volatile citizens, like the Athenians in the time of St. Paul, dearly loved novelty in whatever form it might be offered to them; and when, in July 1815, Madame de Krüdener threw open the doors of the Hôtel de Montchenu to all her friends, rich and poor alike, who cared to take part in her evangelistic services, numbers of people drawn thither either by curiosity or interest flocked to the house.

Here in a salon, destitute of all furniture save a few rush-bottomed chairs and a plain deal table, they were received by their hostess, who was habited, not in majestic sacerdotal robes, as certain chroniclers of those times have depicted her, but in a dark woollen gown, cut in the extreme of simplicity. The services, which began at seven o'clock in the evening, were conducted by Empaytaz, a young divine who shared her wanderings, and consisted of an extempore prayer and an exposition of a portion of the Scriptures. Madame de Krüdener herself usually knelt among the crowd, and took no prominent part in the service, but was always ready to confer with those who might wish to consult her in private. As her fame spread, these private interviews became so numerous that at length she could scarcely find leisure for food or rest.

Among the throng of notable people who, from different motives, attended these services were Chateaubriand, Benjamin Constant, Baron de Gerando, the philanthropist, Grégoire, Bishop of Blois, the Duchesse de Bourbon, and Princess Sophia Volkonski.

Chateaubriand, who had been on intimate terms with the evangelist during her former residence in Paris, seems to have been attracted to the Hôtel Montchenu more by the remembrance of their old friendship, and, possibly, also, as the lady's latest biographer suggests, by the hope of entering into personal relations with the Czar, than by any sympathy with her religious methods. "I infinitely preferred Madame de Krüdener," he says, "when, surrounded with flowers, and an inhabitant of this miserable world, she composed *Valérie*."

Constant, however, carried away with him a very

different impression. He had known Madame de Krüdener in Switzerland, and was now a frequent visitor at her house, "an unchanged Adolphe in the presence of a regenerated Valérie."

To Madame Récamier, after one of these visits, he writes as follows:

"I have spent the whole day alone, and I only went out in order to call on Madame de Krüdener. The excellent woman! She does not know all, but she sees that I am devoured by some frightful grief. She kept me three hours in order to console me. She told me to pray for those who caused me to suffer, and to offer up my sufferings in expiation for them if they were in need of the sacrifice."

It may readily be imagined that it was not long before Madame Récamier found herself drawn to the Hôtel de Montchenu, and a warm friendship sprang up between these two women, each so supreme in her own particular sphere. Unfortunately Madame Récamier's presence seems to have occasionally diverted attention from graver matters, and, accordingly, Benjamin Constant was deputed by Madame de Krüdener to write to her on the subject.

"I acquit myself with no little embarrassment," he says, "of a commission which Madame de Krüdener has just given me. She begs that you will come to her house with as few charms as possible. She says that you dazzle every one present, and, consequently, all hearts are troubled, and all real attention becomes impossible. You cannot divest yourself of your beauty, but, pray, do not enhance it."

Madame de Krüdener, however, in spite of this gentle remonstrance, attached no little importance to the presence of the celebrated beauty at her gatherings, and was as anxious for her conversion as Mathieu de Montmorency had been.

Benjamin Constant, as we have said, was one of the most frequent of Madame de Krüdener's visitors. The evangelist was of an intensely sympathetic nature, and felt great compassion for Benjamin Constant, bowed down as he was under the weight of the universal reprobation which his extraordinary conduct during the Hundred Days had brought upon him, and a prey to fits of bitter irony and morbid self-abasement. Encouraged by her sympathy, it was not long before he made her the confidante of his unfortunate love-affair, whereupon she promised him her help to establish between him and the object of his attachment what Constant, in his *Journal Intime*, calls a "*lien d'âme.*"[1]

Whatever results the publicist may have been led to expect from this mysterious connection, it is clear that they were not realised, for, a few days later, he writes in the same interesting autobiography: "Alas! Madame de Krüdener has not been a prophetess, for Juliette has never treated me more shamefully. Yesterday she gave me four rendezvous, not one of which did she keep; and this evening I have found her a *chef-d'œuvre* of coquetry, deceit, vanity, hypocrisy, and affectation."[2]

The unhappy man at this time appears to have been going through a further transformation. Under the influence of his Russian friend he became a mystic. "He used," says the Duc de Broglie, "to spend whole nights in the salon of Madame de Krüdener, in company with other new converts, sometimes praying on his knees, at other times stretched on the floor in fits of ecstasy;

[1] Benjamin Constant's *Journal Intime*, p. 146.

[2] *Ibid.* p. 147.

all to no purpose, for what he used to ask of God, God occasionally permits in his wrath, but regards with abhorrence. Being in love with Madame Récamier, who, though already on the turn of life, was still beautiful, Benjamin Constant begged of God to turn the lady's heart in his favour, and, as God was deaf to his prayers, the lover made up his mind to apply to the devil, which was more natural."[1] The duke further relates how one dark, stormy night, while Constant, Auguste de Staël, and himself were returning from Angervilliers, where they had been visiting Madame de Catellan, Constant took them into his confidence with regard to the efforts he had been making to strike a bargain with the enemy of mankind. At first they felt inclined to laugh, but as Constant proceeded, he gave the two young men such an insight into his distracted soul, that any wish to make fun of him entirely disappeared.

However, prayers and incantations were alike unavailing, and after 1815 we hear very little of Constant in connection with Madame Récamier. "At the end of eighteen months," says his sympathetic biographer, who, by the way, seems unnecessarily severe on the object of the publicist's misplaced affections, "his passion extinguished itself, like a fire which has burned too rapidly and received no fuel, leaving Adolphe ashamed of himself, wretched, embittered." [2]

In September, 1815, the Emperor Alexander set out on his return to Russia, and shortly afterwards Madame de Krüdener left Paris for Switzerland, whence she wrote the following characteristic letter to Madame Récamier:

[1] Duc de Broglie's *Souvenirs*, i. 286.

[2] Introduction to Benjamin Constant's *Journal Intime*, p. 56.

MADAME DE KRÜDENER *to* MADAME RÉCAMIER.

"BERNE, *November* 12, 1815.

"How I long to have news of you, dear and lovely friend, and how interested I am in you and your happiness, which will not be assured until you give yourself up wholly to God. This is what I ask of Him when, prostrated before the God of mercy, I invoke Him on your behalf. He has touched your heart; and that heart, which all the illusions and all the good things of the world have not been able to satisfy, has heard the call. No; you will not hesitate, dear friend. The trials which you often experience, the hollowness of the world, and the need of something great, infinite, and eternal which from time to time alarms and agitates you, all tell me that you will declare yourself altogether on the right side. I beseech you to be true to those great impulses which you are experiencing, and not to allow yourself to be diverted from them. An agonising grief would be the result of this lapse from grace. Ask at the feet of Christ for the faith of divine love; ask, and you shall receive, and a holy fear will inform you how great is the life, and how infinite the love of the Saviour, who died to save us from the just punishment for sin, which every one of us has deserved. Ah! if one could but look upon our God, who made Himself man in order to die for us—if we could look upon Him with broken heart, and weep at the foot of the Cross for not having loved Him. Far from rejecting us, His arms will open to receive us; He will pardon us, and we shall know that peace which the world cannot give.

"What is that poor Benjamin[1] doing? On leaving

[1] Benjamin Constant.

Paris I wrote him again a few lines, and sent him some messages for you, dear friend. Did you not receive them? How is he getting on? You must be very charitable to a sick man much to be pitied, and you must pray for him. Our journey has been a pleasant one, thank God! Switzerland rests me; it is so lovely, and so tranquil in the midst of this distracted Europe. I have the happiness of having my son[1] at Berne, and we make the most delightful expeditions, and have the most affectionate talks together, for we love each other dearly. . . . I do not despair of seeing you among the Alps, which are worth all the salons in the world.

"Write to me at Basle, dear friend; direct your letter to me, care of M. Kellner. Tell me everything, putting your trust in my tender affection. Have you seen M. Delbel?[2] He is a most excellent man. I am very anxious Benjamin[3] should see him.

"Kind regards from my daughter and myself,

"B. de Krüdener.

"Once more, dear friend, I commend our poor Benjamin to your kind heart. It is a sacred duty."

Poor Madame de Krüdener's last years were clouded with disappointment. Her religious activity was by no means favourable to established church order, while the civil authorities of the various countries which she visited were, not unnaturally, prejudiced against her by the vast crowds of idle and clamorous beggars which her indiscriminate charity drew after her wherever she went. After being directed to withdraw from one German state after

[1] Baron de Krüdener, Russian Minister to the Swiss Confederation.
[2] Curé of Clichy. [3] Benjamin Constant.

another, she became discouraged, and, in 1818, finally retired into private life on her estates at Riga.

In 1820 she visited St. Petersburg, where she had the mortification to find that her influence with the Czar had not survived their five years separation. The cruel and crafty Arakchéïeff and the monk Photius had, in the interim, supplanted her in Alexander's esteem, and succeeded in inducing that generous-hearted but vacillating sovereign to reverse both his political and religious policy. The consequence was that when Madame de Krüdener appealed openly to her former disciple to fulfil his obligations as a Christian monarch, and assist in liberating his co-religionists in Greece from the intolerable Moslem yoke, she was commanded to remain silent or leave St. Petersburg. She chose the latter alternative, and on Christmas morning, 1824, died at Karasu-Baza, in the Crimea, whither she had gone to recruit her health, which had been entirely shattered by the arduous nature of her evangelistic labours. Less than a year later the Emperor Alexander followed her to the grave.

Madame de Staël, unlike the majority of Madame Récamier's friends, had not returned to the capital after the battle of Waterloo had settled once and for all the fate of their old enemy. She had spent the winter and spring of 1815–16 in Italy, in the hope that the mild climate might be beneficial to her young husband Rocca, whose health had been gradually becoming worse; but at length, in the autumn of 1816, she reappeared in Paris, where her salon was soon crowded with representative men of all parties, and the most distinguished foreigners who were then in the city. "Madame de Staël had," says one of her guests, "the rare talent, perhaps, never possessed by any other person of uniting around her the most distinguished individuals of all the opposite parties, literary and political, and making them establish relations among themselves which they could not afterwards entirely shake off. There might be found Wellington and Lafayette; Chateaubriand, Talleyrand, and Prince Laval; Humboldt and Blucher from Berlin; Constant and Sismondi from Switzerland; the two Schlegels from Hanover; Canova from Italy; the beautiful Madame Récamier, and the admirable Duchesse de Duras; and from England, such a multitude, that it seemed like a general emigration of British talent and rank." [1]

But, alas! it soon became apparent to her sorrowing friends that the days of the authoress of *Corinne* were numbered. Madame de Staël's health had been greatly weakened by her flight from Coppet to Russia, immediately after the birth of the child of her second marriage; and the alarm and fatigue which her sudden journey to Switzerland to escape the returning Emperor occasioned, had completely shattered it. Little by little her health became worse, and at length she was compelled to keep her bed.

Still her faculties remained unimpaired. Every morning, as soon as she woke, her maid brought her her writing materials, and she wrote in bed till noon; and afterwards received the visits of her most intimate friends. Her daughter, the Duchesse de Broglie, by her express wish, received in her place the usual company, and would often slip up to the sick-room to report any *bon-mot* or especially interesting piece of news which she had heard during the evening.

The gay world of Paris showed no lack of sympathy

[1] Child's "Madame de Staël," p. 71.

with the suffering of its most distinguished representative. Her house was besieged with callers. Members of the Royal family made daily inquiries after her health, and Wellington came himself every day to ask how she fared. She was to the last full of sympathy for fellow sufferers, and the day after her death a condemned man named Barry, for whom she had made intercession, was pardoned by the King. She expired without pain at five o'clock on the morning of July 14, 1817, at the age of fifty-one. Her young husband, Rocca, survived her but six months. His bereavement greatly aggravated his malady: after the funeral he went to the Riviera to endeavour to find relief, and died at Hyères in the following January.

CHAPTER XI

Madame Récamier's meeting with Chateaubriand—His early life—His visit to America—His marriage—He joins the *emigrés* —He is wounded and escapes to England—His terrible privations—His love affair with Miss Ives—His *Essai sur les Révolutions*—He returns to France—*Atala*—*Le Génie du Christianisme*—Great influence of this work—He is sent as *attaché* to Rome—And as envoy to the Valais—He resigns and opposes Napoleon—Napoleon's opinion of him—He goes to the East—His *Itinéraire* and *Les Martyrs*—*René*—He is elected to the Institute—His address—Fury of the Emperor against him—He is ordered to leave Paris—His pamphlet *De Bonaparte et des Bourbons*—Its extraordinary influence on the course of events—He accompanies Louis XVIII. to Ghent during the Hundred Days—He listens to the cannon of Waterloo—His opposition to the Government after the Second Restoration—His personal appearance—His attraction for women—His admiration for Madame Récamier reciprocated —Ballanche and Mathieu de Montmorency oppose their intimacy—But without success

It was at the deathbed of Madame de Staël that Madame Récamier renewed an acquaintance, made some years before, with a person who was destined to more than fill the place of the beloved friend she was about to lose.

François René de Chateaubriand was born at St. Malo on September 4, 1768—just three weeks after the birth of Napoleon—the youngest son of Comte René de Chateaubriand, the head of one of the most ancient families in

Brittany. Even as a boy, he was of a restless, dreamy, melancholy disposition, a temperament which he seems to have inherited from his father—whose habitual state of mind, he tells us, was one of profound sadness—and which was doubtless intensified by his picturesque surroundings, and the quaint legends and superstitions of the Breton country-folk among whom his childhood was passed.

He was educated at Dol, Rennes, and at a theological seminary at Dinan, and seems to have at one time entertained some idea of entering the priesthood. But he soon abandoned this intention, and, at the age of nineteen, accepted an offer of a commission in the Navarre regiment. A military life, however, was but little to his taste, and, in 1791, he sailed for America, with the object of obtaining immortality by the discovery of the North-west Passage.

The Passage was neither found nor, for the matter of that, even attempted; but his brief sojourn in the New World was by no means barren of result, as it was there that he found his true vocation and the materials for *Atala* and *René*.

On his return to France he discovered that his mother and sister had considerately arranged a marriage for him with a certain Mademoiselle de Lavigne, a young lady of some fortune, a plan to which Chateaubriand consented readily enough, although he had only seen his intended bride on two or three occasions, and was quite indifferent to her. "I felt no qualification for the position of a husband," he says in a characteristic passage in his *Mémoires d'Outre Tombe*. "Lucile [his sister] was fond of Mademoiselle de Lavigne, and saw in this marriage a means of securing my independence. 'So be it,' said I. In my case the public man is immovable; the private individual is at the mercy of any one who wishes to influence him, and, to avoid an hour's bickering, I would enslave myself for a century."[1]

The marriage, although quite devoid of affection on the husband's side, was not an unhappy one. For many years, however, the author and his wife were content to live apart; but when, in 1804, Madame de Chateaubriand suffered a reverse of fortune, her husband behaved in a very honourable manner, and sent for her to share his home. Chateaubriand appears to have always respected the many good qualities of his wife, and graciously permitted her to worship him, which was all she asked. "Madame de Chateaubriand," he says, "admires me without having read two lines of my works; she would fear to meet in them with ideas differing from her own, or to discover that the rest of the world is not enthusiastic enough in its estimation of me."

After the execution of Louis XVI. in January, 1793, Chateaubriand, who, like all the Breton aristocracy, was a fervent Royalist, joined the ranks of the *emigrés*, and took part in the Duke of Brunswick's invasion of France. After the failure of that expedition, in which he was wounded at the siege of Thionville, he made his escape to England. Here his small stock of money was soon exhausted, and he and a fellow exile named Hingant, who shared his garret, found themselves on the verge of starvation.

"We reduced our rations," he says, "as is done in a ship when the voyage is expected to be a very long one. At our breakfast we saved half our bread, and dispensed altogether with butter. . . . When we came to our last shilling I arranged with my friend to keep it, in order to

[1] Chateaubriand's *Mémoires d'Outre Tombe*, ii. 350.

make a show of breakfasting. We agreed that we would buy a twopenny loaf; that we should have the breakfast-things laid as usual, the hot water brought up, and the tea-caddy set on the table; that we would not put in any tea or eat any bread, but merely drink some water flavoured with a few crumbs of sugar which remained at the bottom of the basin.

"In this way five days passed. I was devoured by hunger—felt on fire—and sleep had forsaken me. I used to suck pieces of linen dipped in water, and to chew grass and paper. On passing by a baker's shop the torment was horrible. On a bitter winter's evening I have remained for as long as two hours standing before a grocer's shop or Italian warehouse, devouring with my eyes everything I saw. I would have eaten not only the eatables, but the boxes, bags or baskets which contained them."[1]

At length their friends sent them a little money, and Chateaubriand removed to Beccles, in Suffolk, where he maintained himself by giving French lessons to the sons and daughters of the neighbouring gentry. One of his pupils, a Miss Charlotte Ives, daughter of the rector of Bungay, unaware that there was already a Madame de Chateaubriand, quite lost her heart to the handsome Breton. Chateaubriand, to whom admiration was as the breath of life, cruelly forbore to undeceive her; and it was not until the lady's mother offered the young *emigré*, whose poverty she thought made him too timid to come forward, her daughter's hand and a home under their own roof, that he confessed that he was not free to love.

Twenty-seven years afterwards, when Chateaubriand returned to England as French ambassador, Charlotte Ives,

[1] *Mémoires d'Outre Tombe*, iii. 168.

who had in the interval become the wife of Admiral Sutton, and the mother of two fine boys, but in whose heart time had not effaced the memory of her first love—a fact which Chateaubriand, with rather questionable taste, expatiates upon in his *Mémoires*—called upon him to solicit his influence to obtain for her eldest son an appointment upon the staff of the Viceroy of India. His application was successful, and he was thus able to make the poor lady some reparation for the injury he had done her.

In 1797 Chateaubriand published his first work, an *Essai sur les Révolutions*, which was favourably received, and in 1800, his name having been struck off the list of *emigrés*, he returned to France. *Atala*, a love-story of savage life, the scene of which is laid in the American forests and prairies, appeared in the following year, and established the reputation of its author [1]—a reputation which was enormously enhanced by the publication, three years later, of his famous treatise *Le Génie du Christianisme*, which may almost be said to have paved the way for the re-establishment of the Roman Catholic religion in France.

This masterpiece of literary art, which originally included both *Atala* and *Rêne*, though these stories were subsequently detached, appearing as it did at a time of widespread reaction against the blasphemous buffooneries of the Revolution, met with extraordinary success. It must be admitted, however, that its merit lies rather in the brilliancy of its descriptive passages than in the cogency of its reasoning, for Chateaubriand was never either a particularly sound thinker or a particularly able controversialist.

Bonaparte, whose conciliatory policy towards the Papacy

[1] *Atala* has been translated into six European languages—English, German, Greek, Russian, Spanish, and Swedish.

the opportune publication of Chateaubriand's book had done much to facilitate, rewarded the author by appointing him *attaché* at Rome, where he wrote his *Lettres sur l'Italie*, and quarrelled so much with the ambassador, Cardinal Fesch, that in a few months he was recalled, and sent as envoy to the little republic of the Valais.

While on this mission all Europe was horrified at the murder of the poor young Duc d'Enghien. Chateaubriand, feeling that he could no longer with honour hold any office under a Government which could perpetrate such atrocities, immediately resigned his post, and eventually became as formidable an opponent of Napoleon in the sphere of ideas as Wellington and Metternich were in that of action.

Several of Chateaubriand's contemporaries have asserted that, had Napoleon shown more disposition to acknowledge the great writer's merits, he might have won him over at any time, for Chateaubriand would not have been indifferent to praise from such a quarter; and Madame de Rémusat tells us that the Emperor said on more than one occasion, "The difficulty would not be to buy M. de Chateaubriand, but to give him his price." [1] If Napoleon really did say this, and, as Madame de Rémusat is generally a veracious chronicler, there is no reason to think otherwise, it shows a complete failure to understand the character of the author of *Atala* very unusual in so shrewd a judge of human nature as Napoleon; for in spite of his egotism, his vanity, and his affectation, in spite of the inconsistency of his political conduct under Louis XVIII. and Charles X.—inconsistency due in great part to his unsuccessful attempts to reconcile Legitimacy and Liberty—Chateaubriand was a high-minded and honourable man,

[1] *Mémoires de Madame de Rémusat*, ii. 391.

and no consideration whatever would have induced him to support a sovereign who, to borrow his own words, had not scrupled to use the bleeding corpse of a Frenchman as a footstool to ascend the throne of France.

In 1806 Chateaubriand set out on a tour in the East, visiting Greece, Palestine, and Egypt in quest of fresh material for his work. The result of this journey was his delightful *Itinéraire de Paris à Jerusalem*, and *Les Martyrs*, a prose epic, of which the action passes in the days of Diocletian. The professed object of this latter work was to demonstrate the superiority of Christian over Pagan forms of worship: and although in this respect it was only partially successful, chiefly because the author falls into the error common to most writers who deal with the early Christian era—that of making the Pagans the most interesting characters—the genuine pathos which surrounds the character of the ill-fated druidess Velléda, and the eloquence with which the glories of the ancient world are delineated, must ever suffice to give it a place among the masterpieces of French literature.

Two years before, his most characteristic production, *René*, had appeared, which, like Madame de Krüdener's *Valérie* and Madame de Staël's *Corinne*, contains a fairly accurate portrait of its author. "It paints with wonderful mastery," says an English critic, "the misery of a morbid, dissatisfied soul, the type of a character blighted by over-sensitiveness on the one hand, and an egotism, thinly veiled by poetical sentiment, on the other. René's morbid despondency is but the too faithful portrait of the desolation begotten in his own mind by the unnatural alliance between opulence of imagination and poverty of heart."[1]

In February 1811, on the death of Joseph de Chénier,

[1] "Encyclopædia Britannica," v. 437.

Chateaubriand's friends proposed to nominate him for the vacant seat in the Institute. Chateaubriand was at first unwilling to join what he termed a "den of philosophers"; but eventually he consented to become a candidate, and was duly elected. When the time for the admission of the new member arrived, it was found that in his address, copies of which were being circulated in Paris, he had vehemently denounced the execution of Louis XVI., and called for vengeance upon the regicides, several of whom, like Cambacérès and Merlin de Douay, occupied positions of the highest importance in the service of the State; and had extolled liberty, which, he declared, found refuge among men of letters when banished from the body politic.

The Institute, fearful of the consequences which might follow so much boldness on the part of its latest recruit, appointed a commission to examine the discourse and report upon it. The commission decided that it must be revised. The Emperor, however, hearing of what had passed, demanded that the address should be submitted to him.

Daru, himself an author and critic, was deputed to take the manuscript to the Emperor, who received him alone. Napoleon, it appears, had already a grievance against Chateaubriand, who had recently published an article in the *Mercure*, in which he had compared the Emperor to Nero and himself to Tacitus. On receiving this fresh proof of the author's hostility, Napoleon flew into a terrible passion. "Had this discourse been delivered," he exclaimed, "I would have closed the gates of the Institute, and thrown M. de Chateaubriand into a dungeon for life."

His furious apostrophes of the absent Chateaubriand were overheard in the antechamber, and believed to be addressed to Daru. The consequence was that when poor

Daru reappeared, he found himself, to his astonishment, shunned by the very courtiers who had, on his entry, greeted him most warmly. As for the real object of the Imperial wrath, he was ordered to leave Paris at once, nor did he return to the capital until after the abdication of Napoleon.

In March 1814, at the moment when the fate of the Empire was trembling in the balance, Chateaubriand published his pamphlet *De Bonaparte et des Bourbons*, a scathing indictment of Napoleonic ambition, which Louis XVIII. once declared to have been worth a hundred thousand men to the Legitimist cause.

After the Restoration Chateaubriand was made a peer, under the title of Vicomte de Chateaubriand, and a Minister of State. But he was far too original a character to commend himself to the old-fashioned king ; indeed, the two men appear to have been naturally antagonistic—an antagonism which Chateaubriand described as the dislike of the classical for the romantic. Nevertheless, he accompanied the Court to Ghent during the Hundred Days, and did his best to counteract the influence of the favourite Blacas and the other reactionaries by whom Louis was surrounded.

In his *Mémoires* he describes how, one Sunday afternoon in June, during his stay at Ghent, he was strolling along the high road which led to Brussels, reading Cæsar's *Commentaries*, when his attention was aroused by a noise like the rumbling of distant thunder. He looked up, and, observing that the sky was somewhat overcast, concluded that a storm was approaching. Presently the sound was repeated, and he noticed that the detonations were neither so loud nor so regular as those of thunder, and began to wonder what they could be. He learned afterwards that the noise which had puzzled him was the distant echo of the cannon at Waterloo.

When Napoleon was once more caged, this time for good and all, Chateaubriand returned to Paris, and for a time associated himself with the violence of the Royalist reaction. But he soon became thoroughly disgusted with the set of intriguers who had assumed the direction of affairs, and his brochure, *Monarchie selon la Charte*—a sweeping exposure of the unconstitutional acts of the Government—exasperated the king so much that, in 1816, his name was struck off the list of Ministers of State, and the pension attached to his post taken from him.

At the time of his meeting with Madame Récamier, Chateaubriand was forty-eight, and still as handsome as ever. "He was of middle height," says Lescure, "a little high-shouldered: all his vitality and masculine energy seemed to be centred in the head, which was superb and full of fascination. He had a broad forehead, with black, curling hair, and eyes that had a profound expression, like the sea whose colour they matched; and when he wished to please, he had a smile at once captivating and irresistible, such as Count Molé said he had seen only in Bonaparte and Chateaubriand."

For years he had been the spoiled darling of the salons. Men, while acknowledging his brilliant talents, found his vanity and egotism difficult to bear; but the ladies of the Faubourg St. Germain were quite willing to take him at his own valuation, which was an exalted one, and it was to them that Chateaubriand was wont to turn for consolation in his constantly recurring fits of depression, for he always aspired to more than he gained, and was dissatisfied even with his own aspirations.

Chateaubriand seems to have at once conceived a

profound admiration and devotion for Madame Récamier, and her gentle influence dominated the remainder of his life. She, on her part, found herself irresistibly drawn towards this brilliant man, with his romantic past, his beautiful, intellectual face, and his fine courtly manners, whose respectful admiration was so refreshing a contrast to the rhapsodies of poor Benjamin Constant, and the intense weariness of life which he affected only proved an additional attraction in her eyes. Henceforth it is Chateaubriand who occupies the foremost place in her affections, and those faithful friends Mathieu de Montmorency and Simon Ballanche are relegated to secondary positions, for the author of *Atala*, like the Turk, suffered no brother near the throne.

"Chateaubriand's friendship with Madame Récamier," says a contemporary writer, "was, as he confesses it, a relief to his spirits. She seems to have understood this melancholy man more than the world did. She cheered him, not, perhaps, entering so much into his feelings, as flattering imperceptibly his vanity, which was naturally soothed by a beautiful woman, who had been such a star in the world of society. Often, indeed, the recluse, the bitter philosopher, verging on misanthropy, is drawn back to the world, at least to humanity, by the delicate allurements of a mere flirt. Madame Récamier was little more. She was not a woman of profound mind. Her companionship with thinkers like Ballanche or Chateaubriand was not spiritual, or metaphysical, or philosophical, or speculative; such men did not want such companionship. They had run into superhumanity (if the term be permitted), and they wanted more humanity. They found it in its pleasantest, least offensive, most attractive form in this amiable, agreeable, pretty woman, who had lived to enjoy life, and enjoyed it, and even prized it still. Madame Récamier won back these morbid thinkers by the strength of her very reality. She was their medium between a world "*d'outre tombe*" and a living world, to which they felt, or professed such hostility. Far from angelic, she was a kind of angel to them, who was able to throw a halo of common beauty over the world they detested. The fact that she was a woman, still beautiful, still gay, still full of life, gave her this power. In this respect a woman however commonplace is more than a poet, and Madame Récamier, though a flirt, was not commonplace."[1]

It can readily be understood that neither Mathieu de Montmorency nor Ballanche—who had, on the death of his father, sold his printing business, and settled in Paris, that he might be near his idol—were at all disposed to allow the new favourite to usurp the place which they had come to look upon as rightfully their own ; and one cannot read without a smile the serious way in which both the *dévot* and the philosopher set to work to wean their sovereign lady from, what they considered, her deplorable weakness for the intruder.

Montmorency redoubled his pious efforts at conversion. "I was greatly pained and shocked to-day," he writes, "at such a sudden change in your manner towards myself and others. Ah ! madame, what rapid progress has this evil—which your most faithful friends have dreaded for your sake—made in the course of a few weeks ! Ah ! turn—there is always time—to Him who gives strength, when the desire to obtain it is sincere, to cure all and repair all. God and a valiant heart are all-sufficient. I pray from the depths of my heart, and with all the strength which the

[1] Wharton's "Queens of Society," ii. 35.

ardour of my wishes gives me, that you may be sustained and enlightened, and that by His powerful aid you may be prevented from weaving with your own hands a chain of misery, from which those who love you will suffer as well as yourself."

The philosophic Ballanche devised a more singular cure for Madame Récamier's infatuation: he recommended her to divert her thoughts by translating Petrarch. "You are a complete poem; you are the Muse herself," he writes. "You are an angel that has lost its way in coming to a world of turmoil and falsehood. . . . The work that I want you to do for Petrarch has been done for Dante; but no one has dared to wrestle with the difficulties of the former. This work would do you infinite honour. I go further: I want you to write the introduction. I shall reserve for myself only the editing, which, modest as it is, will bring me great credit, without even mentioning the glory that will be reflected upon me from my association with you. No, you do not know yourself; no one knows the extent of his powers until he has tested them. . . . Your domain lies in the realm of delicate sentiment; but, believe me, you have under your command the genius of music, flowers, imagination, and elegance. Privileged creature, take courage: lift your charming head, and do not fear to try your hand on the golden lyre of the poets!"

Jealousy, a passion from which neither devotees nor philosophers are wholly exempt, no doubt had something to do with the opposition shown by Montmorency and Ballanche to Madame Récamier's growing intimacy with Chateaubriand; but it would appear to have been principally due to disinterested motives. According to Madame Lenormant, these two faithful friends dreaded that Madame

Récamier's peaceful life would be disturbed by contact with a person of so capricious and fitful a nature, to whom the greatest success failed to bring contentment, and who was subject to continual fits of morbid depression.

But, whatever their motives may have been, their efforts were futile. Neither devotion nor Petrarch—of which Madame Récamier did actually translate a small portion—sufficed to bring about the desired cure. Day by day saw her more irresistibly fettered by the influence of the conqueror; and at length Montmorency and Ballanche reluctantly abandoned the struggle and resigned themselves to the inevitable.

CHAPTER XII

Jacques Récamier sustains fresh losses—Madame Récamier determines to retire to the Abbaye-au-Bois—Chateaubriand's description of her "cell" there—The Abbaye-au-Bois becomes the fashion—Chateaubriand the chief personage in Madame Récamier's circle—His character and habits—Madame Récamier's devotion to him—Assassination of the Duc de Berri and fall of Decazes—Chateaubriand goes as Minister to Berlin—His letters to Madame Récamier—He returns to Paris, and is sent as Ambassador to London—The Carbonari—Their organisation and methods of communication—Risings in different parts of France—Coudert and Sirejean—Madame Récamier obtains the pardon of Coudert—Her efforts on behalf of Sirejean—His fate

In 1819 Jacques Récamier suffered fresh losses, and this time his wife's own little fortune, which she had generously but imprudently hazarded in his speculations, was involved to the extent of one hundred thousand francs. A few months previously, Madame Récamier had bought a house in the Rue d'Anjou, where she had established herself with her husband, her father, her little niece, and old Simonard, who was always looked upon as one of the family. She now, however, determined to break up her establishment, separate from her husband, and retire to the Abbaye-au-Bois in the Rue de Sèvres. Her husband, M. Bernard, and his inseparable companion Simonard could share a lodging in the neighbourhood, could dine with her every day, and spend the evening in her company. By this means the expenses of the liberal hospitality to which they had always been accustomed would be avoided, and she would be able to live alone without the appearance of disagreement with her husband, as no men were permitted to reside even in the exterior of the convent.

Her resolve met with the decided approbation of her friends, for the world, usually so censorious, especially where a pretty woman is concerned, was invariably just to Madame Récamier; and she had the satisfaction of knowing that her motives in thus withdrawing from society were understood and appreciated.

The Abbaye-au-Bois, one of the few convents which had the good fortune to escape the Revolution, lies, with its small garden, a little way back from the street, in the Rue de Sèvres, in the middle of the fashionable Faubourg St. Germain. A lofty iron gate, surmounted by a cross of the same metal, gives admission to a quadrangle, on one side of which is the chapel. Several staircases ascend from this yard, leading to apartments rented to ladies who wished to retire into an interesting semi-obscurity. Many famous leaders of society had sought, at one time or another, the shelter of the Abbaye, Madame de Vintimille, the mistress of Louis XV., among the number.

The only suite of rooms vacant at that time in the Abbaye was situated on the third floor, under the lofty old-fashioned roof of the building. It was a small apartment, crooked in shape, paved with tiles, and altogether uninviting. The stairs leading to it were very steep and difficult of ascent, a somewhat serious drawback for visitors advanced in years.[1] Madame Récamier, however, having

[1] Maria Edgeworth, in a letter to her sister, says that there were seventy-eight steps, and "every one came in with the asthma."

once made up her mind, was not one to draw back, in spite of the comfortless appearance of her surroundings. She settled the three old men whose good angel she was in a lodging close at hand, and installed herself in the room which every one else had found uninhabitable. Chateaubriand has described in his most poetical language the "*cellule*" of his beloved recluse:

"The chamber," he says, "was furnished with a book-case, a harp, a piano, a portrait of Madame de Staël, and a view of Coppet by moonlight. On the window-sills were pots of flowers. When, quite out of breath with having climbed three flights of stairs, I entered the cell just as twilight was falling, I was enchanted. The windows overlooked the garden of the Abbaye, under the verdant shade of which the nuns paced up and down, and the pupils played. The top of an acacia was on a level with the eye, sharp spires pierced the sky, and in the distance rose the hills of Sèvres. The rays of the setting sun shed a golden light over the landscape, and streamed in through the open windows. Here I found silence and solitude, far above the noise and turmoil of a great city."

In 1819 the Abbaye-au-Bois was so little known, at least to the fashionable world, that Madame Moreau, when she paid her first visit to Madame Récamier, took the precaution of ordering her dinner an hour later than the usual time, in order to make the journey to a place so remote. In a few days, however, all the world had found out the way, and ere long it became the fashion to be admitted to what Chateaubriand called the "cell" at the Abbaye.

But if the gay world came to her and was made welcome, Madame Récamier resolutely refused to return its visits. She paid an occasional visit to the theatre to see Talma in some new rôle, and was present at Madame Rachel's *début*, but, as a general rule, she never went out except in the morning. Dinner found all her family assembled round her just as in former days, and to the domestic circle was frequently added one or other of her most intimate friends. Mathieu de Montmorency came every night, always late, because his duties as *Chevalier d'Honneur* to the Duchess d'Angoulême required his attendance until she retired to rest. At first there was some little difficulty about his being admitted, as the rule of the convent was that the outer gate should be closed at eleven o'clock; but Madame Récamier eventually persuaded the Supérieure to allow it to remain open until midnight, and until Montmorency's death these evening visits were never interrupted.

At the end of six months Madame Récamier moved to a more commodious suite of rooms on the first floor of the Abbaye, where she was far more comfortable, and able to extend her modest hospitality to a much larger circle of friends. Hither came her old friends Simonard, Adrien and Mathieu de Montmorency, Ballanche, and Madame Moreau; distinguished foreigners like Elizabeth, Duchess of Devonshire, her brother, the Earl of Bristol, Sir Humphry and Lady Davy, Mary Berry, Maria Edgeworth, and Alexander von Humboldt; and literary men and politicians of every school and shade of opinion—Chateaubriand, Benjamin Constant, Lamartine, Dubois (of the *Globe*), Baron Pasquier, and Auguste Périer; and, later, Villemain, Montalembert, Tocqueville, Guizot, Thierry, Sainte-Beuve, and Prosper Mérimée. Here Lamartine's *Méditations* were read and admired before they were given to the public. Here Delphine Gay, as a young girl, recited a poem of her own, which was afterwards crowned by the Academy; and Jean-Jacques Ampère, the son of the famous geometrician, was introduced to Parisian society. Here also Mary Berry, "no longer young, but still beautiful and *spirituelle*"—as one of the *habitués* describes her—made a ludicrous and rather awkward mistake about the Queen of Sweden, to whom, in ignorance of her identity, she related an amusing anecdote, the heroine of which was the queen herself. But by far the most important person in Madame Récamier's circle of friends at the Abbaye was Chateaubriand; indeed, from the very beginning of his daily visits he became the first object of her life. Strange as it may seem in a man of so wayward and capricious a temperament, Chateaubriand was as regular and methodical in his daily habits as any bank clerk. Every morning he wrote a note to Madame Récamier. Every afternoon, precisely at three o'clock, he paid her a visit; in fact, so remarkable was his punctuality that he used to laugh and say that people regulated their watches by him as he passed. Although far from a shy man, he was singularly reserved and exclusive. He detested nothing so much as to find himself in a room full of strangers, and, accordingly, Madame Récamier admitted no one at his "hour" without his consent. All the mixed or casual company she saw came in the evening when he was not there. The change in her life was indeed an extraordinary one. Until her meeting with Chateaubriand she had been the object around which others revolved. It was now Chateaubriand who was the centre of her little world; but there can be no doubt that she was far happier in the self-abnegation now required of her than in the cold and glittering supremacy she had formerly enjoyed. All her habits were modified to suit his tastes; all her interests were centred in him; while his restless, melancholy nature and the vicissitudes of his political career kept her in a continual state of anxiety and perplexity. "It was the one aim of her life," says Madame Lenormant, "to appease the irritability, soothe the susceptibilities, and remove the annoyances of this noble, generous, but selfish nature, spoiled by excessive adulation."

This beneficial mission was only accomplished at the cost of Madame Récamier's peace of mind; and, in this respect, the fears of Mathieu de Montmorency and Ballanche were but too well justified. Still, she had her reward. As time went on, Chateaubriand became less morbid, less supercilious, less egotistical, and altogether more considerate for the feelings of those around him. His admiration and respect for the woman who, by virtue of the pure and unselfish affection she cherished for him, was able to exercise so great an influence on his life was boundless. "You have transformed my nature," he says to her in one of his letters; and he spoke the truth.

Soon after the beginning of Chateaubriand's intimacy with Madame Récamier he asked permission to bring his wife to call upon her. Madame de Chateaubriand was a *grande dame* of the old school, with a manner which seemed to imply that she was conferring a favour upon those whom she condescended to address. She was noted for her charity, and she and her husband had established a sort of hospice, where twelve old men and the same number of old women had found a shelter in their declining years. Thomas Moore, who met her about this time, and who, as a poet, may be presumed to have been a judge of feminine beauty, says that she was still handsome, but chronic ill-health had reduced her almost to a skeleton and spoiled her temper, and she was, in consequence, far from an easy person to live with. Fortunately for her husband, however, she was quite devoid of jealousy, and regarded his friendships with Madame de Duras, Madame Récamier, and other ladies with perfect complacency. She remained on cordial, though never very intimate terms with Madame Récamier during the rest of her life.

The assassination of the Duc de Berry, second son of the Comte d'Artois, in 1820, was followed by the fall of the Decazes Ministry, and Chateaubriand's friends, the ultra-Royalists, came into power. Chateaubriand had contributed too largely to the success of his party to be passed over by them; but the king's dislike to him was so intense that it was impossible to give him a seat in the new Cabinet. They, therefore, fell back upon the usual expedient when dealing with a powerful and independent politician whom it was necessary to propitiate, and offered him the post of Minister at Berlin. Chateaubriand, however, declined to accept it unless his name was, at the same time, reinstated on the list of Ministers of State, from which it had been removed in 1816. After some demur on the part of the king, his request was granted, and on New Year's Day, 1821, he left for the Prussian capital. While there he kept up a regular correspondence with his friend at the Abbaye-au-Bois.

VICOMTE DE CHATEAUBRIAND *to* MADAME RÉCAMIER.

"*January* 20, 1821.

"If it be true that no one is a prophet in his own country, it is equally true that except in his own country no one is properly appreciated. Doubtless they (the Berliners) know who I am; but the nature of the people is cold; what we call enthusiasm is unknown. They have read my works; admire them more or less; look at me for a moment with quiet curiosity, and have no desire to talk with me, or to know me better. M. d'Alopéus[1] will tell you the same thing. It is the simple truth; and I again assure you that this suits me in every way. There is no society here beyond the great Carnival reunions, which end at the beginning of Lent, after which every one lives in the most complete retirement. No receptions are given to the Diplomatic Corps, and I might be Racine or Bossuet, and nobody would care. If I have been at all warmly received, it has been by the royal family, who are charming, and have overwhelmed me with kindness and attention. At a grand fête at the English Minister's on Tuesday, I had the honour of being chosen as a partner by the Grand-Duchess Nicholas, the King's favourite daughter, and her Royal Highness the Duchess of Cumberland.[2] Yesterday I had a long conversation with the Grand-Duke Nicholas. Now, here you have the whole story of the honours which are being conferred upon me, and of my way of life. Every day I take a solitary walk in the park—a large wood at the gate of Berlin; and when there are no dinner-parties or reunions, I go to bed at nine o'clock. I have no other resource, except conversation with Hyacinth.[3] We discuss current literature. What

[1] The Russian Minister to the Court of Berlin, whom Madame Récamier had met at Aix the previous summer.

[2] "The Duchess of Cumberland took, nearly every day, the same walk as myself. Sometimes she was returning from a charitable visit to the cottage of a poor widow of Spandau; sometimes she would stop and say to me, in a gracious manner, that she had hoped to meet me. I visited her frequently. She often remarked to me that she would like to confide to my care the little George, the prince whom, it was said, his cousin Victoria wished to place by her side on the throne of England."—*Mémoires d'Outre Tombe*, vii. 321.

[3] Hyacinth Pilorge, his private secretary.

else can I tell you? I am engaged upon my third diplomatic despatch. Try to find out, through Mathieu,[1] if it gives satisfaction. My recall is certain in April; but you must press it.

"The four little lines were a complete success. They could not possibly be detected, and the fire brought them out as if by magic. You will see that all my predictions will come to pass. I shall return in the spring, and you will find me as devoted as ever."

"*March* 20, 1821.

"You say that I do not tell you of my successes. Here is one. A Moravian preacher gave a most pompous eulogy of me last Sunday in the pulpit. What do you think? He contrasted me with Voltaire, who also lived in this country: he to corrupt it, I to repair the evil he had done.

"I have told you a hundred times that I read you easily, in spite of your fine writing. Give yourself, therefore, no uneasiness on that score. You cannot imagine my delight at hearing that you are again in your little cell. Before two months are over I shall see you. This thought gives me new life and courage."

Chateaubriand returned to France in the following May. In the autumn a change of Ministers brought the Royalists fully into power. Villèle took the Treasury; Corbière became Minister of the Interior; Peyronnet Minister of Justice; and Mathieu de Montmorency Minister for Foreign Affairs. Chateaubriand had looked for the last post, and was naturally much chagrined at being again passed over. He was, however, somewhat

[1] Mathieu de Montmorency, then Minister for Foreign Affairs.

mollified at being offered the embassy in London; and in April 1822 returned to the city through whose streets, thirty years before, he had trudged a penniless and starving adventurer.

About 1820 the Carbonarism which had flourished for some years in Italy began to take root in France, and quickly received from that systematising genius so characteristic of the French an organic character which it had hitherto lacked. The Carbonari were divided into sections called *ventes*, or circles, with a supreme *vente*, or directing committee, presided over by the veteran Lafayette. The deputies of twenty particular *ventes* composed a central *vente*, the latter communicating through a deputy with the high *vente*, which, in its turn, received orders from the directing committee. These orders were communicated with astonishing rapidity and secrecy. No Carbonaro knew any but the members of his own *vente*, and written communications were strictly prohibited. The conspirators revealed themselves to one another by signs, passwords, and sometimes by cards, divided in such a way as to fit to other cards. Carbonarism made great progress, especially among the middle classes—university students, journalists, and subalterns in the army; indeed, the army appears to have been a perfect hotbed of conspiracy.

Fired by the example of their Spanish and Italian brethren, efforts were made by the French Carbonari, in 1821, to raise revolts at Belfort, La Rochelle, Saumur, Thouars, and other towns. They were suppressed without much difficulty, but not without revealing how widespread was the movement, and the Government, accordingly, proceeded to mete out severe punishment to those of the conspirators who had fallen into their hands, with the object of striking dismay into the hearts of the rest.

Eleven young officers, stationed at Saumur, were tried by court-martial at Tours, and three of them named Delon, Coudert, and Sirejean, were condemned to death. Delon, who appears to have been the instigator of the plot, saved himself by flight, and it transpired that the other two had been induced to join him by false representations, and in complete ignorance of his real motives. Leave to appeal was, accordingly, granted them, and, in the interval between the two trials, their friends made great efforts on their behalf. Coudert's brother, although quite unknown to Madame Récamier, presented himself one day at the Abbaye-au-Bois, and besought her to use her influence on behalf of the unfortunate young officer.

Madame Récamier, always ready to assist those in distress, willingly agreed, and exerted herself to such good purpose that the revisional tribunal, doubtless acting upon a hint from the Government, commuted the sentence of death passed by the court-martial to one of five years' imprisonment.

The success which had attended Madame Récamier's efforts on behalf of Coudert encouraged the friends of Sirejean to invoke her assistance in their turn. Sirejean, it may be remarked, was by far the most to be pitied of the two prisoners. He was barely twenty-one years of age, and had, it seems, joined the Carbonari under the impression that he was being initiated into a harmless society akin to that of the Freemasons. He was a member of a very respectable family at Châlons, where Madame Récamier had spent the first few months of her exile, and his aunt, Madame Chenet, called upon her with a letter of introduction from the wife of the prefect of Marne. The imprisoned youth himself wrote to Madame Récamier a touching letter:

"MADAME,—I am at a loss to find words to express my sense of gratitude to you for the interest which you have promised to exert on behalf of an unfortunate man, who is only a stranger to you, and who has been guilty of a crime which the confidence he reposed in the miserable Delon caused him to look upon as a duty. My age, my inexperience of the world, prevented me from perceiving the trap that was laid for me; and I have fallen into a pit from which I shall never be able to extricate myself. What consoles and assists me to bear my remorse is the knowledge that there are hearts like yours, madame, who know that my fault was an unconscious one, and who believe that I am repentant.

"SIREJEAN.

"P.S.—The court will meet next Monday.

"THE PRISON, TOURS, *April* 8."

Madame Récamier laboured indefatigably to save this poor youth, who was so much more sinned against than sinning, and to comfort his parents, who were so overwhelmed by the terrible fate that threatened their son as to be incapable themselves of taking the necessary steps on his behalf. But the Government, in commuting Coudert's sentence, seems to have reached the limit of its clemency, and, doubtless, considered that to spare both the youthful conspirators might savour of weakness. All Madame Récamier's efforts were in vain, and, on April 18, the revisional tribunal confirmed the death sentence.

The condemned man, however, wrote again to his protectress a letter, the handwriting of which plainly revealed the terrible agitation under which he was labouring. He told her that his friends had decided to press for a new trial, as the fugitive Delon had been captured, and was to be tried at Poitiers, and it was confidently anticipated that his evidence would completely exonerate the victim of his intrigues. He begged Madame Récamier to exert her influence to obtain a respite.

She did so, and was gratified to hear that the War Office had informed Sirejean's relatives that a respite had been granted. Her horror and indignation, therefore, may be imagined when she discovered that, in the face of this promise, the poor youth had been shot at daybreak on May 2. Sirejean met his fate with unflinching courage, as became a soldier.

CHAPTER XIII

Chateaubriand in London—His reception there—His dislike of English society—The Congress of Verona—Chateaubriand's anxiety to represent France at the Congress—Mathieu de Montmorency and Villèle ignore his applications—He appeals to Madame Récamier—And is nominated as one of the French envoys—His real object in wishing to attend the Congress—His duplicity—Mathieu de Montmorency and Chateaubriand at Verona—Their letters to Madame Récamier—Indiscretions of Montmorency and intrigues of Chateaubriand—Montmorency returns to Paris—Villèle and the King refuse to ratify his action at the Congress—He resigns, and Chateaubriand becomes Minister for Foreign Affairs—Magnanimous conduct of Montmorency—His letter to Madame Récamier—Chateaubriand declares himself in favour of armed intervention in Spain—The French invade Spain—Chateaubriand's letters to Madame Récamier—Benjamin Constant prosecuted for his publications—Madame Récamier intercedes for him—Success of the French arms in Spain—Triumph of Chateaubriand—Effects of popular adulation upon him—Strained relations between him and Montmorency—Madame Récamier determines to leave Paris—And sets out for Rome

While Madame Récamier was engaged in this work of mercy her interest was being solicited by a very different person, and for a very different object.

On first arriving in London, Chateaubriand had enjoyed the great political importance which attached to his post; and had taken an almost boyish pleasure in parading his fine horses, carriages, and liveries before the eyes of the citizens who, when he formerly lived among them, had hardly deigned to notice his existence. But, ere many weeks had passed, the novelty of his new position had worn off, and he once more began to experience that feeling of weariness and disgust with his surroundings which was incessantly threatening to counteract the activity and ambition of his mind. "My principal fault," said he of himself, "has been *ennui*, distaste for everything, perpetual doubt." A strange temperament in a man whose life had been devoted to the restoration of religion and monarchy!

The fact of the matter was that England wounded his vanity. In Paris he could not enter a salon without at once becoming the cynosure of all eyes; he could not open a newspaper without finding some reference to himself. In London it was very different. As a man of letters, he was known there only by name; while, as a politician, he found himself, to his intense mortification, regarded rather as a successful party man than as a statesman. London, the English Court and drawing-rooms, bored and displeased him. "Every kind of reputation," he says in his *Mémoires*, "travels rapidly to the banks of the Thames, and leaves them again with the same speed. I should have worried myself to no purpose by endeavouring to acquire any knowledge of the English. What a life is a London season! I should prefer the galleys a hundred times."[1]

His letters to Madame Récamier teem with complaints of the monotony of his life and the social duties which his official position entailed, and which he cordially detested.

"Yesterday I made my first appearance in society. I

[1] *Mémoires d'Outre Tombe*, vii. 395, 396.

was extremely bored at a rout. I have been unwell ever since I have been here. I have frightful nights. The climate is detestable. . . . A part of my duty consists in going into society; and, when I have been working all day, I have to dress and go out at half-past eleven in the evening. Imagine what a plague this is to me! . . . I am living contrary to all my tastes and habits. I leave you that I may not annoy you with my lamentations."

He grumbles at the interest which she is taking in the fate of Sirejean, and seems to regard it as a slight to himself. "Alas! we have plenty of personal sorrows without adding to them the griefs of strangers."

As time went on, the monotony, the idleness, the "isolation from the sound of his own name"—as Lamartine aptly expresses it—became almost unendurable. He burned with impatience to return to Paris, resume his place in the Chamber of Peers, and compel the king to acknowledge his claims to a seat in the Cabinet. An opportunity soon presented itself, which enabled him to seek in another direction the excitement and popularity which were to him as the breath of life.

For some time past affairs in Spain had been going from bad to worse. The despicable Ferdinand VII. had been forced by his incensed subjects, in 1820, to accept the Constitution of Cadiz; but he had no sooner done so than he had sought to evade its provisions, with the result that the unhappy country was now given over to all the horrors of civil war. Metternich, whose importance and influence had greatly increased since he had crushed the Italian revolutionaries, had now turned his attention to the affairs of the Peninsula, and urged the Powers to deliberate upon them in Congress. His suggestion was adopted; and Verona was selected as the trysting-place.

When Chateaubriand was first informed of the intention of the allied sovereigns to meet at Verona, he wrote to Villèle strongly deprecating "the insolent interference of the Northern Cabinets in the affairs of the South." He would appear to have been, for the moment at any rate, in favour of the extension of constitutional rights in Spain and Naples, possibly owing to the influence of Canning, with whom he had formed a close friendship. No sooner, however, did he learn the names of the celebrated Ministers and diplomatists who had been accredited by the different Courts to assist at the Congress, than he became feverishly anxious to be nominated as one of the French representatives. He accordingly wrote to Villèle and Mathieu de Montmorency to press his claims; but the two Ministers ignored his appeals. Villèle distrusted Chateaubriand, who, he considered, would be as likely as not to commit the Cabinet to a policy totally at variance with any decision they might arrive at; while Montmorency foresaw that, if the ambitious Breton attended the Congress, there would be an end to all freedom of action on his part; that he would, in all probability, be compelled to yield the palm to him in diplomacy, as he had already done in love; and that, on their return to Paris, Chateaubriand would succeed in ousting him from the Foreign Office, a post which, as he was well aware, he had long coveted. Under these circumstances, Chateaubriand decided to have recourse to the intervention of his friend at the Abbaye-au-Bois, knowing full well that the devoted Montmorency would find it hard to refuse her any favour she might ask of him. He was, however, careful not to allow her to suspect his real motive for wishing to go to Verona.

"You will say that I am terribly anxious to take part

in this Congress," he writes. "Not at all. But it is the road which leads me the more naturally into your cell, without a resignation and without a scene. This is all my secret. I shall await with the greatest impatience the first news from you. Write! Write!"

At the same time, in order to leave nothing to chance, he despatched Marcellus, the First Secretary of the French Embassy, to Paris to represent to Montmorency that, unless his request was granted, his chief was fully resolved to resign his post, and return at once to France.

Montmorency's determination to exclude Chateaubriand from the Congress was considerably shaken by this intelligence, as he foresaw that, in the event of the ambassador carrying out his threat, Villèle would probably be constrained to sacrifice the Foreign Minister himself, in order to buy off the hostility of the man who had already wrecked one Ministry, and might quite conceivably be strong enough to upset another. When, therefore, to the warnings of Marcellus were adde the entreaties of Madame Récamier, whom he feared would attribute a refusal to jealousy of his successful rival in her affections, he reluctantly yielded; and, consoling himself with the reflection that a troublesome colleague at Verona might, perhaps, after all be preferable to a certain competitor in Paris, advised Villèle to send Chateaubriand his nomination.

It is more than doubtful whether Madame Récamier would have lent her aid to the furtherance of Chateaubriand's wishes, had she been at all aware of the secret workings of her friend's ambitious mind. So far from desiring to counteract the tendency of the Eastern despots towards war, as he had led Villèle at one time to suppose, Chateaubriand was strongly in favour of armed intervention in the affairs of Spain. Moreover, he fully intended that it should be he, and not Montmorency, who should decide upon and direct that war, notwithstanding the fact that, in one of his letters to the Foreign Minister, he had declared that the statement, which was being continually made in the newspapers, that he desired his place in the Cabinet was an "infamous falsehood," and that his sole reason for wishing to take part in the Congress was to increase his importance and influence at the Court of St. James's.

Chateaubriand arrived at Verona on October 16, whither Montmorency had already preceded him. The intercourse between the two diplomats was, according to the correspondence which they kept up with the object of their common attachment, courteous, although somewhat reserved. "Our first meeting was very friendly," writes Montmorency. "I trust that we shall continue on the same footing. That is what I fully intend, and he also, I imagine." "We are very civil to one another," says Chateaubriand. They both, it appears, avoided, by common consent, the subject of Madame Récamier. It was still a sore point with the Foreign Minister.

The majority of the French Cabinet was strongly in favour of war; but Villèle himself, the only member of the Government who had the least pretensions to be considered a statesman, was anxious for peace, and desired that, if war should become inevitable, France should maintain entire freedom of action, and should enter upon the struggle as an independent Power, and not as the instrument of the European Concert. He had, therefore, while instructing the French envoys to ascertain whether the Allies would support France in the event of the task of coercing the Spaniards proving beyond her strength, strictly enjoined them to avoid committing themselves to any definite course of action until the opinion of the Ministry at home had been taken upon it.

Montmorency, unfortunately, regarded the Spanish Constitutionalists as the avowed enemies of religion, and was eager for war. Moreover, he was entirely ignorant of the tortuous paths of diplomacy, and was as wax in the hands of such a veteran intriguer as Metternich. Instead, therefore, of contenting himself with obtaining an assurance from the Eastern Powers—Wellington, on behalf of England, refused his assent—of their moral and material support in the event of France declaring war, he subscribed to a resolution, proposed by the crafty Austrian envoy, that notes should be presented by all the ambassadors at Madrid demanding a change in the Spanish Constitution, and to a secret clause, whereby the four Powers bound themselves to withdraw their ambassadors should the Spanish Government fail to return a satisfactory answer to their demands. A draft of the notes to be presented was then drawn up; and Montmorency returned to Paris to submit it to the king before handing it to the ambassadors for transmission to Madrid.

The principal reason that had induced Villèle to consent to Chateaubriand's nomination to the Congress was the belief that he had imbibed the liberal opinions of his friend Canning during his stay in England, and that he would, therefore, serve as a useful counterpoise to the warlike predilections of the Foreign Minister. A word of warning from Chateaubriand might have prevented Montmorency from allowing himself to be made the catspaw of Metternich; but that word was never spoken. Chateaubriand was quick to perceive that not only was his colleague committing the French Ministry to the policy which he himself secretly favoured, but that he was ruining his political prospects by his indiscretion, for it would be impossible for Villèle to overlook such wilful disregard of his instructions, and that his fall would mean his own elevation. He was, therefore, quite content to keep in the background, and leave the conduct of the negotiations entirely in the hands of Montmorency.

The latter was not a little surprised at this self-effacement on the part of a man, as a rule, very far from inclined to hide his light under a bushel, but he does not appear to have had any suspicion of his real motive. "I do not much like the general position in which he has placed himself," he writes to Madame Récamier; "he is looked upon as singularly taciturn; he assumes a stiff and reserved manner, which makes others feel ill at ease in his presence. I shall make every effort, before I leave, to establish more congenial relations between him and his colleagues."

Montmorency had no occasion to trouble himself to secure this result. No sooner had the Foreign Minister started for Paris than Chateaubriand emerged from his shell all affability and courtesy. In a very few days he had succeeded in ingratiating himself with the allied sovereigns, more particularly with the Emperor Alexander, whose indignation against the disturbers of the monarchical institutions of Spain he artfully encouraged, and who, in return, promised him his unlimited support both for his policy and for himself.

Meanwhile Mathieu de Montmorency had arrived in Paris, where Louis XVIII. offered him a dukedom in return for his services at the Congress. The king wished to bestow upon him the title of Duc de Vèrone; but Montmorency would not relinquish his name, even to please his sovereign, and, accordingly, he was created Duc Mathieu de Montmorency, as the head of his illustrious family already bore the title of Duc de Montmorency. During his absence the elections had taken place, and still further strengthened the war party in the Chamber of Deputies; while, on the other hand, the Constitutionalists in Spain were carrying all before them, and the perjured despot's throne, if not his life, seemed in imminent peril.

Such being the condition of affairs, Villèle heard with indignation and alarm how completely his colleague had committed France to the policy of the Eastern Powers. There was no likelihood that the Spaniards, now flushed with triumph, would make the least concession of the kind demanded, in which case France stood pledged, if Montmorency's action was ratified, to withdraw her ambassador from Madrid at once. He endeavoured to persuade the representatives of the other Powers to postpone, for the present, the despatch of the threatening notes, but to no purpose.

Montmorency, in the meantime, was urging on the Cabinet the necessity of submitting a similar note to Madrid, in conformity with the engagements he had entered into at Verona. The king, however, probably influenced by Wellington, who had stopped in Paris on his homeward journey, and warned him against permitting himself to be made the tool of the Eastern Powers, advised delay, and, a few days later, to the intense chagrin of Montmorency, appointed Villèle President of the Council of Ministers.

In virtue of his new position, Villèle at once opened negotiations with the Spanish Cortes, without even consulting the Foreign Minister. Montmorency thereupon called his colleagues together, and, in the presence of the king, read to them the note which he had addressed to the French ambassador at Madrid, and called upon them to approve or disavow his action.

The Cabinet was divided, but the king put a stop to the discussion by siding with Villèle. The same day Montmorency tendered his resignation, which was accepted.

Villèle saw that the resignation of a man like Montmorency, popular at once with the Congress, the Court, the Royalists, and the Church, would mean the speedy downfall of his own Ministry, unless he could replace him by some one who would be likely to satisfy these powerful interests. There was obviously only one person who could fulfil these requirements—Montmorency's principal colleague at Verona. Chateaubriand was by no means a favourite at Court; but, on the other hand, he had won golden opinions from the allied sovereigns at the Congress, and was the idol of the ultra-Royalists and the clergy. Villèle believed also that Chateaubriand would show himself more in harmony with his own views on the Spanish Question than Montmorency had done, and he, accordingly, advised the king to offer the vacant portfolio to the author of *Atala*.

Chateaubriand could with difficulty conceal his delight at finding the post he had so long coveted at last within his grasp; but, prompted either by vanity or, possibly, by some decent scruples for the feelings of his old friend Mathieu de Montmorency, he feigned great reluctance to accept it. "I refused Villèle at twelve," he writes to Madame Récamier. "The king sent for me at four, and kept me an hour and a half preaching to me, I resisting. At length he ordered me to obey. I obeyed. So now *I* shall remain near you; but this Ministry will kill me."

Mathieu de Montmorency was naturally much mortified at seeing himself supplanted by the friend who had so indignantly protested against the insinuation that he had any designs upon the Foreign Office, but he was far too high-minded a man to make a parade of his own feelings, still less to indulge in useless recriminations. "He continued to honour," says Lamartine, "sometimes in retirement, sometimes at the Court, the king who disavowed him, the Minister who dismissed him, and the friend who abandoned him—an example almost unique among those parties and assemblies where triumph hardens the heart and defeat depraves it, and where changes of position are so often changes of language, of cause, and of fidelity."[1] There can be no doubt, however, that a chivalrous desire to spare the lady of the Abbaye-au-Bois the pain of witnessing an open breach between her two most cherished friends had much to do with the courtesy with which he continued to treat Chateaubriand. A few days after his resignation he writes to Madame Récamier:

"I wish, *aimable amie*, to inform you at once of the result of the meeting about which you were inclined to be uneasy. I have just come away from it. I had only to ward off his civilities, excuses, and protestations. I believe that I replied to them quite straightforwardly, without ill-humour, anger, or weakness, and passed on without delay to the business details which I had to give him, and which he took in very good part. We separated on the footing on which we must remain, and in which there is nothing particularly embarrassing for you.

"I am sorry that I cannot see you personally to assure you anew of my affection. Pray send me news of your

[1] Lamartine's *History of the Restoration of the Monarchy in France*, iv. 71.

health, and also *Phêdon*, which will sustain me with sublime thoughts in my retirement."

Chateaubriand had assured Madame Récamier that the post of Foreign Minister would be his death, but we see no sign of dying in what followed. No sooner did he join the Ministry than he flung aside the mask of moderation which he had hitherto assumed, and boldly declared himself in favour of the very policy which had cost poor Montmorency his place in the Cabinet. It was in vain that England tendered her mediation ; it was in vain that his friend Canning wrote expressing his amazement at this sudden and complete change in Chateaubriand's views, and exhorting him to leave the Spanish revolution "to burn itself out within its own crater" ; it was in vain that champions of constitutional liberty like General Foy, and far-seeing statesmen like Talleyrand, denounced the proposed intervention, the one on the ground of justice, the other on that of expediency. Chateaubriand turned a deaf ear to all appeals. His fiery eloquence roused the war-party to a pitch of frenzy against which it was hopeless for Villèle to protest ; the king's speech at the opening of the Chambers virtually amounted to a declaration of war, and, on April 7, 100,000 French troops, under the command of the Duc d'Angoulême, crossed the Bidassoa.

During this eventful period Madame Récamier continued to be the recipient of all her friend's confidences :

"I could not see you yesterday, as the Chamber of Peers adjourned too late. I pass to-day at the Council with the king and in my salon ; and I shall work all night to speak, perhaps, to-morrow, as my speech is not yet finished. The *Constitutionnel* asserts again this morning that I read the speech at the Abbaye-au-Bois. You see how your friends treat you, and how well informed they are. Let it pass. Pray for me, as I do for you. To-morrow or Tuesday will be a decisive day in my political career. I love you, and that sustains me. After my speech, I shall be more at liberty, and wholly yours."

And again :

"Several foreign ambassadors have called upon me to beg me to reply to Mr. Canning's speech.[1] They found me at work upon the very speech which they wanted. You can understand that this has spurred me on a little, by promising me a European success. I am going to bury myself in my work, and I will show it to you. But I shall not be able to see you to-day, which counter-balances the pleasure I feel at my political success. Pardon, and love me a little for the sake of my fame. Till to-morrow!"

Soon after Chateaubriand became Foreign Minister, Madame Récamier's former adorer Benjamin Constant, who had taken an active part in opposing the war, was prosecuted by the Government on account of two pamphlets which he had written, and was sentenced to pay a fine and undergo a term of imprisonment. Constant now visited Madame Récamier but seldom; but he came to the Abbaye-au-Bois on this occasion to ask her to intercede for him with Chateaubriand. She did so, and his sentence was commuted to a simple fine.

Angoulême's campaign in Spain was short and decisive. The Constitutionalists, badly armed, badly led, and divided among themselves, were, of course, quite incapable of coping with disciplined troops. No serious resistance was

[1] This was the speech which Canning delivered in the House of Commons on April 8, in laying on the table the despatches relating to the affairs of Spain.

met with, except at Cadiz, and the triumph of the French arms was used to stamp out in the most merciless way the adherents of liberty. Ferdinand VII. returned to Madrid, and ruled for the rest of his worthless life as the most absolute of sovereigns.

Chateaubriand's Spanish policy has been made the subject of the most extravagant praise on the part of some of his contemporaries; but the modern writer will probably see in it nothing but an utterly unjustifiable interference with the right of a free people to choose their own form of government, with the puerile idea of restoring French prestige by means of a military parade, and, at the same time, identifying his own name with a great public event. However, for the moment at any rate, his triumph was complete. The glory of military successes encircled the monarchy. The Royalists were exultant, and deluded themselves with the belief that Angoulême's cheaply-gained successes had rekindled in the French army something of its old enthusiasm for its Bourbon masters. The clergy saw in the victory of their brethren in Spain a promise of returning power for themselves. The allied sovereigns sent him cordial congratulations and numerous decorations. The journals vied with one another in extolling the statesmanlike qualities of the Foreign Minister. The salons resounded with his praises. He was the hero of the hour.

Madame Récamier sympathised to the full with the success of her friend, but she could not fail to perceive that his acceptance of office had, in a great measure, put an end to the pleasant intercourse which they had formerly enjoyed. Chateaubriand's daily visits to the Abbaye-au-Bois were now frequently interrupted by meetings of the Cabinet or by the sittings of the Chambers; and when he came she saw that he was greatly changed. The temper and character of the great writer, like that of so many other men of letters who have been called to play a prominent part in political life, had not been proof against the intoxication of fame and success. The adulation of the great world of Paris, more especially that part of it to whose flattery he was most susceptible—the fine ladies of the Faubourg St. Germain—had injured, temporarily at least, the pure and devoted affection he still continued to profess for her. Whereas she had hitherto found him, notwithstanding his fits of depression, one of the kindest and most considerate of friends, he was now quick to take offence, absurdly sensitive to the least breath of criticism, fretful and capricious as a spoiled child. Sometimes he would neglect her for days together; at others he would be unreasonably exacting in his demands on her time and attention; and, moreover, she noticed with pain and uneasiness that, as her niece diplomatically expresses it, "he no longer treated her with that respectful reserve, characteristic of those permanent sentiments which she wished only to inspire."

Another source of unpleasantness for her lay in the now very strained relations which existed between Chateaubriand and Mathieu de Montmorency. The latter, as we have seen, had behaved with rare magnanimity towards Chateaubriand at the time when he had sided with Villèle against him, and consequently secured the post which his own delicate sense of honour had prompted him to resign. But it was too much to expect him to continue to do so when he saw the new Minister pluming himself upon the successful issue of the very policy to which his predecessor had pledged himself at Verona. With the tenderest consideration for Madame Récamier's peace of mind, it was impossible for him to altogether conceal his contempt for a man who could stoop to such duplicity to further his own interests.

In the midst of these perplexities, Madame Récamier's niece, Amélie de Cyvoct, was taken ill, and on her recovery the doctors advised her wintering in a warm climate. Madame Récamier welcomed this suggestion as a means of escaping from her difficulties; and, at the beginning of November, set out for Italy. The faithful Ballanche begged to be allowed to follow, which he did, accompanied by Jean-Jacques Ampère, who had become as devoted to Madame Récamier as any of her older friends. "Perhaps nothing," says Madame Mohl, "can show her peculiar charm so well as the attachment of this young man. He had lost his own mother when a child, and he found in Madame Récamier all the sympathy and interest that a beautiful young mother gives so lavishly to an affectionate son."

This departure for Italy was a great effort for Madame Récamier, but, as she told one of her friends some years later, she saw that a temporary separation from Chateaubriand was the only course open to her under the circumstances. By the time she returned to Paris she hoped that Chateaubriand would have come to see that the blame for their recent misunderstandings rested entirely with himself; that the friction between him and Mathieu de Montmorency would be at an end, and that it would be possible for them to resume their former pleasant relations, as if nothing had ever occurred to interrupt them.

Chateaubriand could not but be aware that his own conduct was the principal cause of his friend's leaving Paris, but, true to his egotistical nature, he affected to believe that he was the injured party. "Always fearing to hurt your feelings," he says, "when you think so lightly of mine, I write you this to reach you as you pass through Lyons. I shall be in Paris on Thursday, and you will be no longer there. Well, you would have it so. Will you find me here on your return? Apparently, that is of little importance to you. To one who, like you, has the heart to break up everything, what signifies the future? However, I shall await you. If I am alive on your return, you will find me the same as you leave me, my every thought of you, and never having ceased to love you."

He evidently thought that her journey was but a whim, and that she would soon return, and predicts as much in a letter which he sends her a few days later. However, she did not do so until the summer of 1825; and, after a few months, Chateaubriand took umbrage at her continued absence, and for more than a year there seems to have been a break in their correspondence.

CHAPTER XIV

Madame Récamier arrives in Rome—The Duc de Laval—Elizabeth, Duchess of Devonshire—Her patronage of art and literature—Illness and death of Cardinal Consalvi—Grief of the duchess—The Bonaparte family in Rome—Madame Récamier meets Queen Hortense at St. Peter's—Torlonia's ball—A comedy of errors—Illness and death of the Duchess of Devonshire—Singular conduct of the young duke—A curious story—Madame Récamier's letter to Mathieu de Montmorency—Madame Salvage de Faverolles—Affairs in France—The Septennial and Revenue Bills—Strong opposition to the latter measure in the Chambers—Chateaubriand remains silent—Indignation of his colleagues—His ignominious dismissal from office—His resentment and its results

MADAME RÉCAMIER arrived in Rome at the end of November. Her friend Canova was no longer there to greet her: he had died at Venice more than two years earlier, from a disease brought on by the continual use of carving-tools, and his sceptre had passed to the Danish sculptor Thorwaldsen; but she received a warm welcome from her old admirer Adrien de Montmorency, now Duc de Laval, and French Ambassador to the Vatican. He placed his carriages, horses, and servants at her disposal, came to see her every day, and did all in his power to make her voluntary exile as pleasant as possible. She took lodgings in the Via Baburino, opposite the Greek Church, and her evening receptions went on just as if she had been still in Paris. "Every evening," writes Madame Chevreux, "she is surrounded by intimate friends, such as M. Dugas-Montbel, the Duc de Laval-Montmorency, M. de Girré, the Abbé Canova, Guérin, Léopold Robert, Delécluze, &c. Ballanche and Mademoiselle Amélie remain with Madame Récamier; Jean-Jacques [Ampère] passes part of his days with them. And so the Abbaye-au-Bois is reconstituted in Italy."

The acknowledged leader of society in Rome at this time was Elizabeth, Duchess of Devonshire, who had taken up her residence there after her husband's death in 1814, and enjoyed the friendship of many distinguished Italians, particularly of Cardinal Consalvi, Pius VII.'s able and liberal-minded Secretary of State; while her house was the chief resort of the brilliant throng which flocked to the Eternal City from all parts of Europe.

The duchess, who was a daughter of the fourth Earl of Bristol, had been one of the most beautiful women of her day, although she was now pale and emaciated. When very young she had married Mr. John Forster, who, however, died a few years later. After his death she spent some time on the Continent, and at Lausanne met Gibbon the historian, who gave it as his opinion that "if she chose to beckon the Lord Chancellor from his woolsack, in full sight of the world, he could not resist obedience"; and is said to have proposed to her upon his knees, from which position, owing to the violence of his emotion and his extreme corpulence, he was unable to rise until she had summoned her maid to assist him. She did not return the author's affection, although she was a great admirer of his "History," part of which he read to her before sending it to his publishers in London; and in 1809 became the second wife of the fifth Duke of Devonshire.

She was a munificent patron of literature and art, although the omniscient George Ticknor was of opinion that "she attempted to play the Macænas a little too much." In 1816 she printed, at her own expense, the Fifth Satire of the First Book of Horace, with a versified Italian translation, and, two years later, an edition of the *Æneid* of Virgil, with a translation by Annibal Caro. Both these works were embellished with fine engravings by the most famous artists in Italy.

The duchess was an old friend of the Duc de Laval's, whom she had known as an *emigré* in England, and both he and Mathieu de Montmorency always spoke of her as "*la duchesse cousine*," though there was no tie of relationship between them. Madame Récamier had first met her during her visit to England in 1802, and the acquaintance thus formed was renewed in Paris after the Restoration, and soon ripened into a warm friendship.

At the time of Madame Récamier's arrival in Rome, Cardinal Consalvi was seriously ill, and she became the sympathising confidante of the alternate hopes and fears of her English friend. The cardinal's illness, to the inexpressible grief of the duchess, terminated fatally at the beginning of the following January.

The Carnival that year at Rome was a very brilliant one. The Duc de Laval, the French Ambassador, entertained on a regal scale, and gave several magnificent balls; but Madame Récamier adhered to her resolution not to attend any large gatherings, and during her stay in Rome made but few exceptions to this rule. One of these was on the occasion of some private theatricals at the Austrian Embassy, in which her niece had been invited to take part. Mademoiselle de Cyvoct appears to have acquitted herself with great credit, and her aunt was much gratified by the encomiums bestowed upon her acting. Madame Récamier was accompanied by the Duchess of Devonshire, the first time the latter had appeared in society since the death of her friend the cardinal. "She was very sad," writes Madame Récamier to her nephew Paul David, "and when the hall resounded with laughter, she would look sorrowfully at me, as if to invite my sympathy."

By the treaties of 1815 the members of the Bonaparte family were not allowed to travel or change their place of residence without the unanimous consent of the five Great Powers; but many of them had obtained permission to reside in the Papal States, and in Rome Madame Récamier found Napoleon's mother, "Madame Mère," as she was still called; her brother, Cardinal Fesch, who had one of the finest private picture galleries in Europe; the Princess Borghèse (Pauline Bonaparte); Jerome, ex-King of Westphalia; Louis, ex-King of Holland, and her old adorer Lucien Bonaparte, who had been created Prince de Canino by Pope Pius VII., and was held in much esteem in Rome, although he seldom went into society, preferring to divide his time between his children, to whom he was devotedly attached, and his books. Soon after her arrival the Bonapartes were reinforced by the arrival of the Duchesse de St. Leu (Queen Hortense) and her two sons, Napoleon and Louis (afterwards Napoleon III.).

Madame Récamier met the ex-queen one day at St. Peter's, whither she had gone to listen to the music, and was warmly greeted by Hortense, with whom she had been on very friendly terms until she had the misfortune to fall under the ban of the Emperor's displeasure.

In deference to the feelings of the Duc de Laval, whose

position as the accredited representative of the Bourbons precluded him from holding any intercourse with the rival dynasty, Madame Récamier had hitherto refrained from visiting or receiving any of the Bonaparte family; but she now spent a good deal of her time in the society of the ex-queen, with whom she made daily expeditions to the different places of interest around Rome.

One of the chief events of the Carnival was a grand masked ball given by Torlonia, the banker, at his magnificent palace on the Corso. Madame Récamier and Queen Hortense were very nearly of the same height and figure, and the latter persuaded her friend to break through her rule and attend the ball, and, moreover, arranged that they should both wear the same costume—a white satin domino, trimmed with pearls—in which disguise it would be very difficult, even for their most intimate friends, to distinguish one from the other. As a mark of recognition, Hortense was to carry a bouquet of roses, while Madame Récamier wore a wreath of the same flowers. We will let Madame Récamier give her own account of the comedy of errors which followed:

"I arrived at the ball, escorted by the Duc de Laval, and eagerly scanned the large and brilliant crowd which thronged the rooms in search of the queen, whom I at length perceived in company with Prince Jerome Bonaparte. In passing and repassing each other, we found an opportunity of exchanging a few words, and speedily concocted a little plot. At a moment when the crowd was very great, I suddenly left the Duc de Laval, and, stepping back a few paces, hastily unfastened my wreath. The queen, who was on the alert, gave me her bouquet in exchange, and took my place on the arm of the ambassador of Louis XVIII., while I occupied hers, under the escort of the ex-King of Westphalia. She was soon surrounded by all the representatives of the Foreign Powers, and I by all the Bonapartists who happened to be in Rome. While she was amused at the greetings which, as the companion of the ambassador, she received from the diplomatists—many of whom, no doubt, she knew—I was astonished, in my turn, at the revelation of regrets and hopes which people generally express only to members of their own party. Before suspicion could be aroused, we resumed our places, and, when next we met, changed again; in short, we repeated this jest until it ceased to amuse us, which very soon happened, for everything amusing is from its nature of short duration. In the meanwhile, this ruse, which was finally suspected, had created consternation in our respective circles. It was rumoured throughout the ball-room, that Queen Hortense and Madame Récamier wore the same disguise; and the perplexity of those who addressed either of us, while still uncertain of our identity, prolonged for some time our enjoyment of the joke. Everybody took it in good part, with the exception of the Princesse de Lieven, who never laid aside politics, even at a ball, and who thought it disgraceful that she should have been compromised by association with a Bonapartist." [1]

At the beginning of the spring Madame Récamier suffered a severe blow from the loss of her friend the Duchess of Devonshire, who had never recovered from the shock of Cardinal Consalvi's death, and who died on March 30, after a few days' illness.

The only one of the duchess's relations at that time in Rome was her step-son, the young Duke of Devonshire, to whom Madame Récamier wrote, begging to be allowed

[1] *Souvenirs*, ii. 281.

to see her. In answer to her request she received the following letter:

THE DUKE OF DEVONSHIRE *to* MADAME RÉCAMIER.

"*March* 27.

"DEAREST MADAME RÉCAMIER,—Pray do not think me unkind, if I beg of you to be tranquil. When the time comes for her friends to see her, you will be the first I shall think of, and I will send for you. To-day, no one, not even myself, is allowed to enter her room. Believe me, I fully appreciate your tender friendship for her.

"Your devoted servant,
"DEVONSHIRE."

The following night, however, the duke wrote to her again:

"Come, dear madame, if you have strength to promise me not to enter her room too abruptly.

"DEVONSHIRE."

Madame Récamier hastened to her friend's house, where she found the Duc de Laval, who had also been sent for. They were kept waiting for a considerable time; but at length the duke appeared, and conducted them to the sick-room, where they saw at once that the end was only a question of a few minutes. The duchess was unable to speak, but she recognised her friends, and pressed Madame Récamier's hand affectionately before she died. The next day the duke sent Madame Récamier a ring, which the dead woman had worn until the last, and had bequeathed to her.

The conduct of the young duke in refusing to allow his step-mother's most intimate friends to see her until so near the end was much commented upon in Rome, and revived the old story that the Duke of Devonshire was not the son of the previous duke's first wife, the celebrated beauty Georgiana, but of the deceased duchess herself. According to this account, Georgiana, who was confined of a daughter at the same time that her friend, then Lady Elizabeth Forster, gave birth to a son, consented to the substitution of the children; and the scandal-mongers hinted that the duke had been afraid that the dying woman might reveal this secret. Madame Récamier, however, believed, and the Duc de Laval shared her conviction, that the Duke of Devonshire's somewhat unusual behaviour was to be accounted for by the fact that he had reason to suppose that his step-mother's Protestantism had been shaken during her intimacy with Cardinal Consalvi; and so, fearing that when dying she might desire to be received into the Roman Catholic Church, he would not permit any members of that communion to have access to her until she had lost the power of speech.

As spring advanced Madame Récamier's friends in Paris began to urge her to return, but, partly owing to the wish to completely re-establish her niece's health, and partly owing to the fear of falling again into the old stormy relationship with Chateaubriand, she decided to remain in Italy until the following year. "If I were to return to Paris," she says in a letter to Mathieu de Montmorency, "I should meet again with the old disturbing influences that were the cause of my leaving. If M. de Chateaubriand were on bad terms with me, I should be deeply grieved; if, on the other hand, he was amiably disposed, the result would be an annoyance I am determined to avoid for the future. It makes me sad to have to remain separated from my friends for another six months; but it is better to make this sacrifice, and I confess I feel it to be a necessary one."

Among the friends whom Madame Récamier made about this time in Rome was Madame Salvage de Faverolles, afterwards the devoted friend of Queen Hortense and the confidante of Louis Napoleon's ambitious schemes. She was a tall woman, with a fine figure, a harsh voice, and an abnormally long nose. The Duc de Laval, who was afraid of her temper, used to caution his friends not to offend her lest she should run her nose through their bodies. Madame Salvage had a perfect passion for celebrities, and took a violent fancy to Madame Récamier. The latter, however, did not return her affection, while her friends were by no means prepossessed in her favour. On the other hand, she recognised her sterling qualities, and introduced her to Queen Hortense, to whom Madame Salvage attached herself for the remainder of the ex-queen's eventful life.

While Madame Récamier was living thus quietly at Rome, the condition of affairs in France, both in the Chambers and the Cabinet, was anything but pacific. Two important measures were presented to the Chambers during the session of 1824. The first of these was a Septennial Bill, which proposed to repeal the law by which one-fifth of the Chamber of Deputies retired in rotation each year, and to give the existing House a duration of seven years from its election in 1822. By this means the Government intended to maintain intact the Royalist majority in the Chamber for the next five years, and thus consolidate the Bourbon dynasty. This reactionary measure—one of the worst instances on record of the abuse of a Parliamentary majority—passed both Houses by large majorities, in spite of the opposition of the Liberals and the more moderate Royalists.

The second measure, for which Villèle was mainly responsible, was a financial one, and aimed at reducing the interest on the Funds and compelling the fund-holders to convert their old stock into new, which would represent an amount of capital and interest considerably smaller than they had hitherto possessed. This would have been an equitable and salutary measure enough in England and other countries, where the State borrows a real and definite capital, and naturally reserves to itself the right of paying off the lenders, when it can replace them by others who will be content with a lower rate of interest. But in France the Consolidated Funds represented for the most part interminable annuities—indemnities for the bankruptcies and confiscations of the Revolution—and the Government, in proposing their conversion, violated both the spirit and the letter of their engagements.

The Bill passed the elective Chamber without much difficulty, but it met with determined opposition in the Chamber of Peers, where the Church party, led by Quèlen, Archbishop of Paris, made common cause with the rich capitalists, whose incomes were threatened by the measure, and the Liberals, who opposed it in order to embarrass the Government. Villèle, however, relied upon the eloquence of Chateaubriand to turn the scale in favour of the Ministry, but, to his consternation, his colleague made no attempt to intervene in the debate, with the result that the Foreign Minister's personal following concluded that they were at liberty to vote as they pleased, and the Bill was lost by a small majority.

Chateaubriand's action on this occasion was generally attributed at the time to dissatisfaction with the measure, and he was much applauded for his disinterested conduct; but, according to his own account, given some years later, he was, though by no means enthusiastic about it, in favour of the Bill—indeed, he voted for it with the rest of the Ministry—and abstained from joining in the debate simply because Villèle had omitted to supply him with the financial details necessary for an effective speech. But whatever his reason may have been, it certainly seems extraordinary that he should have taken no steps whatever to inform his colleague of his intentions, after apparently giving him to understand that he might count on his support.

The indignation of Villèle at what he considered Chateaubriand's treason was unbounded. He had never forgiven him for his *volte-face* on the Spanish question, which had forced him to consent to a policy of which he strongly disapproved; and he suspected him, not without reason, of wishing to supplant him, as he had already supplanted Montmorency. The rest of the Ministry shared his indignation, and Corbière, the Minister of the Interior, went so far as to declare that when Chateaubriand came into the Council Chamber at one door he would go out at the other. Villèle, accordingly, confident in the support of the Cabinet, went to the king, and advised him to dismiss the Foreign Minister, representing that it was impossible for him to work in conjunction with so untrustworthy a colleague.

The king, who had always detested Chateaubriand, and had only consented to his inclusion in the Ministry after much pressure, was only too glad of an excuse to get rid of him; and Villèle took care that the royal command should be communicated to his colleague in a manner which should give an additional sting to his disgrace.

An accidental circumstance served to still further embitter Chateaubriand's dismissal. On June 6 (Whit Sunday) he presented himself at the Tuileries to pay his respects to the Comte d'Artois. The previous evening he had attended a meeting of the Cabinet, where his opinion on the matters under discussion had been invited and listened to with the usual deference; and he had received no indication, either by word or look, of the intention of his colleagues to get rid of him. Now, however, while awaiting the prince's pleasure, he noticed that his presence seemed to arouse an unusual amount of interest, and that the courtiers who came and went regarded him with surprise, and exchanged significant glances with one another. Presently an usher approached, and whispered that a gentleman wished to speak to him; and, going into the Hall of the Marshals, he found his private secretary, Hyacinth Pilorge, who handed him a packet, saying, as he did so, "Monsieur is no longer Minister." The packet, it appeared, had been sent to the Foreign Minister's hôtel, but Chateaubriand had not been there that morning, and, in his absence, it had been opened by the Duc de Lauzun, one of the Foreign Office officials. The contents of the packet were as follows:

"MONSIEUR LE VICOMTE,—I obey the orders of the King in transmitting instantly to your Excellency an ordinance which His Majesty has just issued.

"I have the honour to be, &c.

"(Signed) J. DE VILLÈLE.

"*The President of the Council of Ministers.*

"The Sieur Vicomte de Villèle, President of our Council of Ministers, and Secretary of State for the Department of Finance, is charged *par intérim* with the portfolio of Foreign Affairs in the place of the Sieur Vicomte de Chateaubriand.

"The President of our Council of Ministers is charged with the execution of the present ordinance, which shall be inserted in the bulletin of the laws.

"Given at Paris, in our Château of the Tuileries, June 6, in the year of grace 1824, and the twenty-ninth of our reign.

"By the King

"(Signed) LOUIS.

"(Signed) J. DE VILLÈLE.

"*The President of the Council of Ministers.*"

The resentment of the man thus insulted was implacable. He vowed that the jealous mediocrities and servile courtiers of which the Ministry was composed should soon learn to appreciate him at his proper value, and should bitterly rue the hour in which they had had the temerity to drive genius into opposition. To this end all his eloquence, all his incomparable polemic energy, was devoted. For four years with voice and pen, in the Chamber and in the Press, he never ceased to assail the Government from which he had been so imprudently expelled. He succeeded in his purpose of overthrowing his enemy Villèle, but his opposition went much further than that, much further, indeed, than he would have allowed it to go could he have foreseen the consequences of his hostility. Chateaubriand had done more than any man in France to bring about the Restoration; he did more than any man to destroy it. From the day he retired from office, followed by all the intelligence of his party, and by the *Journal des Débats* and all the other Royalist organs, save those in the pay of the Government, we may date those divisions in the Legitimist camp which paved the way for that "fortuitous concourse of atoms," which, within the space of a few years, converted an insignificant minority in the Chamber into an overwhelming majority, and brought about the downfall of the dynasty whose position at that moment seemed so impregnable.

CHAPTER XV

Madame Récamier's opinion of Chateaubriand's fall—She sets out for Naples—Charles Lenormant—Winter in Rome—Madame Swetchine—The bas-relief of Eudorus and Cymodocea—Madame Récamier starts for France—Visit to Canova's native village—Visit to Caroline Murat at Trieste—Harsh treatment of the ex-queen by the Powers—Madame Récamier returns to Paris—Renewal of her friendly relations with Chateaubriand—Marriage of Amélie de Cyvoct—Mathieu de Montmorency is elected to the Academy—And is appointed Governor to the Duc de Bordeaux—His sudden death—His noble character—His widow's letters to Madame Récamier

MADAME RÉCAMIER had not heard from Chateaubriand for some weeks, he having, as we have said, taken umbrage at her continued absence from Paris; and it was a letter from Mathieu de Montmorency which first acquainted her with the change in the political fortunes of her ambitious friend.

Montmorency, who was strongly opposed to Villèle's revenue bill, had forgotten the differences between himself and the fallen Minister, and expressed his generous approbation of Chateaubriand's conduct. "His behaviour," he says, "is simple, noble, and courageous. He has just come into the Chamber, where I am writing, to resume his old place."

The Duc de Laval, however, who had returned to Paris

on leave of absence, took a very different view of the matter, and wrote to her deploring the violence with which Chateaubriand was assailing his former colleagues, and pointing out how seriously he was injuring his political prospects by adopting such a course; while the old Duc de Doudeauville, who was a supporter of Villèle, echoed his complaints, and suggested that if Madame Récamier could see her way to return to Paris at this juncture, "she might be of infinite service in softening these asperities."

Madame Récamier fully shared Chateaubriand's indignation at the insulting character of his dismissal: but she could not help agreeing with the Duc de Laval that it would have been more dignified and more in keeping with his reputation and his interests to have remained silent; and she felt that in this respect his conduct compared very unfavourably with that of Mathieu de Montmorency under somewhat similar circumstances. It was thought probable that the latter would return to his old place in the Cabinet; but his dislike to the revenue bill proved an insurmountable obstacle, and the vacant portfolio was given to the Baron de Damas, who was a great friend of the Duc d'Angoulême, and whose servility to the Court was unimpeachable.

Madame Récamier's regret at Chateaubriand's fall was probably not untinged with a feeling of relief that the principal bar to a renewal of their former friendship had thereby been removed. Now that he was no longer the most prominent figure in his sovereign's councils, and no longer the centre of a sycophantic herd of courtiers and place-hunters, she foresaw that he would soon begin to repent the severance of a connection which had been the chief solace of his life, before the fumes of the incense of flattery had mounted to his brain. She did not, however, on that account decide to hasten her return to Paris, knowing well that the longer she remained away, the greater would be Chateaubriand's need of her companionship and sympathy, and the keener his remorse at having been the cause of her absence.

Towards the end of June, Madame Récamier and her niece, accompanied by Ampère and Ballanche, left Rome for Naples, travelling for the most part by night in order to avoid the heat and the malaria from the Pontine marshes. Brigandage was so rampant in Southern Italy at this time that they deemed it advisable to secure an escort of eighty Austrian soldiers to conduct them along the most dangerous parts of the route; but they reached Naples without any adventures. Once again Madame Récamier established herself on the Chiaja, in rooms which commanded an exquisite view of the blue waters of the sunlit bay and the Island of Capri; but owing to the extreme heat which aggravated a complaint from which she suffered much in later life—insomnia—she passed every night for several weeks in rooms at Capo di Monti on the heights of Naples.

Both Madame Récamier's squires were highly pleased with Naples. Ballanche, upon whose philosophic mind the most beautiful works of art had made but little impression, was lost in admiration at the wonders of Nature among which he now found himself; while young Ampère, to whom this Italian tour was to prove the forerunner of wanderings in many lands, took a keen delight in all he saw, and was the life and soul of the little party. "I do not believe there can be anything more delightful in any place in the world," he writes to his father. "The nights of Greece and the East cannot be more beautiful. We shall go to see Pompeii by one of these delightful nights. The illusion will be more perfect in the ancient city at the hour when the inhabitants may be supposed to have quitted the temples and theatres and to be asleep. I hope to write here, for there is less to be seen than at Rome, and in the long dreamy days on the seashore the waves will bring me many a verse."[1]

Madame Récamier's niece, Amélie de Cyvoct, also carried away pleasant recollections of the syren city, for it was here that she met Charles Lenormant, a young antiquary and one of Champollion's favourite pupils, who subsequently became her husband. Under his guidance Madame Récamier and her friends made many expeditions, taking special pleasure in visiting the scenes mentioned by Chateaubriand and Madame de Staël in their writings.

Madame Récamier returned to Rome at the end of November. She had hoped that Mathieu de Montmorency would have joined her there; but the illness of his aged mother prevented him leaving Paris. She did not lack friends, however, as the approach of the Jubilee brought many visitors to the Eternal City, including Mathieu's relatives, the Baron and Baronne de Montmorency, the Duc and Duchesse de Noailles, and Madame de Nesselrode, the wife of the Russian Foreign Minister. She also made the acquaintance of the celebrated Madame Swetchine, who appears to have come to Rome, imbued with some prejudices against Madame Récamier. These, however, vanished at their first meeting; and she soon became as much attached to her as Madame de Krüdener had been. "I was a captive before I thought of defending myself," she writes to her. "I yielded at once to that irresistible,

[1] Hamerton's "Modern Frenchmen," p. 273.

indefinable charm to which you subject even those in whom you take no interest."

During the winter, Madame Récamier passed a good deal of her time in the *atelier* of the sculptor Tenerani, whom she had commissioned to execute a bas-relief to perpetuate one of Chateaubriand's finest creations, the martyrdom of Eudorus and Cymodocea. This work was completed in 1828, when the author of *Les Martyrs* himself was ambassador at Rome, and was greatly admired. It is now in the museum at St. Malo—Chateaubriand's birthplace—to which it was bequeathed by Madame Récamier.

After Easter, Madame Récamier and her party commenced their homeward journey. On their way they stopped for a week in Venice, and then left for Bassano to meet the Abbé Canova, who had promised to conduct them to Possagno, his famous brother's native village, where a magnificent church, for the erection of which the sculptor had bequeathed the greater part of his fortune, was being built. This church had been intended by Canova for the reception of a colossal statue of Religion, on which he was working at the time of his death, and he had expressed a wish to be buried there The sculptor had been passionately attached to his native village. Every autumn it had been his custom to spend some time there, and give a sumptuous feast to the workmen engaged upon the building of the church. On one of these occasions, it is said, he caused all the peasant girls of the neighbouring hamlets to pass in review before him, and to each he made a present, expending in this way over ten thousand lira.

The abbé took Madame Récamier to see the little church, where his brother's remains lay pending the completion of the new building. It was a bare little place, the only ornament being a magnificent whole-length portrait of the deceased sculptor above the high altar. After the new church was finished the Abbé Canova was created Bishop of Myndus by Pope Gregory XVI.

From Bassano, Madame Récamier journeyed to Trieste to visit her old friend Caroline Murat, ex-Queen of Naples, who was living there under the title of Comtesse de Lipona, an anagram on the name of the beautiful city where she had once reigned. After the judicial murder of her husband in 1815, the ex-queen had retired to a country house in the neighbourhood of Vienna, where for some years she devoted herself to the education of her children. She had wished to join her mother and brothers at Rome, but permission to do so had been refused by the Powers, who considered that it was too near Naples, where the perjured tyrant Ferdinand was only able to keep his throne through the help of Austrian bayonets. They had lately, however, consented to her going as near Italy as Trieste.

Madame Récamier received a very warm welcome from Madame Murat, whom she had not seen for eleven years. The ex-queen was still very handsome, though she had grown somewhat stout, while her manners were as charming as ever. She complained bitterly of the irritating restrictions imposed upon her by the Powers, who seemed to have shared the high opinion of her statecraft which Talleyrand had once expressed, and to have regarded her as the most dangerous of all the exiled family. She was not allowed to live in Italy, the Low Countries, or Switzerland, while France was of course closed to her; nor was she permitted to remain in one place for more than a certain length of time. To add to her troubles, King Ferdinand had on landing seized all her private property at Naples, while the Bourbons had sequestrated that in France, including the estate at Neuilly which Napoleon had given her. In consequence she was now in somewhat straitened circumstances, and her two sons had been forced to seek their fortunes in America. The elder of these, Louis, who settled in Florida, married a grand-niece of Washington, and wrote several commendable books about America and her institutions. He died in 1847. The younger, Lucien, returned to France the year after his brother's death, was elected to the Chamber of Deputies, and supported the policy of his cousin Louis Napoleon. When King Bomba was driven out of Naples by his enraged subjects, Lucien Murat issued a manifesto; but the time had not yet come for delivering Italy from the Bourbon and Austrian yoke, and the French Government declined to support his claims.

Madame Récamier only remained a few days at Trieste, as she was tired of her wandering life, and then, taking an affectionate farewell of her good-natured friend, resumed her journey to Paris, where she arrived on May 3, after an absence of eighteen months. While at Naples she had received the news of the death of Louis XVIII. and the accession of Charles X., events which Chateaubriand had celebrated by the publication of his rather extravagant brochure, *Le Roi est mort! Vive le Roi!* The new monarch shared his predecessor's dislike to the great writer, but it was not as yet so pronounced; and on her arrival Madame Récamier found that Chateaubriand was at Rheims attending the coronation. Mathieu de Montmorency was also absent on the same errand, but wrote, begging her to let him know the result of her first interview with "the melancholy René."

The faithful Mathieu might have spared himself any anxiety on that score. The very day on which he returned to Paris, Chateaubriand hastened to the Rue de Sèvres. No word of explanation or of reproach passed between them; but Madame Récamier's womanly instinct told her at once that it was the friend of the early days at the Abbaye-au-Bois who now stood before her—the friend who had been all the world to her before the intoxication of political success, and the adulation of those who are ever ready to bow down to it, had interrupted the companionship which had been so pleasant to them both; and she rejoiced that her self-imposed exile had not been in vain. All the little misunderstandings, the querulous demands on her time and attention, and the capricious and temporary neglect which had sometimes fallen to her lot, were now at an end. It was, indeed, a keen delight to her to find Chateaubriand resuming his old habits—the morning note, the afternoon call, the hundred and one little kindnesses and attentions which she had come to value so much and to miss so sorely; to be once more the chosen confidante of all his hopes and fears, his triumphs and his defeats, and to feel that her friendship was even more necessary to his happiness than his was to hers.

It was through Chateaubriand's influence that, a few weeks after her return to Paris, Charles Lenormant, the young antiquary, to whom her niece was betrothed, received the appointment of Inspector of Fine Arts, a post which carried with it a considerable salary, and enabled the marriage to take place during the ensuing winter. Madame Récamier, however, was spared the pain of a separation from her adopted daughter, as the latter's husband took a house close to the Abbaye-au-Bois, and she was thus able to spend a good deal of her time with her aunt, and dine with her every day.

In November of that year Mathieu de Montmorency was elected a member of the Academy, a choice which caused general astonishment—for the duke, greatly as he was esteemed, had no literary pretensions whatever—and was mainly attributed to the influence of "*la Circé de l'Abbaye-au-Bois.*" "We owe thanks to Madame Récamier," says Rondelet, "for having witnessed the Academie Française return so appropriately to that ancient tradition of good society, in which a great name passed as a serious reason for competition." Montmorency was, it may be observed, one of the last of the great noblemen to be admitted to the Academy, to give that institution "a perfume of the lady's chamber," as Ballanche expressed it; and, perhaps, it was just as well for its reputation as an intellectual centre that a time was not far distant when the claims of literature were to be the only ones to receive recognition at its hands.

A few weeks later Montmorency was the recipient of another and far more deserved distinction, being appointed to preside over the education of the young Duc de Bordeaux, a selection which was universally applauded. He was not, however, destined to enjoy this honour long. Since leaving the Ministry he had redoubled his religious exercises and mortifications of the flesh, with the result that his health had suffered. On Good Friday, while kneeling at prayer between his wife and daughter in the Church of St. Thomas d'Aquin, he suddenly fainted. He was carried into the vestry, and from there home to the Hôtel de Luynes; but had scarcely strength to receive the sacrament ere he expired.

Mathieu de Montmorency was a nobleman in the

highest sense of the word. The sincerity of his religious convictions in his later years was beyond dispute, his honour unimpeachable, and his charity boundless; while it was his constant endeavour to influence for good the frivolous society among which his lot was cast. His devotion to Madame Récamier was beyond all praise; and it is, perhaps, not too much to say that it was in a great measure owing to his unceasing vigilance that the somewhat pronounced flirtations in which she indulged in early life never developed into anything worse.

Probably no more eloquent tribute could have been paid to the wonderful fascination which Madame Récamier exercised over men and women alike, and the unexceptionable character of her friendships, than the fact that Mathieu de Montmorency's wife, like Madame de Chateaubriand, had permitted herself to be relegated to a secondary place in her husband's affections, in spite of the fact that she was passionately devoted to him.

"I only propose coming to Paris to mingle my tears with Adrien's,"[1] she writes, shortly after the duke's death. "I shall at least make an effort to see you (do not doubt it), but not at your residence. I am afraid I should not have sufficient courage to mount those stairs of which he has spoken to me so often. He was always in such haste to see you! He loved you so much. Ah, madame! make still greater efforts to join in Heaven him who has so well deserved to enter at once into that blissful state." In another: "You are so kind to me; he loved you so much; and you also loved him. Such claims appeal direct to the place where my heart was—that broken heart which beat only for him. I know not if I still have one; yet, when I think of you, I believe I have."

[1] Adrien de Montmorency, Duc de Laval.

A little later the widowed duchess sent to Madame Récamier a packet containing the letters which she had received at various times from her husband, as to one who had a better right to these precious mementos of the dead than herself.

CHAPTER XVI

Fall of Villèle—He is succeeded by Martignac—Ministry of Public Instruction offered to Chateaubriand—He refuses it, and demands an embassy—He is sent to the Vatican—The King and the *Journal des Débats*—Chateaubriand's letters from Rome—First impressions—A little *ricevimento*—His opinion of English women—The tomb of Poussin—A New Year's greeting—An Ambassador's day—An odd stranger—A children's fête—Death of Leo XII.—A Pope's funeral—Political confidences—Election of Pius IX.—A service in the Sixtine Chapel—An Ambassador's expenditure—Chateaubriand returns to Paris

TOWARDS the end of the following year came the downfall of Villèle, for which Chateaubriand and his friends had so long been working. Since the death of Louis XVIII. Villèle had occupied a most equivocal position, retaining his post only at the price of compliance with the Court, now entirely in the hands of clerical reactionaries, which had compelled him to lend the authority of his name to measures which his own judgment condemned. In the autumn of 1827 Charles X., believing his Ministers to be stronger in the country than in the Chambers, exercised his prerogative of dissolution, with the result that the Government was completely defeated, and the Opposition in the new Chamber outnumbered the partisans of the Court by more than three to one.

Villèle had now perforce to resign, and although the

king was at first unwilling to choose his successor from the majority in the Chamber, and even thought for a time of violent resistance, more prudent counsels eventually prevailed; and he, accordingly, sent for the Vicomte de Martignac, a member of the right centre, and the representative of a policy of moderate reform, and directed him to form a Ministry. Martignac urged that it would be advisable to buy off the hostility of Chateaubriand by including him in the new Cabinet; and, much against the king's wish, offered him the Ministry of Public Instruction.

This post Chateaubriand was at first inclined to accept; but his friends declared such a subordinate office to be beneath his dignity, and urged him to wait for a chance of obtaining the controlling voice in the Council, which, as Martignac's Ministry was generally regarded as only a stop-gap one, and unlikely to satisfy either party, would not be long in coming. In the meantime, as he had been far more attentive to fame than to fortune and was in embarrassed circumstances, they suggested that he should apply for the first vacant embassy.

The king and Martignac, who felt that there could be no peace so long as this stormy petrel of politics remained in Paris, eagerly caught at the idea, and Vienna was offered him. Chateaubriand, however, had set his heart on the Vatican, where the salary was munificent, the society congenial, and the duties comparatively light; and nothing less would tempt him to leave France. Unfortunately, the Duc de Laval, who had filled that post for some years to his own and every one else's satisfaction, was by no means disposed to surrender it, least of all to a man of whose public conduct he so strongly disapproved; and the Government dared not go so far as to recall him. Thus once again Madame Récamier found herself placed between the opposing interests of two of her friends. She succeeded, however, in pouring oil on the troubled waters; and, for the sake of his "dear, ever dearest," the haughty head of the Montmorencies eventually consented to leave Rome, and betake himself to Vienna, the climate and inhabitants of which he cordially detested.

The way was now cleared for Chateaubriand, and he, accordingly, prepared to set out for Italy. But before he did so his friends in the Chamber insisted that the Government should pay his debts. This request the new Ministers were afraid to refuse; but, as the first sum given was insufficient, and Chateaubriand still lingered in Paris, the king, in order to relieve them from the presence of so dangerous a competitor, made up the deficiency from his own privy purse.

This, it may be remarked, was not the only sum which the luckless monarch was called upon to disburse at this juncture, in order to buy off the hostility of Chateaubriand and his triumphant followers. At the beginning of his ministry in 1823, Villèle had subsidised the *Journal des Débats*—a journal which, as Lamartine ingenuously observes, "did not sell itself, but condescended to receive subsidies, which, without corrupting its opinions, remunerated its zeal and its services." When, however, Chateaubriand was so ignominiously dismissed from office, the *Débats* immediately repudiated its subsidy, in order that it might be free to further the vengeance of its most brilliant contributor. The king and Martignac were fully alive to the importance of securing the support —or, at any rate, the neutrality—of so powerful an organ of public opinion; and the former, accordingly, sent for Bertin, one of the proprietors of the newspaper, and begged him to be reconciled to the new Ministry.

"This Ministry!" exclaimed this Napoleon of the Press, contemptuously. "It is I who made this Ministry. Let it conduct itself properly towards me, or else I may crush it as I did the last one."

The king was naturally much incensed at this boastful speech, but he dissembled his anger; and it was ultimately agreed that the Ministry might count on the support of the *Débats* provided that the subsidy was continued, and what Bertin called his "arrears"—that is to say, the amount that he would have received but for the defection of his newspaper in 1824—were paid. There were not sufficient funds in the Ministerial chest to satisfy this demand, which amounted to no less a sum than half a million francs, so Charles had again to dip pretty freely into his privy purse.

The king afterwards asserted that a considerable portion of this so-called subsidy found its way into Chateaubriand's pockets; but it is only fair to the latter to observe that this charge has never been corroborated, and, indeed, seems in the highest degree improbable.

Chateaubriand remained at Rome until the following May, during which he kept up a regular correspondence with his friend at the Abbaye-au-Bois. His letters are extremely interesting, if only for the light that they throw upon the singularly complex character of the great writer.

VICOMTE DE CHATEAUBRIAND *to* MADAME RÉCAMIER.

"ROME, *October* 11, 1828.

"You ought to be satisfied. From every place in Italy at which I stopped I have written to you. I have traversed this beautiful country, so associated with you. This association consoled me, without taking away the sadness of other recollections, which I met with at every step. Once again I have looked upon the Adriatic, which I crossed more than twenty years ago, and in such a frame of mind. At Terni I stopped to console a poor dying woman. Rome finds me without any enthusiasm. As I feared, her monuments appear to me coarse after those of Athens. My memory for places, which is both astonishing and painful, will not allow me to forget a single stone. Alone and on foot I have traversed this great city of ruins, without any longing save that of leaving it, with no thought save that of returning once more to the Abbaye and the Rue d'Enfer.

"I have seen no one except the Secretary of State. I am going to have an audience of the Pope. Yesterday evening, at sunset, in order to find some one to talk to, I sought out Guérin.[1] He was delighted to see me. We opened a window which commanded a view of Rome, and together admired the romantic horizon lit up by the last rays of the sun, which seems to me to be the only thing which is the same as it used to be. Either my eyes, or the things themselves, have changed, perhaps both. Poor Guérin, who detests Rome, was so delighted to find that I sympathised with his feelings, that he almost cried. Now you have my exact history.

"Madame de Chateaubriand is no better. Left to herself in a great house, with not even a cat to say to her, 'God bless you!' where she finds everything in this bachelor's establishment arranged in the most ridiculous

[1] Pierre Guérin, the historical painter, at that time director of the French Academy of Painting at Rome. Among his pupils were Géricault, Delacroix, and Ary Scheffer.

manner (*boudoirs in the English style* in a Roman palace !), she bewails the day when she decided to come here. Perhaps she will take more kindly to her new situations when she begins to receive visitors. I do not doubt that she will have a real success ; but her health will always be an obstacle to a society life. Now you have the whole truth.

"For the rest, I have been most cordially welcomed by all the authorities on the journey—at Bologna, Ancona, and Loretto. They quite understood that I was not an ordinary man, but scarcely knew the reason why. Was he a friend ? Was he an enemy ? In Egypt, the politicians and the educated people took me for one of Bonaparte's great generals, disguised as a savant.

"The end of all this is that you must come immediately to my relief, or I shall very soon come back to you. I have not received a single word from you, save a line at Lausanne—nothing at Milan ; nothing at Rome. The post arrives this morning. Will there be anything for me ?"

VICOMTE DE CHATEAUBRIAND *to* MADAME RÉCAMIER.

"*October* 14, 1828.

"Still no letter from you by yesterday's courier. Can it be possible that you have not written to me ? In that case you are carrying your resentment too far. Can any accident have happened to your letters ? I will not repeat to you what I have already said in all of mine. From them, you will understand the state of my mind and heart. Come quickly, or find means to recall me speedily.

"I have seen the Pope ! He is the handsomest prince and the most venerable priest in the world. We had a long conversation. He is full of nobility and gentleness, and a thorough man of the world. I am enchanted with him. The Secretary of State is a very able man. All along the route I was overwhelmed with honours; and I have been remarkably well received here. . . .

"As to society, I know nothing at all about it. I pay my visits by leaving cards. M. de Celles,[1] a very able diplomatist and a most charming man, is the only person I have seen as yet. Come then, I beg of you. Come quickly, and write. Madame de Chateaubriand is not at all well. I foresee that she is about to achieve that social success which you have predicted for her. His Holiness has spoken to me about her. I suppose that you are the only one in Paris who gives a thought to me."

VICOMTE DE CHATEAUBRIAND *to* MADAME RÉCAMIER.

"*November* 5, 1828.

"We had yesterday, so the secretaries say, a very delightful day. Not a member of the Corps Diplomatique was missing from San Carlo, and, what has never been seen before, the Pope himself came. I had Davidde for the singing, so, of course, the church was full.

"In the evening we had a little *ricevimento*—regarded as quite a French affair, because I have absolutely nothing in readiness for receiving people; but all the great ladies, Roman, Russian, and English, came, and the cardinals and the Prince Royal of Prussia. I tried not to forget any artist, whether French or foreign; and I also had invitations sent to the commercial people, which my predecessors have never done, and which seems to have been much appreciated by them. There was a little music. I had Davidde and Madame Boccabadati—that is to say, the best

[1] The Netherlands Ambassador.

talent that could be procured, for I have borne in mind what you said about poor singing. . . . So I think my first reception has been a success; and I hope it will be the last; for you were not there.

"What am I doing here? I can, no doubt, go through with this life of outward display as well as any one else; but is it the life for which I am most fitted? Have I nothing better to do in this world? If I have any ability, is it not a pity that it is not directed into some channel where it might be of greater service to my country? or rather, why does not Time pension me off? I am only one of his old pensioners, who will soon cease to be a charge on his treasury."

VICOMTE DE CHATEAUBRIAND *to* MADAME RÉCAMIER.

"*November* 15, 1828.

"As soon as Madame Salvage arrived, I hastened with Madame de Chateaubriand to call upon her, in order to hear about you, and to see some one who has *seen* you. . . . The Torlonias have given their first ball. I met all the English to be found in the world there. I imagined myself again Ambassador in London. English women have the air of ballet-girls engaged to dance for the winter at Paris, Milan, Rome, and Naples; and who return to London in the spring, after their engagement expires. The skippings of people on the ruins of the Capitol and the general manners of *good* society everywhere, are very strange things. If only I had still the chance of taking refuge among the ruins of Rome! But these ruins appeal to me no longer, and I only pass from *ennui* to *ennui*.

"Shall I have a letter to-day? I almost expect one. You see how faithful I am in writing to you. . . . When shall I be in my Infirmary[1] again? and when shall I see you every day?"

VICOMTE DE CHATEAUBRIAND *to* MADAME RÉCAMIER

"*November* 20th, 1828.

"I have at last received a letter from you, dated the 3rd of this month, by a courier who has been delayed. Imagine what happiness! but, at the same time, what disappointment! A special courier reached me the same day from the Foreign Office, bringing despatches of the 10th; and nothing from you! Remember that a courier now leaves every week from the Rue des Capucines, and that this courier does the journey in seven days. The worthy Henri Hildebrand will come to give you notice, and take your instructions. When you have only time to send by him these two lines, 'I am well, and I love you,' that will satisfy me; it being understood that you are not to neglect the ordinary post."

VICOMTE DE CHATEAUBRIAND *to* MADAME RÉCAMIER.

"*December* 18, 1828.

"... Alas! almost another year has passed over my head. When shall I find rest by your side? When shall I cease to waste upon the highways those days lent me to put to a better use? When I was rich I squandered them recklessly; I thought the treasure inexhaustible. Now, when I see how much it has diminished, and how little time there is left for me in which to love you, my heart is very heavy.

"But are there not long years beyond the grave? Had I but the philosophy of Cousin, I should describe to you that Heaven in which I shall await you, in which you

[1] His asylum for aged people at St. Genevieve.

will meet me once more, full of grace, beauty, and youth. Poor and humble Christian that I am, I tremble before *The Last Judgment* of Michael Angelo. I know not where my future abode will be, but if it is to be where you are not, I shall be most miserable.

"I have told you a hundred times of my projects, and of all my plans for the future—the Rue d'Enfer near you; this is the only New Year's wish that I express on my own behalf. Ruins, years, health, loss of every illusion—all say to me, 'Go away; retire; have done with it all. . . .'

"It was your wish that I should do something to mark my stay in Rome. It is done; the tomb of Poussin will remain; it will bear this inscription: '*F. A. de Ch. à Nicolas Poussin, pour la gloire des arts et l'honneur de la France.*' What is there for me to do here now? Nothing; especially after having subscribed the sum of one hundred ducats to the monument of the man you love the most—after me—Tasso."

VICOMTE DE CHATEAUBRIAND *to* MADAME RÉCAMIER.

"*January* 1, 1829.

"1829! I was awake, and thought sadly and tenderly of you, when my watch pointed to midnight. We ought to feel ourselves less heavily burdened as Time carries away our years; but it is just the contrary; that which he relieves us of is a weight with which he overwhelms us. May happiness and long life be yours. Never forget me, even when I am no more. I shall go to await your coming. Perhaps I shall have more patience in the other life than in this one, when I find three months without seeing you of immeasurable length.

"I received this morning all the French people in

Rome. Madame Salvage dines, for the first time, at the Embassy. I like that woman, because she talks to me about you. I have also made a friend of Visconti, because he always asks me when you are coming. . . . A happy New Year! It will be happy, since in a few months I shall be with you."

VICOMTE DE CHATEAUBRIAND *to* MADAME RÉCAMIER.

"*January* 3, 1829.

"I renew my wishes for a happy New Year. May Heaven grant you health and a long life. Love me above all, and do not forget me when I shall be no more. I have good hope of that, for you have never forgotten M. de Montmorency and Madame de Staël. Your memory is as good as your heart. I told Madame Salvage yesterday that I knew no one in the world so beautiful or so good as you.

"I spent an hour yesterday with the Pope. We talked of all manner of things, including the highest and most important matters. He is a most accomplished and enlightened man, and a prince full of dignity and grace. To complete my political life, one thing only was needed —relations with the Sovereign Pontiff; that crowns my career.

"Would you care to know how I pass my day, and exactly what I do? I rise at half-past six; I breakfast at half-past seven on a cup of chocolate, in Madame de Chateaubriand's room; at eight, return to my study; write to you or attend to business, when there is any— the details for the French establishment and the poor French are quite numerous. At noon, I dress; at one, o'clock I take a large cup of asses' milk, which does me infinite good; afterwards, I walk for two hours in the

Campagna with Hyacinth.[1] Occasionally I pay a formal visit, either before or after my walk. At four o'clock, I return home, and dress for dinner, which is at five o'clock. At half-past seven, I go to a party with Madame de Chateaubriand, or I receive a few friends at home. Between ten and eleven, I go to bed, and always think of you. The Romans are by this time so used to my 'methodical' life that I serve them for a timepiece, as I served your neighbours at the Abbaye. Now, is it not true that I am a very tiresome sort of person, and very different from the Duc de Laval?[2] Never have there been so many strangers in Rome as this year. Last Tuesday, the whole world seemed to be in my salon."

VICOMTE DE CHATEAUBRIAND *to* MADAME RÉCAMIER.

"*January* 8, 1829.

"I must tell you a little story of my last 'Tuesday.' There was an immense crowd at the Embassy. I was leaning against a marble table, bowing to the people who came and went. An English lady, whose name and face were quite strange to me, approached, looked me full in the face, and said, with that accent which you know so well, 'Monsieur de Chateaubriand, you are very unhappy!' Astonished at such a speech, and such a strange way of beginning a conversation, I inquired what she meant. She replied, 'I mean that I pity you.' So saying, she took the arm of another English lady, and disappeared in the crowd; and I did not see her again the rest of the evening. Do not be alarmed. This odd stranger was neither young nor pretty. I was pleased with her, nevertheless, for those

[1] Hyacinth Pilorge, his private secretary.

[2] His predecessor at the Vatican.

mysterious words, which were in harmony with my state of mind, and with what I have written to you.

"No courier has arrived to-day. This frequently happens, now that the rivers and streams have overflowed. Bear this in mind, and do not be uneasy if my letters are delayed. Only, you will be fifteen days without receiving any, and then get five or six at once. On Saturday!"

VICOMTE DE CHATEAUBRIAND *to* MADAME RÉCAMIER.

"*January* 13, 1829.

". . . I have a little story to tell you. You know the poor ladies of St. Denis; they have been to a great extent overlooked since the arrival of the great ladies of the Trinità de' Monti. Without objecting to the latter, I have ranged myself, along with Madame de Chateaubriand, on the side of the weak. For the last month, the ladies of St. Denis have been anxious to give a fête in honour of *M. l'ambassadeur* and *Madame l'ambassadrice;* it took place yesterday, at one o'clock.

"Picture to yourself a theatre, arranged in a kind of sacristy, the stage facing the church; for performers, a dozen little girls from eight to fourteen years old, playing *Les Machabées.* They had made their helmets and their robes themselves. They declaimed their French verses with a spirit and an Italian accent which was the funniest thing in the world, and stamped their feet vigorously in the more sensational scenes. Among them was a niece of Pius VII., a daughter of Thorwaldsen, and one of Chauvin, the painter. They were wonderfully pretty in their paper costumes. The one who played the part of the high priest, wore a long black beard, which was both a delight and a plague to her, as she had to keep on arranging it with her little white thirteen-year-old hand.

"For spectators, there were ourselves, a few mothers, the nuns, Madame Salvage, two or three abbés, and another score of little boarders, all in white, with veils. We had cakes and ices brought from the Embassy. Some one played the piano between the acts. Just imagine the delightful anticipations this fête must have aroused in the convent, and the recollections which will follow it. The finale consisted of a *Vivat in æternum*, sung by three nuns in the church. It is for you that I would like to live for ever. I must close. You must be tired of my letters and my insipidities.

"I have seen in the papers an account of my dinner with Guérin, and the history of our monument to Poussin. Adieu until Thursday!"

VICOMTE DE CHATEAUBRIAND *to* MADAME RÉCAMIER.

"ROME, *January* 20, 1829.

"My attention has been called to two articles in the papers—one in the *Quotidienne*, the other in the *Gazette*. The first says that I have become a Jesuit; the second insists that I am coming back to France—and that I have written to that effect—to make an 18th Brumaire. That makes me laugh, and proves, at least, that people concern themselves about me. You know that on principle I never reply to the papers.

"Concerts are now all the fashion in Rome; soon we shall have balls. When all these calamities are over, Lent will follow, and then Easter, which will bring me back to you. I live only in this hope; it helps me to bear the burden of the days, very heavy indeed as far as I am concerned.

"Above all things, take care of your health. Live

long, long years, that there may be some one in the world to remember me."

VICOMTE DE CHATEAUBRIAND *to* MADAME RÉCAMIER.

"*Monday Evening, February* 9, 1829.

"The Pope is very ill. I am sending off a special courier to Lyons, to transmit a telegraphic despatch to the Government. These two lines will be posted at Lyons. I received this morning your letter of the 27th."

VICOMTE DE CHATEAUBRIAND *to* MADAME RÉCAMIER.

"*February* 10, 9 A.M.

"The Pope has just expired. Is it not strange that Pius VII. should have died while I was Minister for Foreign Affairs, and that Leo XII. should die while I am Ambassador at Rome? Now my position is again changed for the moment; and my rôle becomes one of importance. The death of the Pontiff is an immense loss to moderate men. . . .

"This evening an attaché will leave with a long letter for you."

VICOMTE DE CHATEAUBRIAND *to* MADAME RÉCAMIER.

"*February* 10, 11 P.M.

" . . . What do you think they found the poor Pope doing last Thursday, before he was taken ill? Writing his own epitaph! When they tried to divert him from these gloomy thoughts, he said, 'No, no; it will be over in a few days.'

"Madame de Chateaubriand is quite ill, and has been in bed for three days. All the Carnival pleasures are over, thank God. No more dinners, balls, &c. The

English are leaving, and are going to dance at Naples and Florence.

"I am going to have a multitude of couriers. I shall take advantage of them, and you must do the same.

"I beg you will send for Bertin [1] and read him some portions of this letter. Recommend him to praise the Pope and Bernetti.[2] They could not have been more tolerant or more moderate."

VICOMTE DE CHATEAUBRIAND *to* MADAME RÉCAMIER.

"*February* 17, 1829.

"The Conclave, taking all things into consideration, cannot last more than three months, and probably will be much shorter. . . . Will it change all my political destiny?

"My mission, no doubt, increases my political importance every day; but will it not furnish a pretext for completing the Ministry, without ascertaining whether it is agreeable to me, and giving me any Minister they please—sure, as they will be then, that I shall not give in my resignation during a Conclave, and that my duty will compel me to remain at my post, even though boiling with rage?[3] But will they gain by that? Shall I not tender my resignation the day after the election of the Pope; and, after having rendered some important service in preventing the election of an Austrian or fanatical Pope, shall I not stand higher in public estimation?

"Madame de Chateaubriand is more stormy than ever

[1] The editor and proprietor of the *Journal des Débats*.

[2] Cardinal Bernetti, Secretary of State to Leo XII.

[3] La Ferronnays, the Minister for Foreign Affairs in the Martignac Ministry, had just resigned. Chateaubriand, of course, hoped that the vacant portfolio would be offered to himself.

To-day there is trouble with the servants, and that in the midst of my despatches, the death of the Pope, and Paris political intrigues.

"I was present at the first funeral ceremony for the Pope, at St. Peter's. It was a strange mixture of indecorum and grandeur. Singing, interspersed with the blows of the hammer that was nailing up the coffin of a Pope; the light of torches, mingling with the light of the moon; the coffin, finally, raised by a pulley, and suspended in the darkness, in order to place it above a door in the sarcophagus of Pius VII., whose ashes give place to those of Leo XII. Picture to yourself all this, and the ideas such a scene suggests.

" . . . They have just brought me the poor Pope's cat. He is entirely grey, and as gentle as his old master."

VICOMTE DE CHATEAUBRIAND *to* MADAME RÉCAMIER.

"*February* 23, 1829.

"I am writing to tell you that the obsequies of the Pope were concluded yesterday. The paper pyramid and the four sconces were really beautiful, and reached to the cornice of the church. The last *Dies Irae* were admirable. Its composer is an unknown man, attached to the Pope's chapel. To-day we pass from sorrow to joy. We chant the *Veni Creator* for the opening of the Conclave, which takes place this evening; then we shall go every evening to see whether the votes are burned, and whether the smoke issues from a certain stove: and on the day when there is no smoke, the Pope will be elected, and I shall start to join you—which is at the bottom of all my plans.

"Pay attention to what I am going to tell you. If by chance I am offered the portfolio of Foreign Affairs—which I do not at all believe—*I shall not refuse it.* I should go to Paris; I should speak to the king, and *arrange* a Ministry of which I *should not be one;* but, in order to attach my name to my work, I should make a proposition which would be agreeable to you. I think—and you understand my feelings—that it is necessary for my *Ministerial* honour, and to wipe away the stain that Villèle put upon me, that the portfolio of Foreign Affairs should be given me for a time. It is the only honourable way in which I can return to the Administration. That done, I withdraw at once, to the great satisfaction of all candidates, and pass the rest of my days in peace with you."

VICOMTE DE CHATEAUBRIAND *to* MADAME RÉCAMIER.

"*March* 31, 1829.

"Victory at last! After a sharp tussle, I have one of the Popes on my list—Cardinal Castiglioni, under the name of Pius IX.—the same cardinal whom I supported for the Papacy in 1823, when I was Minister, and the one who replied to me recently, and praised me so highly. Castiglioni is moderate, anti-Jesuit, favourable to the Ordinances, and entirely devoted to France. It is, in short, a complete triumph.

"A few lines, that I am going to have dropped into the post at Lyons, tells all this to Bertin;[1] but send for him in case, by any chance, these lines should not reach him, for it is necessary to take every precaution. Please send also for the excellent Kératry on behalf of the *Courrier*. Give him the information. It will be acceptable to him, and useful to me.

"I am certain that the Conclave, before separating, has ordered instructions to be sent to the Nuncio in Paris,

[1] Editor and proprietor of the *Débats*.

directing him to express to the king the satisfaction the Sacred College has felt at my conduct. What will the *Gazette* say? What am I going to do now? No matter! I am going to see you; that will be my reward and my happiness.

"Yet after all I have never been so miserable and worried as I have been during the Conclave. Everything was, at first, against me. The French cardinals arrived hostile and resolved not to set foot in the Embassy; I discovered intrigues and odious correspondence; I considered myself thoroughly beaten. Well! the cardinals stayed with me; they voted as I wished them to vote; they chant my praises; so you see what it is to be under the influence of your star."

VICOMTE DE CHATEAUBRIAND *to* MADAME RÉCAMIER.

"*Wednesday, April* 15, 1829.

"I am beginning this letter on the evening of Holy Wednesday, on my return from the Sixtine Chapel, where I have witnessed the *Tenebrae* and heard the *Miserere* chanted. I remembered that you had spoken to me of this beautiful ceremony, and, on that account, I was a hundred times the more moved. It is truly incomparable; that light which dies away by degrees; those shadows which gradually envelop the marvels of Michael Angelo; all the cardinals on their knees; the new Pope prostrated at the foot of the altar where, a little while before, I had seen his predecessor; that glorious chant of suffering and of pity rising at intervals through the silence of the night; the thought of a God dying on the cross to atone for the sins and infirmities of men; Rome and all its memories under the vaults of the Vatican. Would that you could have been there! Even the tapers, whose smothered light permits a white smoke to escape—symbolical of a life suddenly extinguished—appeal to me. What a beautiful place Rome is, wherein to forget and despise everything, and to die!

"Instead of that, the courier to-morrow will bring me letters, papers, anxieties. I shall have to talk to you about politics. When shall I have finished with my future, and have nothing more to do in the world than to love you, and devote to you my last days?"

VICOMTE DE CHATEAUBRIAND *to* MADAME RÉCAMIER.

"*April* 18, 1829.

"The special courier, leaving the day before yesterday, the 16th, carried you a very melancholy letter. I was disheartened by yours. Yesterday, Good Friday, I thought that I was going to die, like your best friend.[1] You would have found, at least, this point of resemblance between us. To-day I am quite well: I cannot understand this state of health. Is it a warning to prepare myself; and is death touching me with the point of his scythe? You will find me greatly changed. I look a hundred years old; and it is a century of love that I lay at your feet."

VICOMTE DE CHATEAUBRIAND *to* MADAME RÉCAMIER.

"*May* 5, 1829.

". . . . I presented this morning my letters of credit to His Holiness. As soon as the courier, whom I have been told to expect, arrives, I shall leave matters to M. Bellocq,[2] and set out for Paris. Perhaps before leaving Italy, I shall show Naples to Madame de Chateaubriand. The mischief all this is that the first year of an ambassador's

[1] Mathieu de Montmorency, who died on Good Friday 1826.

[2] First Secretary of the French Embassy at Rome.

establishment is ruinous ; and the entertainments I have been obliged to give on account of the Conclave, and the presence of the Grand Duchess [Helena of Russia] have ended by ruining me. I shall leave Rome to enter a hospital. Unfortunately, my whole edition is sold, my brain empty, and my health impaired ; but then I have not much farther to travel to reach the end, and there is no necessity to load too heavily an old vessel on the verge of being wrecked.

"I no longer reckon upon your letters, as, most unfortunately, you doubtless believe that I have left. I can hardly get away for another fortnight. All will be forgotten in the happiness of meeting you again, to part no more."

Vicomte de Chateaubriand *to* Madame Récamier.

"Rome, *May* 16, 1829.

"This letter will leave Rome a few hours after I have quitted it, and will arrive a few hours before me in Paris. It closes this correspondence, which has not missed a single courier, and which must form an entire volume in your hands. Your own letters make but a very small packet. My heart misgave me when I tied them up yesterday, and noticed how little room they took up.

"I am experiencing a mingling of joy and sadness, which I cannot express to you. For three or four months I disliked Rome ; now I find myself once more drawn towards these noble ruins, to this profound solitude, so peaceful, and yet, so full of interest and memories. Perhaps, also, the unlooked-for success which I have achieved here has attached me to the place. I arrived here the victim of prejudices which had been stirred up against me, and I have triumphed over them all.

"To what am I returning in France? Noise instead of silence, agitation in place of repose, unreasonableness, ambition, contests for place, and the struggles of vanity. The political system which I have adopted is such as will in all probability please no one; and, moreover, I shall not even have a chance of putting it into execution. I would still undertake the responsibility of giving a great glory to France, as I contributed to obtain for her a great liberty; but will they give me a free hand? Will they say to me, 'Be master, dispose of all, at the peril of your head'? No; they are far from being willing to say such a thing to me; they would take any one in the world in preference to me; they would only admit me, after having been refused by all the mediocrities in France; and think they were conferring a favour on me by consigning me to an obscure corner of an obscure Ministry.

"Dear friend, I am coming for you, to bring you back with me. Whether ambassador or not, it is there that I wish to die near you. I will at least have a great tomb in exchange for a petty life. However, I am going to see you. What happiness!"

VICOMTE DE CHATEAUBRIAND *to* MADAME RÉCAMIER.

"LYONS, *May* 24, 3.30 P.M.

"On Thursday, at last! My heart beats with joy at the thought of seeing you again in your little room. I have a letter for you from the Queen of Holland.[1] On Thursday! I dare not believe in that word. Only eight days ago I saw the Sabina mountains, and now I behold those of the Bourbonnais. From the Tiber to the Rhone—to the Rhone, whose waves you brightened with your childish smiles. On Thursday!"

[1] Queen Hortense.

CHAPTER XVII

Madame Récamier's pleasure at Chateaubriand's return—His interview with the King—Reading of *Moïse* at the Abbaye-au-Bois—An awkward predicament—Chateaubriand goes to the Pyrenees—Formation of the Polignac Ministry—Chateaubriand returns to Paris—The King refuses to see him—Death of Jacques Récamier—Madame Récamier goes to Dieppe—Père Lacordaire—The revolution of July—Madame Récamier returns to Paris—Chateaubriand's position—He is sent for by the Duc and Duchesse d'Orléans—His interview with Louis Philippe—And with the Duchesse d'Orléans—His disinterested conduct—Benjamin Constant supports Louis Philippe—His reward—His anxiety to be elected to the Academy—His proposal to Guizot—His candidature—His letter to Madame Récamier—He is rejected by the Academy—His death—Mary Berry's description of his funeral

Madame Récamier's pleasure at the return of her friend was as great as that of Chateaubriand himself. "M. de Chateaubriand arrived here on Thursday," she writes to her niece. "I have been happy in meeting him again—happier, indeed, than I believed possible. . . . This morning I am expecting M. de Chateaubriand, who has an audience of the king, and is coming to give me a full account of his interview. I see a number of people—M. Villemain, whom I find very agreeable, M. de Sainte-Aulaire, &c. ; but it is M. de Chateaubriand's arrival that gives a new zest to my life, which seemed to be wearing out."

The king received Chateaubriand very graciously; but he asked him rather pointedly when he intended returning to Rome, and allowed him to see that whomsoever he might select to fill the vacant post of Foreign Minister it would certainly not be his representative at the Vatican.

Chateaubriand was, naturally, much mortified at discovering how vain had been his hopes in that direction, for it was one of the peculiarities of the great writer that he never could understand the extent to which he was disliked and distrusted by both Louis XVIII. and Charles X. He was, however, in doubt as to which course it would be advisable for him to pursue, whether to return to Rome, or resign his post there and resume his place in the Chamber. At length he decided to go to the Pyrenees to recruit his health and await the development of events, now fast hastening to a crisis.

Shortly before Chateaubriand went to Rome he had completed a tragedy called *Moïse*, which he had been exceedingly anxious to see upon the stage. Bertin, of the *Journal des Débats*, and other members of his party, however, had begged him for political reasons not to allow it to be produced, and he had yielded to their persuasions, though sorely against his will. Before he started for the Pyrenees, Madame Récamier, by way of compensation for his disappointment, arranged a reading of the play at the Abbaye-au-Bois. The reading was entrusted to the celebrated actor Lafont, and a large and distinguished company, including Cousin, Villemain, Lamartine, Mérimée, and many other well-known men of letters, assembled to listen to it. The entertainment, however, came very near ending in a fiasco.

Lafont acquitted himself very creditably in the first act, but, unfortunately, he had not looked at the rest of the play, the handwriting of which left a good deal to be desired. The result was that he hesitated, stammered, made several provoking mistakes, and finally declared that the manuscript was illegible. Poor Madame Récamier was on thorns, fearing an outburst of anger on the part of her irascible friend; but Chateaubriand, noticing her anxiety, by a great effort succeeded in mastering his indignation, and, throwing the blame on the manuscript, took it from Lafont and read it himself.

In July came the news of the dismissal of Martignac and the formation of the Polignac Ministry. Prince de Polignac, an Ultramontane fanatic of the most dangerous type, who had suffered a long term of imprisonment for his share in Cadoudal's plot to kill Napoleon, and on his return to France in 1814 had refused to swear to the Charter, because it granted religious liberty to non-Catholics, became Minister for Foreign Affairs; Labourdonnaie, the champion of the reactionary Terrorists in 1816, Minister for the Interior; and General de Bourmont, who had deserted to the English at Waterloo, Minister for War.

Chateaubriand, quick to perceive the disastrous results which must inevitably follow the appointment of such Ministers, and forgetting his own grievances in his loyalty to the Crown, immediately returned to Paris and demanded an audience of the king, in order to warn him of the danger of thus wantonly provoking a conflict with the nation. The king, however, refused even to see him, whereupon Chateaubriand at once resigned his post at the Vatican.

In the spring of 1830 Madame Récamier lost her husband, who passed away at the age of eighty, gay and good-natured to the last. Since the death of his father-in-law and of old Simonard, which had taken place a few years before, he had lived with his niece, Madame Lenormant, and had dined every evening at the Abbaye-au-Bois. His mornings he spent in the Chaussée d'Antin, his old business quarter, where he had a small office in which he received his friends, whom, in spite of his reverses, he still found means to oblige. On being seized with his last illness, he had expressed a wish to be removed to the Abbaye-au-Bois, where, tended with affectionate care by his wife, he died on April 19.

"It would be difficult to find," says Madame Lenormant, "in taste, temperament, mind, and character two persons more dissimilar than M. and Madame Récamier. They had but one quality in common—that of good-nature; and yet, in the singular tie which united them for thirty-seven years, there had never been the slightest interruption of their friendly relations. In losing her husband, Madame Récamier felt that she had lost a second father." [1]

In July Madame Récamier transported the colony of the Abbaye-au-Bois to Dieppe. Here she made a new friend in Père Lacordaire, soon to become famous as a preacher and orator. He was then a young man of twenty-eight, but already noted for his conversational powers, and Madame Récamier found him a charming companion. Chateaubriand joined her at the end of the month; but he had not been at Dieppe more than a few hours, when he received news of the promulgation of the fatal Ordinances, issued the very day he had left Paris by the fanatical Polignac and his equally infatuated master. He at once set out on his return to the capital, and Madame Récamier, anxious for his safety and for that of her

[1] *Souvenirs*, ii. 384.

niece, who had remained in Paris, followed him the same day, accompanied by young Ampère and her maid.

They reached the city on the 30th, but found to their astonishment that their carriage could not enter the town. They were, therefore, compelled to leave it at the end of the Faubourg St. Denis, and make their way on foot to the Abbaye-au-Bois, through streets in which barricades eight feet high had been erected.

The following morning Madame Récamier received a note from Chateaubriand, who had been informed of her arrival by Madame Lenormant.

"*July* 31, 1830.

"I had just written to your niece to say that you would arrive *at the most unexpected moment.* You see how well I know you. I was *carried yesterday in triumph through the streets:* I do not dare to go out to-day. Come, therefore, when you are rested. Unfortunately, one cannot go about except on foot. I have matters of the utmost importance to talk about. I hope that I am going to play a part worthy of you and of myself, but which may perhaps cost me my life. You will understand what I have to endure from the terrible state of alarm which Madame de Chateaubriand is in. Sleep, and come to me when you are quite rested."

Chateaubriand now found himself called upon to decide between the two principles which throughout his political career he had been vainly endeavouring to reconcile—legitimacy and liberty. "My position is painful, but clear," he writes to the confidante of all his hopes and fears. "I will not betray either the king or the Charter, either legitimate power or liberty. I can say nothing, do nothing, but wait and weep for my country." He felt that he could not be true to the one without being false to the other.

The temptation to a man so ambitious as was Chateaubriand to abandon the cause of the dynasty, whose representatives had treated him with so much ingratitude and contumely, must have been indeed a strong one. While the declaration which was to change the office of Lieutenant-Governor of the Kingdom into royalty was under discussion, Comte Anatole de Montesquiou, a great friend of the Duc d'Orléans, called one morning at the Abbaye-au-Bois, where he found Chateaubriand alone with Madame Récamier. In the course of conversation he mentioned that the duke and duchess were anxious to make amends for the discourtesy with which the late king had treated Chateaubriand, and would be delighted to see him if he would go to the Palais Royal.

The latter was not a little surprised at Montesquiou's advances, but he did not refuse, as he was glad of an opportunity for pleading the almost desperate cause of the little Duc de Bordeaux, the legitimate heir to the throne, in whose favour Charles X. had abdicated.

On reaching the palace, Chateaubriand was ushered into the presence of the duchess, who received him very cordially, and at once began to deplore the dangers which threatened France, and to hint at the great services which lay in his power to render to the nation at so critical a juncture.

Presently Louis Philippe joined them, but, instead of discussing the situation of affairs, as Chateaubriand expected him to do, proceeded to bewail the necessity which had summoned him from the congenial pursuits of a country life to take his place at the helm of the ship of State. He assured his visitor that nothing but a stern sense of duty had impelled him to meddle in politics, and that he asked nothing better than to be allowed to return to the peaceful existence which he had so reluctantly quitted.

Chateaubriand, who was aware that the duke had inherited both Philippe Egalité's ambition and his duplicity, was far from being deceived by this assumption of disinterestedness. He soon contrived to steer the conversation round to the matter which had brought him to the Palais Royal that day, and strongly urged Louis Philippe to support the claims of the legitimate heir, and to content himself with the office of regent during the young king's minority.

While Chateaubriand was speaking he noticed that the duke seemed very ill at ease, and studiously avoided meeting his eye; and he was, therefore, scarcely surprised when, in reply to his appeal, Louis Philippe answered that he feared events were too strong for him; that the masses would not be so easily satisfied; that they might rise and massacre the whole of the Royalists; and that he must now beg his visitor to excuse him, as a deputation was waiting to see him. "I read upon his brow the desire to be king," says Chateaubriand, and returned to Madame Récamier, feeling that the cause of the Duc de Bordeaux was now quite hopeless.

Next day the Duchesse d'Orléans sent for Chateaubriand again, and used every persuasion to win him over to her husband's side. She reminded him of the sacrifices he had made on behalf of the Bourbons, and of the slights which had been put upon him by the late king and his predecessor. She dwelt upon the great influence he possessed over public opinion, and of the value Louis Philippe attached to his services. And finally gave him to understand that, if he wished for the portfolio for Foreign Affairs, her husband would willingly give it him, while if, on the other hand, he preferred to return to the Vatican, that post was equally at his disposal.

Great as must have been the temptation to yield, especially now that it was obvious that no effort on his part would be likely to prevent the Chambers from offering the crown to Louis Philippe, or the latter from accepting the offer, Chateaubriand was proof against it. He thanked the duchess for the high opinion which she expressed of him, and for the flattering proposals she had made him, but said that, as his writings proved, his whole life had been devoted to the cause of the fallen dynasty, and he must decline to stultify himself by countenancing a usurper, even one of the royal blood.[1]

Chateaubriand's refusal to accept office at Louis Philippe's hands does him all the more honour as he was at this time in serious pecuniary difficulties owing to his unbusinesslike habits, and the lavish expenditure which he had incurred at Rome during the Conclave ; and is, therefore, in itself a sufficient refutation of the charges of opportunism which have been frequently brought against him.

The political changes of that eventful year, which relegated Chateaubriand to private life, brought long deferred advancement to another of Madame Récamier's friends. Benjamin Constant had been one of the leaders of the Opposition in the Chamber of Deputies, and had written a series of exceedingly able pamphlets, denouncing the reactionary measures of Charles X.'s advisers. He was in the country whither he had gone to recruit his health, which was much impaired, when the revolution of July occurred ; but, at the urgent request of Lafayette,

[1] *Mémoires d'Outre Tombe*, ix. 351 *seq.*

returned at once to Paris, and used his influence on behalf of Louis Philippe's elevation to the throne. Honours and favours were showered upon him by the new Government. He was appointed President of the Legislative Committee of the State Council, with a considerable salary; while the king made him a present of two hundred thousand francs from his privy purse to enable him to settle his most pressing debts, for his private affairs, like those of Chateaubriand and many other public men of his day, had been left to take care of themselves.

Constant had, however, set his heart on being elected a member of the Academy, a position to which his great literary reputation gave him an indisputable title. He, accordingly, urged Guizot, the Minister of the Interior, to expel a number of Royalist Academicians, as Vaublanc had done the Bonapartist members in 1816, by which means his immediate election would be, of course, assured. Guizot very properly declined to follow so dangerous a precedent; and Constant, reduced to the chances of an ordinary election, offered himself in the following November for the seat rendered vacant by the death of Ségur, the historian. Just before the election took place, he wrote to Madame Récamier to ask for her interest on his behalf.

"I am going, madame, to ask you to kindly get M. de Chateaubriand to promise to be present at the Academy the day after to-morrow (Thursday). I have an excellent chance of being elected, and I am told that the only danger is that there may not be a sufficient number of my friends present. So I am appealing to your influence with M. de Chateaubriand, whose support is more valuable than I am able to explain, and his presence most necessary."

Chateaubriand gave Constant his support, but the rest

of the Royalist Academicians, hearing of the violent measures the latter had suggested to Guizot, were much incensed, with the result that the rival candidate, M. Viennet, was elected.

Poor Constant's disappointment and disgust at his rejection in favour of a person whose claims were so manifestly inferior to his own greatly aggravated the complaint from which he was suffering; and he died three weeks later. High honours were paid to the memory of the deceased statesman. A civic wreath was laid upon the seat in the Chamber which he usually occupied, a mourning crape was attached to the flag above the President's chair in the Hall of Session, and nearly the entire Chamber attended the funeral. "There never was anything to equal the number of people who followed him to the grave yesterday," writes Mary Berry to one of her friends. "From nine o'clock till three there were eight or nine processions at a time crossing the Tuileries Gardens, headed by tri-coloured flags, with his name and *Liberté et Droit* written upon them. The procession reached almost the whole length of the Boulevards; nothing similar was ever seen at Paris, except at the death of General Foy."[1]

[1] Miss Berry's "Journal and Correspondence," iii. 409.

CHAPTER XVIII

Retirement of Madame Récamier's friends from public life—Consequent change in her own life—Her sympathy for sincere political convictions—The Abbaye-au-Bois gradually becomes a literary resort—Royalist rising in La Vendée, instigated by the Duchesse de Berri—Chateaubriand and other Legitimist leaders are arrested—But are soon released—Outbreak of cholera in Paris—Madame Récamier's peculiar dread of this disease—She goes to Switzerland with Madame Salvage—Visit to Queen Hortense at Arenenberg—Hortense's adventures in Italy—The Château d'Arenenberg—Its Napoleonic treasures—Alexandre Dumas *père*—His impression of Madame Récamier—Queen Hortense's musical talents—Memories of Malmaison — Chateaubriand's visit to the château — Louis Napoleon—His character and pursuits—Madame Récamier and Chateaubriand visit the grave of Madame de Staël—Arrest of the Duchesse de Berri—Chateaubriand's pamphlet in her defence—Announcement of her secret marriage to Count Palli—Her release—Chateaubriand's journey to Prague on her behalf—And to Venice—His letters to Madame Récamier from Venice

THE fall of the elder branch of the Bourbons condemned to private life not only Chateaubriand, but the Duc de Laval, the La Rochefoucaulds, and indeed the greater number of Madame Récamier's intimate friends. With it in consequence begins a new era in her own life. During the past sixteen years her salon had been, to a great extent, regarded as a Royalist stronghold, more from the accidental circumstance that most of her friends happened to belong to that party than from any predilection on her own part; for, as we have said, she made it a rule to ignore, as far as possible, all political distinctions. The men whose names are connected with the literature of constitutional France were then but little known, and, with one or two notable exceptions, such as Villemain and Jean Jacques Ampère, either too poor to mix in society, or too proud to frequent a salon so much affected by the chief supporters of the Government, lest by doing so they should fall under the suspicion of wishing to truckle to the party in power. Now, however, the positions were reversed: the *Jeune-France* party basked in the sunshine of prosperity, and men, like Carrel, Cousin, Guizot, Mignet, Thierry, and Rémusat, were only too pleased to avail themselves of the hospitality of so charming a hostess.

At first, the elder habitués of the Abbaye-au-Bois, differing so widely as they did from the new-comers in politics, and smarting under their recent defeat, were inclined to resent their presence, and treated them with considerable hauteur. But Madame Récamier, who always had the highest respect for all sincere convictions, more than atoned for this by the warmth of her welcome, and allowed her Royalist friends to see that, though she might regret the events which had driven them from power, she was far from approving of their unceasing efforts to oppose the national tendencies and cold-shoulder the national leaders. One day, Madame Mohl tells us, the Duc de Laval was recapitulating what the revolution of 1830 had cost the country.

"Yes," he said. "France has spent all this to get rid of the nobility."

"And France," replied Madame Récamier, with a

smile, "does not think she has paid too dearly for it."

During the first three or four years after the July Revolution politics were the absorbing topic of conversation at the Abbaye, and party feeling ran so high that Madame Récamier had not infrequently to intervene—a task which she invariably performed with marvellous tact—to prevent things being said that might wound the feelings of some of her guests. Gradually, however, literature acquired more prominence, and after 1834, when Chateaubriand had finally retired from public life, the Abbaye-au-Bois became the centre of the most brilliant literary society in Paris.

In the spring of 1832 the Duchesse de Berri, who had followed the rest of the royal family into exile, landed at Marseilles, and made her way into the ever loyal district of La Vendée, where a rising took place in her son's favour. It was easily suppressed, and the Government caused Chateaubriand and three other Legitimist leaders—Fitz-James, Hyde de Neuville, and Berryer—to be arrested, on suspicion of having instigated the insurrection. There was, however, no evidence against them, and they were almost immediately released.

At the end of March the cholera, which had ravaged both England and Germany during the previous year, broke out with fearful virulence in Paris. Within a week the mortality reached five hundred per diem, and the cases to four times that number; and in eighteen days no less than seven thousand persons had succumbed to the disease. Casimir-Périer, the President of the Council of Ministers, Cuvier, and many other well-known persons were among the victims.

By a presentiment which, as we shall see, was only too

well founded, Madame Récamier, as a rule lavish in her care of people attacked by contagious disease, entertained an ungovernable and almost superstitious dread of cholera; and, as the Faubourg St. Germain, and the Rue de Sèvres in particular, was one of the quarters most affected by the epidemic, she quitted the Abbaye-au-Bois, and took refuge with her friend Madame Salvage in the Rue de la Paix. This part of the city was suffering but little from the scourge, which was confined chiefly to the left bank of the Seine.

In August she and Madame Salvage set out for Switzerland to join Chateaubriand, who was already wandering in the mountains. While there she received a pressing invitation from Queen Hortense to visit her at her summer residence, the Château d'Arenenberg, on the shores of Lake Constance.

Since their last meeting in Rome Hortense had gone through many trying adventures, and had lost her eldest son, Napoleon. The Revolution of 1830, which dethroned the Bourbons, had excited insurrectionary movements in several countries and among them Romagna, where a rising took place against the authority of the Pope. Both the young princes, in spite of the efforts of their relatives, had joined the insurgents, in whose ranks their presence had aroused much enthusiasm. An Austrian army, however, entered the Papal territory, and speedily suppressed the revolt. Poor Hortense, who had been following her sons in order to rescue them from their danger, found that the elder had died of fever at Forli, and that the younger was ill with the same complaint near Ancona, and on the point of falling into the hands of the Austrians, who would certainly have shot him without compunction, as he had been specially exempted from the indemnity granted to the majority of the rebel leaders. The devoted mother nursed him back to health, and then carried him away, disguised as one of her servants, and, after many perils, succeeded in reaching French territory. The law banishing the Bonapartes, however, was still in force, and the Government of Louis Philippe would not allow them to remain in France. They, therefore, crossed over to England, where they stayed for some weeks, and then returned to Arenenberg.

Queen Hortense had bought this estate in 1817 for sixty thousand francs. The château was a large, old-fashioned house, perched upon a hill, and commanding a superb view of Lake Constance, the Rhine, and the surrounding country. The queen had greatly improved the property, which had been much neglected, enlarging the house and laying out flower-gardens and terraces; while a carriage-way from the high road to the château had been made under the direction of Prince Louis, and carried over a bridge, which he had designed after his engineering studies at Thun.

The château was a museum of Napoleonic relics and a gallery of family portraits. In the hall were several stands of arms, containing swords, lances, muskets, Arab spears, and Turkish scimitars, trophies of Napoleon's different wars. In the salon was Gros's magnificent picture *Bonaparte at the Bridge of Lodi*, Bosio's statue of Josephine, and Prud'hon's full-length portrait of her. An immense cabinet stood in one corner of the room, filled with different objects that had belonged to either Josephine or Napoleon; a pocket-book, marked "J. and N.," in which was kept the private correspondence of the Emperor and Empress—letters written by the former from Marengo, Austerlitz, Jena, and many another blood-stained field;

Charlemagne's famous talisman, presented to Napoleon by the citizens of Aix-la-Chapelle, and worn by him at Austerlitz and Wagram, just as the King of the Franks had worn it nine hundred years before; the belt Bonaparte had worn at the Pyramids; the wedding-ring he had placed on the finger of Madame de Beauharnais, and the portrait of the little King of Rome, painted by Marie Louise, the last earthly object on which the eagle eye of the great captain had rested. The library contained a portrait of Hortense's father, Alexandre de Beauharnais, a handsome, swarthy man, who perished on the scaffold during the Reign of Terror; another, of the equally ill-fated Murat, King of Naples; and a third canvas, on which was depicted the sombre visage of Louis, King of Holland.

Among the guests whom Madame Récamier found at the château, on the evening of her arrival, was Alexandre Dumas, then a young man of thirty, but who had already forced the doors of the Théâtre Français with his *Henri III. et son Cour*. He was staying at Constance, and had been invited to dinner by the ex-queen.

The famous novelist has left us an interesting account of his evening at the château.

"After dinner," he says, "we returned to the salon. Ten minutes later Madame Récamier was announced. She, also, was a queen of beauty and wit, and the Duchesse de St. Leu received her as a sister. I have heard many discussions about Madame Récamier's age. It is true that I only saw her at night, dressed in black, with her head and neck enveloped in a veil of the same colour, but, to judge by her youthful voice, her beautiful eyes, and her soft round hands, I should have said that she was twenty-five. And I was greatly astonished to hear these two women talking of the Directory and the Consulate as events they had witnessed."

Queen Hortense had, as is well known, great musical talent, and composed many deservedly popular songs, one of which, "*Partant pour la Syrie*," her son Louis Napoleon, on becoming Emperor, made the national air of France. In the course of the evening one of her guests begged her to give them some music, a request with which she readily complied ; and, taking her place at the piano, sang several songs which she had recently composed. Presently Dumas asked her if she would sing him one which she had composed during the Empire, "*Vous me quittez pour marcher à la gloire*," observing that it had been his elder sister's favourite song. The queen replied that she remembered the air, but had forgotten the words. The novelist, however, said he recollected them perfectly, and proceeded to recite them.

Vous me quittez pour marcher à la gloire,
Mon triste cœur suivra partout vos pas ;
Allez, volez au temple de mémoire :
Suivez l'honneur, mais ne m'oubliez pas.

A vos devoirs comme à l'amour fidèle,
Cherchez la gloire, évitez le trépas :
Dans les combats, où l'honneur vous appelle,
Distinguez-vous, mais ne m'oubliez pas.

Que faire, hélas ! dans mes peines eruelles ?
Je crains la paix autant que les combats :
Vous y verrez tant de beautés nouvelles,
Vous leur plairez !—mais ne m'oubliez pas.

Oui, vous plairez et vous vaincrez sans cesse ;
Mars et l'Amour suivront partout vos pas :
De vos succès gardez la douce ivresse,
Soyez heureux, mais ne m'oubliez pas.

While Dumas was reciting these verses, Hortense was heard to murmur, "My poor mother!" and when he had finished, she burst into tears. On recovering her composure, she begged him to pardon her emotion, as the song recalled sad memories.

"You know," said she, "that in 1808 the rumours about a divorce were beginning to spread. They had caused my mother terrible pain, and when the Emperor was on the point of starting for Wagram, she begged M. de Ségur to commemorate his departure in some verses. He brought her the words you have just recited; my mother gave them to me to set to music, and, the day before the Emperor left, I sang them to him. My poor mother! I can see her now watching the face of her husband, in order to note the effect of the song which applied so well to their respective positions.

"The Emperor listened to the end, and at length, when the last note of the piano had died away, he walked up to my mother.

"'You are the best creature that I know,' he said to her; then, with a sigh, he kissed her forehead, and turned away into his study.

"My mother burst into tears, for from that moment she felt that her fate was decided. You can understand now, M. Dumas, how many memories surround the song, and, in reciting it to me, you have touched the most sensitive chords of my heart."

Dumas hastened to apologise, and begged the queen not to further distress herself by attempting to sing the song; but the latter replied that, though it aroused sad memories, it also served to recall the great affection which the Emperor had always cherished for her mother; and, turning to the piano, sang with great expression the verses which had so moved Napoleon that evening at Malmaison, twenty-three years before.

When, a few days later, Chateaubriand arrived at Constance, he was at once invited to dine at the château. Hortense received him most cordially, despite the prominent part he had taken in the overthrow of her family, showed him all her Napoleonic treasures, and read to him some extracts from her memoirs. The ex-queen talked a good deal about her preference for a life of retirement and her aversion to greatness ; and her guests were, therefore, not a little surprised to find that Prince Louis was treated *en souverain* by his mother and the whole household. The prince was a grave, studious, taciturn young man, very different from his generous and enthusiastic elder brother, Napoleon, whom Madame Récamier had known in Rome. He lived in a kind of pavilion, standing apart from the rest of the château, full of weapons of all kinds, books, and topographical and strategical maps. Here he spent the greater part of his day, deep in study, never going out until late in the afternoon, when he rode or drove for a couple of hours. He was a superb horseman, and an admirable shot, both with gun and rifle, and had won several prizes at the *tir cantonal.* His tastes were artistic, and before Madame Récamier left, he sketched for her a view in sepia of Lake Constance as seen from the château, and inscribed his name upon it—that name which in after years was to be attached to very different documents.

On leaving Constance, Madame Récamier and Chateaubriand went to Geneva, and while there made a pilgrimage together to the tomb of their common friend Madame de Staël. In his *Mémoires d'Outre Tomb* Chateaubriand gives an account of this visit, written in his most polished style and with genuine pathos.

"The château was closed," he says; "they opened its doors to me; I wandered in its deserted rooms. The companion of my pilgrimage recognised all the places, where she still seemed to see her friend, seated at her piano, coming in, or going out, or conversing on the terrace which borders the gallery. Madame Récamier visited the chamber which she had been wont to occupy; days long gone by returned to her; it was like a repetition of the scene which I have depicted in *René*. 'I wandered through the echoing apartments, where I heard only the sound of my own footsteps. . . . Everywhere the rooms were empty, and the spider was spinning his web on the beds which had so long remained unoccupied. . . . How sweet, but how fleeting, are the moments that brothers and sisters spend in childhood's years, gathered together under the wing of their aged parents! The family of man is but for a day; the breath of God disperses it as a vapour. Scarcely does the son know the father, the father the son, the brother the sister, the sister the brother! The oak sees its acorns springing up around it; it is not thus with the children of men.'

"I recalled to mind also what I have said in my *Mémoires* of my last visit to Combourg, when on the point of starting for America. Two worlds, different, yet united by a secret sympathy, engrossed the thoughts of Madame Récamier and myself. Alas! these isolated worlds, each of us bore them in our souls; for where can two persons be found who have lived sufficiently long together not to have separate recollections? From the château we entered the park. The early autumn had begun to tinge and detach the leaves; the wind died away by degrees, and we could hear the sound of a stream which turned a mill. After threading the alleys, through which she had been wont to ramble with Madame de Staël, Madame Récamier wished to pay her respects to her friend's ashes. At some distance from the park is a coppice, interspersed with larger trees and encircled by a moss-grown and crumbling wall. This coppice resembles those thickets in the open country, which sportsmen call spinneys; it is there that death has thrust his prey and imprisoned his victims.

"A sepulchre had been built, in anticipation of their death, for M. Necker, Madame Necker, and Madame de Staël. When the last-named had been placed therein the door of the crypt was walled up. The child of Auguste de Staël was buried outside the tomb, and Auguste, who predeceased his child, rests beneath a stone at the feet of his parents. On the stone are graven the following words taken from the Scriptures: 'Why seek ye the living among the dead?' I did not go into the wood: Madame Récamier alone obtained permission to enter. I remained sitting on a bench, before the wall of the enclosure, and, turning away from France, fixed my gaze alternately on the summit of Mont Blanc and on the Lake of Geneva. Golden clouds covered the horizon behind the sombre line of the Jura. One might have compared them to a glory extended over a long coffin. I perceived, on the other side of the lake, Lord Byron's villa, the top of which reflected the rays of the setting sun. Rousseau was no longer there to admire the scene, and Voltaire, also departed, had never cared for it. At the foot of the tomb of Madame de Staël how many illustrious persons, who once frequented the same shore, but are now departed, returned to my memory. They seemed to come seeking the shade of their companion and fly with her to heaven, her convoy through the night. At that moment Madame Récamier, pale and in tears, emerged from the funereal grove, as if she herself were but a shade. If I have felt, at once, both the vanity and the truth of fame and of life, and also what it is to be truly beloved, it was at the entrance of that silent wood, obscure and unknown, where sleeps she who had such *éclat*, glory, and renown."[1]

After her visit to Coppet, Madame Récamier returned to Paris, leaving Chateaubriand with his wife at Geneva. That autumn her niece's husband, Charles Lenormant, was appointed by Guizot Assistant-Keeper of Medals at the Bibliothèque Royale, an appointment which necessitated his removing from the neighbourhood of the Abbaye-au-Bois to the rooms assigned to the holder of that post in the library buildings. This change separated Madame Récamier from her niece, who had been in the habit of dining every day with her husband at the Abbaye ; but, as a sort of compensation, they, henceforth, generally spent the summer months together, either at some country house, taken by Madame Récamier, in the neighbourhood of Paris, or on a small estate in Normandy, which belonged to Charles Lenormant.

In October came the news of the arrest of the Duchesse de Berri, who was imprisoned by the Government in the Castle of Blaye. Chateaubriand, who was still in Geneva, returned at once to Paris, and published his *Mémoire sur la Captivité de Madame la Duchesse de Berri.* This pamphlet, which was a violent attack on the Government, and concluded with the words " *Madame, votre fils est mon roi !* " cost its author a lawsuit ; but he was ably defended by the famous advocate Berryer, and acquitted. In the meanwhile the imprisoned duchess had given birth to a son, the fruit of a secret marriage with an Italian noble-

[1] *Mémoires d'Outre Tombe*, x. 261 *seq.*

man, the son of the Marchese Lucchesi Palli. The announcement of this union forthwith deprived her of the sympathy of the majority of her supporters, and a few months later she was released by the Government.

As soon as she was at liberty she wrote to Chateaubriand, begging him to go to Prague and break the news of her marriage with Count Palli to Charles X. The ex-king and the whole of the royal family were furious at the *mésalliance* and its fatal consequences, and all Chateaubriand's endeavours to reconcile them to the duchess were futile. Scarcely had he returned to Paris, however, when the duchess again wrote to ask him to meet her at Venice, where she and her husband were living, and the chivalrous old man at once started for Italy, though he knew his journey was bound to be a fruitless one. During his absence he wrote to Madame Récamier with his usual regularity.

VICOMTE DE CHATEAUBRIAND *to* MADAME RÉCAMIER.

"VENICE, *September* 10, 1833.

"I wish so much that you were here. The sun, which I have not seen since leaving Paris, is just beginning to shine. I have rooms at the entrance of the Grand Canal, with the sea both at the horizon and under my window. I am dreadfully tired; yet, I cannot help admiring the sad and beautiful spectacle of a city so charming and so forlorn. And then the twenty-six years that have glided by since I left Venice to embark at Trieste, on my way to Greece and Jerusalem! Had I not made your acquaintance in this quarter of a century, I should say hard things about it. . . . Yours with all the sweetness of the climate, so different from that of the Gauls."

VICOMTE DE CHATEAUBRIAND *to* MADAME RÉCAMIER.

"VENICE, *September* 12, 1833.

"I spent a very pleasant day yesterday, if there can be pleasant days without you. I paid a visit to the Ducal Palace, and saw those on the Grand Canal once more. What poor devils we are in regard to art after all this! I have all sorts of plans in my head; I am taking notes; it is for this reason that I do not give you any particulars, not wishing to repeat myself.

". . . To day, I am going to continue my course of sight-seeing. I am impatient to behold the *Assumption* of Titian. One comes across his masterpieces here on every side. His colouring is so perfect, that, if one looks at one of his pictures and then at the sky, one can hardly tell one from the other. . . .

"I am devoured by those creatures who have also stung you. Hyacinth is almost blind.[1] I lay at your feet the most beautiful morning in the world, whose light is streaming across the paper on which I am writing to you."

VICOMTE DE CHATEAUBRIAND *to* MADAME RÉCAMIER.

"VENICE, *September* 15, 1833.

". . . I have written you often and quite long letters. I told you that the notes I am taking prevent me from entering into details. I run about everywhere. I go into society; what do you say to that? I pass my evenings in the company of ladies; what do you say to that? I wish to see everything, know everything. They treat me wonderfully well, tell me that I am quite young, and are amazed at my stories about my grey hairs. Imagine how proud I am, and how I believe in these compliments! Vanity is so

[1] Hyacinth Pilorge, his private secretary.

absurd! My secret is that I did not wish to maintain my reserve here, when I heard of Lord Byron's. I had no desire to pass for the copy of the man of whom I was the original.[1] I have converted myself into the ambassador.

"I have explored Venice in a different way from those who have preceded me. I have searched only for those things which travellers, who follow in one another's footsteps, give no heed to. No one, for instance, speaks of the cemetery at Venice; no one has marked the tombs of the Jews at Lido; no one has studied the habits of the gondoliers, &c. You shall benefit by the result of these investigations. . . . St. Francis's Day will see me once more with you."

At the urgent request of the Duchesse de Berri, Chateaubriand undertook another journey to Prague to make one more attempt to bring about a reconciliation between the duchess and her relatives. But she had ruined her party; and the austere Duchesse d'Angoulême was the only one of the royal family who had any pity for her. Chateaubriand returned to Paris at the end of October, reluctantly convinced that thc cause to which he had devoted the greater part of his life was now irretrievably lost.

[1] Chateaubriand always maintained that Byron was indebted for the idea of "Childe Harold" to his own *René*. He was deeply mortified that the poet had not in any way acknowledged his indebtedness, and looked upon himself as "a father whose son had disowned him as soon as he had made a name in the world."

CHAPTER XIX

Termination of Chateaubriand's political career—A politician rather than a statesman—He becomes a martyr to *ennui*—Madame Récamier's efforts to interest him—His *Mémoires d'Outre Tombe*—Reading of the opening chapters at the Abbaye-au-Bois—Great interest aroused by these readings—Anxiety of people to be admitted—Chateaubriand's financial embarrassments—He disposes of his *Mémoires* in return for a pension—Madame Récamier visits the Duc de Laval at Montigny—Louis Napoleon's attempt at Strasburg—He is brought to Paris for trial—And is followed by Queen Hortense—Madame Salvage at the Abbaye-au-Bois—Madame Récamier goes to see Queen Hortense—The ex-Queen's grief at the exile of her son—Her death—Illness of Madame Récamier—Anxiety of Chateaubriand and Ballanche—Baron Pasquier lends her his house—Her recovery and return to the Abbaye—Madame Récamier the originator of afternoon "at homes"—Newcomers at the Abbaye—The most brilliant literary coterie in Paris—Madame Récamier's devotion to Chateaubriand—Sainte-Beuve's tribute to her unselfishness—Jean Jacques Ampère—His affection for Madame Récamier—The two Chateaubriands—George Ticknor's account of them—The Abbaye-au-Bois the last of the old salons—Its characteristics—Madame Récamier's marvellous tact in conducting the conversation—Musical parties at the Abbaye—Mademoiselle Rachel, the actress—Her romantic career—Her avarice and kindheartedness—Anecdotes about her—Her affection for Madame Récamier—Caroline Murat comes to Paris—Pension voted her by the Chambers—Her death

CHATEAUBRIAND'S return from his second journey to Prague marks the termination of his political career. As a statesman, he can hardly be called a success; indeed, it is doubtful whether he has any real claim to the title at all. But, as a fighting politician, as a debater, and, above all, as a pamphleteer, he has had few superiors; and in the troublous years between the restoration of the Bourbons and the July Monarchy he was, undoubtedly, the greatest force in French politics, equally dreaded by his enemies when in opposition and by his friends when in office.

Henceforth Chateaubriand was seldom separated from Madame Récamier for any long period, with the exception of his visit to England in 1843, and her thoughts were constantly employed in giving an interest to his life. This was no easy matter. The great writer had always been subject to *ennui*. It was now a malady. Madame Mohl tells us that she often heard him express a wish that it would settle in his leg so that he might cut it off, as he considered that contentment of mind would not be too dearly purchased by the loss of a limb.

For some time past Chateaubriand had been writing his memoirs, with the intention that they should be published posthumously; and one day Madame Récamier suggested that she should invite a few of their most intimate friends to the Abbaye to hear the opening chapters of the book read. Chateaubriand, not unwilling to have a foretaste of the judgment of posterity, was pleased with the idea; and, accordingly, invitations were sent to some half-dozen of his contemporaries, and as many more of the rising generation, from whose impressions he might be able to gauge the modern taste.

The experiment was a great success. "The readings," writes one of those who were privileged to be present, "began at four o'clock in the afternoon and continued till dinner at six; were resumed at eight and went on till half-past ten. Not only did attention never flag, but no one knew that he had listened between four and five hours. Though the whole has since been published in the *Mémoires d'Outre Tombe*, those who heard the first reading felt as if they saw but the dead body when they read it in print. M. Lenormant, who officiated, was a perfect reader. In some of the scenes, the tears that stole unconsciously down the cheeks of one or two of the audience (the younger portion) gave more satisfaction to the author than all the well-turned compliments of his old friends." [1]

The readings continued about once a week for more than two years. Chateaubriand went on writing, and always read what he had written to Madame Récamier alone in the first instance. The audience rapidly increased, and Madame Récamier was soon hard put to find accommodation for all those who wished to be present. Moreover, it required great tact on her part to make a selection from the numerous applicants for admission, for the *Mémoires* were largely political, and Chateaubriand had, at one time or another, offended each of the great parties. The Bonapartists regarded him as one of the principal agents in the downfall of the Empire; the Liberals as an upholder of the *ancien régime*, and persisted in identifying him with the other Royalist leaders, who themselves had never forgiven him for the violence of his attacks upon the Ministers of Charles X. It was, therefore, necessary to invite only those whose sympathy with the author was sufficient to outweigh their party hostility, or whose literary tastes were stronger than their political sentiments; but she triumphed over all difficulties, and

[1] Madame Mohl's *Madame Récamier*, p. 85.

the readings became so much the fashion, that people who cared nothing for politics or literature, fine ladies, dandies, foreigners, whose knowledge of French was so scanty that they could not possibly have understood half of what was read, vied with one another for admittance.

For some years Chateaubriand's affairs had been in a very unsatisfactory state. Nothing else, indeed, could well be expected in the case of a man who, without any private fortune, had the munificence of a *grand-seigneur*. Handsome as had been his official salary while ambassador at Rome, it had been quite insufficient for his expenditure, and he had contracted large debts, which were still unpaid. On the fall of Charles X. he had very honourably resigned the Ministerial pension to which he was entitled, and since then had been entirely dependent upon his pen. He complained bitterly to Madame Récamier of his poverty, but, though her anxiety on his behalf cost his sympathetic friend many a sleepless night, she could not for some time discover any way of freeing him from his embarrassments.

It happened, however, that the booksellers, hearing that the now famous memoirs were to be published at the author's death, had begun to make proposals to him. These were at first coldly received. No single bookseller could possibly afford to pay the high price demanded by Chateaubriand in ready money, for, as long as the author lived, the publisher would, of course, have no opportunity of reimbursing himself for his outlay. At length, however, a plan suggested itself to Madame Récamier, who communicated it to some of Chateaubriand's Royalist friends who were aware of his difficulties. She suggested that a number of people should be invited to enter into an agreement with one of the leading publishers to pay

Chateaubriand a pension for his life, part of it to go to Madame de Chateaubriand should she survive him. The publisher was to be the sole proprietor of all the memoirs written or to be written, and, after the author's death, he was to repay the subscribers out of the profits. This contract was entered into in 1837, probably the first time a man has sold his life in order to live upon it.

Chateaubriand abhorred this transaction, and often referred to his fate as being worse than that of a galley-slave, inasmuch as he was sold both body and mind: indeed, so repugnant was the bargain to his pride that it is very doubtful whether he would ever have been brought to consent to it, had not the future comfort of his wife been at stake. The previous year he had published a translation of Milton, and this was followed by a life of Rancé, the founder of La Trappe. With the profits of these works and the sale of his house in the Rue d'Enfer he paid his debts; but he was compelled to make over to the Archbishop of Paris the asylum for old people which he and his wife had maintained for so many years. This was a great trial to them both.

In the autumn of 1836 Madame Récamier, with Ampère and Ballanche, went to visit her old friend the Duc De Laval at his country-seat at Montigny, where he had lived in retirement since the July Revolution. This was the last time Madame Récamier saw the duke, who died a few months later, at the age of seventy.

On her return to Paris at the end of October, she learned of Louis Napoleon's unsuccessful attempt at Strasburg. The captive prince was brought to Paris for trial, and was followed by his distracted mother. Queen Hortense, however, did not enter the city, fearing that her presence there might militate against her son, but stopped at Viry with her friend the Duchesse de Raguse, and sent her confidante Madame Salvage to the Abbaye-au-Bois to enlist its powerful interest on behalf of the unfortunate young pretender. Madame Récamier, ever ready to hold out a helping hand to those in distress, and touched by Madame Salvage's devotion to her friend, insisted on her remaining at the Abbaye and occupying her own bedroom, and promised to exert all the interest she possessed in the prince's cause. This was not necessary, however, as, a few hours later, they were informed that the Government had decided not to bring their prisoner to trial, but to banish him to America.

Next morning, Madame Récamier went to Viry to comfort the ex-queen, whom she found overwhelmed with grief. She had already learned that her son's life was to be spared ; but the idea of his banishment to America was a terrible blow, as she knew that she was suffering from an incurable disease, and that their parting must be a final one. Madame Récamier was much moved by her friend's sorrow and the great change in her appearance. She did all in her power to console her, but with little success, and when she left she felt that she would never see her again.

A few days later, Queen Hortense, with Madame Salvage, returned to Arenenberg. The fatigue of the journey greatly aggravated her complaint ; and when they reached the château it became clear that her days were numbered. It is sad to reflect that they were embittered by the thoughtlessness of the French Government, who neglected to inform the anxious mother that they had sent her son on a long voyage before landing him in America, and that this was the reason of her not receiving news from him. She was left in a state of cruel suspense until the end of the following March, when a letter reached her from Rio Janeiro, where the prince's ship had been detained for a fortnight owing to a terrible storm. He had not been permitted to land, and his only distraction consisted in reading Chateaubriand's works, a set of which happened to be on board.

The amiable and accomplished Queen Hortense died on October 5, 1837.

In the meantime, Madame Récamier's own health was beginning to cause her friends grave uneasiness. She suffered greatly from insomnia and a troublesome cough, which brought on a gradual wasting away; and it was feared that her lungs were affected. The anxiety of Chateaubriand and Ballanche was pitiable to witness. "During the worst part of her illness," says Madame Mohl, "M. de Chateaubriand and M. Ballanche might be seen walking in the court of the Abbaye-au-Bois, on a cold winter day, watching the doctor as he came down from her apartment into the court. They did not venture to ring, lest she should find that they were anxious. M. de Chateaubriand's beautiful white silky hair, blown about by a cold wintry wind—his physiognomy the very image of despair—formed a striking picture."

It was about this time that the following note must have been written:

"I am bringing this note to your door. In order to sustain my courage, I tell myself that everybody about me is ill also. I was so terrified at not being admitted yesterday, that I thought you were leaving me. It is I—remember it is I—who am to go first."

And again, a few days later:

"Never speak of what is to become of me without you. I have not done so much evil in the sight of God that you should be called away before me. I notice with joy that I am ill, that I felt faint again yesterday, and that I do not gain strength. I shall bless God for this so long as you persist in not getting well. So my health is in your hands, remember that."

At the beginning of December, Madame Récamier's friend, Baron Pasquier, who had been appointed Chancellor of France, and had taken possession of his official residence at the Luxembourg, offered to lend her his house in the Rue d'Anjou, an offer which she gladly accepted. She remained there until the spring, when she returned to the Abbaye-au-Bois in a much more satisfactory state of health. The doctors had ordered her to the South; but she could not bring herself to leave Chateaubriand, to whose happiness she had become so necessary that her shortest absences filled him with despair. Whenever she announced her intention of leaving Paris, poor Madame de Chateaubriand used to hasten to the Abbaye to ascertain the probable date of her return, and to implore her for the sake of the peace and quiet of the Chateaubriand *ménage* not to remain away long. "But what will happen?" she would ask. "What is to become of my husband? What is he going to do if you stay away as long as you propose?"

Chateaubriand's delight was great on her return to the Abbaye. He came every day at half-past two, and read to her whatever work he happened to be engaged upon; no one was admitted till four o'clock, when other friends began to drop in. Until after 1830 it had been the custom for people to call upon their intimate friends in the evening, but as Madame de Chateaubriand was a confirmed invalid, and never went out at night, her husband, during the last eighteen years of her life, invariably spent his evenings at home with her. This, according to Madame Mohl, was the original cause of Madame Récamier receiving at four o'clock instead of after dinner. Her example was soon followed, and afternoon receptions became the fashion under the name of *les quatre heures.*

Amongst the new-comers who found their way to the Rue de Sèvres at this time, may be mentioned Alexis de Tocqueville, the success of whose great work, *Democratie en Amerique*, had made him the fashion, Frédéric Ozanam, the critic, Louis de Loménie, Charles Brifaut, Sainte-Beuve, and Madame Tastu. A great many women writers came to the Abbaye, but Madame Tastu was the only one who became really intimate there, for Chateaubriand disapproved of women meddling with literature and had a positive horror of *bas-bleus;* and Madame Récamier, of course, deferred to his wishes. He made, however, an exception in the case of Madame Tastu, whose kind heart and sound common sense probably appealed to him quite as much as her sentimental verses.

Madame Récamier's receptions at the Abbaye-au-Bois were now almost as celebrated as those in the Rue du Mont Blanc had been in former days, and strangers who saw her the centre of the most brilliant literary society in Paris, concluded that it was now her ambition to charm the poets and novelists of constitutional France, just as she had once charmed the soldiers and dandies of the Empire and the statesmen and diplomatists of the Restoration ; and envied her accordingly. But they were wrong. The pains which she took to gather round her all the intellectual aristocracy of Paris, and to keep it there, were neither for her own pleasures, though her tastes had always been literary, nor for the gratification of her own vanity, though she was not insensible to the homage so freely offered her, but for the benefit of the friend whose happiness had been for so many years the first consideration of her life.

With advancing years Chateaubriand's health had become much impaired. He had long been a martyr to gout, and at times his attacks were so severe as to almost deprive him of the use of his limbs. In consequence he was becoming more and more depressed; and to keep up his spirits was a task requiring constant and daily effort on the part of Madame Récamier.

"Her whole existence," says Louis de Loménie, "was devoted to seeking the means to *désennuyer* this Louis XIV. of literature, who was as *ennuyé* as the great king himself."[1]

In order to effect her purpose, she pressed into her service all the cleverest young men she could find. Did any one happen to praise Chateaubriand in a book or newspaper, advances were always made to him. Did she happen to observe that any chance visitor to the Abbaye had been able to interest the great writer, he was at once encouraged to call regularly and made a friend of. To the success of her heroic efforts Sainte-Beuve pays the following tribute:

"Madame de Maintenon was never more ingenious in amusing Louis XIV. than was Madame Récamier in interesting Chateaubriand. 'I have always observed,' says Boileau, on returning from Versailles, 'that, when the conversation does not turn on himself, the king immediately gets tired, and either begins to yawn or goes away.' Every great poet, when he is growing old, is a little like Louis XIV. in this respect. Each day, Madame Récamier contrived a thousand pleasant things to interest and flatter

[1] *Nouvelle Biographie Générale*, x. 99

him. She got together, from all quarters, friends for him—new admirers. She chained us all to the feet of her rival with links of gold."[1]

In this beneficent mission Madame Récamier was ably seconded by Jean Jacques Ampère, whose brilliant wit and entertaining conversation had made him one of the most popular figures in Parisian society. Ampère, although of a most affectionate nature, had never married, and after the death of his father in 1836 he was left alone in the world. It was on Madame Récamier, therefore—who filled for him the place of the mother whom he had never known—that he lavished all the wealth of affection which, under happier circumstances, might have been reserved for his own kindred. When in Paris he never allowed a day to pass without visiting the Abbaye, always prepared at her bidding to devote himself to the task of amusing Chateaubriand and of inducing his friends to do the same.

Chateaubriand, in spite of his ill-health and low spirits, could still at times be an extremely agreeable companion—that is to say, to Madame Récamier and other intimate friends. To the world at large he was a very different person. The adulation of the public, who had insisted on setting him upon a pedestal and bowing down before him, had converted him, at first, perhaps, almost unconsciously, into that most objectionable product of modern culture—a *poseur*. When there were no strangers present, and he was alone with people whom he liked and of whose good opinion he was secure, he would unbend, relate entertaining anecdotes of his travels and of the many celebrated people with whom he had been brought into contact in politics or diplomacy, joke and laugh like a schoolboy. But did a stranger enter the room, all was changed; he

[1] *Causeries du Lundi*, i. 107.

would at once resume the mask of a great man and his icy stiffness of manner, as became one who had been Foreign Minister, ambassador, and the author of the most widely read theological treatise and the most famous political pamphlet of the century. George Ticknor in his autobiography gives an interesting description of these two different Chateaubriands.

May 28. (Ticknor meets Chateaubriand for the first time.)—"He is too grave and serious, and gives a grave and serious turn to the conversation in which he engages; and when the whole table laughed at Barante's wit, Chateaubriand did not even smile; not, perhaps, because he did not enjoy the wit as much as the rest, but because laughing is too light for the enthusiasm which forms the basis of his character, and would certainly offend against the consistency we always require."[1]

June 16. (Ticknor is now on very friendly terms with Chateaubriand.)—"The evening I passed delightfully at Chateaubriand's, with a few of his friends—most of whom were members of the House of Peers. He was in high spirits, excited, and even *exalté*, and poured out a torrent of rich and varied eloquence, which made me think almost better of the language than I am accustomed to."[2]

Madame Récamier's salon at the Abbaye-au-Bois was one of the last which kept alive the memory of the ancient order of things, the social habits for which old France was so justly celebrated—one of the last of that long list of brilliant coteries, with their grace, their charm, and their wit, which, it has been well said, impressed their character upon the language itself, and made it in many respects what it is. People came there to see the mistress of the house, and to meet those whom they liked and were

[1] George Ticknor's "Life and Letters," i. 137. [2] *Ibid.* i. 140.

accustomed to meet, not to eat and drink, and flirt, and exhibit the latest triumphs of *modiste* and milliner. In those days it was still possible to have the best society without vulgar display and lavish hospitality. Good manners and good conversation were sufficient attraction The mistress of one of these old salons was once asked by an English friend how she managed to keep out the bores. She laughed and replied, "*Oh, il n'y a pas de danger quand on n'a pas deux cent mille francs de rente.*" The Abbaye-au-Bois, indeed, was, in reality, though not in name, a literary club, constituted, as the smaller French clubs usually are, for the purpose of conversation, with Madame Récamier as its president.

And what a president she made! "Talking little, listening much, judging with acuteness, presiding over conversation with admirable dexterity; questioning every one with infallible accuracy on what he knew best; discovering how to make all merit exhibit itself without offending any one; having the consummate art of making every one pleased with himself, and, consequently, with her." Such is the account given of her by Granier de Cassagnac; while Madame de Genlis declares that no one in the world had ever mastered the great art of listening so thoroughly as had Madame Récamier, a qualification the importance of which to any one who aspires to be the queen of a literary court can hardly be over-estimated.

Certain customs were much observed at the Abbaye-au-Bois—customs which, unfortunately for society, no longer obtain. For instance, every endeavour was used to make the conversation a general one, and *tête-à-têtes*, especially those carried on in a low voice, which find so much favour in a modern drawing-room, were considered the height of bad taste, and rigidly discouraged. If, we are told, any of the younger habitués took this liberty, they received a gentle reprimand in a real *tête-à-tête* when every one else had gone.

"Sometimes," says Madame Mohl, "a chance visitor would come in; occasionally, if a lady, she would sit down by Madame Récamier, and, in a low voice, tell her something extremely unworthy of so much mystery. Meantime the circular conversation was going on, and Madame Récamier could not attend to it. On one occasion of this sort, after the lady had gone, she complained of having lost the thread. Some one said of the whisperer, 'no doubt it was from timidity.' 'When people are too timid to speak, they should be modest enough to listen,' was her answer—which ought to become an axiom." [1]

Another characteristic of the Abbaye was that Madame Récamier disapproved of desultory, as she did of private, conversation, and followed the tradition of the Hôtel de Rambouillet in keeping seriously to one subject at a time, although there was a total absence of the affectation and pedantry which must have so often marred the discussions in the salon of the "divine Arthénice." There were no *Précieuses* at the Abbaye-au-Bois for a nineteenth-century Molière to turn into ridicule. Madame Récamier loved simplicity and detested exaggeration.

The visitors, of whom there were usually from six to a dozen present, grouped themselves in a circle round Madame Récamier, who sat on one side of the fireplace and, so to speak, conducted the conversation. As a rule, two or three of the habitués would stand against the chimney-piece, and speak loud enough to be heard by all present The others would listen attentively, one of them,

Madame Mohl's *Madame Récamier*, p. 99.

perhaps, interposing now and again with some witty remark or pertinent question. "If," says one of her most regular visitors, "a *mot* was particularly happy, Madame Récamier would take it up and show it to the audience as a connoisseur shows a picture." She generally spoke very little, however, and even if she knew an anecdote *à propos* of something, would call upon any one else who knew it also to relate it, though she herself was an admirable *raconteuse*. For the most part she would listen and smile intelligently, and from time to time throw in some observation to show that she understood the person who happened to be speaking.

When a new visitor came in, Madame Récamier would, if he knew anything of the subject under discussion, immediately question him, that the company might be aware of it; otherwise he was expected to try and understand what the conversation was about. From long habit she knew what were the subjects on which each guest showed to most advantage, and on these topics she would start him. The rest was not, indeed, difficult, for the guest, usually a veteran *causeur*, knew his *forte* even better than she did, and seized the thread that led to it.

If she fancied that one of those present had any special knowledge of the subject and was too modest to speak, she would, with a pretty air of deference, appeal to him for his opinion, and thus encourage him to join in the conversation. She had, indeed, a wonderful faculty for drawing out the best that was in people's minds; and some, who, before they came to frequent the Abbaye-au-Bois, had so little confidence in their conversational powers that they could only be prevailed upon to express their opinions in the presence of their most intimate friends, soon learned to speak freely and intelligibly in general company.

In 1838 Madame Récamier, who had after her first year at the Abbaye lived in the small apartment on the first floor, which Chateaubriand called "the *cellule*," took a larger salon on the same *étage*, and received in it until her death. Here she gave musical parties once a week, to which she made a point of inviting any distinguished foreigners who happened to be in Paris. She did not, however, continue these parties for more than three or four years, preferring, when her sight began to fail, to confine herself to her own intimate circle of friends.

It was about this time that the famous actress, Mademoiselle Rachel, first came to the Abbaye-au-Bois, and at once conceived a warm attachment for Madame Récamier. Rachel had had a most romantic career, and was altogether an extraordinary character. The daughter of one Abraham Felix, a Jew pedlar from Alsace, her childhood was passed in the direst poverty, and she and her elder sister were forced to seek a scanty subsistence by singing in the streets and *cafés* of Paris. Through the kindness of a famous singing-master named Choron, who gave them lessons free of charge, the girls were able to gain admission to the Conservatoire, where, however, Rachel soon deserted singing for elocution and acting. In 1838 she made her first appearance at the Théâtre Français, in the part of Camille in *Les Horaces*, and her remarkable gifts as a *tragédienne* being immediately recognised, she speedily became the rage. Her features were plain and her voice naturally harsh, but her facial expression was wonderful, and by constant practice she acquired such command over her voice as to be able to vary its tones with every shade of thought and emotion.

Rachel was not the daughter of a Jew pedlar for nothing, and many amusing stories are told of her avarice and passion for " bargains."

When she was at the height of her fame and popularity she noticed one day at a friend's house an old guitar. She asked the owner to give it her, which he did readily enough, for it was in such a dilapidated condition that it would have been dear at a five franc piece. A few days later it was the turn of one of those gilded youths who are always to be found in the train of popular actresses to notice the guitar, but this time it hung in a beautiful silk net, through the bright meshes of which its dark back was plainly visible, on the wall of an elegantly furnished boudoir.

"What in the world have you there?" quoth the admirer.

"That," said Rachel, in a sentimental tone, "is the faithful companion by whose aid I made a few sous when I was a poor little street-singer."

Forthwith nothing would satisfy the infatuated youth but that Rachel should give him this precious souvenir of her early struggles, which, with much apparent reluctance, she finally consented to do in exchange for some magnificent diamonds and rubies which adorned the window of a neighbouring jeweller, and which she had long coveted.

The happy possessor of the historic guitar, of course, took it home, and exhibited it with pride to all his friends. Unfortunately, one day the original owner of the now famous instrument happened to call, and, on hearing the romantic story, could not contain his merriment, and the murder was out. The poor young man was furious at the trick played upon him, but Rachel only laughed at his credulity, and, needless to say, kept the jewellery.

Whenever Rachel saw anything belonging to her friends which happened to take her fancy, she never had the smallest scruple about asking them to give it her—requests which few of them had the moral courage to refuse, especially when they were made, as they often were, before a room full of people. That versatile writer, Arsène Houssaye, himself a sufferer from this form of her rapacity, is responsible for the following amusing story.

One evening Rachel was at a dinner-party at the house of the Minister of the Interior, Comte Duchâtel, and expressed her admiration of a beautiful silver bowl, which, filled with choice flowers, adorned the centre of the table. M. Duchâtel, thinking, or pretending to think, that it was the flowers that she admired, immediately lent forward, despoiled the bowl of its fragrant contents, and offered them to the young actress. But he was not to get off so cheaply.

"Oh, it was not the flowers, but the bowl I admired so much," exclaimed Rachel, with a demure smile.

The unfortunate Minister, with the eyes of the whole table upon him, had no alternative but to beg her acceptance of the bowl as well.

"Monsieur le Comte," was the answer, "your roses and violets bring joy to my heart, but your centre-piece will be the glory and wonder of my dining-room."

The poor Count had his revenge later in the evening. Rachel had arrived in a cab, and her host had offered her his brougham to take her home. When the carriage was announced, he accompanied her to the head of the staircase himself.

"Mademoiselle," he said, with a sarcastic smile, "I have been much honoured by your acceptance of my bowl, but you will let me have my brougham back, will you not?

In spite of her acquisitiveness, however, Rachel had a warm heart, and was ever ready to hold out a helping hand to struggling genius. On one occasion a young man in very poor circumstances, whom she knew to have talent, wrote a play and sent it to the Théâtre Français, by which it was promptly rejected, probably without being read. Rachel, hearing of his disappointment, asked him to call upon her, and, when he did so, told him that she had a wealthy English friend who had a passion for collecting rejected manuscripts, and had commissioned her to purchase his if he would sell it, at the same time naming a liberal price. The offer was, of course, gratefully accepted by the unsuccessful playwright, and Rachel had the manuscript beautifully bound, and placed it in her private library.

Rachel's popularity in society was immense, and no actress had ever before been so much sought after by fashionable hostesses. She soon, however, got tired of her successes in high life and, after a time, the salons of the Faubourg St. Germain knew her no more. But to Madame Récamier she was always faithful, and never undertook a new part without having given the first recital at the Abbaye-au-Bois. On one of these occasions an old lady, who was extremely anxious to hear the famous *tragédienne* recite, owing to some accident or other, did not arrive until the conclusion of the first act. Madame Récamier happening to speak of her friend's disappointment to Rachel, the good-natured actress at once volunteered to begin over again, and did so, much to the old lady's surprise and delight.

In the summer of 1838 Caroline Murat came to Paris to press her claims for compensation on the French Government. She had at last succeeded in obtaining permission from the Powers to reside in Italy, and was now living at Florence. She had certainly chosen her time well. The constitutional monarchy had replaced the statue of Napoleon on the top of the Vendôme column, from which it had been removed by the restored Bourbons ; the Arc de Triomphe had just been completed ; the Chambers were on the point of voting a large sum for the erection of a tomb for Napoleon beneath the gilded dome of the Invalides, and a demand was about to be addressed to England for the ashes of the great commander.

During her stay in Paris the ex-queen spent a good deal of her time at the Abbaye-au-Bois, where she had the opportunity of meeting several members of the Government, and of exercising her still considerable powers of fascination upon them. Possibly these meetings were not without their effect on the decision of the Chambers to confer a pension of one hundred thousand francs upon the "Comtesse de Lipona."

Poor Madame Murat did not, however, profit much by this tardy liberality, as she died a few months after her return to Florence.

CHAPTER XX

Madame Récamier goes to Ems—Trial of Louis Napoleon for his attempt at Boulogne—Madame Récamier visits him at the *conciergerie*—His letter to her from Ham—Disastrous floods at Lyons—Madame Récamier's *soirée musicale* at the Abbaye-au-Bois—Her beauty in old age—Ballanche elected to the Academy—His gratitude to Madame Récamier—Chateaubriand's visit to the Comte de Chambord in London—His letters—Madame Récamier goes to Auteuil—Madame Guizot and Chateaubriand—Madame Récamier's habits—Chateaubriand's journey to Venice—Blindness of Madame Récamier—Accident to Chateaubriand—Illness and death of Ballanche—An offer of marriage from Chateaubriand—The Revolution of February—Chateaubriand's illness—The June insurrection—Death of Chateaubriand

IN the summer of 1840 Madame Récamier was ordered by her doctors to Ems. She undertook the journey with great reluctance, for she knew how necessary she had become to Chateaubriand and Ballanche, both of whom were growing infirm; and it was only the hope that she might gain sufficient benefit from the waters to enable her to continue her self-imposed task of consoling their declining years that induced her to leave them for a few weeks. "Time steals from me every day an eye, an ear, a hand," writes Chateaubriand. "Were it not for you, beautiful and dear one, I should regret having lingered so long under the sun."

On her return to Paris she found that the irrepressible Louis Napoleon was about to be tried by the Chamber of Peers for his ridiculous attempt at Boulogne. Although Madame Récamier had not kept up any personal relations with the prince since her visit to Arenenberg in 1832, it was thought that she might have been made aware of his designs through their common friend Madame Salvage; and she was, accordingly, summoned as a witness, and interrogated by her friend Baron Pasquier, the Chancellor. Her evidence, however, was of no importance.

The trial lasted a week. The prince was eloquently defended by Berryer, but was condemned to perpetual imprisonment in a fortress; while his companions, among whom was old Comte de Montholon, who had shared the Emperor's exile at St. Helena, were sentenced to various terms of detention.

Louis Napoleon preserved his imperturbability throughout the trial, and when the officers of the Court of Peers entered his cell, and read the decree which consigned him to a prison for the remainder of his days, bowed calmly, and answered, "At any rate, messieurs, I shall die in France."

Alexandre Dumas describes Nogent Saint-Laurent as entering the prince's cell before the officials arrived.

"You are condemned to perpetual imprisonment, monseigneur," he said.

"How long does perpetuity last in France, M. Saint-Laurent?" inquired the prince, with a quiet smile.

Madame Récamier, both for his dead mother's sake and his own, was much interested in Louis Napoleon's fate. Misfortune, especially when allied with courage, always strongly appealed to her sympathies, and there was certainly something of nobility in the fortitude with which the young prince pursued the course he had marked out for himself in the face of, apparently, insurmountable obstacles. She accordingly solicited and obtained permission to visit him at the *Conciergerie.*

The prince appeared much touched by her attention, and when she left escorted her as far as the sentinels would permit. Nor did he forget the visit he had received, for two years later he sent her from his prison at Ham his pamphlet, *Fragments Historiques* 1688 *et* 1830, as a mark of grateful remembrance. For this she wrote to thank him, and received in reply the following letter:

PRINCE LOUIS NAPOLEON *to* MADAME RÉCAMIER.

"CITADEL OF HAM, *June* 9, 1842.

"MADAME,—It was extremely kind of you to take the trouble to acknowledge the pamphlet which I took the liberty of sending you. I have for a long time wished to thank you, madame, for the welcome visit which you so kindly paid me at the *Conciergerie.* I have remembered it with deep gratitude, and I am happy that this gives me the opportunity of expressing my grateful feelings.

"I shall be greatly obliged, madame, if you will hand the enclosed letter to M. de Chateaubriand, whose benevolent interest has deeply touched me. You are so accustomed to make all those around you happy, that you will not be astonished at the pleasure I have experienced in receiving a proof of your sympathy, and in learning that you were disposed to pity my troubles.

"Believe me, Madame,

"Very respectfully yours,

"LOUIS NAPOLEON B."

The letter to Chateaubriand, who had also visited him

at the *Conciergerie*, was couched in the most flattering terms, and contained a request that he would give him the benefit of his advice with regard to a history of Charlemagne, which the prince proposed writing.

Chateaubriand, it may be remarked, appears to have formed a very high opinion of Louis Napoleon's character and capabilities—possibly he was not insensible to the deference with which the prince treated him—and, in acknowledging the receipt of the latter's pamphlet, *Rêveries politiques*, we find him going so far as to declare that "if God, in his impenetrable designs, had rejected the race of St. Louis, if our country had to return to an election which she had not sanctioned, and if her manners did not render republican institutions impossible—then, prince, there is no name which befits the glory of France better than yours." [1]

Chateaubriand, in penning these lines, was only anticipating by a few years the verdict of no inconsiderable number of his own party; indeed, Louis Napoleon was just one of those men of whom it may be said, as Tacitus said of Galba, that they were universally considered as qualified to rule until they attempted to govern.

When, in 1848, Louis Napoleon returned to Paris, as a member of the Chamber of Deputies, one of the first visits which he paid was to the Abbaye-au-Bois. It happened, however, to be just after Chateaubriand's death, and Madame Récamier was too unwell to receive any one; and, so, she and the prince never met again.

The winter of 1840–41 was marked by a terrible disaster—the overflowing of the Rhone and Saône, which brought ruin and misery to numbers of unfortunate

[1] Jerrold's "Life of Napoleon III." i. 280; and *Mémoires d'Outre Tombe*, x. 268.

people at Lyons. In Paris intense sympathy was felt for the sufferers, and special performances at the theatres and many private entertainments were given to swell the funds which were being opened for their benefit. Madame Récamier, full of pity for the misfortunes of her native city, organised a *soireé musicale* at the Abbaye-au-Bois. The price of admission was fixed at twenty francs, but so great was the desire to see this celebrated leader of society in her humble home, that as much as a hundred francs was given for a single ticket. Lady Byron, who was passing through Paris, gave this sum for one which she did not use, but she made it an excuse for calling on more than one occasion at the Abbaye, where Madame Récamier was much interested in the lady who had become so notorious through her connection with the ill-starred poet.

The *soirée* was an immense success, both from a charitable and a social point of view. Rachel, Pauline Viardot-Garcia, Rubini, Lablache, and other famous artistes gave their services, and the rooms were filled to overflowing with all that was most distinguished in Parisian society. So great was the crowd that the grand salon, in which a stage had been erected for the artistes, could only be reached with great difficulty, and when the Turkish Ambassador, Reschid Pacha, arrived, a place had to be assigned him on the first step of the stage, as it was impossible to find him any other seat. There he sat amidst a mass of lace and flowers, a striking and picturesque figure, with his long white beard and fine head, right at the feet of Rachel, who was just beginning her rôle of Esther, not yet performed at the theatre. At that moment, a stranger, who was asking the names of all the celebrities, inquired of a well-known wag that of the imposing-looking old gentleman on the stage steps. "Why, don't you see, it is Mordecai, of course?" was the reply. The entertainment realised no less than four thousand three hundred and ninety francs, a sum which could, of course, have been largely increased, had it been possible to find acccommodation for all those who wished to be present.

Although on this occasion some of the most beautiful women in Paris were congregated in her salon, it was the general opinion that Madame Récamier eclipsed them all. Madame Récamier never really knew old age. Of course, as the years passed by, she lost the bloom of youth, and, moreover, acquired a slight stoop; but she always retained the rare beauty of the smile which had won so many hearts, and the singular grace which distinguished her every movement, and which was one of her greatest charms. She concealed her hair, which had turned grey in 1824 at Rome, under a cap, but otherwise did absolutely nothing to hide the effects of age. "She resigned herself gracefully to the first touch of Time," says Sainte-Beuve. "She understood that for one who had enjoyed such success as a beauty, the less pretension she made the greater chance she would have of seeming to remain so. A friend, who had not seen her for years, complimented her upon her looks. "Ah, my dear friend," she replied, "it is useless for me to deceive myself. From the moment I noticed that the little Savoyards in the street no longer turned to look at me, I knew that all was over."[1] It was no doubt this sincerity which contributed to prolong her charms far beyond the ordinary period.

In the autumn of 1842 Ballanche, who had been an

1 *Causeries du Lundi*, i. 105.

unsuccessful candidate for a seat in the Academy some years before, was elected to that august body. Madame Récamier and all the circle of the Abbaye-au-Bois were delighted at his success, but the philosopher himself seemed to regard his admission to the "immortal forty" with comparative indifference. He had little or nothing of *vanité de l'auteur*, and attached far more importance to the moral and philosophical influence he desired to exercise than to mere literary popularity.

But indifferent as was Ballanche to rewards both pecuniary and honorary, he was, nevertheless, deeply grateful to Madame Récamier for the kindly interest she had always taken in his literary projects, and the encouragement she had always been so ready to extend to him. He regarded her as the providence of every moment of his life, and the inspiration under which all his best work had been accomplished.

"Yes, you are the Antigone of my dreams," he writes. "Her destiny is not like yours, but the lofty soul, the generous heart, the genius of devotedness are the features of your character. I was only beginning *Antigone* when you appeared to me at Lyons, and God only knows how large a share you have in the portrait of that noble woman! Antiquity is far from having furnished me with all the materials for it; the ideal was revealed to me by you. I shall explain all these things one day; I choose the world to know that so perfect a creature was not created by me." And again, after he had finished his great work, the *Palingénésie Sociale*, he says:

"If my name survives me, which appears more and more probable, I shall be called the Philosopher of the Abbaye-au-Bois, and my philosophy will be considered as inspired by you. Remember that it was only through

Eurydice that Orpheus had any true mission to his fellow creatures ; and remember, too, that Eurydice was a marvellous vision. The dedication of the *Palingénésie* will explain all this to posterity. This thought is one of my joys. I believe that I am now entering on the last stage of my life ; this stage may be prolonged for some time, but I know what must be the end of it. I shall fall asleep in the bosom of a great hope, and full of confidence in the thought that your memory and mine will live the same life." [1]

But if Ballanche was confident of the verdict of posterity, it was far otherwise with the greatest of all Madame Récamier's friends. Chateaubriand was haunted by a strange morbid fear that his fame would not survive him, and this, combined with his feeble health and the undignified annoyances of poverty, made the task of soothing his declining years more difficult than ever ; and poor Madame de Chateaubriand found herself forced over and over again to appeal to Madame Récamier, and entreat her interference for the sake of peace and quiet.

In 1843 the young Comte de Chambord, the legitimate heir to the French crown, wrote to Chateaubriand from London, the refuge of all vagabond kings and scheming pretenders, begging him to come to England and give him the benefit of his advice. The poor old man was now so crippled with gout and rheumatism that he could scarcely walk, and, besides, grudged every day which kept him from the Abbaye-au-Bois ; but he did not hesitate to comply. While in England he wrote to Madame Récamier as regularly as before, though his handwriting was now so illegible, that he was generally compelled to

[1] Ampère's *Ballanche*, p. 230.

dictate to his private secretary, a necessity which caused him much annoyance :

"I have been airing my melancholy in Kensington Gardens, where you promenaded as the most beautiful of Frenchwomen. I saw once more the trees under which *René* first appeared to me. Then I was young, youth was before me, and I could strive after the unknown thing I sought. Now I cannot take one step forward without reaching the end. Oh that I were at rest, my last thought being of you ! "

And then, after he has seen the young prince, he sends her a note, which, brief as it is, deserves to be handed down as a beautiful example of that unreasoning loyalty which the cause of the Bourbons, like that of the Stewarts, so frequently evoked.

"I have just received the recompense of my whole life. The young prince has deigned to speak to me, in the midst of a crowd of Frenchmen with all the enthusiasm of youth. If I could I would tell you all about it ; but, as it is, I can't help crying like a fool."

In the following spring Madame Récamier took a furnished house at Auteuil, which possessed the twofold advantage of being in the country, and, yet, so near Paris, that Chateaubriand, Ballanche, and her other friends could drive out every day to see her. Here she had as her near neighbour Guizot, with whose family, and especially with his aged mother, she soon became on intimate terms.

Madame Guizot, who was at this time nearly eighty, was the object of universal regard. She had been a very beautiful woman, but, after the death of her husband, who, although a Liberal, had been guillotined during the Reign of Terror, she cut off her long and beautiful hair, put on a small close fitting cap, which she never afterwards laid aside, and lived henceforth in strict retirement, devoting herself to works of piety and the education of her two sons.

The old lady was a warm admirer of Chateaubriand's works, and expressed a wish to make the author's acquaintance. There was some little difficulty about this, as Guizot, being Louis Philippe's chief adviser, naturally stood in a somewhat delicate position towards such an avowed enemy of the Government as Chateaubriand : but, at length, it was got over by Madame Récamier arranging that the interview should take place in her own garden.

The meeting was a very interesting one. Chateaubriand was at his best, and exerted himself to confirm the good impression his writings had made upon this venerable lady, whose happiness had been shipwrecked by the same storm that had driven him to earn his bread in a foreign land, but whose path had never crossed his until they were both so near the end of their earthly pilgrimage. They parted with mutual feelings of sympathy and esteem, and, a few days later, Chateaubriand sent the manuscript of the first part of his *Mémoires* for Madame Lenormant to read to Madame Guizot.

Madame Récamier passed the greater part of the summer at Auteuil, and in the autumn spent some time with her niece in Normandy. During the last years of her life, whenever Chateaubriand and Ballanche could be persuaded to spare her for a few days, she always made a point of spending them in the country ; and it was from these brief intervals of rest, far from the noise and turmoil of the great city, that she drew the strength to continue the life of self-sacrifice she had imposed on herself.

Madame Récamier had always been very regular in her habits. She rose early, and, in accordance with a practice she had begun early in life at the suggestion of Mathieu de Montmorency, devoted an hour to the study of a portion of the Scriptures or of some religious work. Afterwards she had the newspapers and one or two of the latest books read to her; for few women were more extensively acquainted with current literature. This occupied her until breakfast at twelve o'clock, after which she drove out to visit some of her poor people, or to call on her niece or some old acquaintance who was too infirm to come to her, returning to the Abbaye in time to receive Chateaubriand, who arrived every day punctually at half-past two. The two faithful friends had tea, and passed an hour together, and at four o'clock her other friends, of whom Ballanche was usually the first, were admitted. Everything was delightfully informal at the Abbaye: no visitor was ever announced, and people were at liberty to come and go as often as they pleased in the course of the afternoon.

In the spring of 1845 the Comte de Chambord, who was now living at Venice, again sent for Chateaubriand. Madame Récamier was very unwilling that he should undertake so long a journey in his feeble state of health—his hands were so disabled that he could hardly hold his stick—but the loyal old man could not bear to disappoint the youth whom he looked upon as his lawful king, and insisted upon going to Venice, whence he sadly writes that the inscription in the middle of the Grand Canal, recording the fact that Byron had been there, had already disappeared, and that the great poet was now as completely forgotten "as any poor fisherman of the lagoons." He evidently deduces from this that his own fame will prove as fleeting.

Chateaubriand returned to Paris after an absence of three weeks. He bore the fatigue of the journey better than Madame Récamier had dared to hope, but it was his last effort of loyalty.

As far back as 1839 Madame Récamier's eyes had caused some anxiety to her friends, and in 1844 she could no longer see to read. "Her unwillingness to trouble others with her infirmities," says Madame Lenormant, "led her, even when she became totally blind, to conceal the fact from her friends. Her hearing was remarkably acute, and, with an unequalled tact, she recognised instantly, by the first inflection of the voice, people who approached her. Her man-servant took care to arrange the furniture in her salon always in the same order, that she might have no difficulty in moving about; and many people, who heard her speak of her 'poor eyes,' only imagined that her sight was not so good as formerly."[1]

She was now, of course, obliged to make use of other people's eyes in order to gratify her love for literature; and her nephew Paul David read to her every evening. His elocution, however, left a good deal to be desired, and he saw that Madame Récamier was sensitive to his shortcomings, in spite of her efforts not to appear to be so. He, therefore, secretly took lessons in reading, at the age of sixty-four, in order not to mar the pleasure he was able to afford her.

In the winter of 1845-6 Madame Récamier's friends persuaded her to consult Dr. Druot, a well-known oculist, and for some months she submitted to his treatment, but without deriving any permanent benefit. By the use of belladonna, however, her sight was often restored to her for a few hours, and in the following May she was thus able to see and admire Ary Scheffer's beautiful picture, *St. Augustine and Monica*, which the

[1] *Souvenirs*, ii. 538.

painter sent to the Abbaye for her and Chateaubriand's inspection.

Madame Récamier had dreaded the loss of her sight less on her own account than on that of Chateaubriand, whose mental faculties were now beginning to fail, while an accident had reduced him to a helplessly crippled condition. In the summer of 1846, in stepping from his carriage, his foot slipped, and he fell, breaking his collar-bone. From that day he was no longer able to walk, and when he came to the Abbaye had to be carried by two servants from his carriage to the salon, where he was placed in an arm-chair, and wheeled to a corner of the fireplace. When this was done, Madame Récamier was the only person present, and visitors, who came in after his "hour," found him comfortably settled; but he was sometimes obliged to leave in the presence of strangers, and this, as he was extremely sensitive with regard to his infirmities, was always a most trying moment, although out of respect for his feelings no one appeared to notice when he was carried from the room.

Sometimes, instead of receiving her friends in her own salon, Madame Récamier would arrange to meet those who were most likely to be able to amuse Chateaubriand at the latter's house in the Rue du Bac. By this means the old man was spared the annoyance of strangers witnessing his helpless condition.

During the spring of 1847 Madame Récamier underwent an operation upon her eyes. It was performed by an eminent specialist, and great hopes were entertained that it would prove successful, but circumstances combined to render it unavailing. In her anxiety to resume her former mode of life for the sake of Chateaubriand, who was now more than ever dependent upon her good offices, as he had lost his wife in the previous February, she neglected necessary precautions. She had, moreover, been strictly enjoined to avoid all kind of excitement, but, shortly after the operation, she was called to the death-bed of her faithful friend Ballanche.

The immediate cause of the old philosopher's death was pleurisy, but there can be no doubt that his anxiety and terror at the prospect of the operation which the object of his affections was about to undergo had not a little to do with the fatal termination of his illness. He lodged opposite the Abbaye, but would not consent that Madame Récamier should be sent for, as he knew how dangerous it would be for her to expose her eyes to the light. She learned from some of his friends, however, of his critical condition and, forgetting all her doctor's injunctions, at once went to his rooms, and remained with him until the end, thus losing in tears and agitation all hope of recovering her sight.

Ballanche was buried in the family vault of the Récamiers, where Madame Récamier herself intended to be laid, so that he might rest in death near her whom he had loved so tenderly in life; and Alexis de Tocqueville, on behalf of the Academy, and M. de La Prade, representing the town of Lyons, delivered addresses over the grave.

Madame Récamier's grief at the loss of the friend whose whole life from the time of their first meeting at Lyons, in 1813, had been consecrated to her was very great; but the necessity of devoting herself to Chateaubriand—a task which was daily becoming more difficult—absorbed all her faculties, and left her little leisure to indulge in melancholy reflections.

Like Madame de Maintenon, she now found herself

called upon to amuse a being who was no longer amusable. Chateaubriand's memory was now so much gone, that he had been known to ask for a friend who had been dead twenty years, while he had so completely lost the power of attention that he had given up reading. He knew that his faculties were leaving him, and, "like a poor proud man seeking to hide his poverty," as one of his contemporaries observes, hardly ever spoke, except to Madame Récamier and one or two of his most intimate friends. Yet at times a gleam of his former self would flash up and surprise every one. "One day," says Madame Mohl, "a lady calling at the Abbaye made a speech in praise of Robespierre's virtues (we are not aware in England that a knot of democrats uphold Danton, Marat, and Robespierre as the first heroes of equality). M. de Chateaubriand, all at once aroused from his silence, broke out into a description of the deeds of these men, deeds he had witnessed. Never in his best days had he expressed more eloquent indignation. All were silent with awe. They felt as if a prophet raised from the dead had spoken." [1]

He still continued to come every day with unfailing regularity to the Abbaye; indeed, he only seemed to live during the hours he spent with Madame Récamier, and one day surprised her by entreating her to marry him.

Madame Récamier was much touched by his earnestness, but she was firm in her refusal. "Why should we marry?" she said. "If living alone is painful to you, I am willing to come and live with you. The world, I am certain, will do justice to the purity of our friendship, and will sanction anything that will render my task, of making your old age happy, peaceful, and comfortable, more easy for me. If we were younger, I should not hesitate; I

[1] Madame Mohl's *Madame Récamier*, p. 109.

would gladly accept the right of devoting my life to you. But years and blindness have given me this right. Let us change nothing in so perfect an affection."[1]

Such was the reason she gave Chateaubriand for her refusal to bear his name, but it was not the true one, as she confided to a friend shortly afterwards. "If I had thought he would be happier," she said, "I would not have refused; but the only cheerful moments he has in the day are when he comes to the Abbaye. I am convinced that if I lived with him, that slight excitement which gives a little variety to his life would be lost." In this decision she thought of Chateaubriand, not of herself.

Towards the end of July, Madame Récamier, whose nerves had been much shaken by Ballanche's death and her own unsuccessful operation, was persuaded to go to Maintenon on a visit to the Duc and Duchesse de Noailles. Ampère was also of the party, and she took a mournful pleasure in assisting him in the preparation of his "Life of Ballanche." She remained, however, but a short time at Maintenon, as she could not bear to leave Chateaubriand for a day longer than was absolutely necessary.

So great was her desire to recover her sight, in order that she might be of more service to her friend, that on her return to Paris she had the courage to submit to another operation. But this, like the first, was wholly unsuccessful.

The winter passed quietly away, without any indication of the momentous events which were pending, and in February came the third great revolution that she and Chateaubriand were to witness. The latter had by this time fallen into a sort of speechless stupor, and at times it almost seemed as if his intelligence was gone; but he still

[1] *Souvenirs*, ii. 558.

continued to come to the Abbaye-au-Bois, "where," says Madame Mohl, "like an old oak struck by lightning, beautiful in its decay, he sat, seemed to listen to the conversation, smiled when one of his favourites entered; but in reality was indifferent to all."[1] He roused himself sufficiently to make inquiries about the revolution of February, and when he was told that Louis Philippe's Government had been overthrown, he exclaimed, "Well done!" and once more relapsed into silence.[2]

In May Chateaubriand was in such a weak state that he was unable to leave the house. Madame Récamier, therefore, went every day to the Rue du Bac, at the same hour that he had been accustomed to come to the Abbaye, and a few either of her own or of Chateaubriand's friends generally joined her there.

During the June insurrection few drivers would venture out, as the rioters seized on every vehicle they could find, and piled them up for barricades. Madame Récamier, however, remembered that it was possible to reach Chateaubriand's house by making a detour through some unfrequented back streets; and, after some difficulty, she succeeded in persuading a *cocher* bolder than his fellows to take her this way, and, blind and nervous as she was, never missed a day in coming to the Rue du Bac.

At the close of that month Chateaubriand was compelled to take to his bed, and the doctors declared that the end was only a question of days. Madame Récamier dreaded his dying in the night, when it might not be possible to summon her in time, and was, therefore, greatly relieved when Madame Mohl, who lived on an upper floor in the same house, offered her a room.

[1] Madame Mohl's *Madame Récamier*, p. 115.

[2] *Souvenirs* of Alexis de Tocqueville, p. 255.

The scene at the deathbed of the great writer was inexpressibly pathetic. Madame Récamier could not see him, neither could he speak to her, as he had lost the power of speech for some days. Whenever she, choked by her sobs, left the room, Chateaubriand followed her with his eyes, as if fearing that he should never see her again. At length, in the early morning of July 4, in the presence of his nephew, Comte Louis de Chateaubriand, the Abbé Deguerry, and Madame Récamier, he passed quietly away.

Many years before, Chateaubriand had begged his fellow townsmen of St. Malo to reserve "*un petit coin de terre*" for his grave; and here a simple granite cross marks the spot where the most eloquent of modern Frenchmen is sleeping his last long sleep beside the sea, the music of whose wild waves had so often lulled him to rest in infancy.

CHAPTER XXI

Madame Récamier's grief at Chateaubriand's death—Visit of Béranger to the Abbaye-au-Bois—Publication of the *Mémoires d'Outre Tombe*—Return of the cholera—Madame Récamier removes to the Bibliothèque Nationale—She is attacked by cholera—Her death—The secret of her influence

In losing Chateaubriand, Madame Récamier felt as if the mainspring of her life was broken. While witnessing the physical and mental decline of the great genius, she had struggled with passionate tenderness against the terrible effect of years and ill-health upon him; but the long conflict had exhausted her strength, and a strange pallor now began to overspread her face, which seemed to warn her friends that she would not long survive him.

After a time she forced herself to resume her former habits, and her friends continued to come to the Abbaye-au-Bois. Of these Ampère was now the chief. After the death of Ballanche he had given up a projected tour in the East, in order to remain near his beloved friend, and exerted all his wonderful conversational powers to cheer and console her in her blindness and solitude. But alas! no one, however gifted, could ever fill the place of the two friends whom death had taken from her.

"Madame Récamier," says her niece, "often spoke of Ballanche and Chateaubriand together, always expressing herself as if they were only momentarily absent. At the hour when her two friends were accustomed to enter her salon I have seen her shudder if the door happened to open. Upon asking her the reason, she told me that at times she experienced a thought of them so vivid that it seemed like an apparition. The darkness which for her enveloped all objects must have favoured these effects of the imagination."[1]

Shortly after Chateaubriand's death, Madame Récamier received a visit from the famous song-writer Béranger. This was the first time that Béranger had been to the Abbaye-au-Bois, although she had met him several times at Chateaubriand's house. He had been an intense admirer of the great author—he shared his conviction that Byron had got the idea of his "Childe Harold" from *René*—and his object in calling was to express his sympathy with Madame Récamier in the irreparable loss she had sustained. Madame Récamier was much touched by this attention on the part of the kind-hearted little poet.

The death of Chateaubriand, of course, left the publishers free to issue his *Mémoires*. They disposed of the serial rights to the proprietors of *La Presse*, and early in 1849 they began to appear in the columns of that journal. Their publication in this form had been strongly disapproved of by the author, who had foreseen that the publicity of a daily newspaper would make many of the opinions expressed in the book seem unduly severe and create much ill-feeling. Madame Récamier was very distressed at seeing how entirely her dead friend's wishes had been disregarded, more especially when it became evident that his fears in this respect had been but too well grounded; but she was powerless to interfere.

In March the cholera, from which she had fled in 1832,

[1] *Souvenirs*, ii. 563.

made its reappearance in Paris. She was too old and too infirm to fly from it now; but Madame Lenormant suggested that she should remove to the Bibliothèque Nationale, where she and her husband resided. This appeared to most of her friends a great mistake, for the Abbaye was in a far less crowded part of the town than the Bibliothèque; and they, accordingly, did what they could to persuade her to stay where she was, but without success.

Here she remained for three weeks, and then announced her intention of returning to the Abbaye in the course of a few days. On May 7 Comte de Saint-Priest, who had been selected by the Academy to deliver the customary eulogium on their late colleague Ballanche, called to read her the draft of his address, in which she was, of course, much interested; and on the following day she drove out as usual in the morning, received some friends in the afternoon, and dined with the Lenormants, Ampère, and Madame Salvage. On the 9th she seemed perfectly well in the early part of the day, and her great-niece, Juliette Lenormant, finished reading to her Madame de Motteville's *Mémoires*. At four o'clock, however, as she was dressing for dinner she was suddenly taken ill. Doctors were at once summoned and pronounced the disease to be cholera. In her feeble state of health she had no strength to battle with the disease, and two days later she died, rejoicing in the midst of her agony that she was permitted to do so surrounded by those whom she loved. "We shall meet again!" were her last words.

"Cholera," says Madame Lenormant, "usually leaves frightful traces upon its victims, but by an exception, which I cannot help regarding as a last favour of Heaven, Madame Récamier's features assumed in death a surprising beauty. Her expression was angelic and grave; she looked like a beautiful statue; there was no contraction, neither were there any wrinkles; and never has the majesty of the last sleep been attended with so much grace and sweetness."[1]

What was the secret of the wonderful fascination which Madame Récamier exercised over all who came under her influence—a fascination which was as potent on the day of her death as it had been on her first appearance in society half a century earlier? It is comparatively easy to account for it when she was in the heyday of her youth and beauty and the dispenser of almost boundless hospitality. But it is far more difficult to do so when youth had gone, and beauty had fled, and she had exchanged her splendid mansion in the Rue du Mont Blanc for a comfortless garret in the outbuildings of a convent. The secret, we think, is to be found in the possession in a pre-eminent degree of two qualities, by no means common in themselves, and still more rarely to be met with in conjunction with one another—tact and sympathy.

Madame Récamier's most intimate friends, her most ardent admirers, were politicians and statesmen, often rivals, sometimes enemies, yet, she understood all and did justice to all, not by pretending to sympathise with first one and then another, as most women similarly placed would have done, but by remaining absolutely impartial, and letting them clearly understand that she would be no party to their quarrels, however bitter those quarrels might be. "Your position," writes the Duc de Laval to her, at the time of the diplomatic rivalry between Chateaubriand and Mathieu de Montmorency, "is one of the

[1] *Souvenirs*, ii. 572.

most complicated, most singular, and most embarrassing in the whole of my experience; but I am sure you will get out of the difficulty with admirable tact, that you will enjoy every one's confidence, that every one will be satisfied, and that no one will be disappointed."

The duke was right. Madame Récamier never disappointed or deceived any one. In the midst of the most difficult situations, in the midst of friends who were as bitterly antagonistic to one another as men could well be, she maintained her kind, sympathetic, and conciliatory manner, acknowledging allegiance to no party, to no set of political principles, but making it her business to discover some point of agreement between herself and each of her guests—a point which, as Guizot remarks, frequently became a bond of sympathy which nothing had power to sever.[1]

And if Madame Récamier was resolute in her refusal to recognise political distinctions among her friends, she was equally consistent in ignoring social ones. Of middle-class origin herself, and married to a man whose connections were all of the upper *bourgeoisie*, her own charms and the levelling tendencies of the revolutionary era threw her into the very highest society. Some of her chosen associates were men of fashion, some politicians, some *littérateurs;* some were high-born, wealthy, and famous, others humble, poor, and unknown. But, in the few scraps of her correspondence that have been preserved, and in the accounts given of her by various contemporaries, it is impossible to trace the slightest difference in her way of treating these several classes of her acquaintance. To differences in social position, indeed, to which, even in our democratic age, so much importance is still

[1] See Guizot's article in *Revue des Deux Mondes*, December 1859.

attached, she appears to have been wholly insensible. Nor was this freedom from conventional exclusiveness confined to herself alone; she enforced it on all those who came under her sway. Those magnificent *grand-seigneurs*, the Duc de Laval and the Duc de Noailles, must address and speak of M. Ballanche, the ex-printer, and M. Ampère, the journalist, precisely as if they happened to stand on the same level as themselves. She would no more tolerate distinctions of birth, rank, or position among her vassals in her presence than would the Shah of Persia.

And thus it came about that Madame Récamier was able to fill her salon with persons of every school and shade of opinion, and every class and rank in society, and so to contrive that every one there, whether Royalist or Republican, whether Bonapartist or Legitimist, whether prince of the blood or struggling man of letters, should be made to feel perfectly at his ease. The following anecdote, related by Sainte-Beuve, will serve to show to what a height of perfection she must have brought this art.

"One day in the year 1802, during the brief Peace of Amiens—it was not at her splendid hôtel in the Rue du Mont Blanc, but in the salon of the Château of Clichy, where she was spending the summer—a number of men, representative of widely different interests, had met together—Adrien and Mathieu de Montmorency, General Moreau, several distinguished Englishmen, including M. Fox and M. Erskine, and many others. There they stood, eyeing one another, each unwilling to be the first to speak. M. de Narbonne, who was also present, made an effort to start the conversation, but, in spite of his wit, he failed. Madame Récamier came in. She spoke first to M. Fox, then a few words to everybody else in turn, at the same time presenting them one to the other with some well-turned compliments. In a moment the conversation became general; the natural link between them had been found."[1]

But remarkable as was her tact, her power of sympathising with the joys and the sorrows, the hopes and the fears of those around her was yet more wonderful. We have seen her undertaking a night journey through the brigand-haunted Campagna to plead for the life of a poor fisherman whom she had never seen before, and moving heaven and earth to save the condemned Carbonari from the consequences of their folly; but it was in less important matters—matters which many, even of the most kind-hearted among us, would scarcely consider worthy of attention—that her possession of this rare and beautiful quality was most strikingly evinced. "*Elle était le génie de la confiance*," says one of her friends; and it was this, even more than her personal charms and exquisite tact, which attracted and attached people to her. "All who were admitted to her intimacy," says another, "hastened to her with their joys and their sorrows, their projects and their ideas, certain not only of secrecy and discretion, but of the warmest and readiest sympathy. If a man had the *ébauche* of a book, a speech, a picture, an enterprise in his head, it was to her that he unfolded his half-formed plan, sure of an attentive and sympathising listener."[2]

But her sympathy was by no means confined to her own immediate circle, for Madame Mohl, who resided at the Abbaye-au-Bois, and had many opportunities of observing her, tells us that she was frequently consulted in cases of difficulty by people who knew her but slightly. She

[1] *Causeries du Lundi*, i. 106.

[2] See the article by a personal friend, *Fraser's Magazine*, July 1849.

would ask for time to reflect, and give a frank and conscientious opinion.

And this admirable trait, again, sprang from a deeper and more fundamental virtue, in which it is probable that the ultimate secret of her power lay—her singular freedom from selfishness. We never hear of Madame Récamier asking any favour or coveting any worldly success for herself, although she was always so ready to use her influence for the advancement of her friends, never parading her own opinions, seldom dwelling on her own troubles, of which in later life, it must be admitted, she had her full share. Her interests, it has been well said, were all relative. On one occasion, after she had lost her sight, and she fancied she had neglected some slight act of courtesy, she said, with her charming smile, "It is so inconvenient to be blind." Just as if the chief value of sight was the power of ministering to the needs of others.

"To be beloved," says her friend, Comtesse d'Hautefeuille, "was the history of Madame Récamier. Beloved by all in her youth, for her astonishing beauty—beloved for her gentleness, her inexhaustible kindness, for the charm of a character which was reflected in her sweet face—beloved for the tender and sympathising friendship which she awarded with an exquisite tact and discrimination of heart—beloved by young and old, small and great; by women, even women, so fastidious where other women are concerned—beloved always and by all from her cradle to her grave. Such was the lot, such will be the renown, of this charming woman! What other glory is so enviable?"

INDEX

INDEX

INDEX

INDEX

INDEX

Y

INDEX

INDEX

INDEX

Printed by BALLANTYNE & Co. LIMITED
Tavistock Street, London

www.ingramcontent.com/pod-product-compliance
Lightning Source LLC
Chambersburg PA
CBHW032229010726
47494CB00002B/409
9781434423122